David Crackanthorpe was b[...] county of Westmoreland, whe[...] some eight hundred years. His antecedents include Richard Crackanthorpe, the sixteenth-century logician mentioned by Sterne in *Tristram Shandy*, William and Dorothy Wordsworth and the notorious Daniel E. Sickles, a general in the American Civil War. He studied law at Oxford University and practised as a barrister in London, where he married the Irish actress Helena Hughes, now deceased. He has written a biography of Hubert Crackanthorpe, a young writer of the 1890s associated with the *Yellow Book*. He lives in France where he has worked as a forester, gardener and cultivator of olive trees.

'The French background and the personalities are intelligently conceived and fleshed out'     *The Times*

'Beguiling . . . the ingenious and fresh plotting is matched by a fastidious and striking craftsmanship in its use of language'     *Good Book Guide*

'A tightly woven thriller'     *Daily Mail*

'A thoughtful and evocative reminder of how the mid-century upheaval of the war still casts a dark, foreboding shadow over France . . . Crackanthorpe's first novel, *Stolen Marches*, stood critical comparison with Sebastian Faulks' *Birdsong*; this might be compared with *Charlotte Gray*'     *The Bookseller*

*Also by David Crackanthorpe*

**Stolen Marches**

# David Crackanthorpe

# HORSEMAN, PASS BY

review

First published in 2000
by HEADLINE BOOK PUBLISHING

First published in paperback in 2001
by HEADLINE BOOK PUBLISHING

10 9 8 7 6 5 4 3 2 1

ISBN 0 7472 6086 9

Typeset by Letterpart Ltd
Reigate, Surrey

Printed and bound in Great Britain by
Mackays of Chatham plc. Chatham, Kent

HEADLINE BOOK PUBLISHING
A division of Hodder Headline
338 Euston Road
London NW1 3BH

www.headline.co.uk
www.hodderheadline.com

FOR FRANÇOISE

# Chapter One

'The English client is here, Monsieur Bernard. Waiting.'

'We have an English client? Do I know him, Albertas?' As casual as could be, like that.

'You do indeed, Monsieur Bernard.'

'Oh, I see – if you like to call him a client . . .'

Understanding between Maître Bernard Vipont and Albertas, his chief clerk, ran mostly below the surface as if they'd been married for many years, and long ago swallowed one another's signs and habits. Bernard knew Albertas was enjoying himself now, and he knew why. The information just given would be enough to get his employer off on the wrong foot for the day. All the same, audible beneath the enjoyment was a note of anxiety, because this Englishman's unannounced visit wasn't reassuring in any way. And it certainly wouldn't be anything in the normal line of work, the routines so capably taken care of by Albertas and those under him.

In fact, it was unusual for there to be work of any kind waiting for Bernard when he arrived, generally around ten, at his offices with the splendid panorama over the Vieux Port of Marseille – so peaceful from above, masts gently rocked by the water of the port, the vessels under them someone else's worry. Bernard had enough of those of his own.

'Don't send him at once. I'll ring.'

'As you wish, Monsieur Bernard. All the same, I recommend . . .'

'Yes?'

'Not too long. It's a different mentality, remember. Not our good Latin mentality.'

'You mean he'd be annoyed?'

'Exactly.' That was the prospect making Albertas anxious. An angry Englishman who knew too much could be a lot of trouble. 'An old soldier too, there's another mentality again, and a *mutilé de guerre* into the bargain. They're often terribly short-tempered.'

'All right, all right. One deviant mentality will do.'

Bernard passed into his private office, a quiet room where for the first minutes he often had the illusion of calm. Smooth waters. Like not sailing on the windy side of the law. He shut the door sharply behind him. Albertas had worked for his father – from whom Bernard had inherited the practice prematurely and in brutal circumstances, about the time of the Liberation – and he'd been an apprentice under the founding grandfather, the famous Maître Bernard Vipont, once mayor of Marseille. Mayor for a few months only but mayor all the same, until assassinated in a brothel in 1930 when Bernard was seven and still didn't know in detail, as pupil of a respectable Protestant school, just what you went to a brothel for. Naturally he knew in a way, thanks to the collective unconscious, but had difficulty matching the august person of his grandfather to the function crudely outlined by another boy at the school, a child of the people, with a firmer grasp on essentials – 'Your old *papy* was in there screwing, Bernard,' said the schoolfellow, and the image called up became part of the trauma.

He tried to settle down at his desk, below the paintings he kept here. They were minor items from his collections and soothing, partly because they were so minor. There was a Courbet, showing a windmill turning in the sad air of less happy latitudes, and a Bazille, guileless and stiff, hanging on the wall opposite – a Camargue skyscape with a thin strip of shore, blue, olive, ochre, blue. He viewed them now, these works he'd acquired just after the war, thirty odd years ago when he was a student and a beginner. He'd paid more than they were worth then, all above board and safe. Those items of his collection acquired less safely and which he held as trustee – a lawyer naturally finds a category for a vague situation – those works were stowed away in the attics at home, in the Villa Vipont. One reason he kept the Courbet and the Bazille here in the office in public view was their credentials.

Another was, that his daughter Marion said she didn't much care for them at home, they got her down. She preferred something more energetic, with no reference beyond its own surface, and now that she was in the first flower of beauty it was advisable to keep on the right side of her so she'd be less likely to stray from his universe like an unanchored star. So, resist her whims yet fall in with them in good time. When she was still a child one could afford to be more careless about this. No longer.

Through the open window Bernard watched the gulls turn above the yachts in the port. Did they worry about work or daughters? No. But then they laid eggs every year whereas Marion was his only child. Apart from the gulls everything was very quiet. There were no papers spread about, no in-tray, and no law books lining the walls to take up picture space. Albertas carried in his head all the law necessary for running the practice, work which consisted mainly of fixing ways round the inheritance code for rich clients, or processing dossiers for the Court of Appeal. And he did most of the work, and always had done, since Bernard's father's day. When Bernard qualified as attorney-at-law and nominally took charge it was soon clear that Albertas had gathered into his own hands all the operating controls including the accounts, and had no intention of letting go of any of them. But for his other, his engrossing interests, Bernard might have put up more fight about this than he had. As it was, he accepted a more or less figurative position in the office, an actor with lead billing but not the most telling role.

'Madame Ghazakian rang,' said Albertas, entering without warning as usual. 'With the general being here I forgot to tell you.'

'He isn't a general. Please stop referring to him as a general.'

'Madame Ghazakian was rather . . . indiscreet.' Albertas spoke with disapproval in his voice. He thought that since the untimely death of Marion's mother it was Bernard's duty to remarry and produce a son to inherit this practice which he, Albertas, had so carefully nursed all these years. Bernard wouldn't find a wife in the house of Madame Ghazakian behind its Second Empire caryatids. What he would find there were pleasures suitable for the spare time of established married men, yes, but not for widowers who should be putting their affairs in decent order.

'What did she want?'

'She was excited. I couldn't stop her. She says . . . if only your grandfather had heeded timely warnings . . . Madame Ghazakian says . . .'

'For God's sake, what does the woman say?'

'That the last young person you had . . . dealings with in her house is loth . . .' Albertas seemed to stir within his black suit as he brought the item out, 'she's loth to repeat the mise-en-scène of your visit. Absolutely.'

Calling it a mise-en-scène was what shook Bernard, as if it had no authenticity of its own. It was like a probe laid in a wound not healed up. He stared past the gulls at the sunlit rosy limestone of the Fort Saint Jean, on the far side of the Vieux Port. The Sun King himself had built it so the cannons were directed not outward at the pirates and the sea, but inward, onto the recalcitrant, perverse population of the town. That was how Bernard felt now, targeted in his retreat. 'Send in Monsieur Soames.'

'Mademoiselle Marion also telephoned.'

'What for? I saw her an hour ago.'

'It was not my place to ask,' said Albertas stiffly. The Ghazakian exchange had upset him too, that was obvious. It was a reminder to Bernard of how Albertas watched over him. He felt irritated, but touched. 'I only know she sounded very anxious to speak to you. Here is the general.'

Bernard stood to receive this Englishman whose great height always seemed more intimidating if you sat while he towered over you. Soames and he had known each other a long time without easing into the conventions of friendship. Bernard felt a latent rivalry between them as if they were lovers of the same woman. They'd met soon after the Liberation, in which Soames played a part as an English soldier parachuted into the Cévennes, while Bernard was a nineteen-year-old Resistant, starved and terrified. Later, Soames was received with honours by the association of former Resistants of which Bernard was probably about the humblest member, before becoming honorary treasurer and standing legal adviser. But it wasn't on account of any of that, that they knew one another so well. Soames, a pensioned warrior with half an artificial leg, settled in the Camargue a few years after the war to breed horses, and it was at his place that Bernard first met Luis Karoly, the Romany, straight out of the prison for juveniles.

'My wife asks to be remembered,' said Soames. Was she actually his wife? There was certainly no need to bring her to memory, Bernard remembered her all too vividly. Perhaps it was the reason for that sense of rivalry. The feeling could be just on his side. Madame Soames (to call her that) was Luis Karoly's sister – or maybe even put him in the world, with Gitans you never knew. She was a woman fixed in Bernard's mind – an image polished and distant as a still-life. Once seen, never forgotten.

'And what fine wind brings you today, my dear Soames?' It seemed natural to call him just Soames, the way Luis always did.

'I've had this message from a source I can't check. On the telephone. Sounded like a young lad. So I left the horses to look after themselves and came at once. It seems to me you need to do something right away – urgent.'

With him seated in the leather-covered armchair, Soames's legs, including the artificial one – mysterious, metallic, still capable of pain, Luis claimed – stretched so far that his feet were well under Bernard's desk. You just had to put up with that. Soames was a man used to the open air and a lot of his own way. 'A message. I see,' said Bernard slowly, as if delay could push it back into oblivion. Urgent messages were seldom good news.

'According to this lad, Luis was picked up and taken off in a police van.' Soames was a smoker of long thin evil cigars and now he brought one of these out and lit it. 'Night before last. Whatever he was up to, I don't ask questions. So there's a thing you'd know more about than me.'

Soames was being disingenuous. He'd always known what work it was Luis did for Bernard, though they'd never had any discussion

5

about it. And for a long time now Bernard had been aware that Luis was under pressure from Soames and Madame Soames to retire from Marseille to a safer, straighter life. Maybe Soames believed it was just greed for art works beyond his pocket that motivated Bernard to those risky operations in which Luis and he were by now so expert. Suddenly he felt a strange new need to explain himself. Soames was English and so too, in a way, was he. Far back. A bit of him was English and there ought to be more solidarity between him and Soames than there was. Bernard's life was a lonely one full of worries and he felt the need to open himself. 'Have I ever told you anything about my father?' he asked, hearing himself ask it, and felt to his astonishment the tears come into his eyes. They must have been bottled there a long time.

'Your father? The one who copped it in the cat-house?' Soames had sensed the coming tears and his tone was a reminder that an Anglo-Saxon doesn't weep for a father.

'No. He was denounced. Taken away in 1944. Because they called him the Englishman. Our family came to Marseille from Liverpool. That's in the north of the British Isles, perhaps you know it. Marseille is a town of immigrants, from the beginning. But that wasn't the real reason. They took him away, the Milice, and when Albertas got him back, what was left was sewn up inside a sack. The parts . . . what could be torn off was torn off. Albertas only knew him by an old scar on the wrist.' Bernard's own voice sounded far off to him, like the voice of the boy when this news was first broken.

Soames leaned forward, and extending the bony hand that held the cigar he touched Bernard's forearm. 'I'm sorry. A coal-mine can tear a man up too, down in the lungs. It would have torn my dad up in time but it drowned him instead, blocked in an explosion. Trapped like a rat.' He patted the arm again. 'I'm sorry about it. All the same, it didn't turn me into what you are.'

That was another shock, like the mise-en-scène. To Soames, he was an enemy of society. No, Soames didn't care about society – to him, Bernard was a case, a deviant, even before he'd finished his explanation. At that moment the telephone rang. Merciful, in a way. Bernard straightened himself up, physically and mentally.

'Shall I go?' Soames asked, not stirring.

'Of course not.' You'd think by his tone that any call could only be compromising, yet this was a respectable practice.

'Papa?'

'What do you want, Marion? You know I'm working at this hour.'

'Working?' Marion gave a brief laugh without the usual joy she showed in laughing. She must indeed be worried about something. 'I thought Albertas didn't let you do any work.' She was at a disrespectful age.

'We have dossiers here needing my attention for the highest courts in the land, Marion,' Bernard said severely. Sometimes one let the juvenile derision pass unchecked and sometimes not. Only her forefathers' lucrative practice allowed her an existence so far above the common lot. Did he hear something like laughter across the screen of cigar smoke? Better ignore it.

'I can't find Luis. I waited hours in the Café Phocéa. Then I went to the Vieille Charité to look for him.' Luis lived in a corner of that poor-house built like the Fort Saint-Jean in the Sun King's reign, among the thieves and outcasts who'd always lived there.

'I've absolutely forbidden you to go to the Vieille Charité, Marion. You of all people.'

'But you own a lot of it.'

'That's why. Anyway it's not a lot, only a very small bit, a corner. And it's a place of ill-fame, the whole building.'

'I didn't go inside. I asked. No one's seen Luis for two days.'

If she hadn't been really anxious she wouldn't have taken the reminder of old forbidden things at her age. That proved it. Poor child. She'd been in love with Luis since she was fourteen, and Bernard had his reasons for complaisance. He could see ahead. 'What do you expect me to do about it?'

'You'll think of something. You'll have a brilliant idea. You always do.'

'But Luis is a grown man. He's only five years younger than me. He has the right to go away for two days.'

'He's never missed meeting me if he said he would. He never even keeps me waiting. You must make a plan. Please.'

'I'll think.'

'That's right,' said Marion sounding much more cheerful. Her swings of mood were so abrupt you seldom had time to be really convinced by any of them. That was why, although Bernard took her very seriously in one way, in another everything always seemed a game. A game running on from her first childhood, her first words, one that must never be allowed to end.

'Now I have to go back to work.'

'*Bon Courage*, papa,' she said, almost without irony.

Bernard watched Soames smoking in silence. Despite the easy manner he looked old today, as old as Albertas. You could see he was naturally a man of action mined by some private sorrow. Surely not to do with Luis? He was a father-figure to Luis, obviously, but time stretches that out thin. It was only because he'd lost his own father when he still needed him that Bernard's wound had never healed. Or was it because he was a man whose wounds couldn't heal? No time to ponder that now. No, Soames must be suffering from something else. Perhaps he was ill. Those further explanations Bernard would have liked to offer must wait.

'So what do we do now?' Soames asked.

'That's what my daughter Marion wants to know. At once.'

'Luis, he'll never talk, whatever they do to him. Not him. But I wouldn't want them to try and make him.'

'Neither would I. Naturally. But I don't see what I can do to get him out of . . . wherever he is now.'

'Luis does what he does for you . . .'

'And for himself.'

'All right. He does it because you're supposed to be an ornament of the law with a long arm. You had him trained for the work. He's never worked except for you.' All that was true enough. Almost straight out of the prison for minors, Bernard had apprenticed Luis as a Compagnon du Devoir to become a skilled artisan with stone and metal, especially locks. Luis was a multi-craftsman, he could even manage explosives safely, on a small scale. Not that scale had much to do with it if you were standing too near.

'I must see the Public Prosecutor. He won't like it. It may make things worse.'

'There's your girl Marion to think of.'

'I know how to think of Marion.' There, Bernard let no one tell him his duty. Soames remained silent, but with reflections, perhaps projects, behind his silence. Bernard thought of a general studying the advantages of a terrain – Albertas's fantasy of Soames as a general was catching. 'There's no time to lose. In this country, once questions are put and a dossier opened, it stays open for ever.'

'Can you lean on that Prosecutor?' Soames probably meant lean on him as a professional colleague. That showed his ignorance of the Prosecutor's range of powers.

'Maybe. I don't know.'

'What's he called?'

'Caraman.' Not an uncommon name in the Marseille region. It figured in a pencilled list Bernard's father had left in a hidden drawer of his desk in this very room, but Bernard had never established a link from that Caraman to the family of the Public Prosecutor. The list was still there, a few centimetres from his hand, in the same drawer. It was like a guide he'd followed, along the track of vengeance. 'He'll be in court at this minute. That's where to catch him, well away from the ears of clerks.' No one knew better than he did how sharp their hearing was. 'I'll put on my gown and walk over there.'

'Then I'll be back in an hour or two to hear how you get on,' said Soames.

'Wait here in the cool if you like – the streets are infernal.'

'No, I've another mission to do.' Bernard wasn't surprised to hear it. You can usually tell by a dark reflection at the back of the eyes when someone's planning something.

\*

Bernard and the Public Prosecutor met and talked in the safe open air under the Ionic colonnade of the portico of the Palais de Justice. The language on such occasions is elliptical. Understanding was soon reached.

9

'My dear Vipont, you will repay me the service.'

'Monsieur le Procureur, it will be a pleasure to me the day you mention the service I can render in return.'

'I'm mentioning it now.'

'You have all my attention.' Bernard had a vague idea of what to expect. It sometimes happened that a Protestant lawyer was needed to cope with some more-or-less dirty work involving Mother Church. It was a question not just of discretion but, more important though not stated, of Huguenot rectitude. The Catholic Church had an informed wariness of Catholic lawyers.

'There's a little difficulty up at the Couvent de la Génératrice-Immaculée. You know it perhaps?'

'I plead heretical ignorance.'

The Prosecutor looked at him quickly in case irony was intended. Bernard beamed back harmlessly through his glasses like a dim northern sun. That usually worked.

'It's a house of contemplative fathers under a prior. Estimable holy men. There are also some oblates. I know, your ignorance extends to oblates and what they are. They're lay monastics, that is, not priests but under revocable vows. It's in connection with one of these that the problem has arisen.'

'A problem in such a peaceful community is easily resolved as a rule,' said Bernard. 'I remember at the Abbey of—'

'The problem comes from outside the community. An oblate who died a little time ago has become entitled, post mortem, to an inheritance. He left a will naming the community as sole heir, in the usual way. Unfortunately his father happens to be still alive. Very regrettable.'

'And this father claims his part under the Civil Code?'

'Exactly.'

'Can't they let him have it? After all, they're fathers too, in a way. They sow seeds of piety, I suppose . . .'

'Ignorance, Vipont, can soon go too far. Much too far. No. The fact is, the inheritance in question consists of a house and small farm adjoining the domain of the Couvent. The only spring in the vicinity rises on it. The community has worked the land for years and uses the buildings for ... I don't know what they use them for but that's of no importance. The property can't be divided up and we ... that is, they haven't the means to buy out the father's interest. They're a community of poor men.'

'They hope to play for time? Exploit the delays of procedure until the father follows his son into the country from whose—?'

'No, that solves nothing. The father has inheritors, a pair of daughters of indescribably rapacious character. The Prior wants the services of a discreet man of law to find some definitive technical solution. I had already thought of you.'

Had he? Bernard's suspicions were easily aroused. That list of names was never far from his mind in circumstances like these. Whoever had caused his father to disappear would never lose sight of the fact that the Vipont practice still existed, and perhaps its records. The years had erased neither the crimes of those days, nor the scores still to settle. This wasn't Liverpool, this was the South. 'Is that why Luis Karoly was arrested?'

The Prosecutor seemed to gather himself together in outrage. 'Do you impute partiality in the exercise of my functions?'

No. It wouldn't be that. As far as Bernard knew, the Prosecutor had no art works in his possession, and it was possession of art works that gave the list its significance; he'd worked that out, with Albertas, quite soon after he found it. There were two columns of names in his father's small, precise hand. One mostly Jewish; the other, a few names repeated several times, corresponding each time to an entry in the column opposite. Nothing indicated the nature of the connection between the two columns except their obvious involvement, like figures in some equation. Elementary research demonstrated that the Jewish names belonged to people who had disappeared, and that they had been solid citizens, big investors, owners of goods. Albertas had helped, through the universal network of clerks in law offices passing to one another – according to an infinitely complex balance of mutual obligation – the better part of their employers' secrets.

'I know what you're doing, Monsieur Bernard. I warned you for your own safety not to.'

'You don't have to know more about it than you want. And I don't disturb your authority in the office.'

'I don't want to know anything about it at all.' But without Albertas's help, the information would never have been gathered, and he gave it.

It turned out that all the solid citizens were collectors in one way or another. Some had been clients of the practice and the inheritances they would have left behind for Bernard's father to ease past the eye of the fiscal authority had gone up in smoke, like the owners. At first, Bernard supposed that these people had been denounced by those named in the second column. Then he saw the true meaning of these lists. His father had learned, or, still more dangerously, believed, that works owned by the collectors in the first column had been misappropriated by the others. And he must have had good reason to think this, and his good reasoning must have been found out. Probably he'd intended, when the Liberation came, to right these wrongs. He hadn't been allowed the life-time. Bernard had taken it on himself, patiently, perilously, with Luis's help. He would like to explain this to Soames. He wished he had, before they parted company. Whatever Soames was planning, the knowledge might have modified it.

No, there was no strong reason to identify the listed Caraman with the Prosecutor – nevertheless, the arrest of Luis had drawn Bernard closer into his range of observation, and it could have been meant for just that. It could be some kind of trap, and Bernard had passed much of his life on the lookout for traps. Perhaps vengeance made you paranoid. 'No indeed. But may I ask, without indiscretion, how you come to be dealing personally with the problems of the Couvent?'

'The Prior is my brother.'

The Prosecutor's father, if Bernard remembered rightly, had been a judge of the Court of Accounts and Treasurer of the Archdiocese. A high functionary well placed to have advance notice of the arrest and deportation of Jewish patrons of the arts. 'In that case, need I say that no effort will be too great?'

'We're agreed then. Your matter will be dispatched at once.'

'This morning?'

'This afternoon. It's nearly midi.'

'I just fear that a dossier could make its way . . . leave a trace . . .'

'If there's a dossier it will come to me. And your attention to the affairs of the Couvent de la Génératrice-Immaculée will ensure the eventual fate of any dossier.'

So that was that. Luis would be released back into the world within hours, Marion would be grateful again to the resourceful father she couldn't live without, and the Prosecutor with the help of his brother, the Prior, would follow Bernard's progress. It did mean work, unpaid work, but what if it led to identifying these Caraman and locating some treasure they had no good title to? The over-mighty could be brought low, with luck.

'The Couvent de la Génératrice-Immaculée occupies a magnificent site below the Mont Puget, near the sea. There is no telephone. To reach it you take the road past the prison of Les Baumettes and then turn westward along a track. There's a shrine and a signpost among the trees. The shrine is for offerings. The Prior will expect you.'

'Good day, Monsieur le Procureur.'

'I hope you find it an instructive case.' The Prosecutor turned back with what Bernard had come to know as his smile. 'And profitable, I mean in the historical sense. The discipline of an enclosed order is among the most beautiful of the donations of the Latin peoples to . . . proselyte cultures. You will be seeing it at close quarters. It's an example, my dear Vipont.'

*

Should he go straight back to the office and ring Marion now with the news? Or walk up the Canebière and over to Caroline Ghazakian's in the shade of the Allées Léon-Gambetta? That was tempting. The usual feeling of being driven from below invaded an awareness occupied, a moment earlier, by worries and plans. It always happened like that. The ritual that till now he'd always been able to put in place within Caroline Ghazakian's walls came to mind and forced out other considerations. That didn't matter in itself, plenty of other solid citizens took the same route to get there, under the avenues, but it would leave him feeling less ... intact when he reached the door. Better wait till nightfall. That was a discipline to set oneself. Also there was the problem reported by Albertas, the new unwillingness of Caroline's personnel. That meant another telephone call, feeling out the ground.

'I don't want to be disturbed, Albertas. Please connect me to an outside line.'

'I can think of no reason for disturbing you, Monsieur Bernard. Your signature on one or two papers tomorrow morning will do quite well.'

When Albertas wanted to make him feel dispensable that was all he had to say. If, on the other hand, he felt like implying that Bernard neglected his duties and left all the work to others he could create a mountain of dusty dossiers from nowhere and carry them in. 'I will see no one,' said Bernard unnecessarily. He waited long enough for the connection to be made and to feel reasonably sure Albertas wouldn't have the patience to be still listening in on the office switchboard.

'Marion?'

'Oh papa, I've been waiting and waiting for you.'

'Everything's arranged. With great difficulty I must say. If I wasn't who I am—'

'I promise to always speak with respect about the office and all your work in future. Where is he?'

'You're to stay at home where you are, Marion. We must be very discreet. Luis will show up in his own time. He knows about discretion, no one better.'

'I can't stay here and just wait, really ...'

'Marion, I order you to stay at home.' That was taking a risk and asking for trouble, normally.

'Very well, if you say so. If that's what you want.'

He didn't like the sound of it. Experience made him sceptical. But it was no good insisting further in the hope of hearing something more convincing. It would be counter-productive. 'For once I insist, Marion.'

'What do you mean, for once? You've spent my life insisting.' Her voice had risen. She paused and evidently thought better of it. 'But you know how much I listen when you do insist.'

What a liar she was. And he loved her all the more when she lied because her lies made him anxious. There was a term for that. He'd read it in an article dealing with the dynamics of dependent love and immediately thought of himself. Double bind, that's what it was, if he had it right. 'We'll talk about it all this evening when I come home.'

'When will that be?'

'Six o'clock.' He would get there an hour earlier to make sure of her. It was for her own good, and it would still leave plenty of evening ahead of him.

'Monsieur Soames came to the house.'

'He had no business to do that.'

'He didn't come on business. He wanted to talk to me. And bring a message.'

'From Luis?' No, of course not, that was impossible. But who else could send Marion a message through Soames?

'From Madame Soames.'

'What message did she send? It sounds very unlikely to me. Soames was up to something.'

'I can't explain it all on the telephone.'

'Then logically you shouldn't have started.' The conversation was turning into an argument. Love went like that.

'I'll expect you at five this evening, papa,' said Marion and rang off.

He'd managed that reasonably well. After talking to Marion the sound of her voice continued always to echo for some time in his ear. He let it repeat the words she'd used, the tone they'd been said in, the slight hoarseness from her deplorable smoking habit. He sat back in his chair and let this process run its course, visualising her for himself at the other end of the line. Marion was more beautiful, in his eyes, than her mother had ever been. Perhaps that was partly because he saw in her some faint improved element of himself, rendered graceful by femininity, luminous by youth, elusive by the

15

mystery of procreation. Now if he were to telephone Caroline Ghazakian that would round off the day's work.

There was a pause at the end of the line after he announced himself. 'I will find Madame,' said the one known as the secretary because she presided over details like timetables, work-shifts and accounts. Caroline very capably saw to it herself that there was no liability to professional tax, a punitive imposition on any business at a good address. The *maisons closes* had ceased to exist officially a long time ago now. Her house was a private one.

'Good morning, my dear Bernard,' said Caroline, arriving fairly promptly. Her round contralto voice sounded guarded. You wouldn't have known what a staunch client of her house he'd been, from the tone of it.

'Listen, Caroline. I don't want to hear about any problems on the telephone. I've enough trouble already with my daughter. I'll come this evening in spite of the . . . difficulty you mentioned to Albertas. We'll discuss it then. Just you and me. I expect nothing else today. But if you can't continue to accommodate me – well, draw your own conclusion. I'm a client like another, only more generous.'

'Not quite like another. We cater for many requirements, but –'

'Not on the telephone, I told you. I'll come about ten.'

'Very well, as you wish. It's noted. For you, we must always keep an opening in our agenda.'

'Thank you, Caroline. And by the way, I met the Public Prosecutor today. A tax evasion matter working its way through the penal courts. He asked me to render him an important service. I shall be seeing more of him.'

'Until this evening then, dear friend. A glass of champagne together at ten will be like the old days. Not so very old, either.'

'Goodbye, Caroline.'

That too had passed off not badly. Women had to be kept in line when possible, threatened if necessary, and when nothing was possible one must be philosophical and make do with what was offered. He wasn't reduced to that yet. Caroline was a sensible woman anyway, and after all there was nothing truly repugnant about his requirement.

Certainly nothing on which the Criminal Code had anything to say. Heaven forbid. It was merely histrionic and he looked forward to another rehearsal soon. If things don't progress they go backward. On the parquet of the corridor he could hear the unequal sound of Soames's footsteps, the artificial leg striking the floor more heavily than the other as if it was weighted with lead, like a club. Soames entered without knocking.

'Well?'

'Luis will be released into the world some time this afternoon. I know he won't come here. If you want to see him, go to the Vieille Charité. But be careful.'

'The first infernal circle. I like it there.' You had to remember that about the English. They had an easy-going approach to borderlines. Bernard had heard that this was due to the tradition of liberal pragmatism, and felt a vague swelling of atavistic pride.

'Be on the lookout all the same. I never go alone. Albertas accompanies me when it's a question of . . . inspecting property. Seeing about complaints and so on.'

'Complaints?'

'For example, from the police.'

'Pretty frequent?'

'Endemic.'

'You go rent-collecting too?'

'Luis pays no rent.'

'No. It's a service tenancy, what he has there in that slum.'

Bernard heard the contempt in this remark, which at the same time betrayed an intention to remove Luis from his control. Maybe Madame Soames and Soames himself were as possessive about Luis as Bernard was of Marion. Everyone seeks an immortality, somewhere or other. 'Luis chooses to live there. And you know he hates people like the ones who denounced my father even more than I do. Didn't he execute one once, all on his own? Those are the people we attend to. Luis believes we have the right. He's not exploited.' Bernard was leaning forward and speaking earnestly, as if in court. It wasn't the best way to convince someone in private talk, not if they knew you as a lawyer. He sat back again. 'And Luis is very well paid for using his skills.'

'It's his skill with the horses he could make a decent life with, somewhere else than here', said Soames, and Bernard felt a jab of warning in the region of the heart. Because as well as their work of just retribution he counted on Luis to keep Marion at home by staying in Marseille himself. Supported by Bernard and his interests, a dependant of a kind, protected, semi-captive. When he'd said Luis wasn't exploited he hadn't meant this.

'I don't think Luis would want to live anywhere else.'

'If your Marion did, he might.'

So that was it. Soames had been to see Marion with some scheme in his mind. He probably thought she was malleable and planned to subvert her. Bernard would ask no questions, he hardly needed to. This must be countered. Luis must be made sure of. And for as long as there were serious accounts still unsettled – still names on the list – Bernard felt almost as sure of Luis as of himself. It was the law of the Mediterranean world. Perhaps being a real Englishman, not like him, Soames didn't quite understand this.

'She's a lovely girl, that girl of yours. Over age now, I dare say,' Soames said.

'Thank you. Yes, Marion's at a woman's most beautiful moment of life. The first flowering,' said Bernard, not drawn. There was nothing really for him to find out. Soames's scheme was transparent. Bernard crossed his legs and leaned back comfortably, feeling satisfied with his grasp of the situation.

\*

Usually, Luis would re-enter the Vieille Charité by what was popularly called the secret way, passing under the road and emerging in the crypt of the chapel through the empty tomb of a seventeenth century rector whose bones like his spirit had been evacuated. Luis preferred that his exits and entrances be known to as few of the inmates as possible. But it was in the so-called secret way they'd picked him up two days ago. Years could pass without the police ever going near it but every now and then they swooped, and that was what had happened, at an unlucky moment. Looking for drugs, they said, and taken him in, though they all knew he never touched the stuff. Then enquiries had started on a wider front. A good few of these *flics* were younger than him now. That made it strange. You'd kick them in the crutch sooner than answer their questions, a thing you'd hesitate to think of in the case of older men to whom, in principle, respect was due.

So this time for once he used the only other way in to the place, the main entrance. *Caserne de la Charité*, it said in eroded letters over the gate, *Troupes Coloniales*. That was for the benefit of those of the Senegalese who could read and it dated from a long time ago. These days the population here were people of any colour without rank or papers. Most of them had no state either. They were like a mixed species of animal squatting in a burrow dug years ago by creatures of a higher form. Among the hundreds, Luis was practically the only occupier with a proper title to be there, as guardian or licensee for the landlord of part of the building, Bernard Vipont; apart from the nuns, who were tenants of Bernard's too. He passed in, moving quickly and head down, skirting the rusty cars that littered the vast courtyard and were home to some of the inhabitants, the lines of washing between the trees, the provisional but permanent rubbish dumps growing like cancer on paving stones. Unless you moved smartly enough you got something thrown at you – from a tree – from one of the three stories of arcaded galleries heart-breaking in neglected beauty – from the roof. The people here didn't like lingerers with time to look about them. And they didn't care for you to be a rightful occupier, paying rent for all they knew.

Being a craftsman, Luis knew what a jewel this building was under all the dirt and ruin and rot, the bushes growing out of the walls. In his mind he could see it restored, blackened stone turned to honey and rose in the sun, vaulted arcades to crisp shadow. The oval dome of the chapel standing in the centre of the courtyard had a breach in it like a broken eggshell and the rains had been entering for longer than anyone could remember. In a heavy storm the water drained through the Rector's tomb and flushed out the secret way, running in a torrent

19

to the other side of the road and into a cellar where the exit was. Luis had heard that once someone had been caught in there by a cloud-burst and drowned. Perhaps one day the rainwater had siphoned the Rector's bones away to end in the common graveyard with those of the destitute.

He must get a message to Marion. When there was trouble he always laid low for a bit. It was a cycle of feeling he passed through. Women had them so they should understand that. First there was the risk, then the bright moment of success; and if anything went wrong, a feeling of shock like a pain squatting there inside. Nothing had ever gone seriously wrong but the pain got worse with age, every time it looked as if something might. I'm getting past it, losing it, Luis thought. Better get out, cultivate a couple of fields and leave society's unrighted wrongs for others to take care of. Or follow the way of the forefathers and take to the road. The road. Not behind a horse these days, along international byways, but in some awful motorised home from one municipal park to another. They said it was happening even in England where the hills and the roads were free. Now they make the children go to school. At least I never did that, thought Luis, except for the *compagnonnage* and whatever Bernard pretends, that was only a couple of years. Not an education.

Watching him from behind a tree was that sharp lame boy he gave cigarettes to for making himself useful, the one who said he knew how to use a telephone. He could be sent to call Marion. The boy would never have spoken to a beautiful girl before, her arms leaning on a table, breasts reposed in the crook of her elbows. That's how Marion would be when she answered. Luis would mention enough to the boy to get him interested in doing what he was told. And what should he be told? Having thought about her, Luis realised he wanted to meet Marion again as soon as possible. As soon as he felt all right again. The boy must give a rendezvous with no names mentioned and Marion would know what that meant. Tomorrow. He'd say tomorrow. Thinking about Marion and tomorrow would soon make him all right. He called the boy over by whistling low, three short sounds repeated.

'There's a man waiting for you up in your place, Monsieur Luis,' said the boy.

'A policeman?'

'No. The very tall Englishman. The one I telephoned.'

'How did you know to telephone him, Pierrot?'

'I saw him here before. He told me to, if ever there was trouble.'

'Did he give you cigarettes?'

'No. He gave me a photo of his horses. And some money. Not much.'

'Just for the telephone?'

'And a bit more.'

'He must have trusted you.'

'He could see I'm a boy you can trust.'

'Only because you can't keep up with the other boys. If you could, no one would trust you,' Luis said, giving Pierrot a packet of cigarettes and just enough money to call Marion. There was no point in corrupting the child.

Upstairs, Soames was sitting there puffing away at his foul cigar. 'Salut,' said Luis, closed the door by its one working hinge and opened the window to let the smoke out. It was high up in the building, this bolt-hole of his, and from the window when the shutter was back you saw a triangle of water between the houses one way, a corner of the Cathedral the other, and beyond, straight ahead above the roofs, the islands lying out in the sea like shipwrecks carved in stone.

'Listen to me, Luis,' Soames began. That meant he was going to lay down the law or say what was best to do. He was usually right but Luis pretty well never listened to him these days. It was different when he was younger, then Soames had been a power in his life, steady as a lighthouse. He still was, if you thought of it, but it was wrong to make things easy for him. Soames mustn't be allowed to ease off and get old.

'I'm listening.'

'I've seen Marion.'

'Yes?' Luis turned to face him.

'What use d'you think you'd be in prison to her or anyone else?

21

You don't tell yourself she'd wait, do you? Haven't you been where she lives? Lots of young fellers with money and push and eyes open, up that way. An only child too. Snapped up quick, that's what she'd be, and filled up with babies. Big breeders, are the prosperous classes in this town.'

'I'm not going to any prison.'

'Not this time. But in most ways, you're in one. You're not independent. You're not safe. Or in regular work. You're forty-five if you're a day and you still have to have it off in the back of some car when you get the chance. I know what you do and I know why you do it. I reckon you've paid your old scores by now. It's time to clear out of this run-down port, Luis, before you're old. Before you're caught.'

Luis laughed at him. Neither of them wanted the other old. Derision was the best defence against excellent advice anyway. 'This isn't some English seaside town. It's the shithouse of the Mediterranean world. The hub. Where the action is. I've rewards here I'd never get in some cesspool in the Camargue. And there are still some waiting to catch what's coming to them.' He went to the window and looked out. He hoped his words had given offence. In his heart was a large place for Soames and a place with no limits for the woman known as Madame Soames – Luis's only relation in the world – and the desire to hurt and annoy was in proportion to their hold on this inner space of his.

'You can't give all your life to sorting out a few buggers who'll soon enough be dead anyway. As we all will. You need to leave something behind you when you go.'

'I only give it part of my life. I'm thinking about all the rest.' The sun was going down under the face of the sea, almost dead ahead in line with the islands. All the sky and sea on this still evening burned with the fire dropping out from one to drown in the other. It seemed as if the town, set here in the middle of this immense natural disaster, must contain the last of all living things on earth. 'Look at that. How could you walk out on it?'

'You wait and see,' Soames said, blowing a stinking puff from his dying cigar. 'I've a plan may shift you yet, when you find out about it. Tell me what you think's wrong with the Camargue cesspool, then.'

Luis laughed again, to himself, in the red light pouring in through the window. Soames always treated him like a child, really. That meant the world hadn't changed and never would. The space in his heart with its sitting tenants was safe enough.

# Chapter Two

MARION, TOO, WAS watching the fiery sea, from the terrace of the Villa Vipont behind its walls above the Corniche. Bernard saw her through the long windows of the salon and studied her for a moment, turned half away from him, reading her expression in profile and the sideways view of her eyes. As usual, she looked to him like a young woman ready and open to all life's pleasures but impatient – too impatient – of the intervals in between. According to plan and theory, she was a sensible graduate waiting to take up a first post in the University laboratory at the end of the summer; but there was no getting away from it, Marion was at a moment in a girl's life when the demands of the world can be at drastic odds with the bacchanal surges from below.

Bernard went into the dining room to fetch his evening whisky. That was what one did, wasn't it? He poured a large amount into a cut-glass tumbler and added bottled Highland water from Hédiard's shop in Aix-en-Provence. That too was what one was supposed to do. He took a small mouthful of the mixture and swallowed it without pleasure. Then he put the glass back on the table and walked out onto the terrace. It was still hot, steam seemed to rise from the flat surface of the sea, motionless to the horizon. Marion turned and smiled at him. The flavour of an affinity, of a douceur unlike any other pervaded Bernard's being, as if feasting on the honey-dew. That was how it always was.

'I didn't hear the car,' said Marion.

'Of course you didn't. You're not supposed to hear it. It's an English car, not some Italian flasher.' Bernard drove a twenty-year-old Bentley serviced at huge cost in Nice. He believed it to be the envy of the maturer members of the Marseille Bar. 'So, Marion, you see? I said six and it's six. Not five.'

Marion considered him with that impenetrable look out of black, immigrant eyes. Marion's mother had been of Spanish stock, poor woman. Bernard's own eyes were a brownish grey behind his glasses, as far as he knew – he used them without seeing them. But Marion's eyes were of another world, where beauty and existence, if not truth, were one and the same. 'Was there lots more work?' she asked, scepticism plain beneath good intentions.

'We have plenty of work. Plenty,' said Bernard. He looked behind him at the balconies and balustrades on the roof of the Villa Vipont. 'Otherwise we couldn't still be here, happy in our eponymous residence.' That was a joke between them and Marion let it pass. Concealed behind the balustrades were the oval windows of the attic with its stored trophies. 'And it supports others than just you and me. Not, I admit, in surroundings like these.'

'You mean Albertas?'

'I meant Luis.'

There was a silence. Officially, Luis was employed for the delivery by hand of dossiers and documents. Bernard's office was a street away from the Palais de Justice, but some of the advocates he dealt with had theirs in distant, insalubrious quarters of the town. In fact, Luis was never used for this service but being on the payroll gave him a status and status gives papers and papers give protection, up to a point. Marion's expression had almost closed, a change only perceptible if you were familiar with the look of her moods. She knew that Luis's employment was an alibi. But being so young she was unlikely to know more than that.

'What was Luis doing, papa?'

'Doing?'

'Yes. What you had to be so clever with the Prosecutor about. What was it?'

Her mother never used to ask all these questions. Marion hadn't asked this sort of question before either. It was the result of the

University. And now that she was going to have paid employment and the status of a functionary she would ask a lot more, all the time, and insist on answers. In a way, this was the forfeit he paid for having her still at home with him. If he'd parted with her to a husband instead of to the University there wouldn't have been the questions but he, Bernard, would have been left to live on in this absurdly big eponymous villa full of echoes and memories without her.

'I don't know what Luis was doing, Marion. As I said, he's a grown man—'

'You know as well as I do he can't look after himself. Not in our world.'

If Marion's mother had lived longer, means would have been found for putting a stop to her precocious passion for Luis – a convent in Spain, God knows what – but Bernard had seen further with his bespectacled eyes. Luis was inappropriate, hugely so, and that was his great merit. Passion for the inappropriate Luis, whose life and movements could be bought, was less exclusive in its effects than servitude to a husband, an appropriator. And Bernard could preserve Marion in the attic of his heart. Held there in trust.

'Nonsense. Luis is perfectly well able—' he was saying when the telephone sounded through the open window. Marion was already running in. Bernard leaned over the balustrade at the edge of the top terrace to look down to the next one where the orange trees grew in a line in the shelter of the wall. His property descended in these ledges planted with incense-bearing trees as far as the Corniche road, hidden by a range of giant cypresses over whose crest you saw the absolving sea. Bernard didn't believe in absolution on land. His antecedents prevented him, that was one of his misfortunes. Marion had been brought up a Catholic and she had no problem with absolution. She could behave as she liked and there was a safety net. His thoughts turned naturally to the meeting later in the evening with Caroline Ghazakian. The ritual carried out in her house and in others over the years was like a rite of healing that didn't heal, a rehearsal without catharsis.

'Papa,' he heard Marion call from the house. What if she was taken from him, as the price of his healing? Everyone knows that the gods who absolve have no tenderness. You pay for what you get.

'What is it?'

'Come here.'

Who had the right to give orders like that, in the Villa Vipont? He was the one who had the right. He recognised his weakness. He came from a tribe of men. He had no sisters, no she-cousins or aunts. It was a terrible disability in training for life and it left you vulnerable to the whims of your own daughter. What a disaster it was. The only women in his life, you could say, were the girls at Carole Ghazakian's or some similar, expensive house (and he esteemed them, those girls, for the deal they offered) or Marion's mother, who'd passed her life in the shadow of the soutane – or Marion herself. Also the first one – far back . . . above the sea . . . not too distant, as it happened, from the magnificent site of the Couvent de la Génératrice-Immaculée. That had taken his breath away, when the Prosecutor told him.

'I'm coming. You shouldn't shout for me like that.'

'Do hurry up.'

He went through the dining-room window. Marion had his whisky glass in her hand. 'That's not a drink for young girls,' he said.

'You mean just for men of a certain age? Why didn't you drink it then?'

'I dislike the taste.'

Marion didn't argue or point out how illogical it was, in that case, to pour out such a big glass of it. He respected this in her. It meant she took for granted certain prerogatives, including the right of a father to be illogical. She drank a bit more and said, 'Well, I like it quite a lot.'

Bernard advanced on her and confiscated the glass. 'It's a terrible thing to smell strong drink on a young woman's breath,' he said, though the tariff he could afford had largely spared him the experience.

'Poor papa, you live all in a world of your own.'

It was true, and he preferred it. Anyone of reasonable means lives to some degree in his own world. No, that didn't cover it. There were men with no means at all sleeping in the streets near the Palais de Justice whose world was much more their own than most bourgeois could claim. He knew a couple of these men and often took them a bottle of wine on his way to the office. They looked out from their world with eyes innocent of ambition and greed. Their innocent eyes were their means.

'Who was that on the telephone?'

'It was a message.'

'Obviously it was a message. That's why a telephone rings. Who from?'

'It was for me.'

'From Luis?' Marion was on her way out of the dining room, not, in his opinion, to go anywhere in particular or because she had something more important to do, but because she didn't want to give information when it was asked for. Why had she called him in then? As if reading his thought she turned her head when she was already through the door.

'Thank you for helping Luis,' she said with unusual formality. 'No one else could have done that and I don't know what would have . . . but I don't want you ever to have to do anything like it again. The necessity mustn't arise.'

'Why should it? You needn't worry.' He spoke easily, without stress.

'I'll probably be going away for a bit, papa. I'll need some money.' That was a good thing. Even after she started work in September she would still need money, because the salary was small and her expenses large. Promotion in the University laboratory service was very slow too.

'Of course you will. I'll go to the safe.'

'I don't need all that much.'

What she meant by 'all that much' was too variable for an exact guess. But anyway that wasn't the point. 'Marion, you must always have plenty of money with you, wherever you are. Always. You're the last of the French Vipont.'

She laughed, not unkindly. 'I suppose there are still plenty in Liverpool,' she said, naming that end of the world which neither of them had ever visited, the imaginary city.

'So where are you thinking of going for a few days?'

'I'll ring you when I get there. Then I can say where I am. That's the best,' Marion answered as she disappeared from view.

Bernard foresaw no difficulty. He knew what to do, only the detail needed filling in and that depended on chance and expert knowledge. He went into his study to turn the question round in his head. He would go out again presently in the Bentley, and Caroline Ghazakian would surely give him a light supper after the glass of champagne she'd spoken of. If Marion was busy with her plan for tomorrow he was unlikely to see her again this evening anyway. He called his housekeeper on the internal line.

'I'll be going out again quite soon, Juanita. No need to think of any dinner for me.'

'It is prepared already, Monsieur Bernard.'

'I'm sorry.'

'You are the master of this house, Monsieur Bernard. It's yours. You do what you like in it. The master can be as egotistical as he pleases. No one can stop him.'

This exchange could put him in a nervous frame of mind quite quickly if not brought to a close. Juanita had imported from her native land the same temperament as Marion's mother; complaining, servile, resentful and fundamentally domineering. She'd have domineered if she'd been housekeeper to a curé but Bernard had the feeling – one he always chased from his mind – that Juanita didn't consider him at all in the same light as she would a curé. 'Marion has an excellent appetite,' he said. 'I expect she'll eat enough for two.'

'I hope you will come to no harm, Monsieur Bernard, out in the night in this town of criminals and immigrants.'

'Goodnight, Juanita.' Another encounter from which he emerged, as usual, not unscathed but not completely outgunned either. He had no illusions of a life in which he would really be the master of anything and these reminders, like Albertas's overbearing ways, were part of the price he paid for being looked after in the way he was used to. He noticed, as if observing the reactions of someone else, a twinge of regret when he heard Juanita replace the telephone. The unconscious was to blame, obviously. The wretched unconscious.

He turned to more important thoughts. Soames's visit and the mention of Madame Soames so-called, put him in mind of those days when he'd first known them. When Luis was straight out of detention. He'd been told that Luis, hardly more than a child, had fired a revolver at some Minister's personal assistant, from a train. It seemed so unlikely even for the turbulent days of the Liberation that he'd asked Luis about it, long afterwards. Luis was reticent.

'It was a pederast,' he said. 'He'd been bothering me.'

'How did you know him, if he worked for a Minister?'

Luis had then explained. Apparently it was part of a sad story. Madame Soames – Ida – had brought Luis up and then in the war they'd both been put in a special camp for the Gitans, in the Camargue. An interim solution. She had a lover which wasn't surprising, seeing how she was to any eye. An Englishman in the Resistance, a friend of Soames, that's how it had been. He got her out of the camp but the enemy caught her and sent her over the Rhine, to Birkenau with many other Gitans. She was one of the very few ever to be seen again.

'How did she get back?'

'She walked. They found her because the Englishman knew how to blackmail the Minister.'

'What became of him, this Englishman?'

'The Minister made sure he was shot, for knowing too much. On the same train as I shot the pederast.' It wasn't exactly a clear narrative, but Luis never gave detail just for the sake of clarity. He gave the detail that occurred to him as he spoke, and nothing more. You had to make do with that.

'And then Soames took her over?'

'That was when he noticed how she was. Till then he'd kept away, because of his friend.'

So Soames and Luis and Ida had been joined together like the sides of a triangle ever since the days of victory and the tragedy of the train.

'And you and Soames . . .?'

'You mean did I mind him? Because he's not a Gitan and she's my sister? Well, even if a sister was all she was, I wouldn't mind. He was always our friend. He forgot about his country and his people to stay with us. After the Liberation a Gitane off the street with a boy from prison – what d'you think would have happened to them? Why do you think they built special camps for us when they had the power to put people in camps? Because we belong at the bottom of the shit heap, that's why. Soames saved us from that. But the people who helped send Ida to Birkenau are still around. Still on top of the heap.'

For Luis that was a long speech. And Bernard didn't think it quite did justice to his own part in Luis's post-war rehabilitation. But justice to himself had never much interested Bernard. He liked delivering justice to enemies and so did Luis, for similar reasons – on account of the death camps and the torture rooms and the continuing prosperity of the ones who profited from them. So, returning to immediate concerns, what bait could make sure of Luis in the time between now and the start of Marion's employment at the laboratory? After which, Bernard felt pretty sure of it, she would start to see the world differently, and then a new vigilance would be needed if he wasn't to lose her. Stave off the unthinkable. High risk was what the ideological bait must be flavoured with, for Luis who loved risk. That Derain up there in the attic – the cypresses with a blue mountain, just the contour of the Mont Puget, in the background – that was an example. It was the latest of their trophies, removed from the house of a local politician who lived surrounded by bodyguards in leather coats, and Luis had been very content with the exploit. Leather clothing had a negative connotation for him. But at present nothing sprang to Bernard's mind. True, there were the storerooms of the Musée des Beaux-Arts, he had a file on them. The provenance of some of the works there was questionable. But the Musée des Beaux-Arts was a locality they'd never seriously contemplated. The risk was certainly high enough for anyone. He fetched out the file from the safe.

Yes, they were said to keep some Puvis de Chavannes sketches for the frescoes on the museum staircase down there. Well there was no possible link between those and any collector long vanished into the night. What else might there be, according to report? Ah. A Bonnard kept in store, too. No word on where it came from. One of those naked women in a bath, more dead than alive. Crippen-Bonnard. Why kept in store? Where had it come from? Though there was no reason to connect any past director of the museum with his father's list of names, over the years Bernard had somewhat widened the terms of his mission. Under the Occupation which so many people wished to forget there had been plenty of transfers of paintings to museums, so he believed. It was a serious possibility. The Musée des Beaux-Arts was no doubt impregnable, but the storerooms were another matter. The hillside the building stood on was practically man-made – a Second Empire water-tower full of aqueducts and tunnels, feeding fountains and conduits leading to . . . wherever the water was then distributed from. It wasn't Bernard's business to know the logistical details. It was a good enough start to know that the storerooms were part of a subterranean complex structured like a Gruyère cheese. It would be for Luis to research. The architect's drawings of the original project were probably in the public library or the departmental archive; Second Empire architects had total confidence in their engineering genius and left tomes of inventions for posterity as if each ranked himself with Leonardo.

More must be found out about the museum, its past directors, their policies. He wondered who their legal adviser was. Sometimes, if there was a balance of obligation due to him from an advocate he could gain access to information unavailable otherwise. But in this case he was in the dark. Albertas could enquire through the clerks' underground, that was always the best way in the end. More urgently, Albertas must contact Luis before Marion met him. Bernard picked up the house telephone again and called through to Marion's apartment in the garden pavilion.

'It's me,' he said when she answered.

'Juanita's very angry with you. I have to come over and eat your supper,' Marion said.

'I apologised already.'

'If you're not more considerate you'll lose her.'

'I don't think you need worry about that. I suit Juanita very well. I give her temperament free play. Almost no one else would.'

'I don't know what you mean.' Marion didn't like references to temperament. They were an intrusion on a woman's domain. 'What did you want me for?'

'I find I have no money to speak of in the safe here, I'll have to get it for you in the morning. What time were you thinking of leaving for your expedition to wherever it is?'

Marion hesitated before answering. Possibly she saw through this ruse without grasping its purpose, anyway it left her with no room for manoeuvre. 'Well I can't go anywhere till you bring the money,' she said crossly.

'I can come back from the office at midday. Will that do?'

'Yes, papa, that'll do all right.'

So her rendezvous with Luis must be in the afternoon or evening. Plenty of time for Albertas to arrange a meeting. He rang Albertas's home number.

'Albertas, please arrange at once for a meeting with the person you know. The usual place.' He took precautions, these days.

'The evening is not part of my hours of work, Monsieur Bernard.'

'It's urgent.'

'The nuns transmit all messages. You could telephone yourself.'

'I'm very careful about the telephone, Albertas, you know that.'

'Because your pursuit is making you paranoid, Monsieur Bernard.' Odd he should say that when Bernard himself had thought the same thing that very day.

'Without fail please, Albertas.' Bernard put the telephone back in place. Albertas was reliable as a rock if you insisted. Good, that left nothing more, for the moment, to attend to. Bernard would see Luis in the morning, at their habitual meeting place among the sarcophagi in the crypt of Saint-Victor. Examining the carvings and identifying martyrs of the Roman epoch one could have a murmured conversation and appear to be making notes like a couple of the scholars who sometimes haunted the place. No one had ever noticed or disturbed them there in the past . . . not even a paranoid subject could have anything to worry about in the crypt of Saint-Victor.

*

It was time to go over to Caroline Ghazakian's. He always left the Bentley in a garage he rented for the purpose on the other side of the Canebière and walked the last part, taking one of several alternative routes. There's a difference between a good client of a brothel of standing and a middle-aged habitué. One didn't want to be taken for that, treading always the same path, a little slower, less spring-heeled each time. The house was a fine one, built around 1820 for a family of merchants on the way up in the world. The next rung would have been a bastide out in the hills, with a short avenue for the nightingales and a pond for the mosquitoes. The Vipont family had never taken that step, not for want of means but, so Bernard believed, because of their origins. Where they originated, the elect either lived in the city or at the heart of a landed estate making these bastides – so it seemed to him – appear somewhat comic opera. He possessed a book devoted to the English Country Home in its Landscape, and he had his ideals. Moreover his theories were being borne out these days, since the bastides were rapidly disappearing as the city rushed on them with the kiss of death. Surely no one would ever do that to the English country home?

There was plenty of bronze, marble, and polished brass around the front door below the caryatids, bare-breasted Second Empire forms advertising determined pleasure. He rang. Caroline herself opened the door, with the hulk of Umberto, butler and bodyguard, at her shoulder. In the background other figures seemed to eclipse themselves like phantoms going off duty. It looked as if orders had been given to disperse on his arrival. Never mind. So far today, all the main difficulties had been circumvented, if not overcome. At his age Bernard knew it was too much to hope for final victory over difficulties – he was still too young. 'We won't go to the salon tonight,' Caroline said. 'We would have no privacy there, it's like a railway station.' She sounded displeased by this affluence of custom as if the burdens of administration out-weighed, for once, the profits of the turnover.

'You run a very successful house, my dear Caroline.'

'There are days when one wearies of work.'

'It's the same in my office. Though I'm not sure Albertas ever wearies, he has me to torment with responsibilities. Which brings me to—'

Caroline interrupted him with her low contralto laugh, a sound like a strong pulse of water filling a pool from below. Her laugh was one of her principal charms, now that custom had gone a long way to stale the others. She still dressed well, in fact better than ever, with a certain heavy splendour like a carnival Coptic pope. 'Your responsibilities,' she said, still laughing. 'He had something to say about those, on the telephone. I expect you can take them lightly. He does.'

'Don't forget they led me to a meeting today with the Public Prosecutor.'

'Ah, the Prosecutor, poor man, he's not part of my clientèle, I wish he was. His predecessor was – very regular. A friend should bring this gentleman to me one of these days. I'm sure we could distract him. Now there *is* a man with responsibilities.'

'Maybe he goes to a different sort of house. Who knows? He has connections in the Church.'

Caroline only shook her head, causing her jewellery to vibrate like the feathers of a ruffled bird. The possibility of a Prosecutor with tastes beyond her reach must seem too outlandish for comment. They had entered her little boudoir overlooking the enclosed garden at the back of the house. The statues there, various coupled figures of myth and legend, were floodlit, discreetly. No sign of any special requirements in all that. Just the synchronism of desires. There was a bottle of champagne and two long glasses on a table between the chairs. Caroline hadn't taken his hint about the Prosecutor, that meant she'd thought about it and had time to arm herself. A hint like that with covert menace was only good for one mention, he should know that by now. She'd risen above the repetition. Perhaps she already had a lead on Caraman through some other client. Caroline had always been a smart mover. 'Please pour the champagne, dear friend,' she said.

It was a Piper Heidsieck with emanations from the fields, some hint of harvest but earlier in the season. Bernard felt a lift of happiness which he knew would be brief, but without it no day was quite bearable, not from end to end. Caroline had always shared his taste for champagne.

'A suggestion of apples . . . or preserved pears, is that it?'

'No.' Bernard wasn't going to let her pre-empt his own analysis, even in her own house. 'Certainly not either of those. Let me see. Ah. Not a doubt. Mown hay!' He felt triumphant, another passing moment. 'Hay mown on northern slopes.' Caroline had probably never been further north than Avignon and would find nothing to say to that.

'You may be right. But I still get a finale of pears. Red pears.'

'In that case you should drink champagne rosé.' She didn't rise to this insult, any more than to the veiled threat a minute ago. That was a bad sign. She would have risen if she'd wanted to please him. He went over to the attack. 'It was very indiscreet, Caroline, unlike you I think to speak as it seems you did to Albertas. Concerning—'

'Your ways that have upset my personnel. It was time. I have responsibilities too, to my girls and their families. Many of them are still minor and confided to me by their fathers. We live in a maritime city and you know what that means. Clans. These fathers are all part of one clan or another and they don't lose sight of their girls just because I give them regular work. Quite the contrary. It's an investment for them. And this is a house with the reputation that no girl comes to any harm here. I can't afford enemies.' She waved a hand around at the décor, the furniture, the copulating statues, the bottle on the silver tray. 'All this is built on good faith.'

'You don't suggest I harm these girls?'

'You frighten them. You insist on the youngest and they're not ready for histrionics.' Caroline drew herself up in her chair, throwing the advantages of maturity into prominence. 'Always the youngest. I understand it, whatever you may think.' She lifted her shoulders in pity. 'Men of your age either require the youngest, or the most skilled at raising the dead.'

'I'm a long way from that,' said Bernard firmly.

'But yours is the most specialised skill I've ever been asked for.'

'Oh come. One sometimes hears strange sounds here . . . from other floors.'

'Routine. Pure routine.' Caroline leaned forward from the waist, holding out her glass for more. The movement seemed to suggest that it was with champagne she was so well topped up. 'In a theatre you might find willing collaborators. Here the girls are simple. They have sensibilities, and religion. Clients must take that into account. They're essentially conventional girls, not actresses.' She drank off the rest of her glass at one go. 'Just very human little girls, most of them.'

'I think they've gone downhill, your girls. Their predecessors took the rough with the smooth and didn't complain. Your recruits are effete, Caroline.'

'For the youngest ones I must be watchful as a mother,' Caroline stated definitely.

Bernard was beginning to feel worried. When Caroline took that line it meant she was thinking of closing her doors to someone. These women had you between finger and thumb like a specimen. If you preferred a house with a high tariff and a certain distinction like this, you might think yourself exempt from exclusion. Error. The better the house the more vulnerable you were to this kind of thing.

'All that's necessary is a little schooling in advance. I've never asked for any of these girls of yours to be thrown into the deep end unprepared.' He laughed lightly, hopefully. There was no response. She was thinking.

'It happens I have a quite new one. Inexperienced. I've had a talk with her. I've done this for you as an old friend. But I warn you, it's my last effort. If only you would go in for something simpler – sado-masochism, for example, is much in vogue. Chains and things – have you thought of that?'

'It turns no locks in my libido.'

'It's my last attempt,' Caroline repeated.

'I doubt if just one occasion—'

'I said nothing about one occasion. You've always known me as a reasonable woman. And you're not the only man in the world driven to darkness so they get full pleasure no other way, believe me.'

'It's called conditioning. The early sexual plasticity of the psyche.' He was ready to go on about that at almost any length. 'It's imperfectly understood. A boy's like hot wax till some accident stamps on him. Then it sets.'

Caroline considered this, holding her glass so her nose was just clear of the surface of the wine. 'Men are locked, from beginning to end. This is where you see it best. They're like hostages chained to a radiator. All of them the same – even the priests.' She held out her glass again.

'I prefer the image of the sealing-wax,' said Bernard. 'So, Caroline, this new recruit of yours. You've spoken to her already?'

There was no answer. Caroline's head swayed gently from side to side over her glass and her eyes appeared half shut. Surely she wasn't dropping off? He stamped lightly on the parquet with one foot. 'Caroline.' A sudden apprehension came to him from nowhere. She must be suffering from petit mal. He'd had no idea she did. Perhaps the champagne had brought it on, a first attack. She'd been drinking too quickly. A curious, strong, rank flavour came into his mind, like an odour without a source. Yet he knew nothing of petit mal, he'd only heard of it as something children sometimes had. 'Caroline!' he said again, much louder.

'What is it?' She was back, thank God for that. He wouldn't have known what to do if she'd bitten her tongue or foamed at the mouth. Didn't that sometimes happen? Not with petit mal . . . but can't it turn into the other kind? Bernard felt at sea. 'You're shouting,' said Caroline with her underwater laugh. She seemed refreshed, as if she'd slept for an hour. 'Champagne can make a man shout when he thinks he's murmuring sweet nothings.' She laughed again. 'We'll send Umberto for the girl.' She stood up, perfectly steady on her feet, and pressed an electric bell set in the wall. Umberto appeared almost at once, a presence menacing or emollient according to how you took him.

'More champagne, Madame?'

'No. Go and bring me that girl who came yesterday. Sonia. It's not her real name of course,' she said when Umberto vanished as he'd appeared, like a jinn from a bottle. 'One has to give them a suitable name. They arrive here called Marie or Jeanne or Yvette. Clients of a house like this expect something with a touch of fantasy.'

'Did her father bring her?'

'You fear the clans, like me? No. She came on her own. A volunteer.'

'But if she's a minor?'

'She's an orphan. She had a letter from the priest of her parish. Very respectfully worded.'

Bernard wondered about comparative anachronism among the European peoples. This all sounded like something in a novel by Zola, cast long ago. In a way, Caroline herself was an anachronism in 1975, but Marseille was Marseille, a special case, the cradle, the port of Gyptis and Protis, the first immigrant lovers. And full of new migrants, wave on wave, since the beginning. Thinking of novels brought Joseph Conrad to mind, a story-teller Bernard really enjoyed. Now there was a man. His aspiration was to become an Englishman, to Bernard it was like aspiring to reach the poles. A forerunner of Caroline's could well have entertained him in her house when he came here to make himself into a sailor. A pilot of the Third Company. Admirable man. Only, Conrad wouldn't have been able to afford Caroline's tariff then – or later, probably. It made Bernard sad to think it.

Umberto was back, followed by Sonia, like a gorilla towing a member of a frailer species. 'The new girl, Madame,' he announced in his bass voice, propelling Sonia forward into the room with an irresistible bristly paw. She was young and dark, and only frail by contrast with Umberto – one of those solid young Mediterranean women built like a barque for coastal navigation, short hops from port to port. She might have appealed to Conrad, after the long oceanic haul. Bernard found she appealed to him too. That was often how he experienced appeal, by putting himself into the imagination of someone more admired than it was possible for him to esteem himself.

Caroline stood up, smoothing down her creaseless vestments by habit. 'Don't leave without saying goodnight to me, dear friend. Umberto will fetch me when you ring. You know the house,' she waved towards the panelling in which a neatly fitted door led into another room. 'For this evening, you're at home here.' When she'd gone Bernard turned to Sonia.

'Madame Ghazakian has spoken about—'

'Oh yes, Monsieur. I understand.'

'It's only like a game. No need to be frightened.'

'Or Madame won't let you come any more.'

The small black eyes – eyes with none of the Spanish lustre of Marion's – expressed no fear or indeed anything much else, just the alienation of an animal from another world. It was annoying that she knew about the threat of exclusion, it gave her part in the charade a false note. It all underlined how the situation had changed for the worse. Bernard was used to unquestioned privileges, now he saw how they could be whisked away. He took from his pocket a little bracelet he'd brought just in case it seemed called for. And clearly it did.

'I expect you'd like it if I came again, wouldn't you, Sonia?' he said, handing it to her. It was quite a pretty thing, enamelled leaves linked together and ornamented with garnets like berries. There was a shop near the law courts where you could get this sort of thing very reasonably.

'I don't know yet,' said Sonia, accepting it without comment and putting it at once onto her wrist. It looked as if she had her head screwed on. He wasn't any longer so sure Conrad would have taken to her. Never mind. He, Bernard, was here on pressing business and a shrewd little novice wasn't going to get in the way of that.

'You know what I expect, don't you?' He didn't wait for the answer because it was too late now to risk wasting time with misunderstanding. 'You must seem willing right up to the last moment. Then you must fight back as if it was to save your life.'

'All right,' said Sonia. Maybe she'd already experienced that, out in the real world.

'You're not a virgin?'

She shook her head, but inconclusively, no doubt calculating that he didn't really want a straight answer. 'Is that all?' she asked. 'It doesn't sound to me like something worth making a big fuss about.'

41

'No. But in this fight . . . not too soon . . . you'll know how to tell, if you're not . . . you must make as if there'd been a misadventure.'

'Misadventure?'

'A fatal one. D'you see how I mean?' It was awful how crude it sounded. But who could put such a thing into words without sounding crude? Suppose Conrad had some compulsive ritual concerning mermaids, or midshipmen, say? It was sacrilege even to think it, but Bernard doubted very much if the master mariner would have found any specially dignified way to express it.

'That's all right,' Sonia said. 'I don't mind that. If you're careful.'

'What do you mean, careful? It's bound to be a bit rough.' Bernard had taken her plump brown hand in his and was tracing the outline of the fingers like a zoologist at work. 'Surely you take your precautions correctly?'

'I mean what you call the misadventure. Careful it isn't a real one. You look like a good strong man. Not as strong as Umberto, but . . .' She was being tactful, for a beginner, and he felt surprised and pleased.

'I can see you're a sensible girl,' he said as he drew her to the door and into the other room. He knew the surroundings by heart and they were well-appointed. One started off with every advantage here, even if there was a microphone in the wall. Sonia stood in the middle of the room as she was told and Bernard removed her clothes, murmuring to himself and folding each item as if neatness now would make up for disorder to come. When she was naked she looked what she was, irreducible, a thing hard to define, always the same and always different. Being young she made a homogeneous design, focused in the centre of the room like a figure of Praxiteles. With a kind of dread, Bernard knew it was time to go on.

Sonia was a better performer of her part than you might expect, seeing her nerveless demeanour. She fought back with a vengeance as if she had hidden reserves of fury, and then timed the decease faultlessly, leaving a good margin before climax. That was essential – it was the disregarded braking distance, the margin for remorse. And afterwards she was excellent, marmoreal, motionless. Bernard dressed quickly with his usual post-coital aversion to his own body.

'Was it all right?' Sonia asked, sitting up. The performance didn't seem to have taken a feather out of her, that was one good thing. She would give a fair report of him to Caroline.

'Yes, poor child, it was all right.' But it wasn't all right. It was defeat again. A day of difficulties circumvented had ended in this unvarying disaster. He'd found no exit from the libidinal code that made this the only way to full release. He was driven by a force in the dark, whipped on by devils. He felt like weeping as he reached again in his pocket and brought out the usual extra bank-note. Perhaps if he'd been a poor man he'd have found an exit in the back streets, or out in the hills where this had all begun. But it was part of his misfortune to be locked into an upper-income bracket and he could only look in places like this, with girls like Sonia, again and again. So long as the doors still opened to him.

# Chapter Three

THE VIELLE CHARITE was what Luis called it – the historic shithouse of the old town, of the shore, the docks, the harbour. A grandiose, rotting seventeenth-century prison for the poor and mutilated, still housing whatever society rejected and almost nothing else. And Marseille accepted most things, leaving the Vieille Charité to go to ruin with what was left over. Only Luis and the nuns in one locked corner were exceptions. The nuns owed their situation to Bernard and the patronage of the archdiocese which had always maintained a chaplaincy here for the wretched, and Luis owed his just to Bernard. No, that was incidental. Luis could have lived somewhere else; Bernard supplied him with more than enough to live comfortably, serenely, above the treetops in some bourgeois boulevard near the beaches. But Luis preferred the Vieille Charité where life had that keen value you put on it, suspended to a rock face.

Albertas could get messages to Luis through the nuns, and for safety he rang them from a call-box. Two of them would then proceed, like lepers no one dared lay a finger on, through the shadows of littered courts and stairs, immune from assault, robbery, rape, and so climb to Luis's lodging under the roof. Because Luis was said to resemble Che Guevara no nun would cross his threshold. They would knock and silently pass him a page of notebook, with the barest instructions preceded and followed by a handwritten cross like a sign against beauty's evil eye.

'*Merci, mes soeurs,*' Luis would say, unable to keep the sarcasm from his voice. He didn't believe in the convent vocation. These were girls, old or young, not ghosts, under their shrouds.

'May our Mother in heaven keep you from wickedness. And from tempting the weak,' they would reply, and at least once he'd seen the gleam of irony in the eye of one of them but she was never sent on this mission again.

The message was to meet Maître Vipont in the usual place at nine-thirty when the public was admitted to the crypt of Saint-Victor. Bernard always entered beforehand by the Private Benefactor's door, to which he had a key because he'd contributed to a magnificent new ecumenical altar some years ago. It was a master-work of the Compagnons du Devoir, and Luis sometimes eyed it with the same sarcasm as he eyed the nuns. Those boys were obsessed with *devoir* to the point of aberration. He wondered now if he would obey the summons. He was to meet Marion in the afternoon at the Café Phocéa and the thought of meeting Marion usually drove all other projects from his mind and timetable. Not that he lived by timetable, he was like a poacher living by darkness and the weather and animal essence. He turned up for appointments as a poacher sets snares, by instinctive adaptation to life's terrain, but often enough it was he who got caught in them. Well. Bernard never sent for him without having some interesting idea. Bernard was a fount of interesting ideas, when roused. Luis believed that was due to the fundamental Englishness of the Vipont family. The English had imagination, he knew this not only from legend but by personal experience. Soames had imagination and it had rescued Luis from trouble more than once in his life, even if that was to be only grudgingly admitted. Yes, he would go. Bernard with his imagination was like an older brother with a foot in two camps – within the law and outside it. One of these camps was Marion's world, and it had always seemed natural to Luis that it should be with him that Marion must one day go away. He and Bernard were so close in many ways, Luis believed, aspects of each of them matched to aspects of the other. For example, Luis knew that they both loved Marion as if they were trees growing side by side and she the sap. Was it right to love as much as this? It was natural for Luis, but was it right for Bernard? Luis didn't know. He wasn't a father, and he wasn't a judge. All he knew for sure was that this shared love bound the Gitan and the Marseille lawyer, like it or not. They weren't free and neither of them sought the freedom.

*

Luis was not the only member of the public outside the fortress-basilica of Saint-Victor at opening time, which was unusual. There were several northern tourists, reformed pilgrims, and a doubtful shrinking figure dressed in some sort of monastic gown under a black raincoat. To Luis's eye, he looked as if he had something to hide, under his raincoat and gown. It was a splendid morning, already hot. Saint-Victor was taken over by the curious except on special occasions, and clergy was seldom seen there. Perhaps this man had an interest in early Christian inscriptions, like Bernard and Luis. Luis followed the others in by the portal of the Tower of Isarn, pretended to pray in the nave for a minute or two, then slipped down the stair to the crypt. He was very familiar with this vast labyrinth of stone. The arches and pillars and chapels, the burial holes cut into the rock for the humble deceased, the carved sarcophagi for the great. Bernard had explained about that word, it signified the stone that eats flesh; so the sculpted lid of the sarcophagus of Isarn portraying the saint's head and feet under a tablet naming his merits would not just represent, but actually *be* his remains, the body cannibalised by its resting place. The idea appealed to Luis's imagination, a Mediterranean one. The assigned meeting place was by the epitaph of the martyr Fortunatus, an inscription set in a dark corner of wall. The lighting down here was new but piously dim and left many recesses of shadow. Luis, moving like a shadow himself, saw Bernard before Bernard saw him. He smiled. Although there was no obvious likeness to Marion the simple presence of her father was enough to make Luis smile. Besides, they'd known one another a long time and Bernard had yet to give Luis any reason not to trust him implicitly. He approached, and they stood side by side studying the epitaph – two scholars of the underworld.

'It was a lot of trouble getting you out, you know,' Bernard said. The reproach made Luis smile even more.

'An accident.'

'What were you doing?'

'Burrowing back. Like a rat. Nothing on me.'

'Nothing on you? What d'you mean? Nothing was . . . set up.'

'I mean they had nothing on me. Just suspicion. They don't like my ideas, they say. Gitan ideas, they don't like that.'

Bernard put a finger on the carved lettering in front of him, tracing a word as if decoding the lines of a hand. He always tried to give verisimilitude to their pretences even though no one ever saw them here. Somewhere behind them another shadow moved among the pillars. 'This Fortunatus fellow got himself burned alive just on suspicion, and because they didn't like his ideas.'

'Not so fortunate after all,' said Luis for whom the martyr's only reality lay in his name. It might have been different if a sarcophagus enclosed him. Isarn inside his was as good as an old friend dozing along the centuries. Luis sensed the moving shadow a little nearer them. He put a hand on Bernard's arm and murmured even lower than before, 'Go over to Lazarus's pillar.'

'Why?'

'Just a gitan idea.'

The pillar of Lazarus is not built but grown from the rock itself, bracing floor to ceiling like a bone. Beyond it is a sacred cavern called the confessional of Lazarus and a column of masonry carved with the serpent and the tree of life. The place always had an effect on Luis's mood which became tense and exalted standing between Lazarus and the serpent, as if he was once again capable of anything – like when he was a boy, and first executed the justice neglected by society by pushing a man of the Milice into the Rhône in flood, to be washed away to sea. He looked behind him into the vaults and tunnels. The shadows were all still now. Not even the flickering of a candle. He sensed that Bernard was about to speak.

'In the Occupation – when you were a child in that camp . . .'

'Yes?'

'Bad things there.'

'Very bad.'

'You don't talk about them, Luis.'

'It isn't talking about them does any good.'

'Was Madame Soames in there, in the same place?'

'They sent her away to Birkenau. I told you before – everything.'

There was a long pause before Bernard spoke again. 'They say survivors feel bad about surviving.'

Luis had heard that too. 'It's Jews who feel that, not Gitans. No Gitan minds surviving.' He laughed at the idea, but quietly because of the people asleep in the sarcophagi.

'I don't think all the works of art stolen from people who went to the camps ended up in private hands. There were the museums, the churches, trustees . . .'

'Never trust anyone who says he's a trustee. He's sure to be hiding something.' Luis was carefully examining the carving of the face of Lazarus on the head of the pillar. He wondered if Lazarus would have looked so cheerful about being raised from the dead if he'd known of the camps to come, for people of the wrong race. Then Luis wondered how personally Bernard was going to take his joke about trustees. He'd always known there was something under cover in him but he'd never troubled to wonder much about what it was. Everyone had something hidden somewhere. For a minute, neither of them spoke.

'I believe some of those works have ended up in the Musée des Beaux-Arts here,' Bernard said. He sounded defensive. Or like trying something out.

'I've never been inside. Wouldn't they be recognised by someone, on the walls?'

'They're not on the walls. If I'm right they're in the storerooms. In those days if the directors of a museum coveted a work in private hands, it was easy enough to get the owner sent to a camp. You denounced him.'

The word 'camp' was a trigger, to Luis. 'What can we do about that?'

'Begin in the archives.' Bernard explained about the Gruyère cheese and the designer's drawings. 'The architect was called Esperendieu. Hope in God. Say you're making a historical study. Can you use an American accent?'

'Anyone can try.'

'When will you start?'

'What about now?'

'I thought you were busy this afternoon.'

'Did Marion tell you that? Just for an hour or two. Time to go down to the Café Phocéa and back to the archives.'

'She could make trouble.'

'A man must work to live,' Luis said.

Bernard looked carefully around in the labyrinth. There were too many perspectives confused among the shadows and shafts of rock to be sure there was no observer. 'Listen, Luis. I'll leave supplies in the pocket of Isarn,' he said, referring to a crevice they used in the stone at the side of the holy man's sarcophagus.

'I don't need a lot.'

Bernard smiled as if he'd heard that before. 'You should always have enough about you. You're an American researcher now,' he said, and slipped away into the depth of the crypt.

After a short wait Luis followed him, picked up the bank-notes from Isarn's sleeping pocket, and then set out for the municipal library in the quartier Saint-Lazare. It was Lazarus's day. As he walked he found himself thinking about Soames. Soames would be angry if he knew how he was playing with fire once more. Still, Soames respected his principles, even if he was ironic about them. 'I know about you, Luis, you fancy you're the sheriff in the sky,' he said, but he also knew about society tiring of the effort to remember. It's easier to issue a general amnesty and forget, leaving the dirty work to freelances like Luis. It was like Soames to take an ironic view of the things that go deep. Not of Ida, though. Luis thought of her without irony too, a long way now from the railway arches when he was a child and she not much more than one herself, before they were sent to the camps; and without irony of how she earned their keep in those days. She was the tree of life, whatever she'd done, like the carving on the column facing Lazarus. It was sad that even trees grow old, limbs wither and fall. He stopped himself thinking about that. She would always be there for him, old, or unwithered and young like under the arches.

He took the ferry across the Vieux Port, a haunt at certain times of day for the clan of local pederasts. Luis hated pederasts and how they looked at him, and it amused him to imagine tossing them into the oily waters. Soames had once pointed out that this was a primitive reaction and that tolerance was a sign of understanding the world. Luis didn't claim to be on equal terms with the world so he could offer it understanding. He had feelings and they guided him, that was enough. On the opposite quay, bright awnings like sails spread above the balconies of the rich. Luis knew that Bernard owned some share in these apartment buildings, put up on the site of the old town blasted to dust by the Germans. People said the landlords had had a complicity in that, it had been a quick way to demolish slums and disperse the inhabitants to make way for those able to pay big rents. At least Bernard had been in the Resistance at the time so he couldn't have anything like that on his conscience. What he had on it was something else, Luis was sure, something much closer to him. Behind the apartment blocks and up the hill began what remained of the old streets, dark even in this sea light, filthy rotten as the Middle Ages, with the Vieille Charité at the heart of it. As he approached the library Luis put on the heavy-rimmed glasses he kept, not for disguise, just to draw notice off that famous Guevara resemblance. He knew as soon as he'd thought of it that he could never pass himself off as American. He was a stranger on all the earth, but not that strange. He'd been to England, he might imitate Soames's accent and imagine himself an Englishman. It was a funny feeling, imagining that. He caught sight of his reflection in a window as he passed, as stiff as if (like the popular saying) he had an umbrella stuck up him somewhere. He kept going the way a good soldier would – like Soames and his foot.

*

Bernard was used to self-disgust after his visits to Caroline's house, but this time the feeling was more brutal. While he was with Luis in the crypt he kept it at bay but now, out in the open, he was swamped. Was it because the girl Sonia was so young? Or was there something about her that brought back the original, the paradigm, some detail surfacing

51

from the dark? He didn't think so. What all these girls had was just the femininity of their few years, a sort of carnival mask, not a particular variable characteristic. He felt polluted by his responses because of the charade necessary to call them out, not on account of any puritanism. No, it must be her convincing performance that left him in such recoil.

To reach the office he only had to cross the Place Saint-Victor and once there he would be safe with the innocuous image of the Courbet windmill. Nevertheless he hesitated. Below were the masts and the water and the sleek-riding yachts. The sun was hot but not roasting, and there was a movement of air from the sea. Bernard had taken two baths since last night in the hope of washing the pollution away but now he wanted to dive in salt water to scour himself from end to end. He could take the ferry out to the islands, strip on a rock and plunge . . . no, of course he couldn't, he'd promised Marion money at midday. It looked as if she wasn't going to need it after all in the way she'd thought. Luis had been nobbled – side-tracked, a more elegant word – but pretences must still be kept up. The islands and the scouring sea would be for another time. Perhaps destiny didn't yet judge him fit. Those islands were for straight lovers.

'Monsieur Caraman was on the telephone,' said Albertas as Bernard passed through the outer office, hoping not to be noticed.

'Already?'

'You must ring him back immediately. He mentioned a dossier you discussed with him. It's now in his possession.'

'What did he say about it?'

'The matter is in suspense.'

'Only that.'

'That was all. But my impression is that the suspense is as conditional as suspense can be.'

'What a serpent the man is.'

Albertas hissed as he did when amused. 'If you say so, Monsieur Bernard. I don't permit myself an opinion on the magistrature.'

Oh but you do, you do, Bernard thought, and beside yours mine are kindly ones. 'Please get him on the line and interrupt the conversation after one minute. Say . . . just say there's a client who can't wait.'

'The English general.'

'Yes, announce a general. Even a Prosecutor bows to a general. Especially a Catholic Prosecutor.' Bernard passed into his bureau and stood for a moment studying the Courbet. Would he have been a better and happier man if he'd lived in a land where willows lined the sodden fields and the sails of windmills turned under grey skies like prayer-wheels in the eternal stream? He'd asked Soames, once in their long acquaintance, about life in the north of England where he believed Liverpool to be situated.

'You'd go mad,' Soames had said.

'Why? If my family came from there the people would think me one of them and I would be integrated.'

'I don't recommend trying it,' was all Soames had to say.

One day he would make a journey to this northern region and find a way of forcing Soames to accompany him. He believed he'd prove more integrated there than Soames himself whose presence would thus serve to underline how at home Bernard could be, among the native tribes of his people. The telephone buzzed, making him jump back disagreeably into reality. It must be Caraman.

'Listen to me, Vipont. I saw my brother yesterday and promised him you would lose no time in coming to offer your services. Yet I hear this morning he's still waiting for you. What has happened? Kindly remember that my good offices were given on the spot and at once. I expected the same in return.'

'I understood there was no telephone up at the Couvent de la Génératrice-Immaculée?'

'What has that to do with it? I explained how to get there.'

'I ask only because you say you heard this morning that your brother's still waiting. It's eleven forty-five. How did you hear?'

There was a pause. It looked as if this approach had succeeded. The Prosecutor was thrown off course. 'Word came,' he said, sounding guarded.

'How?'

'Does the mode of communication between me and my brother have anything to do with your advice promised yesterday on an urgent matter?'

'Of course it has. There are questions of confidentiality where a client is without a telephone, in our day. Means of communication are fundamental to . . .' What were they fundamental to? Actually, to forming an accurate picture of the time-links between the convent and the outside world, but one couldn't very well say that. This was the sort of situation where Bernard's skills showed themselves insufficient. He lacked a glib tongue. He would start off some diversionary tactic, only to run out of formulae. 'To assessment of the logistical elements within the juridical coordinates.' There. Nothing could be more meaningless than that and in a moment Albertas would do his duty.

'Get out there at once, Vipont, in your own interests. I've no time to waste on the telephone with you. Your friend's dossier is in front of me and it seems this is by no means the first time he's attracted the attention of the forces of order. He's a marginal. One of the degenerates existing at the Vieille Charité, apparently. I believe you have property interests there too. In 1945 this friend of yours fired on the Chef de Cabinet of the Minister of the Interior and we know what that gentleman has since become. One who can go no higher. Imagine it. From a train. A boy of fifteen. There were rumours too of some murderous incident during the so-called cleaning up. If you care to associate with a delinquent of that breed, and from what I learn allow your daughter an association of the kind, that's your concern, Vipont. But don't look to me to cover you for long. Time presses, here and at the Couvent de la Génératrice-Immaculée.'

Why did it press? To impart a sense of urgency and disguise a trap? The band of those holding looted art-works wouldn't dare complain of their loss when it came, not in the climate of the post-Holocaust world. But they would arrange the elimination of whoever was depriving them, the moment they identified him. That would be the paranoid's conclusion. 'It will be a pleasure to counsel your brother at the earliest moment,' Bernard said. 'A religious order where no one speaks anything but the truth will be an exception among clients.

54

We'll see. I suppose he sent someone down to the nearest telephone cabin to call you?'

'As it happens, an oblate I'm acquainted with came on a motor-bicycle. He saw you in Saint-Victor where he stopped to make his devotions.'

'And how did this oblate know me?'

'You were in Saint-Victor this morning?'

'I'm a Benefactor of the basilica. It's an ecumenical centre.'

Caraman ignored the pretext as if it was so transparent as to be invisible. 'Remember, you go past the Baumettes prison. You'll have no present occasion to stop there.' He spoke with emphasis and rang off just as Albertas announced the general.

*

At the Villa Vipont at midday Marion looked penitent. She hated upsetting Bernard, and every time she did so in pursuit of her right to her own way she put on this touching face of sorrow. Bernard, on his side, hated her to be disappointed and so wore a look of guilt which she would have been quick to notice if it hadn't been for her own problem. He could see all this quite clearly. As long as this kind of emotional cross-current ran in their relations, the relations remained alive. What he dreaded was the day when Marion's remorse dried up, then he would be left to perish like a Portuguese man-of-war on the empty sands of love. Tears of self-pity came to his eyes at the thought.

'I'll ring tomorrow to say where I am when I get there,' Marion said, seeing them.

'Yes, my darling, you ring me then.'

'All this money will last me for ages,' Marion said, flicking through the notes but sounding already doubtful. That was how it went. He knew she was spoilt, he liked it like that. Spoiling her gave him a pleasure which he recognised as akin to love's spasm, the tremor that shakes the building. His spoiling of Marion was sublimation, of a kind only open to a father with a deep pocket.

'It would see me through to nearly the end of my life,' said Juanita in a voice loaded with grievance, as she laid out her trayful of *tapas* on the terrace, under the azure awning and ultramarine sky, before the spread of the sea.

'I've told papa he must be more considerate to you, Juanita,' Marion said.

'When that happens, the last snows of the Sierra Nevada will melt at the Saviour's nativity,' Juanita answered.

'I warned you,' said Marion when she'd gone. 'She's resentful.'

'If you'd known your own mother as I did, you wouldn't pay any attention to all that. It's just their way of saying that sinful as they are, they don't deserve the happiness life brings them.'

'You shouldn't mock my poor mother now she's gone where she can't defend herself from unkindness,' Marion said absently. Poor child, her mind was on the adventure she thought lay ahead of her.

After lunch Bernard went into his study to look at the large-scale map of the surrounding hills. Where Caraman said the convent was, the map showed no sign of a religious house or installation. But there was a big bastide isolated in the pine woods out there beyond the prison. That must be it, beyond a ridge at the end of a private road. The monks must have acquired the bastide from a family of notables who had either gone bankrupt or moved to Paris, as the pretentious tend to do. Unless of course it had been the property of the Caraman family, and this convent was a private creation for the benefit of the brother who was Prior – an occupation for a younger son probably no good for much else. That wasn't unusual, there was a mass of little religious communities dotted about the coast in the sunshine, between Marseille and the Italian frontier, some of them believed to be simply a tax haven for rich families avoiding the succession duties. Bernard smiled. It didn't take him long to work it out. You create a charitable association under the law of 1901 and endow it with part of your property which then escapes assessment – your bastide too big to live in, with its land and contents . . . and perhaps works of art among them. Ah yes. And one of your sons or brothers or daughters becomes head of the community thus set up. Very simple. A generation or two later, your inheritors re-acquire it all, once the locality is ripe for development – at a valuation as at date of endowment. The bastide comes down and the apartment blocks go up. The unassessed art works are re-integrated into your *patrimoine*, as the saying is. All quite harmless, only a judicious exploitation of the possibilities of the Fiscal Code. Well, it didn't look so much like a trap after all and he would get out there now with a clearer idea about this nest of holy men.

But looking again at the map he felt a revulsion against passing so close to the sinister mass of the Baumettes prison, its gross over-crowding, the cruelty of its existence just there, in a situation almost as paradisiac as the Villa Vipont between hills and sea, the islands hung like coral about the throat of the roadstead, visible from barred cell windows. He could see that another track led away from the bastide, through the woods and down the flank of the ridge towards the new University campus at Luminy. He would approach that way, and needn't pass the prison at all. As he stood up from his chair a wave of darkness, almost black it was so dense, came over his vision so that he had to steady himself by the side of the desk. He knew the reason without putting it in words. It was *there*, on the scented hill between what was in those days the virgin forest of Luminy and the sea stirring and lapping in the calanque far below, it was *there* that it happened. Within sight of the sea, within earshot of the distant rumble of German tanks beyond the crest, crashing along roads into the town. That really was why he now chose to go that way, where he'd never returned from that day to this. An echo summoned him there, calling him by name from the reaches of memory – it was his own voice calling, the voice of a youth of nineteen suddenly finding himself the only living thing among the rosemary and myrtle bushes of the hot hillside.

\*

And it's hot now, very hot. Bernard has left the Bentley near the school of architecture building site at Luminy and is walking uphill through the pine wood. From the crest-line ahead you can look back towards the town in the distance or plunge down to the inlet of the sea, a deep cleft between limestone crags. As you mount, the pines get smaller, the soil thinner, until near the top only scrubby kermes oak about your ankles reminds you of the forest you've left. He walks quietly, quickly, a discreet shadow under cover of the trees. There are many paths, ancient, unused, winding erratically among the plants of the garrigue, skirting a rock, dying out at the foot of another. Impossible to know which of them it was he took that day. Suddenly he feels he knows that mass of piled stones around a hollowed-out bowl in the ground. A lime-kiln in ruins. He remembers it, he passed this way, by this path, rising to the few stunted pines on the crest, a shelter from enemy view . . . and there, over the ridge and beyond on the seaward side is the tall cistus shoulder-high, and rosemary and gorse far up in the marine light above the calanque . . . he recalls every detail, or summons them from imagination, which is as good.

Now he sees a young man slipping in among the stunted pines up there, like a hunted animal, furtive and quick. It's someone familiar, he feels a sort of love for this figure in the distance, a profound empathy links them – because it's himself he sees . . . after so many years . . . face unlined, hair denser, body lean and moving with easy precision under the maquisard's clothing, dirty, dun-coloured to fade into the vegetation, torn in places and with no identifying detail. Bernard feels warmly towards this blameless former self – that bland brow.

In the shade of the pines and with the cicada sound filling the air Bernard allows the chronological images to run across the screen of his closed eyes. Cicadas bend time, they wrap it in their violent dimension. The young Bernard, in hiding with his Resistant unit in the forests of la Sainte-Baume, has had a message from Albertas and is making his way at great risk down the valleys to Marseille where his father has been arrested and taken away. At first light there was an air raid over Marseille – allied planes and anti-aircraft fire audible from the forests. And it's known a general strike has been called. The invasion is imminent and the occupying forces are concentrated in the town, men have been seen from afar, quitting the blockhouses along the coast. But now young Bernard changes course, he heads uphill, risking exposure on the skyline where a patrol could pick him out. Why? Here above these steep narrow creeks where no landing would be feasible, patrols will be infrequent, the men needed elsewhere, and the older Bernard's mouth lifts at the corners. This young Resistant has heard the sound of goat bells. In peace, the goats are tended by boys, in war and under occupation, by girls. He hasn't seen a girl for some months, at an age when you need one all the time, even – or especially – if due to lack of opportunity you're still a virgin. So he's following the path through the scrub oak like a goat its instinct. Tension rises in the Vipont organism. The goatherd may be a wizened grandmother, or some mountainous virago who can crush you like a boulder as soon as look at you. But just possibly one might be in luck. From the crest, prone under the stunted pines, young Bernard sees the herd shifting about like breaking crests of waves among the cistus. Where's the goat girl? Kindly Providence, allow that it be a girl and not her aunt. Providence provides. There's a girl down there, her face turned towards the sea but the general outline unmistakable, lying on her side in the shade of a rock. Dreaming, as girls are said to do. He moves stealthily down to cross the short space of open ground between the pines at the ridge and the cover where the goats are at work. But now his stealth falls from him like a phase of childhood and he walks upright with a strong stride, danger forgotten. One instinctive impulse has flooded out another and he walks like a man, in this landscape of Eden.

The older Bernard, down in the wood at Luminy, blanks out the screen. The light has become too fierce, the close-up too ominous. But blanking out the screen isn't going to stop what's going on over there among the cistus and rosemary bushes. Once libido turns its reel it runs the course, that's another commandment of nature. So after a short struggle the censor is overruled and the images resume. They've been getting on with it, the two young people, while he battled with himself. Young Bernard has one hand in the girl's shirt which is now unbuttoned, and the other under her skirt. They're side by side on the ground while the goats, neglected, drift away with the special contrariness of their kind. The girl calls out in a harsh voice – is she calling them back? Raising some protest in this deserted place? It isn't a genuine protest, it can't be, her own hand has moved down to discover what it is, pressing into her side – like horn of goat. The images speed up, the motions flash past the eye as if death, impatient as Eros, winds the reel to a close, to darkness. But not yet. There's something more to see, something essential. Slow the rush of images, this essential element must be caught, he must know. Know how it was, how it happened. The girl is naked, skin of honey. This shows some elegance on the part of young Bernard. Many rough men sequestered up in the hills wouldn't trouble with delicacies like that. They would part the woman's legs, lash into the golden opportunity and ejaculate like an act of war. This is a young fellow with a bit of sensibility. He removes his own clothes. Normally in such circumstances you don't watch a man do that but this is his own young self he sees. How smooth the skin is, how tight the waist, how like a bent bow the muscles of the thigh. Or is it narcissism sending back that image?

They are coupled. Bernard has his back against the rock and the girl is astride him. That's not a position of rape. It's beautiful, in mutual acceptance, entwining arms, give and take. The reel now is almost wound in. But suddenly she arches her back, her head is thrown up, teeth clenched, her arms free themselves and beat at him, his chest, head and face. She makes a loud sound like an anguished yawn, a jackal. What can it mean? The young Bernard doesn't pause to ask the question, it's too late for questions, his arms tighten around the girl like iron hoops. She seems to cry again hoarsely. Behind closed eyes the images accelerate. Now the form of the girl is lifeless. She's astride him, a mere weight. Blood runs from the corner of her mouth, nowhere else. So it wasn't that. It's a locked scene with the key thrown in the sea.

What does he do? What can he do? He shakes the girl lightly, she pivots on his groin and her head rolls about as if a linkage in the neck is broken. He disconnects, withdraws. Horror notwithstanding, there's a last sweetness in the withdrawal ... When he stands, she folds heavily in on herself. And what does he think? He leaps to a conclusion on the rebound of feeling. He has somehow killed this goatherd, God knows how or why. She was willing, she lay all lascivious on the thorny ground alone with her desires, and welcomed him with parted lips. He's killed her. Snapped her neck in the convulsion or crushed her with iron hoops. Is it Huguenot conscience that knots responsibility to his back? The boys up in the hills, the companions of Resistance, they wouldn't let that happen, they'd see it was the woman who'd failed the test. Latin culture and its devices would come to the rescue. Bernard's bad luck is to be born outside that confessional fold.

*

He looks about. Sky and hills are still, vegetation motionless in the sun except for the gentle stir of the goats, the sea far below moves no more than a leaf. There's no boat or aircraft in sight. A gull swings in a wide arc a long way out. Here, above the rosemary, flights of butterflies hover and rise, blue butterflies, escort for the goatherd's spirit. He covers her remains with the clothes lying about, as if that could somehow make things simpler to work out. She had a canvas bag and he places it between her hands. A knife slips out of the bag, a horn-handled weapon with a recently sharpened blade. It's a time when people disappear without trace, especially girls, if they have the misfortune to fall on occupying soldiers or a sentry with hours of duty to while away. So she had the knife for defence and made no attempt to use it. She was willing, surely very willing. Nevertheless, she's dead. It seems to him that one of her hands has taken the canvas bag in its grip. Has it moved? Is that possible? Bernard kneels and puts his ear to the left breast. The heart is silent. He looks again at the hand and there's no doubt, the fingers have closed tight on the canvas bag. It must be a muscular reflex to an extra-sensory signal from beyond. The supposition spreads through his mind like a dye in water and fixes into certainty. On her wrist there's something he hadn't noticed before. A thin leather thong carrying a steel medal. Some sign on it, like a Y with curling arms or a two-branched palm tree, a Greek Y it seems to Bernard who makes nothing of it. He turns the medal. On the reverse are inscribed the names of the three kings – Caspar, Melchior, Balthazar. It's a mystery to add to the mysteries. Maybe she belonged to some guild or band of girls vowed to constancy. The

61

thought shakes him like a secondary tremor. He feels as if he's raped and wiped out a sisterhood. Doubled up on the ground Bernard tries to utter a prayer, that the girl be kindly judged and that he one day find peace in the world. The prayer brings no feeling that he's heard or consoled; the universe, like the sun lowering towards the sea, beats down on him with savage indifference.

He stands again. The slope below is a scree of stones and rocks as far as the cliff which falls directly to the deep water. Rosemary growing between the stones, even from here you can scent it in the heat of evening. An idea comes to young Bernard. Knowing what it is, the older one marshals the argument. Nothing can be done for this girl now; the boy belongs to a Resistant unit and if taken will be tortured for information about his companions which he can't trust himself not to give. He's a boy and even men have given information. The Gendarmerie, reputed friendly, might shelter him, they would come out to find the body, inform the family – but the gendarmes have been ordered by the Provisional Government to quit their barracks and join the maquis in the hills. That leaves the State Police, accomplices of the enemy and the more vicious as their own day of reckoning approaches. Out there on the blank face of the sea, over the horizon, are the ships the landings will be made from – today, tomorrow, in a week. He goes down among the scree in search of a place.

Near the cliff edge he sees some animal like a rat disappear under a rock, and squatting down he finds a crevice, narrow at the mouth but widening into a hollow. He must find a way to unseat the rock that partly occludes the opening and shift it downhill. And afterwards, move the bigger rock from above, sealing it up. It will take time, and deserted though the landscape is, a patrol could any moment pass along the crest, or a plane fly low. He needs the promise of darkness. He looks back up the slope. As the light goes the goats will make for home. It will be milking time and goats have a mind of their own. Home will be a *mas* and a few hectares of vines below Luminy, not far off and before long someone will come in search of the missing goatherd. There's only one way to gain time. The goats have their track and use no other, already one or two are moving off in the direction of the stunted pines. He must get ahead of them and light small fires on either side of the track when he finds it. On this still day they will burn off a patch or two of vegetation and die out when they reach the surrounding rocks. Before then he will be finished and the girl will have a decent burial. It's a great risk but the spirits demand it of him. He runs uphill and overtakes the leading goats which at once accelerate to follow. He tries to wave them back but they take this as a challenge and advance in a body, heads lowered. He runs ahead with a strong stride and near the top crouches among the dry scrub. In his pocket is the note from Albertas telling him his father is arrested. He has a match and lights a corner of the paper. As soon as the goats see flames and wisps of smoke they halt, yellow eyes troubled. Bernard lights a second fire and the sere vegetation flares as easily as Albertas's note. He advances on the goats and this time they turn tail and stampede down the slope, re-grouping near the cliff edge.

The sun has already dropped behind the hill of Luminy and the constant sound of bombardment and firing in the town still echoes round the sky. The enemy is busy. Until dark Bernard tends the fires, keeping under cover where he can and allowing them to spread only seawards, pace by pace. One of the pines, shallower-rooted than the others, can be torn from the ground. Now he returns with it to the crevice and goes to work. On this steep slope he must destabilise the rock and use all his strength with the pine tree as lever to edge it downhill.

The goats watch the fires, then they watch Bernard with the same suspicion, approaching and retiring, every now and then sending up querulous cries as they turn. They've found the girl and inspected her remains without great curiosity. They're of a race with no sense of the meaning of death. For them, there's life and not-life and they have no awareness of a passage from one to the other. Bernard's straining at last succeeds. The rock moves, he works another stone out from under it, gives a last leverage and it goes – a turn, two turns on the slope, gathering momentum it bounds towards the cliff edge and soars into the void over the sea. So still is the day he hears the sound as it hits the water far below.

The body has stiffened, the limbs are setting. The stiffening naked body is a weight he will carry always. On a chain round his neck Bernard wears his grandfather's gold Huguenot cross with the Paraclete and heart, engraved on the back with their name. He lifts it off and puts it round the neck of the girl. He forces the body into the opening, flinching from the numb injuries inflicted, the head going last. His hands are on the head, pushing forward as you load a shell into the breach of a gun. Suddenly there's the sound of falling stone within the crevice, a sliding noise and the body disappears into the dark interior. He'd looked no further in than to make sure of a chamber not more cramped than a grave. Now he understands this is the mouth of a cave going down who knows how far into the heart of the limestone. It's better like that, it's an underworld she's gone to, not a cell.

At work on the rock above the opening, he first notices the breath of wind, cooling him, blowing from inland, from the north, beginning to stretch the flames of his fires seaward. Alone, he has no chance of fighting that and finishing the work at the same time. The lid-stone must be shifted and lodged. Below the opening he makes a bulwark of smaller stones to stop the rock before it gathers momentum. He looks a last time into the dark, remembers the clothes and throws them in, then murmurs a word of committal without sense and applies his lever. The rock lurches once and settles into position. It might have been there since the last ice age when the sea was lower and this place was halfway up a mountain and the shore forty kilometres out to the south. It's finished, she's gone, with his cross and her canvas bag and knife.

The agitation of the goats alerts him to the advancing flames. The whipped fires are angry, they lean down in vengeance. Escape by the ridge is now impossible, the flames mark an unbroken barrier and beyond them on the crest he seems to see the silhouette of moving figures. He runs to the cliff edge. The sea is only fifteen metres down and the water deep. It would be like a dive from a third-storey window. But he's a boy incapable of leaving a herd of goats to jump or burn. This is just one of many moments in his life when prudence and character are opposed. He sees the girl's shirt still on the ground, forgotten. He gathers it up and runs in the direction of the cleft in the limestone at the head of the calanque, calling the goats, waving the shirt, pausing, slipping on the loose scree, calling, cajoling the frightened animals. At last one of them follows. From here there's a way down if they reach it before the flames. He flourishes the shirt above his head like a flag for a troop, calling, calling. The herd moves to him.

By the water's edge all is stillness again, the surface is like oil, the wind passes far overhead. The goats act as if it had all along been their plan to come down here, they nose about peaceably, issuing self-satisfied coughs and bleats. A trickle of fresh water falls from a rock face forming a pool which they soon find. They ignore Bernard, you wouldn't know they owe him their life at the risk of his own. It's almost dark, the sky shows a faint violet colour over the western sea, no more. Only the light of the fires. This is a deserted calanque, no cabins, no quay, no boats drawn up, it's as it must have been when the rising level of the sea first reached it. He hears shouts far up on the hillside and the nearer sound of approaching planes. He leaves the girl's shirt near the edge of the water. She'll be mourned as a casualty of these days – one who tried to escape the fires by swimming, or that the ubiquitous enemy took. By morning the goats will go home, udders bursting. He again removes his own clothes, folds them into a bundle tied by his belt and enters the sea. The water is warm, caressing. He swims out into the deeper sea of the calanque and then changes course eastward in the dark, away from Marseille, towards the next inlet where there's a track he knows, running back the way he came across the stony ridge and into the pine forests. He can't go to his father now, wherever he may be, that's something else to carry through life. He holds the bundle of clothes at the surface and swims clumsily. Floating a moment on his back he watches the fires at the edge of the cliff, still under the wind lashing them towards the sea. The he turns and swims away, he hopes for ever, from this theatre of crime and grief.

*

It's been an exhausting experience in the lime-kiln under the pines – the painful detail, the straining in heat and fear, the orgasm by proxy. Bernard is sweating and his heart pounds. It was the intense living of hours compressed into fifteen minutes' screen time. But he chose to come this way, this theatre is part of him. It will be evening by the time he reaches the Couvent de la Génératrice-Immaculée but the Prosecutor and the Prior like angry deities must be propitiated. And there's the bait of curiosity drawing him on. He'll be tired but calmer when the Bentley rolls into the forecourt of the great bastide in the shelter of the woods, far from the telephone lines, away from the world of gain, duplicity and sin.

# Chapter Four

'THE COMMUNITY IS at prayer at this hour, Monsieur. We do not receive.'

'The Prior expects me.'

'No instructions were given to that effect.'

'I'm sent here by his brother, the Public Prosecutor in Marseille. I am Maître Bernard Vipont, attorney-at-law.'

Unimpressed, the monastic at the door – which he held open by no more than twenty centimetres while speaking suspiciously through the gap – opened it a little wider and viewed the Bentley superbly resting at the foot of the steps. He then looked hard at Bernard, peering into the depths of his eyes – to gauge his sinfulness perhaps. It was to be hoped he would get no reading. 'I have to insist that you wait outside,' he said, 'my instructions are formal.' He was a young man but one apparently born old, with a dry manner and dry, flaking skin around the creases of his face. 'I am Brother Alain.'

'You're an oblate?'

'That happens to be so.' Brother Alain sounded sharp and closed the door without saying any more. It wasn't quite the traditional reception at a hospitable house of God. It looked as if hospitality wasn't the raison d'être of this order, whatever they were. Of course if Brother Alain's instructions gave him no room for initiative that would add a frustration to the biological ones he must already suffer. Bernard felt sure that the mentality and motivation of these celibates would be easy enough to fathom. From deep within the building came the sound of a tolling bell, a single note like a light at sea between long spaces of darkness. Was it to ring devotions into the divine ear? Bernard liked to be ironical about Catholic ways, ever since the trying years of his marriage. After a long wait the door reopened and Brother Alain stood before him, hands joined under a kind of narrow apron forming part of his black habit – a scapular, Bernard believed it was called.

'Father Prior will receive you despite the hour. Be good enough to follow me. In silence.'

Brother Alain turned on his heel, kicking the door shut with the sole of the other foot as he did so by extending his leg behind him. It was a deft and casual movement. Bernard noticed, walking after him, that he was small and slight like a big child masquerading as an adult. He walked quickly, scuttling along as if driven by the scourge of some cruel temptation. The interior was dimly lit but you could see in the half-shadows all the flamboyance of décor that went with social climbing – masses of gilt, fancy plaster-work and heavy pillars. The staircase rose a dozen steps and then curled back to right and left to reach the first-floor landing, under a glass lantern high up in the roof. A huge brass chandelier hung there in the dark and the staircase went no higher. This was where the principal rooms would be, a piano nobile. Anyone going further up could use the back way. On the landing and equidistant from the two arms of the stair were double doors of carved walnut. Brother Alain tapped on one of them and opened it.

'The attorney-at-law, Father Prior,' he announced, his voice deeper than you'd expect from his frame, and then remained standing in the doorway as Bernard went forward with outstretched hand to meet the Prior. He hoped this was the correct proceeding. With bishops and abbots you made some token gesture of reverence, kissed their rings or just bowed if you wanted to keep your independence. But with a mere prior, surely . . .?

The Prior took his hand without returning the pressure. His own must be reserved for blessings. 'Good evening, Maître. I'm glad you managed to find your way to us at last. You may go, Alain.'

'You don't need me to take notes of your talk with the attorney?'

'Leave us.'

'I left my breviary somewhere in here . . .' Alain began to ferret about among the books and papers on the huge table in the centre of the room. Even Bernard could see this was a pretence. He was in no hurry to go. The Prior sighed. Bernard was struck by how this reaction resembled that of any man failing to win compliance in his household, a situation he was very familiar with. The sigh was philosophical. Maybe like a wife with a dowry, Alain was another oblate with expectations and had to be humoured. But Bernard's late wife had no dowry, come to think of it, and it was just the same.

'An oblate need not use a breviary. In fact he should not. He has no office to say.'

'I make it part of my voluntary devotions, Father Prior.'

'Beware of too many voluntary devotions, my dear little Alain. They lead easily to spiritual pride.'

Alain's persistent movements about the room suggested that he thought himself exempt from the risk. His lack of physical advantages let him off. 'Here it is,' he said, still lingering. The Prior waited silently and without moving. Clearly this was his technique for getting rid of Alain so Bernard did the same. At last the reluctant oblate edged towards the door. 'You require nothing? No refreshment?'

'You know quite well the whisky I keep for guests is here in my desk.' Bernard's spirits sank. More whisky.

'Very well, Father Prior, as you wish,' said Alain and departed like a child who loses a battle but, with time on his side, is far from losing the war.

'Alain is a young religious attached, too attached, to my person,' said the Prior with a shake of the head but in a tone of self-satisfaction. 'And he tries to please in case . . . complaint is brought against him.'

Bernard wasn't yet interested in the internal politics of the convent. 'Is he the oblate who saw me in Saint-Victor this morning?'

'Alain? Oh no. Alain doesn't ride a motor-bicycle.'

'You have many oblates, Father Prior?'

'Only two remain since the passing of Brother Raimond whose affairs you're here to discuss with me.'

'So who's the other one?'

There was a hesitation. People often hesitate when a lawyer asks them a question and you learn to interpret it. But possibly this was just the necessary interval for the Prior to get the whisky bottle and two glasses from a cupboard in his desk, an elaborately carved piece of furniture in Renaissance style. 'Our other oblate is a man of mature years retired from the world to give himself to a life of contemplation and prayer. He leads . . . a very withdrawn and spiritual mode of existence here.'

'But sometimes rides a motor-bicycle down into Marseille.'

The Prior, having indicated the chair where his guest was to sit, put himself into a kind of throne, a seat of authority behind the desk. Bernard sensed something inauthentic about this arrangement. The Prior looked hard at Bernard before answering. 'Occasionally, yes. We have no telephone and he carries any urgent message I need to send into the secular world. We are a reclusive order.'

'I've been giving thought, naturally, to the problem the Prosecutor outlined to me,' said Bernard, dropping the matter of the oblate for the time being. It would keep. He looked carefully about him in a way he hoped would leave him seeming unconcerned with the surroundings. A few devout pictures, obscure saints immolated by the death wish, likenesses of forgotten popes. At the darkest end of the room was a painting in a gilded frame, showing a Tuscan or Provençal landscape with antique ruins, in the manner of Patel but mediocre, Bernard judged from where he sat. Not a thing a solid Jewish collector would look at a second time. 'Of course I'll have to examine all the documents with care but *a priori* a technical solution suggests itself. I won't at this stage go into details, I must economise your time, Father Prior, so late in the evening.' That was how to leave the door open. Curiosity must be respected, it was the best way of spotting traps before they snapped shut on you. 'With your permission I'll return tomorrow morning.'

The Prior opened a drawer in front of him. 'Here is poor Brother Raimond's will, in his own hand. If only he could have lived longer . . .'

'Yes, the survival of a testator's parent can be a calamity for other parties.'

'But you think there may be a way . . .?'

'Of side-stepping the father? There may be. Delicate but not impossible.'

'Take the will with you if you wish.'

'No, thank you. When I come back I'll bring my books and you'll give me a corner here where I won't be in the way. Then I can examine everything with a bearing on our question – deeds of property, the statute of your endowment, the rule of the order under which oblates are engaged and received, family records of the late Brother Raimond including any correspondence between him and his father, boundary maps, wills, donations, and valuations – these may be important if we have to apply to the court.' Bernard reckoned this list was enough to be going on with and to give him a lasting upper hand. 'I'll know then what else I may need to look at.'

'All the material you mention will be ready for your arrival tomorrow. You can work in the library. A table will be cleared for you.' Was there a dim light at the back of the Prior's eye as if the library was for some particular reason where Bernard was intended to go? The Prior himself escorted him to the doorstep and they paused outside on the perron, under the stars. A nightingale, a bit off tune so late in the season, sang a love hymn in this celibate enclosure.

'A beautiful domain,' Bernard said. 'I almost envy your oblate who has retired from the world.'

'Our business is with spiritual beauty,' said the Prior reprovingly, 'and the burden of upkeep is what we mostly feel about the domain.'

'The bastide seems in a good state.'

'The structure's good. Our forefathers . . . but much of the carving on the exterior is degraded. There seems to be a sickness in the stone. The balustrade on the roof is dangerous. Pieces fall on windy days.'

'Do they,' said Bernard looking upwards in the dark. 'My own house, the Villa Vipont, has a balustrade on the roof which gave trouble not long ago. I've an excellent artisan still working for me. A Compagnon du Devoir, an expert in stone. I'll bring him up to look at yours and advise you. You'll allow me to offer his work at my expense. Your brother, the Prosecutor, is an esteemed colleague which will make it a pleasure.' Was he going too far, too fast? That was the danger of upper-hand situations, you got over-confident and plausibility ran away with you. Anxiety, less amusing, was really safer.

'Agreed,' said the Prior promptly, and bowing very slightly he stepped backward into the doorway. 'Good night, Maître. I look forward to the visit of the Compagnon.' The door closed with the thud of massive woodwork, shutting out nightingale song and other natural resonances.

\*

The evening was a difficult time for Bernard. Before Marion grew up the evenings when he stayed at home had been easy, delightful, filled with the pantomime of a relationship not yet dangerous. Dangerous? One mustn't exaggerate. Still. Never mind how . . . and other evenings he would go to Caroline's but today his heart wasn't in it. The pantomime of Marion's growing up had been an impromptu by players amusing each other, a rehearsal of games. But now the game was a double pretence, they pretended nothing had changed except that feelings were matured. But the change was far more fateful than that. There was imbalance. His love continued to grow like a parasitic plant on the limbs and branches of her adolescence and now her adulthood, while hers . . . well hers stayed what it had always been but reduced in proportion as she grew. She viewed him, he supposed, as a part of herself to be managed by the right methods of control. Weaned of too much dependence.

He was nearly home, the Bentley nosed its way round the roads above the Corniche like a horse to manger. Bernard was reminded of the homeward flow of the goats at Luminy. The portals of the Villa Vipont opened at the command of his remote control and closed again softly behind him. The churning of his own gravel under his wheels in his own forecourt, the reassurance of all these things almost drove out the memory of the goats and the burning hillside and the rock. But they didn't drive out his fear of seeing Marion disappointed.

She wasn't in the house. 'Hasn't she telephoned?' he asked Juanita. 'No,' said Juanita. She was lying. He knew that because her eye when she lied had the opaque glaze that the eye of Marion's mother always had in the same circumstance.

'I expect she has but she ordered you not to tell me anything.'

'Marion doesn't order me. She's a polite girl, from a good convent, not an arrogant and overbearing man. And not a heretic. She requests me.'

Juanita's hands were on her hips which was always the sign that she was in a good mood. That was because she could see Bernard at a disadvantage. 'So she requested you not to say anything about what she's doing?'

'Every father must lose his authority in the end, Monsieur Bernard. Even a papa with a big cheque book. The cheques get bigger but the authority just shrinks, and the papas get older and they shrink too.'

Damn the woman. She was like Albertas, she thought herself indispensable. It was his own fault, he was too good to everyone around him and he knew what that was supposed to mean. A longing to be loved. But they'd got it wrong, the gurus who thought that up, he had no need to be loved. All he needed was to know why, on that hot scree on the hillside in the summer of 1944, that girl had died, skewered on him. 'One day you'll annoy me and I'll give you notice, Juanita.'

She laughed, looking round at the walls of the Villa Vipont, a laugh of derision without humour. 'And that day you'll be really all alone here with your locked-up attic,' she said, and clicked her tongue after she'd spoken, like a castanet. 'You'll regret me then.' Probably she was right and he would. There was time to see about that, find out what it meant. The future, where everything was always a surprise.

Could Luis have changed his mind and let him down? Perhaps Soames had turned up again. Or perhaps it was just that Luis was ageing too, becoming less calculable, less interested in his career. Bernard was on his way to the telephone to tell Albertas to institute enquiries when it rang, the sound tearing through the empty house like a siren. His heart leapt. It might be Marion.

It was. 'Juanita?' she said.

'It's me.'

73

'Oh.'

'Where are you?'

'You told Juanita you were out till late this evening. I thought you were at your club.'

'I don't remember telling her that and if I did I've changed my mind too. Anyway I never go there.'

'What d'you mean "too"?' Marion sounded suspicious.

'I expected to find you at home.'

'Oh.'

The conversation was becoming impenetrable, they each had too much to hide. 'Where are you?' he asked again.

'I'm at the Phocéa.'

'Is Luis there too?'

'He had to go to work.'

'You know you shouldn't be out alone at night, Marion, you know that.'

'That's why I rang Juanita.'

'I don't see what she has to do with it.'

'To see if there were any messages for me.'

'You mean from Luis?'

'Or anyone.'

'Stay in the Phocéa and I'll come and fetch you. Don't go out in the street now, it's too late. It's a dangerous part of the town. Are you listening?' Now she would have to come into the open, he thought. There was a long silence. 'Do you hear, Marion?'

'I'm thinking,' she said, and then added, 'I told you I was going away.'

'But you're not going away.'

'How do you know that? And why did you expect to find me at home?'

He'd tripped himself up. Marion wasn't a lawyer's daughter and a Vipont for nothing. Now she was more suspicious than ever. And he knew how suspicion can be the sign of someone fearing for their liberty. Perhaps paranoia was a hereditary inclination. He knew that whatever he said she would go on fearing for it but he couldn't stop himself. It was like the breath you have to draw to live. 'I hoped you'd thought better of it,' he said.

'You can fetch me if you like,' said Marion in the small voice she used when she saw there was nowhere further for the exchange to go. In a way it was a sign of the despair that had come into their dealings.

'I'll be there in fifteen minutes.'

He would take her to a restaurant. She must guess that he was responsible for Luis's defaulting, even if Luis had said nothing. No one was better at keeping his mouth shut, except possibly Soames. It was one of the things that made them resemble each other. He would order champagne, she adored that, she could have as much as she wanted. He liked it when Marion was slightly drunk – it softened the Iberian core.

It was clear she only wanted to talk about Luis. Naturally, because if her plan hadn't aborted she'd be with him now, far from Marseille. Bernard refilled her glass. Probably he was the only person she could really discuss Luis with quite freely. She certainly couldn't with her bourgeois friends and colleagues at the University. It meant that Marion was very much alone, in some ways. She needed her father more than she knew.

'Why is it you like Luis, papa?' she asked suddenly.

'I've known him a long time. Ever since the Liberation almost.'

'That's not why you like him. You've known a lot of people you don't like for a long time.'

'I admire his independence.'

'He's not independent of you.'

That was a thing to be neither admitted nor denied. 'I like his difference,' he said, putting it another way.

'He's a Gitan.'

'Yes.'

'You know I love Luis, don't you papa, you know that, don't you?'

'Yes, I know.'

'Can I have some more champagne?'

'Of course you can.'

Marion seemed to fall back into reflection, it was as if her mind turned in an ellipse, passing the same points, never quite coinciding with the last curve of her thought. 'I don't really understand why you just leave me to love him, just like that.'

'I can't stop you loving anyone, Marion.'

'You'd do your best if you hated him. But you don't.' She sounded almost aggrieved, as if his acquiescence defrauded her of something.

'Perhaps some of what you love about Luis are things I appreciate too. He believes in justice at any price. That's an example. And he carries it out if he sees it's needed. Did you know he once executed a collaborator? When he was only a boy, because no one else did it. I admire that.'

She brought her attention back and with it her eyes settled on him. What was she wondering about, from her shore of the divide? One thing was sure – it was impassable. Did this action of Luis's mean anything at all to her? Or was the context too remote, just leaving violence as the kind of outbreak a woman has to expect? 'Is that what gives you a hold over him?' she asked.

'I don't think I have a hold on anyone, Marion. Not Albertas, not Juanita. Not you. We're useful to each other, that's all.'

'You didn't say "not Luis".' She put a hand onto his where it lay on the table next to his glass. There were tears in her eyes. 'Anyway, with me it's more than just usefulness.' She must be feeling sorry for him all of a sudden. It wouldn't last but it was pleasant for the moment. He took her hand between both of his.

A little wind had got up at nightfall and from beyond the open windows of the first-floor restaurant you could hear the rattle of cords on all the boats in the Vieux Port. The sea was stirring, bringing itself back to mind, ceaseless as the stir of the senses. 'Between us usefulness is a word, only a sound. It stands for whatever we want it to mean. We don't have to say more than that.' Marion didn't answer but her hold on his hand tightened before she let go of it to pick up her glass which she held out for more. 'Did you see Luis this afternoon?' he asked.

'Oh yes, I saw him. I told you so on the telephone.'

Uncertainty of the way forward had made him repeat his question. She'd seen Luis, he'd left her to go about his and Bernard's business, and until he made contact there was no way of knowing what he would do next. 'When will you see him again?'

'When he tells me.'

'You mean he didn't tell you?'

'Tomorrow, I expect. Or the day after.' Sometimes champagne made Marion excited and other times sleepy. Now it was making her sleepy. Her eyes were closing by degrees and her voice losing buoyancy. They were only halfway through the meal but she lit a cigarette. Bernard made no protest.

'So you're coming home after all.'

'After all.'

'You know you can always go away because I'm so glad when you come back. You know that, don't you, Marion?'

Once again she didn't answer. Because of course she could go away when she wanted, whenever she wanted. She was free, the only freedom she didn't have was the one caught inside, somewhere in the maze of childhood. She would always come home, unless one unlucky day she found an exit from that maze. But perhaps for as long as they both lived the maze would hold her fast. It was one of the things he counted on.

\*

He decided against summoning Luis again, he would rather give him the illusion of autonomy, it was more decent. Better for now that he continue his researches at the library, leaving Bernard time to look around at the Couvent de la Génératrice-Immaculée. What was needed, to make sure of Luis for a month or so, was something more feasible than that stop-gap project at the Musée des Beaux-Arts.

'I shall be out all day,' Bernard told Juanita.

'You won't even eat here at midi?'

'I said, all day. Until tonight, probably quite late.'

Instead of welcoming this unusual programme as he'd expected, she seemed to take it as a personal affront. 'Your own house sees less and less of you,' she said furiously. 'Soon you'll forget how to find your way back from . . . the *company* you frequent.'

How illogical she was. It made him wonder, not for the first time, if Juanita was secretly waiting for some sort of proposition from him. Surely not. But she often behaved like a wronged woman, bellicose, perverse and self-righteous. He'd never given her any reason to expect advances, as far as he was aware. But he knew that certain perfidious signals can be sent and received unconsciously, and Juanita was handsome, rather more than just handsome, and there was a lot of her to catch the eye. The priests who heard her confession every week probably had dreams about her afterwards, Bernard thought sarcastically. He'd had one or two himself, actually.

Brother Alain was at his post at the door and this time there was a slight unbending in his manner as he surveyed the Bentley. 'Father Prior mentioned you would bring a young artisan to look at our stonework. But I see you haven't,' he said. 'The Prior will be disappointed.' In fact disappointment was clearly written on his own face. Presumably his was a life with not much social variety.

'He may come with me tomorrow.'

'You expect to be still working here tomorrow?'

'Quite possibly I may,' Bernard said in a final voice. Alain hadn't so far given enough sign of goodwill to get a lot of questions answered.

'Father Prior instructed me to show you to the library. He hopes to meet you at midi. You're invited to eat with us in the refectory.'

'I look forward to that,' said Bernard. The refectory was another important room to be inspected.

'The late Brother Raimond was a sad man,' said Alain, showing a new side of himself, purveyor of gratuitous information. It was an aspect to be cultivated.

'Wasn't he happy in the monastic life then?'

'We don't expect happiness here below. Service is our highest aspiration. Even the service of prayer.' Something didn't ring quite true about this statement. As a lawyer, Bernard was quick to sense things not ringing true.

'Perhaps Brother Raimond was made for something different,' he said trying to sound incurious, as they approached an arched doorway at the end of a long corridor on the ground floor of the building. The principal rooms were on the piano nobile, here the ceilings were vaulted and low and the floors paved with stone. In the days of the bastide's prosperity all this would have been part of the domestic offices, storerooms, spaces for the paraphernalia of sport, a billiard table somewhere perhaps, a gun-cabinet, stuffed birds and boars.

'When he was young he planned to marry his cousin. But the young lady disappeared.' Had Alain ever met one of that species? He sounded as if to his mind it was natural for a young lady to disappear in a puff of smoke, never to be seen again. It had happened to the *génératrice immaculée* after all.

'How old was Brother Raimond?'

'About the same age as you, Maître, at a guess.'

'I see. I'd imagined him much older.'

'Because he's dead? One can die at any age.'

Alain was becoming not exactly familiar but a little too much at ease without waiting to be put there. All the same, he mustn't be discouraged before his usefulness could be assured. 'And Brother Raimond's girl . . . what became of her?'

'No one knew. He said she went out one day and never came back.'

'Where was he at the time?'

'He never told me. It was too sad. But wherever he was, I'm sure he aspired always to serve,' said Alain mechanically. 'Here's our library. Father Prior has had all the documents he thinks you may need put here on this table in the window. No one else may use the library as long as you're here. You will ask me if anything more is needed.'

'Where will you be?'

'I'm the doorkeeper of the convent. Therefore I'll be by the door.'

When Bernard had passed an eye quickly over the documents he thought of his books still in the Bentley. He didn't really need them, he was familiar with all the legal ploys the case demanded, but there was no hurry to let that be known. He left the library and returned along the corridor. The doors onto the perron were open with hot air pouring in and there was no sign of Alain. He stepped outside and looked about him. No other building was in sight, yet there must be other buildings – stables and coach houses and premises for the farm. Round the other side and in the trees, no doubt. In the centre of the gravel was a large stone basin for an ornamental fountain from which no water ran, marking the austerity of the bastide's present being. He went down the steps to the Bentley. And there was Alain, on the other side of the car with the door open, bent down to examine the running-board. He straightened up when he heard a step on the gravel. His flushed face was lit with excitement and shadowed by apprehension.

'Thrupp and Maberley,' he said, pronouncing these names with difficulty. 'Here's their plate. The coachmaker of your car. I knew where to look because I knew a lot about English cars once. A long time ago it seems now. It was a childish interest.'

'From before the aspiration to serve got the better of you and drove it out.'

Alain giggled, disclosing teeth too discoloured for his age. It was an odd sound he made, high-pitched, quickly repressed, contrasting with his deep voice. 'I learned from cigarette cards and magazines. I've never seen a real one so close. It took my mind away from my breviary.'

'Get into the driving seat,' Bernard said. 'Can you drive?'

'If anyone saw me doing that . . . frivolous and selfish . . . there'd be a severe penance for me. Brother Michel would make sure of it.' All the same, temptation had taken hold, you could see it at work.

'The other oblate?'

'Yes.'

'Has he the right to give you penances?'

'He reports me . . . unless I . . .'

'Unless?'

'Brother Michel and I must cooperate, it's our religious duty to do so without complaint from me. And he's much older. He's been in the world. He's renounced so much more. I am subordinate.'

'I can say I asked you to fetch me something. Go on, just get in and hold the wheel. It may be the only time you'll ever do it in your life. They can't want to punish you for that.'

'Brother Michel has his own ideas about what should be punished.'

'If he can ride a motor-bicycle down into Marseille surely you can step into a car in the forecourt if I ask you to?' Bernard felt determined now to have his own way about this. There was something in Alain's fear that roused a desire to score over Brother Michel who, anyway, had already earned his suspicion by reporting him to the Prosecutor. Obviously a natural petty denouncer. Alain was already in the driver's seat, the top of his head not far above the arc of the steering wheel. He looked as if he was getting an advance on the ecstasy promised for the after life. Bernard stepped in on the other side.

'To start the engine you push that shiny button there,' he said. 'It's so silent you may not even hear it. It's a very powerful engine all the same. A real tiger.' His unconsulted law books sat on the back seat and the Prior's pile of documents lay neglected on the library table while he enjoyed himself out here in this new role. It was much more entertaining, better value altogether. It was unforeseen experience. Alain put out a hand, his index pointed at the starter. Then he drew it back.

'It would be wrong, even if Michel didn't see me I'd know it was wrong. Childish things must be put away. It would be indulgence.' One expected the extraordinary in a convent for monks but this was absurd. Bernard wondered how long it was since Alain had indulged to the extent of masturbating. Perhaps never. Now he was trembling like a rabbit in a snare. Bernard took his hand firmly in his own like a child's, and pushed his finger onto the little silver dome of the starter. At once a soundless tremor ran through the bodywork.

'There you are. You see it wasn't impossible to do what you wanted.'

Alain was already half out of the car. 'I must return to my post,' he said, and ran across the gravel past the dry fountain to the door. But Bernard felt he'd won a hold in his mind. He'd shown him he wasn't as completely cut off from delight as he thought, and that the essence of true temptation is to be irresistible. Alain had learned something he didn't know before.

Back in the library, Bernard took stock of what it contained. It was beautifully cool in here under the vaults. The space was L-shaped and at each end was a barred window buried in the wall. The shelves carried many vast dull histories approved by ecclesiastic authority, theological works in Latin and German, lives of the saints and popes. Just looking at the collection from a distance created an anguish of boredom and resentment. Nothing, nothing whatever, recalled the existence of the things that make life tolerable. Beauty might never have been born and woman never invented. Bernard turned his attention to the walls. Sombre prints in black frames – the Arènes at Nîmes and Arles, the Pont du Gard with northern tourists in the foreground looking up from under their top hats. Nothing else. At one place was a hook high up in the masonry, and if you looked closely enough, a hint of a quadrangular shadow on the wall below it. Something had hung here, and not long ago, traces of cobweb from behind it still stuck to the plaster and drifted minutely in the movement of his breath. Bernard felt his instinct alerted. The item seemed to have measured a little over half a metre high and slightly less in width, big for a print, comparatively small for a painting. It certainly couldn't have been a life-size portrait of the order's founder or patron saint, nor one of those pious images to elevate thought, they were usually enormous. This blank had the proportions of half a landscape. So why had it been removed? To hide it? To draw him on? And where to? He must try and sound out Alain on these questions. He was sure that very little would go on at the Couvent without Alain knowing something about it. He had the physique and personality of a spy, passepartout, ferrety, unprepossessing.

The midday meal in the refectory was eaten in silence but for readings from Bossuet's *Sur l'Unité de l'Eglise*, chosen, so Bernard suspected, specially for him. The reader was the oldest member of the community and his ancient voice soared nasally for panegyric passages and sank like lead in a pond for lyrical ones. Bernard ate little though the meal was a good one, the monks weighing into it like labourers – which most of them were, straight off their fields – and the wine from Cassis was solid and copious. Bernard found the reading countered appetite but that gave him the more opportunity to observe. The community numbered thirty present. They were of all ages between the reader at one end and Alain at the other, but the preponderance was of Bernard's own age and above. These were men who would have been of fighting years at the outbreak of war and fit for Resistants under the Occupation if they hadn't already been soldiers of Christ in an enclosure. Alain sat at the bottom end of the table, farthest from the Prior, and if anything was wanted he got up to fetch it. Bernard caught his eye once and winked but got no response. Which of the company was Brother Michel, the denouncer? If he met another eye he would know. But no one else looked his way at all, they ignored his presence as if it was part of their rule. Probably it was. Guests from the world might bring with them the virus of desire.

The Prior, come to think of it, had given him a cool reception in the minutes they were together before the meal. Maybe someone had seen Alain with him in the Bentley and reported it already.

'You're comfortable enough in the library?' asked the Prior with a note of irony, Bernard thought.

'Perfectly.'

'And the documents? You have what you need?'

'I believe so.' Short answers tend to elicit other questions and you can sometimes learn from a question.

'Do you think of putting your car out of the sun? You'll find an old coach-house behind the main buildings. You won't need anyone to direct you. The afternoon will be very hot and your return journey would be more comfortable. The car, shall we say, is a conspicuous object for a house like ours.' Bernard gave a slight shrug without replying and the Prior turned away impatiently. Men used to easy authority don't like to be thwarted on their home ground. The Prior had betrayed a weakness. Looking round now at the community at table, Bernard felt the collective force of their certainties, the conviction of rightness. The law taught you that was always a delusion. He waited patiently until the ancient reader closed his volume and then he spoke into the silence in a carrying voice.

'The late Brother Raimond brought a fair endowment to the convent, Father Prior – or rather, it seems he thought he'd brought it. I wonder if that's so with many of your community?' The eating, nearly at an end, now stopped altogether. Bernard read in the eyes

turned on him a pleasurable shock and anticipation of awful consequences. The Prior laid a hand on his arm.

'Our rule of silence is to be respected,' he murmured but Bernard
pretended not to hear him, breaking in before the sentence was out.

'I can understand a monk under vows choosing to give away his
inheritance, but an oblate – I find it more surprising. He can return to
secular life at any time, can't he? Brother Raimond could have gone
out from here and married and had children to leave it to. Or not
married and left natural children. Of course, I didn't know him, he
may have been suggestible . . . I don't mean influenced, of course . . .'

Now there was a scraping of chairs and sounds of wordless protest.
The thought of careless reproduction by one of their number was too
much for most of them. But there was one face among the rest where
Bernard caught a smile, possibly sarcastic, with a glint of gold among
the teeth halfway back. Hardly the right fillings for a poor friar. He
knew he'd succeeded in flushing out Brother Michel. The Prior rose
and with a sign dismissed the assembly. 'Please follow me,' he said.

In the wide corridor outside the refectory he turned furiously. 'I
fear your remarks could offend some of my brethren, Maître Vipont.
This is a community of simple men, not cynical lawyers. We work the
fields and Raimond's legacy consisted of fields, no more.'

'Yes, I've studied the plans. His fields lie near the outskirts of the
town, Father Prior, those spreading outskirts. Development land in a
couple of years. They're a prize which the succession laws will give
back to his family unless the right steps are taken. Discreetly and
quickly.' There. Now he possessed the detail of the documents it was
too late for the Prior to drop him and ask the Prosecutor to send
another attorney. The community was committed. He was their legal
adviser.

'I sense a hostility to our way of life, our discipline. You're not a
Catholic, I think. I can only hope your work here will be soon
finished.' The Prior seemed nervous, his anger having met an obstacle
that didn't move. 'Perhaps by this evening you'll be ready to make
your report.' That didn't make it sound as if the removed picture was a
lure to keep him here. More as if it was hidden to keep it out of his

sight. But of course that would make it all the more alluring, once suspected. If this was a trap it was a deep game.

'I doubt it,' said Bernard. 'The courts are loth to allow exceptions to the Civil Code on inheritance, it's one of the Napoleonic corner-stones. I need time to study all the documents in detail and prepare a dossier . . . for more ample reflection, in the office. By my collabora-tors.' Usually the word dossier was enough to halt everything. A dossier can take years of life, just by being a dossier, like a tortoise wandering the African bush. 'I shall need to come back over several days. And I haven't forgotten my promise, Father Prior. I'll bring you my artisan tomorrow. And I swear to hold my tongue in the refectory in future.'

*

About halfway through the afternoon Bernard decided he'd spent long enough on the documents. He rearranged them meticulously in the order he'd found them. There was only one letter among the rest, apparently from Brother Raimond's father. He hadn't noticed it until now. It wasn't long, a minute or two to read, no more. A peasant's commonplace message to his son, no doubt, about the vines and olives. Bernard settled back in the chair with the letter in his hand. It was undated but the lined paper was old and creased, stained and worn along the folds as if Brother Raimond had kept it near and often looked at it, folding and unfolding with fingers thickened by manual labour. He felt an instant sympathy with the dead oblate.

My dear son,

I hope your work for the reverend fathers gets you their good opinion but I hope too you will come back before long to me and your mother. There's work for you here, work enough for both of us. The fathers can always find someone else, you know that. Someone not needed at home perhaps. Now you're nearly a man you must be brave about what I have to tell you, Raimond. Your mother says I shouldn't tell you in a letter but I say it makes no difference, there's a war and he's nearly a man, others have worse things than this, in the war.

Your cousin, the little Julie, she's gone away. We don't know what happened – your poor aunt, you imagine, she's torn in pieces. Julie went out with the goats and only the goats came back to be milked. Perhaps the Germans took her. I don't like to think it and your mother and your aunt won't say what they think. The poor women, all the poor women in this dirty war. My heart breaks, Raimond, to tell you this. You must be a man, if only we knew what that really is. She won't come back, I think. And you know she had that sickness still. You know another thing, they kill them, perhaps I shouldn't say that to you. When they finish with them they kill them and throw them in a hole.

Come back to us, Raimond. With poor Julie gone your aunt has only you to inherit her fields next to mine. You and Julie would have had them all. Come back – and when the wound heals you will find someone else.

Your devoted father.

Bernard was sweating, an icy sweat like a sheet coiled round him. 'They finish with them and throw them in a hole.' The stain of atrocity spread into his conscience. But Raimond, in spite of the letter, hadn't dared be the man his father hoped for. He'd hung on to the skirts of the Church and worn his loss like a scapular, a long black apron screening his virile parts from the day and the world of action. Because Bernard, the young Bernard, had cheated him of his girl and her inheritance of little fields. Now Maître Vipont the attorney stood up, tall but burdened. At least he knew what he could do, even if it was too late to do Raimond any good here below. He could make sure of those valuable fields which Raimond, after his own death, had inherited at last from his aunt, the poor goatherd's mother. And now Bernard the attorney could ensure they went back to Raimond's father, never to the convent, the family of the Prosecutor, the hungry treasury of the Church. It was in his power. The claims of fathers were naturally close to Bernard's heart.

It sounded from the letter as if the goatherd had no father. Bernard remembered the skin of honey, and the rest. The image could be Marion. The goatherd hadn't been much more than a child

86

– neither had he. And he'd destroyed the daughter she'd once been to someone. Bernard's heart accused him. Law and conscience could be countered with reason. Not the heart. The heart would only answer to reparations and amendment.

But what would the Prosecutor do about Luis and his dossier then? Caraman was a wilful man with a high sense of what was due to him. Well, one would see. One must take one's time. Amendment was a patient process. And Bernard felt sure now that there were other discoveries to be made about the affairs of this convent. There were things hidden here, issues of conscience guilty as his own, he could feel it. Investigation, then action, that was the way, the best way always. Resolve laced with possibilities of vengeance made him feel better. The burdened heart would follow in its own time. He knew himself, he always resurfaced, he was his own life-belt; his nature was like a ring of cork bearing him up when the going turned rough.

It was time to go and find Alain.

He was sitting in an alcove near the door, breviary in hand, back towards that whore of a Bentley. 'I hope Brother Michel didn't report you, at least?' Alain said nothing but raised a warning hand. They were already complicit in something like a conspiracy. Alain was to be seduced, he longed for it. 'Come and help me carry my books to the car. I left them in the library.' On the way Bernard put a friendly hand down on Alain's thin shoulder beside him, holding it a little with a pressure just more than its own weight. 'I've come to feel a great sympathy for Brother Raimond and his sadness,' he said. 'His life had no colour in it. He was made to be a farmer with a young wife.' Tears of genuine empathy and remorse came into Bernard's eyes as they entered the library. 'A life inside these thick walls with no pictures even, to bring a bit of light. And he was a man of the *pays*. Our Provence with all its brilliant colour. Think of it. No wife. No light. No colours. No picture. Bare walls.'

'There was a picture here with a strange light in it . . . before . . . until . . .' Alain said, and broke off.

'Was there? Well the place needs it. Why isn't it here any longer? Was it too much of a distraction?'

'It was taken down,' Alain said in a closed voice, picking up almost half Bernard's pile of heavy volumes.

'Is that where it hung, over there?'

'Yes. I think so. I don't have permission to use the library. The library isn't for oblates.'

'Not even for Brother Michel with his gold teeth?'

Alain looked at him quickly, and away. 'It was Michel who took the picture down.'

'How do you know that, if you don't use the library?'

'He carried it upstairs.' Alain motioned with his head.

'Did he? I see. Well, now we'll go back to the Bentley with all these great tomes and you'll have a good excuse for another look inside. Next time I come perhaps I'll take you for a little drive in it. As far as the coach-house where the Prior wants me to hide it decently. You'll show me the way and we'll open the bonnet and you can see the engine. If no one's looking you can even drive it yourself, across the coach-house yard.'

Alain's lips moved in hopeless prayer against the irresistible. But prayer was no use to Bernard, he was earthbound and must live with what he'd done, and what he'd learned.

# Chapter Five

In Luis's life he could never remember it better than this – in fact never as good, probably. His hands still wandered about the body beside him, not urgent now, just a continuation of idle wandering at low tide. He thought of a poem about wandering hands that Soames had shown him. Soames claimed that old soldiers liked poetry due to the sadness of war, and he'd tried to educate Luis because Gitans were sad anyway, war or no war. 'Here, you'll learn plenty of useful English in this,' he'd said – 'behind, before, above, between, below' – that poet knew what he wrote about, that's why Soames approved of him.

Marion seemed asleep but he knew she wasn't. When she really slept her mouth opened a little and a sort of shadow appeared round her eyes. Of course Luis had never yet seen her sleeping at night when you'd expect long shadows. Just in the afternoon. It was strange to think, after so many others, that this one was a lifelong love. Well, not quite lifelong since it only started when he was already about forty, but love while he lived, he was sure of that. Anyway, this was a feeling and therefore true, not a time-table which only had to be accurate. This was like what he had under his hand now. And if truth to feeling would do for Soames's poets, it was good enough for him.

'I felt when you came . . . never like that before.' Why did she say she felt it? Surely she always did. Still, it was good if it wasn't just the same every time. 'I mean inside.'

'I always have you inside, Marion, always.' Luis saw himself suddenly again like long ago, the half-starved sun-scorched boy out of a camp in the Camargue for people of his race.

She opened her eyes and looked at him, weighing this up for a moment as she'd learned to do at the University. 'You're talking metaphorically, Luis, because you're only a man,' she said. After she'd thought about this she added, 'but never mind. I know I never could love anyone else but you. I do love papa, of course.'

'Oh yes, of course.' There was a long silence.

'In a different way.'

'Of course,' said Luis though not absolutely convinced. As a nominal orphan he had no direct experience of the Oedipal situation, but his feelings about Ida were what made him doubtful of Marion's statement. Without going into it too carefully he knew his love for Ida wasn't different in kind from what he felt for Marion, just in priority.

'I must always remember to think of him,' she affirmed as if Luis had argued with her openly.

'I know.'

'Whatever I do. You see that.' Perhaps she wanted him to argue, perhaps that was it. But he wasn't going to. He respected prior claims, they turned, with time, into the claims you had yourself.

'You're right.'

Marion sat up straight so she was looking down at him. He could tell by her expression that she was about to legislate for them both for the future. He put a hand on each of her arms and listened carefully. 'We must think about what we're going to do, Luis. We can't go on like this for ever.'

'No, Marion.' She didn't look satisfied by that. Her education had made her expect longer answers you could get your teeth into.

'What do you mean, no?'

'You're right,' he said again, 'right about everything.' He leaned forward and kissed a shoulder.

'Unless you listen to me properly I'll put my clothes on.'

'I am listening to you.'

'You trust Monsieur Soames, don't you? He says he knows of a house with land, near him in the Camargue. For horses or bulls. He's going to try and buy it.'

'Soames always has solutions. He's a fountain of solutions.'

'It's to help us. You should be grateful.'

'It's to make me do what he thinks I should do.' He could see she took that seriously, because it had to do with freedom, one of her principles. Marion was consistent about freedom.

'What is it you do for papa, that you're always there to be sent for when he wants you?' she asked, trying another tack.

'We have business interests together.'

Marion laughed. 'You and papa. Business interests. You've got as much interest in business as he has. None. I'd love to do business with either of you. You wouldn't have a chance. I'd skin you alive.'

'It's not that sort of business, Marion. It's more like an idea of what's just and putting it right, and so we both know what to do. It's about freedom, in a way.' He chose what to say, carefully, to appeal to her beliefs.

'Papa is free. I don't see what you mean.'

'I don't think he's free in his heart.' This was as close as Luis could get to his perception of Bernard's difficulties in living.

'You mean me.'

'No, that's not what I mean. Not quite. Apart from you, I think he's in some trouble he can't solve. I think he always has been.'

Marion's clothes were on the floor, perhaps because she thought it was cleaner there than on any of the furniture in the bedroom of this one-star hotel. Probably she was right. She got off the bed and stooped down to pick them up one by one. Watching her, a kind of peace spread over Luis's mind. 'When will I see you again?' Marion asked.

'I don't know. Soon. I hope.'

'What d'you mean by soon, Luis?'

'I must see what your father . . . I have to see him about that business we're working out.' He'd never spoken so incautiously before. It was because this time he was emptied of reserve.

'It's so cruel for papa to control how we live.' Marion's face was decomposing like the face of an actor on the screen but better, much better. The tears when they came would seem the natural overflow of a spring. Luis felt sabotaged at the prospect of these tears, as if Marion

91

wept in a language of which he commanded not a single word. He stood up, holding his shirt in front of him like a shield from the storm. 'And what's worse I don't even know how he does it.' Now the first tears were there, not many but enough to make Luis very unhappy. Should he approach and hold her, dropping the shirt? The likely effect of that would be to excite him and cause Marion to misinterpret the gesture. So he put his trousers on while she stood there watching him, with eyes full of tragic fury. 'Why don't you speak?' she demanded at last. 'Or has papa taken your tongue away so you can't tell anyone anything?'

Now he understood better the ratio of anger to distress in her feelings and was glad he'd decided against any attempt at physical comforting. That would have made it worse. He sat on the edge of the bed with bent back to give an impression of tractability and calm. 'Perhaps I'll tell him. I mean, tell him I can't work for him any more. Then we could— '

'No, no,' Marion interrupted. 'You mustn't tell him anything. As soon as you tell him something he starts thinking. It's much better for papa not to have to think at all. Then you can guess what he's going to do. As soon as he thinks, he's unpredictable. Like a startled animal.'

'We're all like animals.'

'We all are animals, Luis. I mean papa's a dangerous one, when he thinks.'

'I don't think he's very dangerous. He's a kind man. Generous. Just.'

'Being kind only makes him more ... redoubtable.' Her tears seemed to have dried up at source. Perhaps she was secretly pleased with her papa for being so fearsome. Or she might just be interested in an intellectual way. In all his dealings with women, Luis had never had an intellectual before and it brought many surprises. Feelings so easily reversed into the gear of analysis and back again, it made you dizzy.

'Well then, I'll just go on with ... what we're thinking about him and me and then afterwards I'll disappear without saying anything more. And you can follow. I'll go to Soames,' Luis said.

'He mustn't suspect it in advance.'

'I'll be careful.'

'Even so, I think he'll work out a way to keep you back. He sees ahead. And he wants you near us.'

'Why do you think so?'

Marion didn't say anything for a moment but looked at him and then at the bed, the doubtful furniture, the thin bars of white light in the shutters still closed. It was as if she was looking for somewhere to hide something. 'I don't know.'

'At the beginning I thought he'd hate me being with you. I'm old enough to be your father myself. I corrupted you from the young men with money and houses and families and work. I've no place in your world.'

'That may be what he likes about you. You appeal to the anarchist in him. You know papa's not very grown-up, not really.'

Luis hadn't known that, nor did he know what she meant. Bernard was older than him and seemed to Luis a pillar of society and righteousness, even if it had to be underground righteousness. So what was being grown-up supposed to be? But it was no good worrying over these meanings. If he and Marion lived in the Camargue and worked for their life with the horses instead of at the University, she would gradually stop being an intellectual and then she'd be happier and easier to understand. That was what to plan for, without saying it. She would always be easy enough to love, he knew. 'We'll do whatever you want,' he said.

'We must keep very quiet. I was stupid already, I made him suspicious about Monsieur Soames. We must go on the same as before, Luis, until we're ready. I won't even tell Juanita, not everything.'

'That'll hurt him you know, Marion. We'd both be hurting him when we should both . . .'

'I'll make it all right afterwards. I know how to do that. It'll be all right.'

Luis had dressed himself and they stood facing one another. He held out his hands and she took them. 'I won't use that boy at the Vieille Charité any more,' he said. 'Albertas knows about him. I'll leave messages with Soames. You do the same.'

'Yes, Luis,' she said, as if they were already on their ranch where orders would be orders. Luis laughed with relief and because he enjoyed Marion's comedies, usually. 'I know it'll be all right in the end.'

'We just have to reach the end,' Luis said.

\*

'I slept badly, Juanita. I had nightmares. The weather must be going to change.'

'It's because there are rats up there in your attic.' Juanita stood over Bernard while he finished his coffee. 'I can hear them. Rats are the messengers of the evil one.'

'Rubbish,' said Bernard.

'If it's secret papers you keep up there, they'll eat them. They'll work their way right through all of them.'

'I don't keep papers there.'

'I can't go on living in a house with rats. You must let me go into your attic with the poison.'

'You certainly won't ever set foot inside my attic, I promise you that, Juanita.'

'If it's not papers, what is it you keep locked away up there then?'

'If you want to know, if you really want to know . . . this time I'll tell you . . . they're my collection of sacred images – reminders of man's inspiration within himself.'

'You are an irreligious man, Monsieur Bernard. You're nothing but an atheist. You have a pagan heart.' She sketched the gesture of crossing herself, but perfunctorily, because it was her enquiries that interested her here and now. 'You should be careful of making jokes at the expense of the faith. One day an account of your words and actions on earth will be required of you.' In fact he believed that a lot of her Catholic zeal was a pose – it was the costume for the part she'd cast herself in.

'And on that day I'll call you as witness to my good nature and long-suffering tolerance,' Bernard said.

'I believe you have pornographic materials you're ashamed of, up there. And aids for the act of sin.'

Bernard laughed. In a long history of outrage Juanita had never gone quite so far. It was her lubricious imagination irritating her. It made him more than usually conscious of her physical volume, a mass of suppressed desires. But he would never do anything so foolish as to . . . besides, he wasn't free in himself. As Caroline might have said, he was a hostage of conscience, chained to a radiator. 'I don't need any aids, thank you, Juanita. I don't suffer from jaded Latin appetites.'

'The English are vicious people, everyone knows it. Naturally an appetite is less jaded if you tickle it with aberrations.' Having worked out this crushing reply Juanita picked up the tray that had carried his breakfast and moved towards the door. 'Marion intends to spend the next few days studying. She asked me to tell you. She will be staying in her apartment where you can call her if you have to. But she will be very busy.'

'I see.'

She turned at the door. 'We have oysters from Portugal today at midi. They're recommended for restoring a tired organism.'

'I'll make sure and be home punctually.' There was no harm in letting her feel she'd come off best. Bernard believed everyone had a right to their particular pleasures and he didn't mind being Juanita's occasional butt if that made her life here at the Villa Vipont more tolerable. Besides, she was . . . under his protection, and occasionally had a role in his dreams. The first of these reasons might be old-fashioned, the second was quite convincing.

Actually, only a part of the attic was locked up, but the systems there were the most secure that money could buy. Quite a small space, very crowded. If fire swept through the Villa Vipont everything up here would go because no one but Bernard knew the codes. But he didn't worry much about fire. What worried him was burglary. If the works were stolen, they would fall into other hands and he was as jealous as any trustee. There was no time this morning to look around in his usual studious way. He stared for a minute or two at the Derain with the cypresses which he'd thought about two days ago. He was still fresh to it, it was a newcomer to his field like the girl Sonia, at Caroline's house. How devious was the contrivance of its flat planes and colours. It was an enigmatic landscape to die in . . . like the vicinity of the Mont Puget . . . with the sea as neighbour. But there was no sea in the painting, only the sky suggested that element inseparable from death. He knew he was considering the picture in the wrong way, he was seeing it in the light of autobiography, past and future. It wasn't a sound critical perspective. It was out of date, as Marion could have told him. Bernard locked up and went down to the Bentley.

Luis would be waiting for him in the shade of the trees on the Avenue du Prado, on the way to the racecourse. The vicinity of a racecourse was one where Luis wouldn't seem out of place and the driver of a Bentley could very well stop in the ordinary run of business. Bernard attended the races regularly in the Bentley precisely for the purpose of giving verisimilitude to this useful ruse. Also because he enjoyed watching horses, at a safe distance. One of these days he would go with Soames to that legendary course at Liverpool and witness the Grand National Steeplechase. What a magnificent title for the event – only the English could imagine bringing the house of God into a horse race. He would mention this to Juanita. There Luis was, leaning against one of the last of the old plane trees. As always, Bernard's aesthetic sense responded to Luis's appearance, so relaxed, so easy against the tree as if he grew from it like Daphne and the laurel. When Bernard had first known Luis as a boy, he'd seemed to him only distinguished from other strays as one coin varies from another by the beauty of the profile stamped on it. Now this distinction was at full maturity and Luis, leaning against the tree, looked more like Apollo resting in the huntsman's grove.

'Luis!'

'Salut, Bernard.' Luis got into the back of the car, discreetly like the client of a client. 'Sorry, I didn't see you.'

That was unusual, very unusual. As a rule Luis never apologised for anything because if things went wrong it was not him but the *baxt* that was responsible. His people's fatal law. The *baxt* had willed it so. Bernard's internal alarm system was alerted. What was passing in that Romany head to make him apologise suddenly? Something must be on his mind. He must be watched.

On the way up to the Couvent, Bernard explained Luis's mission –

to keep his eyes and ears open for anything out of the ordinary.

'What's out of the ordinary in a convent for men?' Luis asked. 'Everything would seem out of the ordinary to me.'

'I don't know. Anything that looks like covering up. A picture was moved out of the library as soon as it was known I was going to be working there. It may be nothing at all. Or it could be a decoy – to draw us in.'

'And you want to know which.' Luis knew almost as well as he did how the powerful hereabouts looked after their interests – a body thrown in the sea – or by a roadside – some chance fall of rock . . .

'Exactly. I do.'

'Do we know who moved it or where?'

'Brother Alain probably knows where it is.'

'Brother Alain?'

'You'll see him when we arrive. He keeps the door and the Bentley excites him.' Bernard might have added 'almost to orgasm' but Luis was prudish and had never taken to joking about such matters. In fact Luis rarely joked. It made him dangerous, in a way.

'Is he a priest?'

'No, he's an oblate. His vows are provisional. He can retire into civilian life if he wants to. There's another oblate and you should look out for him. He has gold fillings in his teeth. His name's Michel. He's the one who moved the picture.'

Luis was silent. They were passing the University buildings at Luminy and he was staring out of the window.

'That's where Marion's going to work,' Bernard said, pointing towards the Faculty of Sciences.

'If she goes to work there she'll never . . .'

'Never what?'

'Never . . . look back.'

Bernard didn't believe that was what Luis had first meant. Did he mean come back? You had to take Luis unawares to learn what was hiding in his head. The Bentley advanced slowly along the sandy road from Luminy to the convent.

'Is this the only way in and out?'

'You can get here by going past the prison and turning into the woods near the quarry.'

'This is better. You could ride this way.' In the forecourt Luis looked up at the façade of the bastide and its elliptical bay. 'They're well installed here, these monks. I thought for them it was meant to be a life of poverty.'

'It's like Brother Michel. These places always have plenty of gold filling in the background. There's Alain now.'

He must have been waiting for them. Bernard patted him familiarly on the shoulder when he reached the top of the steps. 'Shall we take her round to the coach-house straight away, Brother Alain? You know what I promised you. I always keep my promises.' He felt slightly ashamed of himself, as if teasing a child with the lure of fruits just out of reach. Alain's eyes were fixed on the car with the look of an obsession born there and then. You'd think he'd recognised his fatality in that polished four-wheeled article out there on the gravel. His responses of yesterday were nothing to this. Luis was out of the car and standing with his back to it, studying the roof-line and the balustrade above the windows.

'Did you hear me?' Bernard asked.

'No. Oh no.'

'I said—'

'Who's that, there?'

'It's Luis. The artisan.'

Alain turned back into the house. Bernard thought he heard a whimpering sound come from him. Perhaps Michel had been bullying him in some way. It was high time to make the acquaintance of this oblate of mature years who led, according to the Prior, so withdrawn an existence up here, ever at his prayers. 'No. Oh no,' Alain repeated, with his back against the closed half of the door.

'It's all right Alain, nothing to worry so much about. We'll do it another time. When you like.' Bernard could see he'd gone too far. Sin was real for Alain. For him too, come to think of it, but at least Alain had the confessional, so he shouldn't take it so seriously. Bernard wondered how secret and remedial the confessional could really be, in a small closed community like this one. He'd dipped into one or two accounts of Freudian theory and it seemed likely to him that elements of transference would enter into the relations of pardoner and pardoned in a place like this. Maybe there was transference between Alain and Michel, from both sides. A little domestic drama, tyrant and victim as in many homes. Bernard waved to Luis through the open door to follow him up the steps.

'This is Luis Karoly, stone carver and metal worker. Luis, Brother Alain. I don't know your family name . . .'

Luis held out his hand. 'Monsieur,' he muttered.

'*Perdu . . . perdu . . .*' Alain said. Bernard was unsure if this represented his patronymic or not. If not, what did he mean? How or where was he lost?

'Luis is here to examine the balustrade. I'll leave you to show him the way. I shall be working in the library.' He looked back at them as he turned the corner into the long corridor leading to the library door. They were still standing there in silence like schoolboys, Luis looking down on Alain and Alain with his back to the door and eyes searching the ground as if he'd mislaid his soul or faith. Was the skin near his eyes moist? A pitiable air of distress seemed to hang over him like a swarm of flies circling some dead or dying thing. Bernard felt sorry about it but Alain was, after all, not his business. His present business was that mysterious picture from off the library wall. Enquiries were a matter of patience. Luis must see what could be got out of Alain even if at the moment he didn't look like a promising source. On the other hand, when people are distressed their defences often go down. He might be less cautious than usual. Bernard settled down at the table in the library with the papers and pretended to study them, just as he did when anyone came without warning into his study at the office.

*

He must have nodded off. The table was under one of the windows and now the sun was streaming onto the back of his neck, trenchant as a guillotine. He looked up from the book spread open before him. He'd known without seeing that there was someone there on the other side of the table, watching him; it felt as if these watching eyes and not the sun had woken him. They were eyes to alert you certainly. Large and blue-black as the sea far out where the predators are. Bernard pulled himself together. This was only Brother Michel, smiling to half-reveal his fillings. 'Maître Vipont, I think?'

He wouldn't have said that if the Prior had sent him. He was here for reasons of his own. Bernard felt his own eyes close up so that as little as possible should leak out, no suspicion. He smiled. 'Quite right,' he said. 'As you must know, since it's only two or three days ago you recognised me in Saint-Victor.'

'That's possible,' said Michel.

'It's certain. The Public Prosecutor told me so. And to recognise me then you must have seen me before. I wonder where that was?'

Michel had a ready answer for that. 'It was on the day of the consecration of the master-altar by his Eminence, the Cardinal Archbishop.' He lowered his eyes in veneration. 'An ecumenical occasion. There were plenty of photographs in the newspapers, yours among them. I still have them in my files.'

'You filed the photographs?'

'I'm a devotee of the Friends of Saint-Victor. And I've always followed the activities of prominent citizens with interest.'

'I'm not a prominent citizen.'

'Perhaps more than you realise, Maître. You're too modest. You're known as one of the ornaments of the Palais de Justice.'

Strange that Soames too had used the word 'ornament'. It must be ironic in both cases, but with Michel the irony could be loaded. Bernard didn't like the sound of any of it. This Brother Michel was a gatherer of information. Energies which should go into prayer where they could harm nobody were being spent on curiosity. Why? His personality didn't seem to match the Prior's account of it and the Prior must know that better than anyone. Michel had some status here beyond that of oblate, the humblest rank of monastic hanger-on as far as Bernard could make out. Michel was more like an official seconded from another service and a good deal higher up the ladder. 'You've come looking for me?'

'Little Brother Alain quit his post at the front door without permission. It's a serious fault. He claims you sent him on an errand. I came to ask if this is true.' There was another light now in Michel's eye, the gleam of a gratification sanctioned by duty. Bernard felt an inward shudder. There was something here in alien code.

'Of course it is. He took my artisan up to inspect the balustrade.'

'Ah, your friend the artisan.'

Yes, he'd seen them together in the crypt of Saint-Victor, he was the shadow moving among the shadows. That, and not so much the persecution of Alain, was the real reason for his interest now. He was on the scent of information. 'Karoly is a very skilled reproducer of antique stone carving. He's made a study of early Christian sarcophagi.'

'I believe the Prosecutor Caraman knows him too,' Michel said.

So that was it. This man was some kind of agent of Caraman who must know all about his taste for information. Unless he'd planted him here to keep an eye on things. There was a third possibility – that he'd placed Michel in the convent to keep him safe. It was by far the least likely. Anyway, he and Luis would have to be very careful, Bernard could see that. Possibly even abandon enquiries about that picture. Luis must be warned. Still . . . it would be a pity never to know what it was, and why this Michel had moved it . . . since one was here on professional business . . . unchallengeable by a mere pawn . . . Bernard was brought up short by an awareness of contradiction. Until now he'd only taken in the gold fillings and the eyes. Now he studied the whole appearance more closely. No, not a pawn. Knight or bishop, rather. The nose of a falcon, bones carved in stone, the skin almost Arab in shade. Michel's head was a work of art in its way. What an unnatural hiding place for an alien code.

'Tell me, Brother Michel, have you been an oblate in this convent for long?'

'I've been here fifteen years.'

'Fifteen years. A long time to give, in the prime of your life. Always as an oblate?'

'It's the condition I aspired to.'

That wasn't a straight answer. The information-gatherer played it too close to his chest. Fifteen years. How old was he now? About fifty? And before that?

'You give me the impression of a man who's been out in the world. Excuse my interest. It was Caraman himself who told me to profit by the examples I'd find here. He thinks I need it – and I believe he's a man of unusually strict observance, for the Mediterranean world.'

A smile like a sneer passed across Michel's face. Obviously the Mediterranean world wasn't the one he was native in. You could always tell, by the sneer on northern faces. He must come from somewhere beyond the frontier of the olive tree. 'Surely we mustn't admit that strict observance in public life is unusual? Even the Jews . . . the Pharisees . . .'

'Brother Michel, I wonder if you have some free time? I've spent long enough on these papers' – Bernard waved a hand over the pile on the table which had already sent him to sleep once – 'I need fresh air before it gets too hot. I'd like to walk about the grounds with you – and listen to the nightingales while we talk.'

Michel laughed, showing the full range of his gold reserves. 'It's too late for nightingales. *Post coitum omne animal* . . .' When his laugh ceased it was cut off abruptly as if humour itself had been executed on the spot. 'But I'll walk under the trees with you – where they sang with the prospect of love still before them. There's a way out into the park at the end of this corridor – we needn't use the main door.'

'Not even to see if Alain's at his post?'

'Alain's case can wait. It'll keep.'

The side door gave onto a parterre of sandy earth and parched grass near the building with a grove of plane trees further off, on ground falling away beyond the trees so you saw nothing there but blue between the trunks. The Mont Puget was out of sight behind the bastide and this blank blue was the sky over the town, far off.

'Does an oblate know about the prospects of love by empathy? Or experience?' They were under the trees now, the canopy high above them and the great trunks all leaning slightly towards the Mont Puget, driven by the Mistral.

'Before being an oblate, he could legitimately know it.'

'Like Brother Raimond.'

'Raimond was feeble-minded.'

'Feeble-minded? You mean incapable of making a valid will, for example?'

'It's not for me to say. He was a degenerate.'

'That's a strong word. What do you mean exactly, Brother Michel?'

'There was gitan blood – a grandmother I believe – backward peasant miscegenation.' The last word was spat out with the sound of disgust that can betray a secret desire.

Bernard walked on through the grove in silence, Michel beside him, silent also. The virulence of the prejudice was surprising; he'd have expected from a religious an expression more feline. You'd think there was something sexual there – victim and master. Round the side of the bastide the outbuildings were visible, usually sheltered from view by trees – coach-houses, stables, farm buildings, a small house for the factor, probably. But now there wouldn't be one of those, the brethren themselves did all the work and the Prior oversaw them. They took no outside help.

'Did you never think of entering the priesthood?' Bernard asked. 'Oblate seems subordinate, for you.'

'The priesthood's a calling, not a club or a rank in the police. To become a priest a man must be free to answer God's call if he's one of those chosen to receive it.'

'Weren't you chosen?'

'That wasn't the question.'

'What was the question, Brother Michel? You've given so much of your life to the convent to advance so little . . . a man of your authority and energy. I'd have expected you to aspire to be at least the head of a community not its second humblest member. You have a head made for the mitre.'

'As I said, one must be free.'

Obviously that hadn't been the case. What was the tie? There was a lot more here than showed at the surface. Bernard felt convinced that Michel's role lay outside the community and was related directly to the Prosecutor. The position he appeared to hold here was a blind. He thought back to whatever he'd ever heard about the relations of State and Church in recent years. The Public Prosecutor was a powerful functionary and the State had an insatiable appetite for information. That would include information about the inner councils of the Church. If Michel was an agent, what intelligence could he hope to collect up here? Unless by any chance the Cardinal Archbishop . . .

'This is a wonderfully peaceful place, away from the city but within reach. I have a friend, a Madame Ghazakian, who sometimes entertains his Eminence at her soirées. I hear he complains of having no retreat to hide from his secretaries. I'll mention the Couvent to her . . .'

'I'm surprised to hear his Eminence complains of that. He's a frequent visitor here. The Prior keeps special rooms prepared for him. A saintly man.'

'Ah,' said Bernard. 'How admirable.'

As he spoke a figure flitted from the trees ahead of them and ran downhill towards the outbuildings. A girl dressed in dark clothing. Michel was looking another way and hadn't seen her. She passed behind a tree, paused and turned for an instant. One breast was bare, her blouse pulled apart from the waist up. Bernard lifted a hand in salute and at the same time, attracted by the movement, Michel turned back. An angry sound came from him and he raised his fist.

'Get indoors, *salope*,' he shouted; then repeated the word even more violently – '*Salope*!' The girl had already turned and was running again with a flurry of black like a nun startled out of cover.

Bernard decided to ignore the incident. It was something to find out about at the right moment, not now. All the same, there were inferences to draw. The first was that Michel had a vulnerable side. Anger like that came out when a weakness was surprised. Clearly the girl wasn't a stranger – 'get indoors,' he'd said. That meant she belonged in the interior. Who was she? Bernard knew that no women worked here, the community gave no employment in the locality. So the girl belonged inside because she lived here and not on account of her work. Besides, she didn't look to Bernard as if she did any work.

The bare breast proffered round the bole of a plane tree suggested to him eccentricity, perhaps neurosis, not trade. If she lived here with no other women and a houseful of celibates a stone's throw away any neurosis would soon show up, the flaunting and withdrawal of invitation at a safe distance. And where did she live? Bernard found that all his thought of abandoning research here at the Couvent had evaporated. Luis must get onto this. He didn't hide from himself that Luis was irresistible to women. He always had been, it was only necessary for him to look at one, apparently. They went down like ninepins. Sometimes Bernard envied him this fatality, at others he pitied him for it. It could become a burden.

'Thank you for your company,' he said politely to Michel. 'The outbuildings of the bastide are very handsome. Plenty of style. The family who built this place had imagination.'

'They had pretensions,' Michel said with bitterness perhaps stirred up by what had just happened.

'Was it the family of the Prior himself?'

'I'm sure you know the answer already, from studying the documents and property titles.'

'Then you're aware that it was.'

'I don't concern myself with private histories, Maître Vipont,' Michel said, 'but I know that for a lawyer, no histories are private.'

'Yes, they all interest me.'

'You won't find any here. Raimond had one perhaps but the monastic life is poor in private histories. It excludes them. Prayer takes their place.'

'I saw a girl a moment ago who must be – surely? – part of a private history. What can she be doing here where prayer fills the woman's place?'

'It's a history I advise you not to interest yourself in. She's a sick girl related to a member of the community and she has nowhere else to go.'

'No one else to look after her? I'm sorry for her if that's so.'

'Your pity will help no one. And no one needs it. She's well enough looked after.'

'Which member of the community is she related to, poor thing? Not Alain, I presume.'

Without answering, Michel turned away and started to walk quickly back towards the bastide. Then he stopped, turned back again with his hands joined under his scapular and spoke with that smile which Bernard now found so much more arctic than even his usual expression. 'I know you'll ask the Prior the same question before long,' he said. 'He'll give you the same answer. She's considered a relation of the house. Till another place is found for her.' In spite of the smile there was something behind the eyes – hidden in the head – something that struck a chord of empathy in Bernard. Only a love secreted there could do that.

*

At first, Luis took Alain just for a sorrowful religious to be respected in a vague way as representing the spiritual order. Not that Luis was much interested in the spiritual order. The beauties of the world stood in for that as far as he was concerned. But he recognised it. And Alain seemed the image of everything Luis thought of as in the sphere of the spiritual. Selfless, sexless, sacrificed.

'No need to come onto the roof with me, Brother Alain,' he said, feeling embarrassed about the hoisting up of Alain's skirts and the helping hand he'd probably need. 'I'll find my own way down again when I've seen what's to be done.'

But Alain was watching him as he took the first rungs of the ladder. Watching him? That meant, usually, at eye level. Luis understood what was happening. It was something he'd always hated and had suffered often enough ever since he was a boy. Even in that camp in the Camargue. He'd hated it, those other men seeing him as an object of envy or desire. What did they lack, to need anything from him? He hated them and when he could he punished them for it. He'd even shot one once, years ago when he was a boy, but only in the arm. The bullet should have gone in nearer the middle and lower down.

Alain, however, was different. He was a pitiful small animal you wouldn't crush under your wheels if you could avoid it. You'd urge it to hop away.

'Maybe you want to come and look at the balustrade with me? Were you ever up here before?' Luis was unsure how to treat him gently, get rid of him painlessly and not have to think about him any more. Alain didn't answer and this made Luis look at him more closely. Those moist hollows weren't due to perspiration. Alain was weeping, silently. The tears were running more freely now as if his heart was breaking. 'What's the matter with you?' Luis felt ashamed and angry at the same time. Alain was a man, even if not much of one. His emotions were getting the better of him and they weren't proper emotions for a man, anyone could tell that.

'I should be at the door.'

'Go back then. I don't need you. Thanks for showing me the way.'

But Alain was still there, motionless except for his tears, at the base of the ladder and looking up. With all his experience and lore of the road, Luis had never felt himself so much the object of longing. It lifted the situation out of the run of ordinary affairs of desire or even love, and he felt humiliated by the scale of the thing. Besides, it was absurd, it was like in a theatre. Just seeing it, you were exploited.

'Go down where you can keep an eye on the Bentley,' he said roughly, recalling how Bernard had linked the Bentley to the then unknown world of Alain's desire. 'It isn't locked.'

There'd been a shift in Alain's expression, an adjustment of light there. 'I'll come up onto the roof with you,' he said in that voice which sounded like a child imitating a man. Coming to a decision made him seem more of a man too. There'd been a struggle and an outcome. Bernard had said to see what could be got out of him. He might yet be useful.

'All right, if you want.' Luis climbed to the top of the ladder which gave onto a parapet between the slope of the roof and the balustrade. A moment later Alain's head appeared through the opening, like a weasel. 'Keep down behind the balustrade. With your height no one'll see you.'

'What are you going to look at?'

'Everything.' In fact this inspection was a formality. Part of the balustrade had broken away because a small chimney had fallen on it.

The parapet ahead was still blocked by the rubble of masonry. All he needed to do was measure the number of elements missing and make a profile drawing. But he would take his time, make a tour of the roof and inspect the other chimney-stacks, that would justify his presence while he memorised the layout. Ways onto and off a roof can be important if you're in a hurry.

'It goes all the way round,' said Alain, as if answering a question.

'Then we'll look all the way round. Be careful where it's missing. It's a long way down.'

'I've got a head for heights. I used to climb rocks in the park of the orphanage.' He was bent almost double and held the skirt of his habit in one hand. He really was still like a child in an orphanage; he looked quite happy now, with a child's sudden switch of moods. Evidently he'd had no father, any more than Luis himself . . . but Luis had had Soames . . . Perhaps Alain's apparent longing was really no more than to be treated with affection and carried across into the world of men. This time Luis felt ashamed of having read more into the situation than was probably there. It must be that he expected people to be fascinated by him. That was a fault he'd better correct before he got old and the fault turned dangerous.

'There's a gap here, at this corner. You'll have to jump. Keep your weight on the side by the roof in case you slip.' He turned, saw Alain hesitate, and held out a hand. He knew as he did this that now he was the exploiter. Alain took the hand and held it tightly as he made the short jump over the void where the chimney had broken through. He didn't release the hand at once, hanging on to it like a rail at the side of a ship. Now Luis knew his first assessment had been the right one but it was too late. They were linked by Alain's rush of emotion and the advantage Luis had tried to take of it. Alain had entered a new phase, you could read it in his eyes. There was a tenacious look, like a dog that's known you five minutes and decided to adopt you for ever. The only way out would be the brutal one, kicking the dog away. Luis wasn't capable of that, he was still too near a stray himself.

The striking thing was that this little monk appeared in the space of half an hour to have dropped the monastic way of thought like a skin.

Had his beliefs gone too? Or did they just mean so much less to him now he'd discovered passion? The form of the question added to the shame Luis already felt. They were round the side of the building with only a great canopy of trees in front of them. Luis stopped, leaned back against the slope of the roof and lit a cigarette. 'Won't your superiors wonder where you've got to?'

'Only Michel.'

'And he isn't a superior?'

'In a way he is.'

'What way?'

'He sets himself over me. Watching for faults.'

'Faults?'

'Of discipline. Wrong thoughts.'

'Thoughts? But perhaps that needn't worry you so much . . . now.' Luis observed himself without complaisance. He was sounding the depth of Alain's change. He offered him a cigarette, and after a moment's doubt, Alain took it.

'Not as much as before.'

'Before?'

'Yes.'

'Why? How did Brother Michel manage to worry you so much more before?'

'He devised penances. He has a fertile imagination. Degrading ones.' Alain looked distressed again, but only for a moment.

'Degrading penances? For your thoughts?'

'Yes. Sometimes.'

'But surely he couldn't . . .'

'He said he could. He said it was the right way to the imitation of Christ. It's what Pascal said, Michel says.'

Luis's philosophy rose up like an army in the night. 'Fuck Pascal and the imitation of Christ,' he said. 'I'll fix your Brother Michel sooner or later, you can count on that.' Why did he care? What was it to him? Didn't he have his own problems? Was it because Alain had become his self-appointed dog and any previous tormentor had it coming to him? 'Why didn't you tell the Prior? Don't you ever see him to talk to?'

'The Prior's afraid of Michel.'

'Afraid of what?'

'I don't know. Everyone's afraid of him.'

Luis drew the last smoke from his cigarette, stubbed it out on the tiles and looked at Alain smoking his. He held it in front of him as if he was sucking a thumb, puffing dutifully to the end. It must be the first time. He'd probably be sick in a minute. 'Listen. This Michel, who is he?'

'I think he's someone important.'

That was what Luis thought. Important enough to terrorise the Prior and everyone else. 'We must find out about him, Alain,' he said. 'Maître Vipont – he's a good friend, a real one, I've known him since I was a boy and you can trust him – he says this Michel moved a picture from the library just before he was going to work there. Did you know that?'

'I saw him carrying it.'

'Yes, that's what Bernard – Maître Vipont – that's what he said. What was the picture?'

'I only saw it once, when I was sent to the library for something. It's very old and dirty and dark. There's an old woman in it, and two young people. I think the old woman's a . . . Gitane,' he looked carefully at Luis and spoke the word in a low voice. 'It isn't a holy picture at all. Perhaps that's why they moved it.'

'I don't think so. Where was Michel taking it?'

'He put it in his Eminence the Cardinal's room.'

'The Cardinal isn't afraid of him as well?'

'I expect he can't be. But just Michel being here – I think the Cardinal's afraid about that.'

'Why do you think so?'

'In the refectory, when the Cardinal's here, he looks at Michel like a sore on your skin that won't heal up.'

'You seem to keep your eyes wide open.'

'Perhaps it's what unhappy people do.'

'Haven't you ever been happy here?'

'I liked Brother Raimond. He was a peasant.'

'He didn't know about Pascal.'

Alain laughed for the first time, a laugh with humour in it, not loud but pleased. 'No, I'm sure he didn't. Raimond was simple. He just knew about goats.'

'Maybe you shouldn't live here, in a convent like this. If you were never happy.' This was another wrong move, combining kindness and calculation. Alain was looking at him now and all the implications of what he'd just said must be clear to both of them. The dog would try to follow, running along the road whatever happened.

'Will you be working here?' Alain asked.

'I expect so.'

'How long for? A long time?'

'No. A few days.' Luis thought quickly and added, 'It could depend on you.'

There was a light now in Alain's eyes, like fire on a hillside. 'How on me?'

Luis studied him for a moment before answering. It was a big risk, he wasn't sure Bernard would approve. But he'd always followed his instinct and Bernard had mostly approved that so far. 'I'm interested in that picture,' he said. 'I'd like to have a look at it.' That after all didn't commit him too much. He was an artisan with artistic interests. There would be plenty of time to see how dependable Alain really was, once he'd seen the picture.

'I'll show you,' said Alain. 'I know a way. We'll have to be quick. Michel must be looking for me already.'

Shrinking from the gesture, Luis patted him on the shoulder. 'Well, Alain, now we know each other better, now we're friends, you can tell Michel to stuff his imaginative penances . . . in the place he knows. That's the place for penances.'

Alain laughed again, with the same sincere pleasure, not laughing for show. 'I'll tell him something pretty well like that,' he said. Luis felt quite sure he'd be dependable to the end. The only trouble was, what would be done with him then? And who would do it? What he needed was a woman, to put him to rights.

# Chapter Six

AS A FOREIGNER, Soames had to apply in person every few years for an extension to his residence permit, even though he was a war hero who'd fought with the Resistance in the Cévennes, and was invited annually to the reunion of former comrades in Nîmes, along with many respected local figures. The people in offices who oversaw permits and liaised with police and security services weren't at all the same kind as attended the old Resistants' booze-ups. They were men and women trained in Paris in the best methods of buggering the peace-time citizen, so Soames believed. Above all the citizen from abroad.

'If you were married to a Frenchwoman, Monsieur, you could be naturalised as of right,' said the official at the Marseille Préfecture. She turned over some unattached sheets of typewritten paper, brown with age, then slowly turned them back. 'It appears you live with one in concubinage.'

'I'm too old to marry,' said Soames. 'Marriage is for young folk like you, in the prime of hope and beauty.'

The official flushed slightly and gave a small strict smile. She wasn't bad to look at, in her pin-striped coat and skirt. Her shoulders curved round and forward in a friendly way, her bust was ample and in a word she looked made for better things than sitting in this office full of dossiers. 'If you imagine that gallantry can distract a French functionary from her duty, you delude yourself, Monsieur,' she said. 'In your own country it may be different. Here, we have a sense of what's fitting to time and place.'

The effect of this remark was to make Soames picture how she would look in more fitting conditions, stripped of the pin-stripe suit. He mustn't let this show. The woman here had the power to make things extremely difficult for him. Why, come down to it, had he and Ida never married, just to be regular? Perhaps because they lived alone with their animals in the Camargue like the first man and woman, for whom marriage wasn't necessary because there was no Civil Service at that time. If they'd had a child, they'd have gone through the formality, of course. As it was, there was just Luis, who came and went, seemed to draw near and then distanced himself again. The lady was examining her pages more carefully. When they were slow like that it didn't necessarily mean they were new to the work, or taking special care not to make a cock-up. Being slow was a skill in itself, part of the training.

'Your concubine . . .' she double-checked that what she was about to say rested on a solid bureaucratic base . . . 'I may have been wrong to say that by marrying her you would acquire a right to naturalisation. It's not certain that she's a Frenchwoman.'

'She's a Gitane. They ignore frontiers.'

'For the Republic, frontiers define the citizen.'

'She isn't a citizen. She was a woman before there were any such thing as citizens. If you saw her you'd understand.'

'My predecessor seems to have been negligent about this. What papers does she have? No papers are listed here. I shall have to summon her to the Préfecture for an interview.'

'She would never come.'

'There are sanctions for not obeying such a summons. She could go to prison, in the last resort.'

Soames rose from his chair. An expression of alarm crossed the woman's face, turned up at him far above her. He slapped with his open palm on the table between them – not loud, but firmly. 'She's ill. She'll be dead before your sanctions for disobedience get to her. Does that satisfy you? I've come for my permit, not an inquisition.' He sat down again. He'd been led away and gone too far. 'I don't believe you're a person to make trouble for two people in distress. You look kind.'

'Kindness has nothing to do with it, Monsieur.' The look of alarm hadn't faded. That was to do with his height, Soames realised. Height had advantages and drawbacks. One of these was that women in positions of authority sometimes felt threatened by it. She lifted the telephone and spoke a couple of words he didn't catch. 'Apparently, Monsieur le Chef de Cabinet of Monsieur le Préfet wishes to see you. Wait here.' This command was issued on a note of bravado, as she was already halfway to the door. There was no doubt, she was trying to shelter behind a higher power. It was a bad sign, because the higher power might decide to take it out on him, hero or no hero. When she came back she was accompanied by a young man with an eager, carnivorous air to him, as if he was looking forward to the mincemeat he would soon make of Soames. Without speaking, he ushered him into an adjoining office, a much larger room containing solid nineteenth century furniture instead of the flimsy modern issue of subordinate spaces. Above the desk, on the wall, was a framed and enlarged photo portrait of the President of the Republic, Henri Fernand-Félix – a political marauder whose path Soames had crossed at the time of the Liberation. It was uncertain then whether his Vichy past would interfere with what looked like a brilliant Republican future. It hadn't turned out to matter at all.

'Sit here, Monsieur Soames.' The Chef de Cabinet sat with the light of the windows behind him, the sun blinding Soames as he faced him. 'I have a note here that concerns you. Your visit spares me the trouble of sending for you. You've come about your permit? I believe it's already expired.' He held out a hand. 'Can I see it? Ah yes. You should have applied six months ago. Your situation is now irregular. Theoretically, you could be expelled from France at once. Theoretically, you could be taken straight from this building to the airport. The Préfet has power to order it.'

Obviously this had nothing to do with the alarm of the junior lady next door. It must be to do with Luis and his recent arrest. The fact that there were no internment camps for Gitans any more didn't mean they were free of the State's disapproval. Soames had always known this, living with Ida – and it wasn't just the State, it was society.

Romanys, for the Republic, were mongrel, lawless, outside folk. 'I've lived here thirty years,' he said, as if in all that time he hadn't learned that sentimental claims mean nothing in the schools where this functionary got his training.

'Yes.' The Chef de Cabinet had no need of notes or dossiers. He had the case at his fingertips, and all the apposite regulations. He inspected the fingertips now. 'You live with the woman Ida Karoly. A displaced person who entered France in 1945.'

'She re-entered France then. She'd been deported to Birkenau.'

'There's no record here of any papers to prove that. A large number of people crossed frontiers at a time when frontier discipline was suspended.'

'The people who knew her can vouch for it.'

'Who are they, Monsieur Soames?'

'Myself. Some of my colleagues in the Resistance. Luis Karoly . . .'

'I was coming to him. In his case, it seems there's no lack of papers. With good reason. He spent two years in a detention centre for minors. However, there's nothing about his parentage. Is he the son of Ida Karoly?'

Soames felt his anger mount again. 'She's his sister. If the truth is that she brought him into the world, it's no business of yours.'

'And his father? Would that be you?'

'No, it would not. Since he was a lad, I've tried to give a helping hand any time he needed it. But that wouldn't figure in your categories.'

'You're wrong. We rely for a lot of information on helping hands. I expect you'd be glad to do anything you could to spare Ida Karoly and this Luis any problems with the administration? The Police? The Ministry of the Interior?'

'I remember when Fernand-Félix was Minister of the Interior. A friend of mine caught a bullet, for worrying that Minister. An Englishman. He knew a bit too much for his own good.'

'So I see, here. Seagrave, a political agitator. I hope you don't know too much yourself, Monsieur Soames, for your own good. The Englishman fell in the same incident when Karoly wounded the Minister's secretary.'

'That was a pederast who'd been bothering him.'

A brief smirk passed across the hungry features of the Chef de Cabinet. Perhaps it was a piece of information he could make some use of, on his way up the ladder. 'That gentleman is now an Ambassador of France,' he said thoughtfully.

'At the court of Sodom and Gomorrah, I wouldn't wonder,' Soames said.

The Chef de Cabinet swept this aside. 'Since then an eye has always been kept on Karoly. And now, he may be in a position to help us – in exchange, of course, for certain judicial latitudes . . . tolerance, in short . . . which in his current situation he may badly need.'

'You mean you'll buy something you think he knows.'

'Not from him, Monsieur Soames. From you. To put it in a word, both Karolys are precariously placed. And so are you.'

'What do you want to know?'

'Karoly is said to work for an attorney of Marseille – Maître Vipont. You know him?'

'By repute. A respected lawyer.'

'Vipont is a source of anxiety . . . in higher places.' A slight inclination of the head in the direction of the Presidential photograph showed where they might be found. 'He may be one of those harbouring out of date rancour from the period of the Occupation. In those high places –' there was another inclination '– it's felt that the time when the French had insufficient . . . fondness one for another is better buried. Forgotten. Forgiven.'

'There could be plenty to forgive, if you were packed off to Birkenau.'

Visibly, the Chef de Cabinet decided to overlook this detail of history. Then he hesitated. 'You're probably not a Catholic, Monsieur Soames. So you may not appreciate the power of pardon of the Church. *Par don*. By gift. A gift denied to the puritan conscience, more's the pity.'

'But Vipont isn't pardoned the anxiety he causes.'

'Maître Vipont is an officer of the Ministry of Justice. His position is almost unassailable.' The Chef de Cabinet leaned forward. He held his official stamp in one hand and the draft of Soames's new permit in the other. 'But his activities could be checked, and your peace of mind – for yourself and your friends – restored for the rest of your lives.'

'So what do you want?'

The stamp fell on the draft and the Chef de Cabinet signed it with a quick flourish. 'We think Karoly could tell you about the work he does for Vipont. And we believe that then Vipont could be encouraged . . . urged even, to modify his interests and forget his rancours. Talk to Karoly about his work for Vipont. Ring me on this number.' He passed Soames a card. 'Your discretion is the price of ours. Cooperation between allies. The most natural thing in the world.'

The permit, of course, only symbolised the suspension of threats. Soames knew a bit about sequestration pending enquiries, in this land he'd come to love so much. France was to be loved for the land and the people, not its administration of justice. Nor, he thought as his eye rested on the foxy likeness of Fernand-Félix, for its President. 'Leave it to me,' he said. He stood up, took the permit from the hand of the Chef de Cabinet without waiting for it to be extended, and knocked twice on the floor with his artificial leg, a technique he'd found useful. 'Cramp. I'll give you a buzz on this number. I think I can guarantee to get Karoly out of Marseille for good. He doesn't know it, but he may soon become a chef de famille. Like you being a Chef de Cabinet. Delivered of a child with the right papers. So you can count on me, as an old soldier. A fount of information. Old soldiers know about keeping their mouths shut and opening them, in any country. Mercenaries, the whole lot.'

For the first time, the Chef de Cabinet looked less than sure of himself. 'But Monsieur, knowing how to keep one's mouth definitively shut is . . .'

'A life-saver. Don't worry. You play it straight with me, I won't fuck you up.'

They would have to work it out for themselves and wait and see, these regimental clerks, blokes in soft shoes. And Soames would keep his side of the bargain. Without Luis, Bernard's vengeances would come to an abrupt end. And Luis was irreplaceable. There would be no need for the authorities to have Bernard assassinated. Soames didn't intend to pass any information to anyone, just shift Luis once and for all out of Bernard's orbit so he'd become what he should have been long ago – a secret man, a Camargue horseman.

\*

There was a note from Albertas on Bernard's table. A flowing, compassionate hand which didn't seem to fit the crabbed personality Albertas liked to project. His handwriting was the signature of his humanity.

Ten thirty hours. Monsieur Caraman telephones. Signs of agitation. He wishes to hear from you urgently. Don't make an enemy of the Prosecutor, Monsieur Bernard. A Vipont can never be safe.

Midday. Monsieur Soames arrives. Says he must make a will and thinks you should advise him. In reality, I think he is interested in Mademoiselle Marion. He mentioned her several times. I'm told Madame Soames is very ill. I think you should be on your guard with Soames. A general always has a master-plan, I believe.

Seventeen hours. The secretary of his Eminence the Cardinal Archbishop telephones. A Monsignor. His Eminence is angered by reports that the devout existence of the Couvent de la Génératrice-Immaculée at Luminy has been disturbed. He demands that you surrender the dossier at once to the Prosecutor. Who telephones ten minutes later, even more agitated. You are summoned to his personal bureau at ten tomorrow. I call your housekeeper at seventeen thirty hours and advise her to put your telephone on the answering machine.

It was already dark and the shutters were shut but Bernard at once turned out the lights and retreated from his own room into the blind offices at the back. There was no one here at this hour and Luis was coming for consultation. He'd had a sight of the missing picture and they were going to look into some of the art histories Bernard kept here, try at least to identify the genre and period. Luis had a sensitive eye but not much instruction.

Also, there was something he hadn't mentioned to Luis, coming back in the Bentley from the Convent, and that was about that girl in the wood. For some reason he'd felt reluctant. And he had a strong sense there was something Luis hadn't mentioned to him. Of course that was often so, in fact Bernard believed himself surrounded by people not mentioning things to him as they might, with a little more goodwill, but today Luis seemed particularly reticent. This must be to do with Marion, and great subtlety would be required to find out what it was. Subtlety in the form of patience, probably. He opened Albertas's cupboard with his pass-key and borrowed a bottle of Burgundy. Clos Vougeot. That might help. Luis always entered from the street at the rear by a concealed door which looked like part of the neighbouring building. It was one of the advantages of the site and dated from the time under the Occupation when Bernard's father had received a number of dangerous visits, but the concealed door hadn't saved him. When Bernard remembered the body in the sack he began to shake and sweat, wherever he was when the image reached him; its disfigurements, the slow passage over the frontiers of pain they evidenced, were his. Thank God, there was Luis now, Bernard heard his soft step on the back stairs. If this office had windows, from here one would see across the Vieux Port to the oval dome of the Vieille Charité just emerging from the roof line of the surrounding slums. One day that part of the town would be redeveloped and Bernard, who owned quite a slice of it, would clean up. It was another reason to feel like a pariah. If it wasn't for Marion he would promise the money to some charity, something supported by the Anglican Church of Marseille, for example.

'Salut,' said Luis in a distracted manner. He was still like a youth, in many respects. He had no way of stepping outside the context of love. Bernard poured the Burgundy into two tumblers he'd found in the cupboard alongside the bottle.

'Santé,' he said.

'Santé.'

A silence followed. The Vougeot, in spite of being opened at the last minute, was sublime. Bernard looked at the label. 1953 – just for the odd tipple in the office. That was how it went in the world of clerks.

'The Archbishop's on to us,' he said. 'We'll have to be quick about making an assessment and then disappear and let the dust settle.'

'Disappear . . .' said Luis.

'I mean lie low for a bit. Not long.' That had been a slip. Luis mustn't on any account think that disappearance was on the programme. The summer stretched in front of them, beguiling, endless – the sea, the sand, the shore of the love that's for ever – the summer must be weathered and Marion delivered safe and registered at the University in mid-September. 'Have a look at these illustrations. From what you said the picture's probably a copy of a minor Tenebrist – Salini or Manfredi. But maybe more interesting than that, you never know. In which case it would have been a piece . . . for a collector.'

Luis turned a couple of pages without much attention. 'You'd better see the picture for yourself, Bernard,' he said.

'Just look at these. Say how it strikes you. I know the painting's dirty, just think of the outline and the feeling.' He paused. Luis must be brought back. 'There's something I don't like the smell of, up at that convent. And now the Cardinal. That man, Michel, I doubt if he's a real monk at all . . .'

'He may be. I don't know that but I know one thing about him. He has a taste for . . . domination. That's what they call it.'

Yes. There was that girl – 'This Michel seems to be the guardian of the painting. Either for himself or for someone else. And if it's someone else it must be Caraman and then this would be a trap.'

'I don't see how it can be for himself. Don't they make a lasting vow of poverty or something? I thought they couldn't have even a photograph of their mother let alone a painting of a Gitane . . .'

'A Gitane? You didn't say there was a Gitane.'

'I couldn't see her properly. The Cardinal's shutters stay closed when he's not there. Alain was afraid to turn the lights on. But he says there's a Gitane in the picture. He whispered it – just . . . not to annoy. Gitans aren't real Christians. Only scrap for the Vieille Charité. The shithouse.' Luis spoke lightly but Bernard knew that denial would be taken for disguised assent and silence for the assent that dare not speak its name.

'She'd be a soothsayer I expect, someone of special gifts. People always consulted them. Like lawyers.' As he spoke he felt a stir of excitement in the back of his mind. Whose work portrayed sooth-sayers? 'I must see that painting, Luis. Tomorrow could be the last day. By evening Caraman will run me to earth.' He thought for a moment. 'How did you get Alain to take you?'

'By a back way. There's a service stair, for emptying piss pots.'

'I meant how did you persuade him to do it?'

There wasn't any doubt, Luis didn't like the question and that was why he'd taken it like that. Even Luis could be devious. 'He's a boy I feel sorry for,' he said.

'You didn't need long to decide that.'

'You don't need long to get to feel pity for a victim.'

'Of Michel?'

'Yes. And himself, how he's made.'

'You mean stunted in growth?'

'That about describes it.' Luis must know, after all these years of close association, that Bernard would sense there was more behind the answer than on the surface. Luis had discovered some other handicap in Alain than his obvious disadvantages.

'He's not mentally deranged, is he?'

'No. Or yes. Depends what you think of it.'

'Of what?' Bernard poured out more Clos Vougeot and raised his glass to Luis. 'Santé,' he said again.

Luis moved uncomfortably in his chair. 'I've always hated them before but this time I just feel sorry. He's not really a man, that's why.'

'I see.' Bernard at last saw the obvious. It hadn't taken Luis long to pity nor Alain long to fall in love. He should have seen it at once, when they were at the door with the Bentley paraded on the gravel. He felt quite sorry for Alain too. He didn't share Luis's particular aversion and Alain's love was a desperate affair. But in a way it would be a kindness to make use of it, give him at least the feeling he'd managed to do something with it before the love object vanished, leaving him to eat his heart out in his convent. 'Tell him to show me to the Cardinal's rooms. You do a few drawings of the balustrade with measurements and I'll present you to the Prior. Spin it out. Convince him he's getting a lot of restoration work for nothing. Go into detail. And while you're doing it Alain can lead me up that service stair. I'll take a strong torch.'

'And Michel? He's always on the lookout Alain says.'

Bernard laughed. He liked solving problems like that. 'That's easy. I'll pick you up as usual by the hippodrome. You go into the post office there and send a telegram to the Prior in the Prosecutor's name. There's no telephone at the convent. The telegram will be delivered an hour later and we'll get there about the same time.'

'What do I say in it?'

' "Send Michel" – that's all. He'll get on his motor-bicycle and we'll have a couple of clear hours and when he gets back he'll bring a message from Caraman telling me to present myself at once. We'll have caught them on the wrong foot and we'll have an alibi for the telegram.'

'What sort of alibi?'

'The Prosecutor's been ringing Albertas. If I was avoiding him I wouldn't arrange for Michel to go down and report where I was. The suspicion won't even cross his mind.' Luis looked at him with a more wary admiration than he used to show for this sort of invention. That was because of his relations with Marion. These days Luis viewed his ingenuity in a new light. It couldn't be helped. They were becoming adversaries now, still needing each other.

'So will you present yourself later on?'

'Yes.'

'What for?'

'To see what his idea is. If he's like the Archbishop and in a hurry to get me away from the convent, then they may have something to hide there but it isn't the picture. If he isn't in any hurry, then that picture's bait, as I suspected, and they're waiting to see if we swallow it. If we do, then it's us someone means to get rid of. We must find out all we can while they're still not sure.'

'A couple of hours isn't much, for finding things out,' Luis said.

'No.' Bernard reflected, his thoughts turning to Michel. What sort of man was he, in the private domain? If he enjoyed tormenting Alain it could be partly due to suspicions about his proclivities. That was a common motive for victimisation. In other words, Michel's own were not inverted, whatever else they might be, and if he wasn't a genuine monk then riding his motor-bicycle into a town like Marseille would put ideas into his head or fire up those already simmering there. Maybe that was one reason for his visits. This was a case for a specialist. 'As soon as we finish this bottle I'll call on Madame Ghazakian,' he said. 'Michel must be waylaid and we'll gain a full morning at least.'

'Perhaps he hasn't got the money.'

'Don't be a fool, Luis. This isn't a commercial occasion. I'll pay. She must send a devout looking girl to catch him. That's probably the way.'

'I know he plays at penances. Like in magazines for perverts.'

'I'll tell Caroline that. It'll help her prepare the young penitent.' They both laughed, with the abashed laughter that fails to still the voice of scruple. This wasn't the right moment to mention that girl up at the convent. It would look like systematic exploitation of the weaker sex. After all, one was a gentleman and so was Luis, by nature. Marion said so and she should know. The wine was finished. Bernard took the tumblers into the cabinet where there was a tap and rinsed them before putting them back in Albertas's cupboard. He pencilled a note and put the bottle in the waste-paper basket. Albertas was going to pretend to be very annoyed.

'It looks a bit like this,' said Luis suddenly, one of the books open in front of him. 'Solid outlines and shadows. It was too dark for detail but there's also . . . it's like this light to one side.'

'It could only be a copy,' Bernard said, his heart beating a bit faster. 'There are only about forty Caravaggios in the world but hundreds of copies and imitations. Also the picture at the convent's too small, going by the mark on the wall.'

'But perhaps whoever decided to move it doesn't think it is a copy.'

'Perhaps. It all depends who they are and what they know. We must start earlier. That post office opens at eight. I'll be there waiting for you.'

'If the Prosecutor wants to take the trouble they'll be able to trace the post office. I'm easily recognised, I know that.'

'Sending a telegram isn't a crime. I've read the English send jokes by telegram.' They were silent at the thought of such jocularity that stopped at nothing.

\*

'I've written a preliminary note for you, Father Prior. The problem's thornier that I first thought. Brother Raimond was engaged to marry his cousin and the property was her sole heritage, had she lived. The problem is that no trace of her was ever found. The assumption of death is reversible in such cases, and there have been many from the period of the war. I need to interview Raimond's father. The question needs investigation.' Bernard settled comfortably into the chair facing the Prior's throne of authority, across the vast space of the table.

A series of reactions disturbed the Prior's features. First came anger, then fear. Investigation, that was the word that triggered it. You could see the Prior cursing the day Bernard came up here to help and advise. 'Is my brother aware of this?' he asked.

'I hope to meet him tomorrow. Or the day after. But there's no escape from the fact that Brother Raimond's cousin's unresolved disappearance all those years ago carries the matter into the public domain. The Inheritance Code, if I may put it like this, is one of the multiple breasts of our republican Artemis.' He enjoyed bringing that out. He had a sculpture of her at the Villa Vipont.

'A matter in the public domain is surely my brother's concern, not yours.'

'Any lawyer is concerned if it's forced on him in the course of professional duties. Devising means to use the Inheritance Code to advantage is quite legitimate. Defeating it by concealment's another thing altogether.'

'What is it you really want here, Maître Vipont? I received you as a friend of the Couvent. Now I feel you're an alien element in our affairs. His Eminence himself . . .'

'I know. A message was left for me. But not even the Archbishop can obstruct the workings of the Civil Code.' Bernard wasn't so sure of this but it sounded good. He could see now why the Prior's family had put him out of harm's way in a convent. He was inadequate, a shadow behind the form of his authority. If there was a scheme for laying a trap, he wouldn't be part of it. He looked shaken and advantage must be taken of that. Forensic experience suggested surprise. 'Tell me, Father Prior, who would be Brother Michel's usual confessor?'

'Myself.' As soon as he spoke the Prior's eyes showed the shock he felt at giving this answer. So, assuming that Michel observed at least some of his religious duties, the Prior must know what his position here was. The implications of this needed thought.

'I assure you, Father Prior, I'm here to help. And Karoly, my artisan, has drawings and specifications to show you. As I said before, his work's a token offering. It's a privilege to be consulted without fees on the affairs of the community. I'll call him.'

As soon as Luis produced his drawings and measurements the Prior looked happier. There was no moral dimension to a balustrade and parapet. When the sound of a motor-bicycle quitting the stables and heading for the track came to them, Bernard, with smiles and encouraging gestures, left to go down and wait for Alain in the library. He was already there behind the door. They inspected one another more closely than before. They were embarking on an enterprise perilous for them both, if carried beyond primary research. Alain, the prey of passion, appeared in a much more sympathetic light to Bernard, even if the passion was aberrant. Anyway who could say that? What was aberrant? Where were the limits of the normal? No one had that worked out yet. More interestingly, what was Alain thinking? Or does passion burn up thought as fire consumes air? In that case only the name and image of Luis would mean anything to him. 'The Prior and Luis are fully occupied for quite a time,' Bernard said. 'Luis made some beautiful drawings. He's a talented draughtsman in his own line.'

'Please follow me very quietly,' said Alain, but at the name the mistrustful look in his eyes had yielded.

'Brother Michel's gone out.'

'Never count on Michel's goings or comings.'

'Luis will take care of Michel, I think.' On a fatherly impulse Bernard put a hand to Alain's shoulder, offering a kind of comfort. 'Let's go and take a look at that picture. I've brought a torch. A quarter of an hour will do.'

They sidled along the passages of the bastide like trespassers. What sort of background did Alain come from? Oh yes, from none, he was an orphan, Luis had said so. He'd been a trespasser all his life. The service stair was at the back of the building and must lie directly behind the principal staircase which rose from the centre as far as the piano nobile. This one went up to the top and was lit by windows where one saw the distant haze of pollution in the sky above the town. There was no wind today to blow it out to sea and the heat was already stifling.

'Through here,' said Alain, leading the way into a low narrow passage like a tunnel in the wall. At the end was a stone chute with a big brass tap above it. Presumably for sluicing the chamber pots.

'Is this still used?'

'When the Cardinal's here, of course.' It must be one of Alain's duties. 'In here.' He opened a door high enough for him but not for Bernard who had to stoop low to pass through. The Cardinal's rooms were above the library, occupying all of one of the short sides of the building. The ceilings were high, as in the Prior's study which must be the next room along. The only light came from a single heart-shaped aperture cut into the centre of each of the eight shutters like an impossible run of aces in a card trick. They stood in the semi-darkness and listened carefully. There was no sound. 'The walls are very thick,' Alain whispered. Bernard turned on his powerful torch and swept its beam round the rooms. Excitement made him delay the moment of lighting up the picture, whatever it might be. He paused to size up the furniture, the tapestries, the carpet, the panelling, the plaster-work of the ceilings.

'It's here,' said Alain. He was standing beside a canopied bed in the second room. 'This is where his Eminence sleeps.' It looked enticing for the pallet of a clergyman, Bernard thought, as warmly welcoming and upholstered as Caroline Ghazakian herself in her prime.

'Where?'

'On the floor here against the wall.'

Bernard had never before felt this trepidation in the face of a possible prize. His hand was unsure and the torch beam shifted about first between the floor and the frame, then at last around the canvas. The painting must have hung a century or two over a fireplace. Only wood smoke on windy days could give that dense bituminous overlay. The forms were so darkened they seemed sunk like stones in a well. But solid, a great solidity as Luis had said. And that light, dim now but once warm as candle flame, flowing in from one side of the scene onto the forms half hidden there. Their colours drowned in smoke.

'So that's it,' Bernard said. The banal phrase came out almost like an apology for all the trouble he'd given himself and others to get this far. But he hadn't the least doubt about it, intuition and all his knowledge told him he was looking through the gloom at some sort of masterpiece. Whatever a masterpiece might be. But recognition was as sure as Alain's must have been when his eye first fell on Luis. Bernard went closer, bent down and peered at the figures in the dusk of time and dirt. An old woman examined a man's palm, exploring it with her finger while a young one stripped his purse. The effect was so covertly erotic that Bernard glanced at Alain to see if he registered it. You couldn't tell. Like the boundaries of the aberrant, his expression was impossible to read with certainty. Bernard looked back at the canvas. The textile planes of the representation, silk and wool and leather covering skin and muscle, seemed to leave them all the more defence-less, like tortoise flesh under shell.

'Are you very disappointed?' Alain asked. His voice sounded sad. It must look to him as if his exploit for the sake of love had come to nothing.

'No, no.' Bernard smiled at him reassuringly in the dark. 'I think this painting is something extraordinary. I don't know what exactly, not yet. But I'm sure of it.'

'Like you can be sure of the love of God and not know exactly. Till you find one day you'd only believed it was there.' Alain sounded so utterly forlorn that Bernard felt the need to say something, useless though it would be.

'Everyone's loves are part of the love of God. That's why you mustn't ever turn away from them whatever they are.'

'You can't, anyway,' Alain said.

It wasn't a fruitful exchange, but a muddled platitude might still be better than nothing at all. The famous love of God had gone up in smoke. It was like a paper dragon, exciting, gorgeous, magically real up there in the sky until touched by the flame of the elemental thing itself. Bernard had done his best and he wasn't here to console the inconsolable. He straightened up and turned off the torch. A plan must be made. But to do what? A glimpse of a fouled canvas by the light of a hand torch wasn't much to go by. What they needed was a closer, longer, better-lit examination of the picture. Followed by research into its provenance.

'How often does the Cardinal come here?'

'We never know. His secretary comes half an hour before his Eminence arrives and the rooms are got ready.'

That was no help, certainly. Evidently his Eminence was as capricious and as fond of surprise as Juanita. Maybe, like a lot of bishops, he was of Spanish extraction. 'Has he been here since the picture was brought up?'

'No.'

'Won't he wonder what it's doing here?'

Alain gave a little laugh, not without sarcasm. 'You don't know his Eminence. He'll suppose the picture is only here for his greater honour and glory.'

'Do you think this picture belongs to the Archdiocese? Or the Priory perhaps? Or the Prior's family?'

'Do you ask because you want to try and buy it? Is that why you came to look at it?' In Alain's voice there was an odd mixture of disappointment and resignation, as if he'd been brought to the brink of something secretly gratifying which turned out to be quite ordinary in the light of common day. Perhaps he had some vengeances of his own to work off, because of the orphanage and the humiliations of his short life. The thing to do was feed his excitement without giving anything away.

'No, I'm not a buyer.' He put a gentle emphasis on the last word.

'I don't think it belongs to any of them.'

'Whose do you think it is then?'

Alain hesitated. He must have an answer, he'd already betrayed that, but it seemed there was something more which he didn't want to betray at once. After a short struggle with this reticence he let it out. 'I think it belongs to Mado. That's what she says.'

'Mado?'

'A sick girl who lives here.'

'What's wrong with her?'

'I don't know. It's in the head, perhaps. I don't know what kind of thing makes a girl sick.'

'Do you believe her? D'you think the picture does belong to her?'

'Perhaps she just said it because nothing else does. She's like me in a way.'

'What way, Alain?'

'She doesn't seem to belong to anyone either.'

'I think I've caught sight of her, outside. If she doesn't belong to anyone how does she come to be here? This isn't an orphanage. But perhaps that's why you're friends with her?'

'I'm not friends with her. She hates me, I think.' Bernard could understand that. The girl he'd seen would come to hate any young monk who proved immune to enticement. She probably didn't believe in the love of God as an alternative to reality, either.

'She wouldn't have told you about the picture if she did.'

'That was before.'

'How long ago?'

'A year ago.' So the picture wasn't a recent import. But that proved nothing. It could have been here ever since the trains of deportation pulled out of the Gare Saint-Charles. And Bernard's curiosity had got the better of him. He loved to reconstruct, that was it. And now he could see something clearly. These two young people in a grim little adult society had been drawn together by the mere fact of youth. For

Mado, that had promised more, unlikely though it seemed looking at Alain. But not for him. So ever since the rejection she flaunted herself among the trees, luring and vanishing like an ignis fatuus. It was very sad. All the poor neglected girl wanted was . . . what the goat-girl had wanted among the cistus and the rosemary.

'I don't really think the picture can be hers,' Bernard said. 'If she belongs to no one . . . unless of course someone gave it as an endowment to the convent to look after her. Not knowing what it was . . .'

'I think Michel looks after her.'

'Ah.' And the picture. He looked after that too. There must be a connection. 'How does he look after her?'

'He used to teach her . . . Mado's never been to school.'

'Because of being sick?'

'I expect so. Or just because Michel wouldn't let her out.'

Alain's knowledge of the case seemed to come to an end there. His voice showed it, tailing away on the last words. His thoughts were elsewhere, that was obvious. Bernard shone the torch again on the canvas, trying to memorise as much detail as possible. An extensive literature on Caravaggio existed, naturally, and there would be the usual legends about missing works turning up and the claims made for them. He leaned down to examine marks that might be part of a signature. In this light it was indecipherable. Caravaggio had a lot of early followers, especially after his death in a brawl like – who was it? The Englishman Marlowe, that's right – around the same time. Or did Caravaggio survive the brawl and die soon after of some fever? No matter. He and Marlowe were both murderers and lived and died in a shadowy nocturnal world full of shifty villains like themselves. And what Caravaggio painted was a nocturnal world of solid forms.

'We can't stay any longer,' Alain said. 'The others will be coming in from the fields. I have to go to the kitchen.'

Pity for Alain drove out thoughts about Marlowe and Caravaggio, those two brawny bisexuals long since departed. Alain wasn't brawny, and he was still alive and suffering. He must be helped, within the limits of the reasonable, and made use of. That was one way of helping him.

'Did you know the Prior wants me to finish my work here today and not come back?'

'And . . . Luis?'

'I expect he'll be allowed to work a few days on the parapet. Would you like it if he did?' They were back by the stone sluice and through the little window above the brass tap there was visible, in the far distance, a narrow segment of sea and an island of rocks between two worlds of blue like a paradise you couldn't reach but where passions would be assuaged.

'If he didn't come back, I couldn't live.'

'If he does come, will you help him? With anything he asks you?' Alain didn't even answer. He didn't need to. There were tears again on his face. 'Even if it means disobedience to the Prior and the rule here?'

'Yes.'

'Don't be frightened of Michel. We'll see about him quite soon.'

'I'm not frightened of anyone any more. But you have to be careful of Michel. I expect you think he's only an oblate in a little convent in the hills and he doesn't matter. But I think he's something more than that. Something else.'

'Yes, Luis said so.' Bernard didn't add that this was also his opinion, because he'd learnt in his profession that opinion has to be substantiated to be worth anything, that was the difference between theory and practice. Luis must find out more. Starting with the girl, Mado – though Luis didn't know about her yet. Bernard felt a twinge of compunction, not on her account but because of Marion. But the twinge didn't trouble him long. It was all for the best in the end. Once Marion started work in September her need for Luis would become less all-engrossing. 'Where does Mado live?'

'There's a little house by the stables.'

'She can't live there alone, surely?'

'When she was a child Michel lived there too. But now she's big he sleeps here in the house and locks her up at night.'

'Doesn't she ever see another woman?'

'There aren't any other women here.'

'You said she didn't belong to anyone but it sounds to me as if she belongs to Michel.'

'I don't know about that. What I said was, she felt she belonged to no one.' Bernard looked sharply at Alain. He had a knack at times of giving answers that could make him quite a useful lawyer. Like a lawyer, he must keep a lot hidden. 'I must go now,' Alain said, and slipped away down the stair keeping close to the wall like a refugee.

Bernard returned to the library to wait for midi and the tolling of the convent bell. Michel had been away two hours, which suggested that Caroline's emissary had made contact. If he didn't show up for the midday meal it would be a certainty. Bernard pictured him with amusement, the bushy eyebrows knotted in lust, the apparatus of devotion – breviary, rosary, scapular – shelved like stage props till next time. There was something theatrical about Michel, as if his personality had more mobility than one based on mere humdrum essence. He seemed, to Bernard, sitting in the cool of a vaulted library facing the vacant space where the masterpiece had hung, very much a shifty inhabitant of a Caravaggesque world, staged in shadows and deepened by night. For no evident reason the image of Juanita sailed like a galleon into his mind. There was nothing shifty about Juanita, she was too cumbersome to shift with agility. (Wasn't that why the Great Armada had failed?) He liked that about her. If it wasn't for her religion . . . On the end wall of the library within the curve of the vault there hung, like a gamekeeper's trophy nailed to a door, a sombre crucifix, nearly life-size. How that image from the Middle East had polluted the Mediterranean dream with the fantasy of redemption! Bernard thought of the scree above the calanque where he'd entered by misadventure into an unredeemed life. There were no crucifixes there, only the light, the stone, the sea, the fire. If he'd been a Greek three thousand years ago that would have been myth, not sin.

\*

Luis sounded as if he hadn't much stomach for the mission. 'I know what'll happen,' he said.

'You known what you *think* will happen. That's your old vanity, my dear Luis. It may not go that way.' Bernard was being disingenuous. He knew as well as Luis that the moment Mado set eyes on him, all other concerns would flee her mind. Luis was the stuff of obsession, that's what it was. Bernard recalled Madame Soames – once seen never forgotten. 'I'm not a gigolo,' Luis said dispassionately, as if he accepted that it had indeed been one of the avenues open to him.

'Of course not. Be kind to her but not enterprising and she'll think of you as a sort of uncle . . . or something like that.'

'I've heard uncles are the ones who get into most trouble.'

'Only careless ones. All you need do is keep your distance. A kindly, tactical distance.'

Luis laughed without humour. 'If Marion heard of it, I don't like to think how she'd be with me afterwards. Luckily you're the only person who'll ever know and you won't tell her.'

He was right about that. Among Bernard's scruples were some that he believed couldn't be dodged, and one of these concerned his relations with Luis. They needed each other too much for double-dealing. Of course, there was an element of affection too, but that wasn't supposed to count between partners in the business of retribution. 'That's the little house, down there.' They were on the parapet, on the pretext that Bernard needed to know what work would be undertaken for the convent at his expense.

'I can see the roof needs a bit of a mend.'

'Good. I'll tell the Prior you'll go down and see to it. But look out for Michel. He'll be back any time.'

Luis smiled, his white teeth a perfection of sharpness and proportion. 'I'd enjoy a little talk with him,' he said.

'Cautious talk, Luis.'

'Don't worry.'

Luis must be left to it. Bernard trusted his aptitudes because he was elusive, and on account of the *baxt* which you had to trust because it was ineluctable. If Luis had been a man based in bourgeois society he couldn't have been trusted the same way. But he had no base. He was an exile even from his own travelling race. 'You must find out what she knows about that picture.'

'And about Michel.'

'The picture's the thing that matters, Luis. Michel's secondary.' Bernard spoke with the confidence that came when things were under way at last.

'Perhaps,' said Luis. 'I'll see.' There was no good reason to take his doubt too seriously. To redress justice by depriving the villainous had always been enough for him – except once long ago when he knew no better . . . and had taken a fatal step further. But he was more mature now, more stable. He'd slowed down, Bernard thought.

# Chapter Seven

'OHE! OHE! MONSIEUR Luis!' It was the lame boy who was useful for messages. 'Monsieur Luis!' He looked excited, his eyes needle-sharp.

Luis crossed the ruinous space in front of the gate of the Vieille Charité, a huddle of slums too structurally unsafe for habitation even here. The boy was hobbling towards him but he waved him back. Better meet accidentally under the walls. 'What is it, Pierrot?'

'I've heard something that'll interest you.'

'How do you know what interests me?'

Pierrot didn't bother to answer this question. He was already light years ahead in cunning. 'I heard some of the boys talking. They didn't mind me because I could never get out that far.'

'As far as what?'

'And I can't swim.'

If it hadn't been for the lameness, Luis might have dealt him a tap on the ear to urge him on. 'Have they found an island, or what?'

'Not an island, oh no. It isn't an island they found. All the islands are known anyway.'

'What then?'

'It's not above the water. It's under it.' Now he was going too far. Luis walked on with the boy limping in his wake.

'Monsieur Luis! Wait. I'll tell you.'

Luis turned. 'If you annoy me any more I'll never pass you another cigarette, and you get through a few.'

Pierrot smiled. As a threat that was fair enough and it put them on an equal footing. Luis had cigarettes and he had information. 'Can I have one now?'

'No. First I want to know what you're talking about.'

'Round by one of the calanques. The boys were diving from the rocks . . .'

Had they found a Greek bronze? That had last happened over near Agde and the piece was now in the Louvre. Luis's thoughts raced ahead. He would sell it to an American, there were plenty of those about. Not in Marseille of course, but in the resorts along the coast where you could buy the right sort of cocktails. And then he could take Marion away – like a man of his race, with enough resources to put a woman into her own . . . here the thought broke down. He wasn't like a man of his race in any of the ways that mattered. Marion would probably be more at home in a house on wheels than he would. He offered Pierrot a cigarette. 'What did they find?'

'They didn't find anything. They saw something.'

'Lying on the bottom?'

'Well, no.' Pierrot gave him a sizing-up look. How many cigarettes were there in a piece of information which could be a serious disappointment? 'Between the bottom and the surface.'

'Listen, Pierre. I'm not interested in hunting jellyfish. If you're playing with me, I'll make you sorry your mother ever had you.'

'They think they know where there's a cave. Under the water. Can I have another cigarette?'

'You're still smoking that one.'

'For later.'

'Come with me.' Luis went round under the western arcade to keep in the shade. The sun, your friend in the morning, was an enemy by the time it floated down broad and fiery to the skyline. Pierrot followed at a distance to avoid the impression of common purpose. In this place, a complete lack of apparent purpose was safest. It was an enclosed world watched over without goodwill by thousands of eyes. When he reached the staircase in his corner of the court, Luis waited to make sure Pierrot wasn't being followed. The stairs were wide and easy as if they'd been built for the fortunate of the world and not the outcasts, rising through the second arcade which was the most crowded and on to the third, under the sky where it was hottest and there was no running water except through the roof when it rained. Luis valued this lack of amenity, it was the opposite pole to the bourgeois world. Pierrot was painfully slow on stairs. On the flat he could get along fast like a crab but steps required working muscles he was deprived of. 'Hurry up,' Luis called down because the boy mustn't think he was pitied. He'd know too well how to profit by that.

'I finished the cigarette,' he said when at last he got to the top.

'Here you are.' No doubt it was wrong to feed him cigarettes, it would shorten his life. But Luis, safe in the field of his own magnetic force, didn't believe that Pierrot's life should be dragged out at the expense of about the only usual pleasure he was likely to know.

'Thank you, Monsieur Luis,' Pierrot said in a voice already hoarse from smoke and effort. 'No one else in the Vieille Charité ever gives me one. Not even the end of one.'

'Why should they? I only give them when you're useful to me.'

'One of the others could be more useful. One who got about quicker. You give them because you're a good man with no children of your own.'

'Bullshit,' said Luis without much conviction. The boy was getting him tied up already.

'You do have some children?'

'Listen, Pierrot. I brought you up here to give me information, not ask a lot of insolent questions.' Pierrot looked pleased. To him, insolence was a virtue that was its own reward as long as you got away with it. He was very thin all over, not just his wasted arm and leg. Insolence probably didn't get him much to eat. 'Are you hungry?'

'Oh yes.'

Luis went into the cupboard under the tiles that served him as a kitchen and came back with a sausage and a loaf of dry bread. 'So am I. We'll share this.' He poured himself a lot of red wine into a glass on a turned stem given him by Soames some years ago. 'It's a special one for *baxt*. Don't you ever go and break it,' Soames said, 'that'd fuck things up good and proper.' Pierrot eyed the glass with longing. Luis remembered his own childhood. Wine had never been denied him then if he wanted it, least of all by Soames. He fetched another glass, a former mustard jar. They boy ate ravenously and drank with caution. That was a good sign, if he'd made up the story about the calanque and the cave he'd be drinking faster to fire his imagination and silence doubts.

'Now then. What else did those boys tell you? Or did you just overhear them?'

Pierrot didn't pick up this distinction, but from the look in his eye he grasped its importance. If he'd been a mere eavesdropper he wouldn't have access to more from the same source. 'They know the cave under the water goes up and comes out on the hillside.'

'Does it? Yes, yes.' You had to remember that hillside had once been a long way above sea level. It was a mountain then, with the blue water up against the southern horizon. And rainwater creates its own labyrinth in limestone. 'How do they know that for sure?'

Pierrot turned the wine round in his mouth before he swallowed it. He could never have learned that by example in the Vieille Charité. Perhaps he was an accidental offshoot of a family of vignerons and knew it in his genes. Maybe if he had his birthright he'd be a landowner in the Rhône valley worth a million a year. Nothing could entitle Luis to territorial stability and a million a year.

'One of the boys has a brother who works up the rubbish dump, he works for the town.'

'Well?'

'They use stuff they pour into holes in the ground to see where it comes out. Something brightly coloured. For tracing the pollution.' Pierrot looked proud of this information and rightly so. The other boys were probably thick like most, and it was he who'd worked it all out.

'Did the boys have the idea?'

'I told them.'

'So they borrowed some—?' Luis was enjoying the recital. Intelligence was a beautiful thing.

'They'd found this hole in the rocks. It goes down a long way they say.'

'Have they been down it?'

'Only a bit. There was something that frightened them.'

'What?'

'They didn't say. But they poured the stuff into the hole and there was a storm, and next day it began to come out into the sea. Down under the water like I said it would.'

A picture of this labyrinth in the limestone began to form in Luis's mind. Maybe he wasn't intelligent like Pierrot but he had intuition, the Romany gift, Ida said. And in that labyrinth his intuition showed him painted walls.

'What are you smiling about?' Pierrot asked.

'Nothing. A gitan idea. Now you tell me what made you think I'd be interested in all that?'

'I thought, because you like secret things.'

'Like secret telephone messages?'

'Yes. And—'

'And?'

'You're . . .'

'A Gitan? Who'd help himself to secret things?'

'I think everyone does that,' Pierrot said, 'only the Gitans are much better at it.'

Luis laughed. This child had a certain diplomatic sense. Probably if you had such disadvantages and couldn't run away as quick as others you developed it. 'Listen to me now, Pierrot. I want you to talk to those boys again. You're a lot cleverer than them and if you go about it the right way they'll do what you say.'

Pierrot took another sip of wine and an expression of great vigilance and craftiness came into his eyes. He said nothing and was obviously waiting to hear about what there was in it for him.

'How much cash do you get your hands on in a month?'

'It doesn't grown on trees round here. Mostly none at all.'

'No. Well, I've always given you cigarettes when you were useful and this time I'll give you enough money to buy your own for a long time. You won't have to come round me scrounging for more.' Luis felt in his pocket and pulled out a handful of change. He didn't count it up but he knew there was at least thirty francs there in mixed coins. 'Here. This is to go on with.' He put the money on the table in front of Pierrot, not into his hand. This was a deal, not a gratuity. Pierrot just nodded at the pile of coins. It was like his manner with the wine, thousands of years of Mediterranean commerce stood behind him and told him how to be.

'What do you want the boys to do?'

'Tell them in your own way I'll make it worth their while to keep their mouths shut about that hole. Well worth it but not as much as I'll make it worth to you.'

'Will I have a commission on what they get?'

'Not from me. And I don't suppose from them. But I'll pay you . . . a salary from now till I know if there's anything in this story.' Was he exploiting a child and perhaps putting him in danger? A few francs was a fortune to Pierrot and nothing to him. But it was a few francs Pierrot wouldn't get into his pocket otherwise.

'If they find out I've fooled about with them they'll beat me.' He had the fatalistic look that came from being beaten often, whenever it suited anyone.

'I don't think so. It'll be you that passes them the cash. You'll see, they'll crawl. That's what cash does. It's more powerful than muscles.' Pierrot smiled again. It was a truth he'd probably worked out for himself long ago.

'Are they to go and have another look down the hole and see what there is further down?'

'Yes, you tell them that.'

'But if they know you'll pay just to know what's in there, they may try selling it to someone else.'

'Are they all boys from the Vieille Charité?'

'Yes.'

'Then they'll know if they double-cross me, I'll come by with a few gitan friends. We'll find them wherever they are and castrate them one by one. In front of the others.'

Pierrot laughed at this macabre joke, with a distinct touch of anxiety.

\*

Luis kept no car, it was part of his philosophy – if he thought about it – to live stripped of inessentials. So when he went over to the Camargue he took the train as far as Arles and Soames met him there. Soames liked fast cars but never had enough money for a new one and therefore changed them as often as they let him down or failed to live up to their promise. What he had now was a sleek-looking Jaguar saloon about twelve years old but which went, according to him, like a bomb.

'I expect it does about five kilometres an hour more than a Renault four and uses ten times the petrol,' Luis said as they took the road for Saint Gilles.

'This car has genius, that's the point of it,' Soames said.

'I don't much like the sound of the engine. You've got piston slap in that engine of yours.'

'Look, Luis. When you were a lad did I ever tell you you were a right *emmerdeur*?'

'No.'

'That was a serious oversight,' Soames said and they drove on in silence for a bit. When he was with Soames, Luis could appreciate how part of him had stayed behind in childhood.

'Are the horses all okay?' he asked, to prove goodwill.

'Yes. But your sister isn't so very.' They always called Ida his sister.

Luis turned towards him, his whole body pivoting on the leather seat. 'What d'you mean?'

'They don't tell you much.'

'Women don't?'

'Doctors don't.' Luis returned into his silence which was like sand about your head. 'What it is, she sometimes bleeds,' Soames said.

Luis knew he should ask where she bled from. If her life blood was running away it must be stopped. But he was afraid to ask. His share in her was in the outward presence only.

'Is it much, the blood?' he asked in the end, and at once thought it was what a child would ask, to protect its ignorance.

'A fair bit.'

'She doesn't have pain does she?' That was childish too.

'You know she'd never say if she did.'

It was in the camp for Gitans at Birkenau that she'd learned this silent fortitude, to get her out of there alive. In fact, as she got older she said less and less about anything, as if existence itself called for silence.

Luis counted the horses he saw on his side as they drove along. Would he reach fifty before they arrived? These were ordinary Camargue horses, not the Arabs Soames bred and sometimes sold. Luis had never known just what Soames and Ida lived on. Soames must have a pension from the English for his leg; the land belonged to them both but they did nothing to cultivate or exploit it – it wasn't flooded for rice or ploughed or covered with cabins for tourists from the land of Birkenau. Just the Arab horses. And these two lovers – left over. Soames must have a nest egg in England.

'Doesn't it cost a lot of money to go to the doctor all the time?' Luis asked, never having been to one in his life.

'There she is, standing there,' said Soames.

She was in the shade of the terrace in front of the *mas* waiting for them, leaning against one of the stone pillars. Her hair was as she'd always worn it – long and gathered in behind her neck with a ribbon – but there seemed more grey in it that the last time Luis was here, nearly a year ago. And she was thinner; her face was thinner, that's what you noticed first, eyes wider apart than ever now the bones were more outlined under the skin. They looked too big now, as if she was watching something you shouldn't really see. As the car stopped she smiled at Luis and raised a hand. He got out and went to her, holding her hard against him for a moment.

'Where's your girl? Why didn't you bring her? Is she afraid to come?' she asked.

'She's all right, she's studying, ready for the University in September. She'll have a salary then.' As soon as he'd said it, Luis knew how unnatural it sounded.

'If she works there she'll always have a man over her, ordering her about. She should come here to the Camargue.'

'Don't you think there are men in the Camargue to order her about?'

'No one ever orders me.'

Luis looked round for Soames. He was leaning on a fence at the start of the land where his horses grazed, looking over to where they were in the distance. Probably that was his way to forget. 'Not even Soames?'

She laughed. 'You know as well as I do, for him orders are a joke. Even in the army.'

'Not when he lost his foot. That wasn't much of a joke.'

'Specially then.' That was a lot of talking for her and it showed how she was pleased to see him. Not that she needed to prove it. Now she looked tired suddenly.

'What's this about you're not well?'

'That's my business,' she said, and turned away to go back into the house.

Luis seldom went into her house. For him she existed in the open, like when they lived under the railway arches. They belonged to the road, the line, the dusty tracks not marked on frontier maps. He caught her hand and held her. 'Don't go yet,' he said.

'I don't go anywhere. Others go.'

'Who?'

'You. The caravan has to move on.'

She meant the dead were forgotten people, left by the roadside. 'I'll never move on with the caravan,' said Luis to appease her spirit, as you should. But she went off inside all the same.

'How would tha like to go riding, Luis?' said Soames as he came up. Luis knew he was upset or he wouldn't have spoken in English.

'I'd like it well enough.'

'Come and saddle up then.'

They didn't ride the Arabs, they went off for a leisurely tour of the land on two *camargues* solid as timber. The Arabs were for ceremony, breeding and display. They were for beauty. Their beauty was fantastic, it was excessive. Luis knew that for Soames it corresponded to the beauty of the woman indoors. He cursed beauty and all its works and sorrows – it created anxiety, that was the work it did. As soon as you recognised it, the fears began – of losing it too soon, of not grasping it before the caravan moved on; holding it, knowing it. Those Arab horses – if you tried to catch their beauty it would only fly up like a spark in the sun. Even Brother Alain was the victim of the same thing, Luis thought without vanity. That was just a painful twist of life.

'You've to have clean water for those horses,' Soames said. 'Some of the mares were ill last month. I thought I'd lose them. A dog or a *camargue* will drink just about anything but if one of those Arabs drinks it, you can too.' So you have to worry about their water as well. You probably have to get the priest to them when it's time to die. Would she have a priest when it was her time? A priest of what? Luis thought he knew her like himself but now he saw there was something he didn't know. He'd never been near any priest, any more than any doctor, but what about her? Had she learnt to pray at Birkenau? Or did she discover there that there was nothing to pray to? Luis was never in any doubt about that but women know a different logic. They often see past the obvious things that make the surface of your reality so solid.

'The stallion you had . . . what did you call him?'

'I called him Xerxes, the one you knew.'

'That's not an Arab name.'

'It's Persian. Who says they didn't have horses? Look at them – they're from the ancient world all right.'

'Have you still got him?'

'He jumped at a fence and broke a leg.'

'You'd think he'd have the sense not to try anything too high, for knocking his balls on it. You'd think he'd know his safe height that way.' Luis felt resentful about the accident to Xerxes. There's a duty to survive, every one knows that. A duty to keep your wits about you.

'He was getting old like me. He didn't see the ditch on the far side.'

Luis didn't ask what had needed to be done. Beauty had been put out like a spark in the sun. 'Have you found another one?'

'There he is, over there. Only just full-grown. Scarcely knows what's what.'

'You mean he's still a virgin?'

'He knows where it is but he's yet to go there.'

The new stallion was in a separate enclosure with a donkey to keep him company. Luis preferred the donkey. No one could call that beautiful, it was obstinate, cunning and close to the ground. That was the way to be. He wished he was like that himself but then Marion mightn't still care for him. All the same, they were said to have prodigiously long—

'You'd better think, Luis,' Soames said. 'You've seen her now. It's time to think.'

'Yes.' There was no point in contradicting Soames any more. The age of contradiction was over. They were going to need each other, Luis believed.

'See that mare? She's far in foal from old Xerxes. He's gone but he left his flag flying.'

More than you or me, thought Luis. We're slaves to beauty, old Xerxes probably didn't see it, he just got nature's whiff coming at him across the fields. 'You never thought . . . about . . .?'

'She couldn't, not any more. But you, Luis – you were meant to get on with it and prepare the generations like the poet said. Just don't leave it too long. Mind you, it doesn't have to be your choice.'

What did he mean? Luis registered the remark, to think about some other time. 'How long d'you think there is?'

'A year, maybe.'

They were at the limit of Soames's land, and standing in the stirrups Luis thought he could make out the sea, a thin grey haze below the skyline and above the prairie and reeds and sheets of muddy water between here and the sand dunes of the delta. Beyond the tall fence was an unenclosed wilderness dotted with the black forms of young bulls. Why hadn't Soames bred those instead of Arab horses too exquisite for the rough world? Because of his dream. If he'd lived with an ordinary woman taken from the local population he might have gone in for small black cattle and had grandchildren of his own. Instead beauty had snared him.

'That's a short time.'

'It is,' said Soames, and they swung back like compass needles in the direction of the house, hidden from here by trees.

'You know what it is with me. There's Marion.'

'Fetch her here. It's all she wants. And children.'

'How do you know that?'

'We talked, Marion and me. It's time . . . a thing that waits for no man. As any woman will tell you.'

'That's not all. There's her job at the University. She thinks a lot of her father. The time's got to be right. I don't forget him either.'

'That man – he's a parasite on people's loyalties. He's a specialist.'

'He's always been a good friend to me.'

'I'm not arguing with you, Luis. A man chooses his friends. But you fell on the emperor of all the egoists there.' Soames's legs were so long they reached under the horse's belly. With his good one he now gave it a kick and they broke away at a canter. He was half a metre too tall for those little Arabs anyway, Luis thought, as he followed and overtook him, galloping now along the track between ditches. A *camargue* only gallops in short bursts and they stopped before they reached the trees. Soames came up more slowly.

'I'll tell him myself,' said Luis. 'If she told him he'd work out how to stop her.'

'Whoever tells him, he'll try. Don't say a word is my advice.'

'It would be like stealing.'

'Would it now,' said Soames. 'Not the sort you go to prison for.' He seemed decided to leave it at that.

On the way back to Arles in the Jaguar, Luis felt he should say something more. He didn't know what, but he knew he was going away and leaving them to carry the rotten *baxt* alone. 'I'll be back,' was the best he could come up with.

'Make it soon, Luis. A mare takes eleven months to foal. A woman can do it in nine but that's still long when a person's time's as good as counted. Nine months from around now, that wouldn't surprise me,' Soames said as Luis stepped out of the car. 'And there's good money in those Arabs, whatever you think, Luis. It's international, like the Romanies. All in the breeding.'

*

It had been a punishing day and Bernard thought he'd earned this glass of champagne in the comfort of Caroline Ghazakian's boudoir. The Prosecutor had been particularly rebarbative, seated behind his enormous Empire desk while Bernard was on an upright chair a metre the other side, isolated in the centre of the room like an exhibit at an anatomy lecture.

'You have prepared a dossier on the affairs of the Couvent?'

'I have, Monsieur le Procureur.' Caraman extended a hand, white and thin, from a black sleeve. Bernard passed over the dossier and added, 'I have a copy in my file, naturally.'

'Consider yourself discharged from any further concern, Vipont. That's the express wish of his Eminence. You no longer need a copy. Your clerk will hand it over to mine. This morning.'

'I must reflect on the question. It raises issues of deontology.'

'Not at all. No such thing.' The Prosecutor's voice rose sharply but the indignation didn't convince. It was assumed. 'You've already occasioned disturbance and offence in a community of unworldly men. I sent you there on a professional mission, not as a mischievous provocateur.'

'There you go a little far, Monsieur le Procureur.'

'I'm ready to go much further, believe me, Vipont. Unless I'm satisfied that the monks have nothing more to fear from your curiosity, I intend reporting the case to the Council of your order and if need be the Minister of Justice himself.'

Was this still a show? Or was Caraman a blameless functionary who meant what he said? There seemed only one way to find out. 'From the deeds of the Couvent, I see that when your late father endowed and in fact brought into existence this private order, he wisely reserved an option of repurchase.'

'That's perfectly normal. It was part of his family inheritance. He was sentimentally attached to it.'

'Repurchase at a totally anachronistic valuation. And the option has passed to you and your brother who, being celibate, will leave no direct heir. So his portion will fall to you.'

'That's the inherent structure of the code of succession. The consequence doesn't concern you.'

'But it concerns you, Monsieur Caraman, very closely. I fear the Council of the order and the Minister of Justice wouldn't accept a complaint from you as disinterested. The Ministry of Finances, still less. That land is development land. Corbusier could erect a whole new suburb on it. Immaculate Generation city. The capital gain will be astronomical.'

The Prosecutor thought for a moment, one white finger tapping gently on the rosewood surface of his desk. If he'd set out a lure for Bernard it might now seem to him that he'd been snared himself. 'To turn to another matter, Vipont, I think you should know I have the dossier of your protégé Karoly here among those awaiting early decision.'

Bernard was ready for this, in fact it gave him the opening he wanted. 'At this moment Karoly is rendering artisan services at my expense to the community. The community made him welcome. Especially the oblate members. Brother Alain and Brother Michel. The good Brother Michel . . .' There'd been, definitely, a tightening of Caraman's bridled features. 'I had a conversation with him. Interesting man. Well-informed and much attached to you if I'm not mistaken. I mean in the sense of reciprocal service. It seems these oblates are dependents one way or another. In need of understanding, like Alain. Or shelter from the world like Michel . . .' Bernard paused. There'd been no sign of denial. 'Protégés, in a word.'

The Prosecutor picked up the telephone and spoke into it. 'I'm called to court, Vipont,' he said. 'We must both reflect.' He looked more relaxed as if his own reflections were already complete. He knew now that nothing would keep Bernard away from the convent – not the Archbishop, nor the Minister of Justice. So if he was relaxed, he must have intended just that result. 'Remember, any indiscretion will be heavy with consequences.' Surely if that was a threat . . . The trouble with paranoia was that you could never tell a shadow in the dark from the pulse in your own eyelid.

'That's something I've never forgotten in my life, Monsieur le Procureur,' Bernard said.

\*

He'd finished his glass of champagne and was just about to go over to the table where the bottle sat in its bucket, when Umberto came in to see how he was getting on. And no doubt to keep an eye on him.

'Madame will come down in a few minutes. She's a little preoccupied today. It's her health,' Umberto said, filling the glass to the brim the way Bernard liked so he could watch the golden meniscus for a minute before he drank. Umberto understood this. Bernard sometimes even wondered whether he should keep a butler at the Villa Vipont but the idea always sank out of his mind as soon as he thought of another male presence permanently under his roof. Prying about. Sexually colonising. Perhaps even unsettling Juanita. Umberto was an object lesson in himself, relentlessly inquisitive. You could feel the man's eyes boring into the back of your head. Imagine him gliding round the house like a submarine.

'Tell me something, Umberto.'

'With pleasure, Monsieur.'

'Without indiscretion, of course.' The eyes turned harder than ever. 'To oblige me, Madame Ghazakian sent one of the girls over to the Palais de Justice yesterday.'

'Indeed, Monsieur?'

'She was to look after a friend of mine who leads a lonely life.'

'How sad that must be,' said Umberto with real feeling.

'I think she probably carried out her mission very successfully. My friend was away quite a long time.'

'How happy for us there are all kinds of women to help us bear this hard world.'

'I'd like to reward her.'

'She receives her wages from Madame.'

'This would be a little extra present.'

'If the monsieur . . . if your friend thought to show appreciation in a special way, that would be normal. But at second hand – excuse me, I express it clumsily – at second hand, this could look like subornation.' Did Umberto have a vocabulary for each client modelled on the client's professional jargon? Probably. His situation gave him plenty of opportunity for topping up his income by extorting bribes.

'I can always ask Madame Ghazakian.'

'It's Madame herself who instructs us in our duty – *il segreto professionale*.' There was nothing for it. He must be bought.

'I'd like some champagne, Umberto.'

'To the brim, Monsieur?'

Bernard reached into his breast pocket and withdrew his wallet. 'Which girl was it?'

Umberto accepted the wad of notes without looking at it. Why should he? If the amount wasn't right there'd be plenty of time for an augmentation. The byways of service here were so various. 'I think you know the girl, Monsieur.'

'I know a lot of the girls. Even some who've retired.'

'You're thinking of Véronique . . . or poor Marie-Claire?' Umberto looked ruminative, turning old roll-calls.

'Hurry up, Umberto. Madame Ghazakian may be down at any moment.'

'It was the new girl – Sonia. The one you saw recently.'

'Ah.' Bernard had another trifle for her in his pocket, but that wouldn't be enough to get the information he wanted. The rules here were strict and an offender could find herself back on the street without a second chance – especially a novice. Fear was encoded in the employment. He'd put his wallet away but now he took it out again and laid it open on his knee. 'I'd like you to have a little word with her before she and I meet this evening. A rather firm word, Umberto. I have one or two questions to put to her. Nothing that could ever in any way involve anyone else in the house.'

'Madame would be very angry.'

'We must spare her that, you and I.' In his wallet were two bank notes of higher denomination than the ones he'd already handed over.

He'd meant them for Marion, so she wouldn't forget him while she got on with her studies. He half drew them out of cover. 'I hear a voice,' he said, turning his head towards the door. Umberto stepped a pace nearer with his hand at the ready.

'You can depend on me, Monsieur.'

\*

'You look a little tired, dear friend. Lovely but tired.' Bernard said when Caroline sat heavily in the other armchair as if her robes weighed her down. Her face was grey and there was fine perspiration like a haze of dew on her brow.

'It's been an infernal heat today.'

'I admit, I relish it.'

'Your time passes in pleasure. Mine in duty.' She sounded not in the best of tempers. It would do no good to argue the point.

'I see I mustn't keep you long,' Bernard said. 'Albertas tells me my company's a burden to the busy. But I came hoping to arrange a . . . promenade with that little Sonia.'

Caroline rang the bell beside her. 'Bring Sonia to the apartment for special clients,' she said as Umberto emerged from nowhere.

'My dear Caroline, believe it or not, all I want this evening is to walk in the shade of some avenue in pleasant young female company. I'd like to take Sonia for a ride in my Bentley and return her to you safe and sound in an hour or two. That's all. The usual terms, of course.'

Caroline looked extremely suspicious. 'Just a promenade? Why?' She waved Umberto away. 'Have you some problem of erection? There are all sorts of expedients for that these days.' She'd brightened up. 'It's much commoner than you think. Pour me some champagne, Bernard. We'll see about your erection and its ups and downs straight away.'

'There's no problem, I promise you. Good for years to come.' Bernard hoped that was so. On the other hand, considering all the trouble it had given him he wasn't so sure. A rest could be welcome. 'No, I just want a walk under the trees, not alone.' And far from that special apartment and its microphones.

'It's outside my usual practice.' She considered the question. 'The girl's new and your speciality's a demanding one.'

'There's nothing demanding about going for a ride in an automobile. You're getting slow, Caroline. You react without imagination, like a civil servant.'

He was wrong to snap at an old friend like that. She sat there now with her head back and eyes half-shut, sweat on her brow, saying nothing. His impatience had upset her. Or was it something else that was happening? He leaned forward to look at her harder. Her eyes were turned up behind the half-closed lids, staring at the blue of the ceiling painted like a sky. It was the petit mal again, that's what it was. Her legs had straightened out in front of her. Then it was over, without transition, as it had begun. She opened her eyes, drew her knees back, and smiled as if refreshed.

'We'll ring for Umberto again and he'll warn the girl she's to go out for a drive with a fatherly client in his magnificent motor-car. As for the erection, don't forget to tell me at the first sign of flagging. These things must be picked up early. We have a common interest.'

Bernard felt light on his feet as he crossed the Canebière with Sonia at his side, making for the garage where the Bentley dozed. It was as if they'd been let early out of school. She looked pretty and not without style in the open air away from the place of business. Her arms and legs swung freely like the limbs of a dancer escaped from the slavery of work and practice.

'Why don't you bring your car to the house?' she asked. 'Is it that you're ashamed of visiting us?'

'Of course not.' The question, put like that, placed the whores and their company into the category of the oppressed, those whom it was incorrect to exploit. If you were caught paying your way but concealing your interest you were a male fascist. Even here in Marseille the advent of a new age of opinion had been rumoured. 'I keep it in a garage because it's an unusual car.'

'I expect it is. That comes to the same thing. It might be recognised.' She danced ahead in the sunlight as far as the next tree on the avenue and then came back. Perhaps she was afraid if she went too far and failed to give satisfaction he would drive off without her. And then Madame wouldn't be pleased. Nor Umberto. Bernard felt pleasure in this power of drawing her back to his side and down to his pace. It was a power he'd as good as lost, with Marion.

'Where are we going?'

'We'll drive out along the Corniche and have a look at the sea. I'll show you where my house is. Then we'll double back into the hills towards Luminy.'

'I don't know it there. I come from the other side.'

'There are woods. You can walk over the crest to the calanques.'

'Will there be any other people?'

'I expect so. Part of the University's at Luminy.'

She looked relieved. Out of the shelter of the house she must be more aware of dangers, being alone in the open with a man whose requirement was a long way out of the ordinary. It was a chastening thought.

In the car he put a reassuring hand on her knee and looked down at it. It looked more threatening there than reassuring, even to him. 'Don't worry. I only want to have a little talk with you. Away from the walls with ears.' But if that was all he could have talked with her in a bar or at the seaside. He was making for Luminy with nothing in mind but the imperative to go there.

'Umberto did say you wanted to talk.'

'And did he tell you to answer my questions?'

'He advised me to.'

'Advised?'

'He said it would be better for me if I did.'

'You don't have to be afraid of Umberto.'

'That's what you think.' One needn't imagine what that implied. So much the better. It was Umberto's job to keep order and his duty to deliver goods properly paid for.

'I think you went to meet a client outside the Palais de Justice yesterday?'

'Yes.'

'You weren't afraid of him too, were you?'

'He was sad. Very handsome and lots of class but sad.'

'What do you mean?'

'You don't know what we call sad? It's when a man isn't pleased. It's so important to them,' she added.

'Not pleased with you?'

'Not pleased with himself.'

'Did he want something special . . . to help him be pleased with himself?'

'Oh yes, but that's nothing.'

'What was it?'

'You want to see the little marks?' she asked with a sideways smile. Was it a smile of perfect indifference to what seemed to Bernard an abject depravity, or was it a smile of complicity with it? Even whores might have their tastes.

'Did he talk to you?' Bernard knew from cases in court that men dissatisfied with themselves in the sense meant by Sonia often seek relief in talk.

'A bit.'

'About himself?'

'I didn't really listen to him.' That was a lie. The girls always listen. In that situation there's nothing else to do.

'Try and remember.'

'I told you, I didn't listen.'

Bernard drew the car into the side of the road. They were already in the fringe of the woods at Luminy, among the oak trees growing in deeper soil watered by torrents from the limestone above when it rained. 'Look, Sonia. I don't mean you any harm. Now or any time. I like you too much. In fact I've got a present for you. But you must answer me or I'll have to complain to Umberto.'

'He needed to talk. That's all. Lots of men do.' It was the syndrome of confessional, consulting room, bed. *Il segreto professionale*.

'Go on. Did he tell you what he does here? What he's doing in that convent? D'you believe he's a proper religious?'

'No. He talks differently from them. I know about the fathers.'

156

'So you did listen to what he said after all?'

'Some of the time.' She was reluctant but they'd get there in the end. 'I don't like it here,' she said. This part of the wood was under a bluff and the evening sun was now masked behind it. It was dark under the branches while on the other side of the valley were the rocky, striated slopes of the Mont Puget like a giant layered cake, still in sunlight.

'We'll go higher up into the open,' Bernard said, and the Bentley sailed on in silence and without a tremor over the rough ground and back onto the tarmac.

'It's quite a nice car, even if it's old,' Sonia said in the voice she might have used to comfort a client a bit past it.

'Do you like walking?'

'I never have the chance now that I work inside.' There was regret in her voice. Her profession denied her life in every way except the act itself. She was still young but her humanity was sacrificed. No, it was compromised, that was all. It seemed that Michel had somehow reached it. Perhaps by his air of a knight or bishop. Perhaps just by his inability to perform. Unvarying potency must seem so monotonous – repetitive, mechanical.

'Those are the University buildings. We'll walk from here. When you get to the ridge up there you can see the sea a long way down below you in the calanque. In good weather it's quite easy to swim round to the next one.'

'I don't know how to swim,' she said. 'You told me there'd be other people here.'

'It's the vacation. The students come back in September.'

'We have no vacations,' she said as she got out of the car. There was fatalism in her voice and expression. She'd wanted other people around and now she knew there weren't any, she knew she had to go on with this cross-examination, because she was just a whore with a compromised humanity. He felt some pity for her but only a grain.

'This evening will be like a short vacation,' he said, not believing it. She didn't believe it either, he could see that. Here she didn't run on ahead as under the trees of the Canebière. She walked beside him but

157

half a pace behind as if held on a chain. Her fatalism removed the grain of his pity. If that was how she thought then she must expect to be used. In a sense, exploitation was reciprocal, probably always is. She reduced his humanity to nearer her own level. 'Did that man tell you his name?'

'It's Michel.'

'His other name.' Everything was going to have to be dragged out of her.

'Weiss.'

'It sounds German.'

'How do I know? It's not my fault if it sounds German.' She was beginning to be resentful, with the easily cured resentment of something at the end of a chain.

'Where does he come from?'

'The east.'

'How do you know that?'

'He said his homeland was where the new sun came up to fill the old world with fresh light. That's exactly what he said, if you want to know.'

'Usually the rising sun means Japan.'

'I think he meant when he was young – what he hoped for. A better time.'

She'd been a thoughtful listener then. Bernard looked in her eyes to see if this showed in the light of intelligence. But any light was shuttered by what she was and what had been done with her.

'So he came from the east – Metz or Strasbourg perhaps – to Marseille when the sun didn't rise the way he hoped.'

Sonia looked at him, and away again. 'From Nancy,' she said. She must have decided to stick as near as possible to the truth.

'So he talked to you for quite a time.' He tried to think what he knew about Nancy. Nothing, except that he had a colleague there. It could be useful.

'We went to the cinema and sat right at the back. It was nearly empty.'

'And he talked through the film?'

'Very quietly.'

'So how did you hear him?'

'His mouth was next to my ear.' It sounded as if Michel had needed the dark to unburden himself. 'I could smell his breath. I don't thinks he's been to the dentist for a long time.'

'Half his teeth are gold.'

'It must be the other half.' So there'd been a time when he invested in his teeth and a moment when he stopped.

'Perhaps he hasn't talked to a woman for a long time either. There aren't any where he is.'

'There's his daughter, he says, but I don't think he talks much to her. I think he loves her but they don't talk. Perhaps she doesn't love him. A man can have a lot of women and even a daughter and not be loved ever.'

Yes, of course, that was it. Daughter. Something in common in spite of all. 'You're an understanding girl, Sonia, it's why I like you. Is her name Mado?'

'He said no one knew.'

'I've got a daughter too. You can guess if a man's a father. Especially if it's a daughter.'

'They're lucky.'

'Who?' She didn't answer. The grain of pity returned, augmented. She was somebody's daughter, lost in the hard world. 'Why do they live in the convent? And why does no one know about her?'

'He just said it's a sanctuary. That's what he called it, over and over – they owe me the sanctuary. I don't know what he meant. He was like talking to himself really. His lips touched my ear but it was himself he was talking to.'

'Then it means he's hiding.'

They were near the crest, walking among the stunted pines and the rosemary. Below them, down the valley, a huddle of brown roofs emerged from among the cover of some big trees. Was it the Couvent de la Génératrice-Immaculée, sheltering secrets, giving sanctuary? It must be. It was the only bastide shown on the map of the area. The little peasant farms of Raimond's family would be buried out of sight in the forest of tall crowns. 'What happened to the girl's mother?' he asked suddenly. They always talk to the whore about the wife, especially if things go wrong.

'He said she was no good. She left a long time ago.'

'Back in Nancy?'

'She wouldn't come to the Midi.' So somewhere in the world outside convent walls there was someone – other than the Prosecutor – who knew who Michel was and why he was here. 'I'm tired,' Sonia said. She got no exercise for her legs in that house of Caroline's apart from opening and closing them. She might as well have been a door. No climbing, no going along a distance. Those few free steps on the Canebière had been the limit of her escape. Bernard thought of Raimond's cousin, the goat-girl, with her outdoor limbs. This poor creature here, Sonia, she was made to be a victim, born to be used and broken. The other had been free, down among the stones and the cistus with her yellow-eyed animals and the sea moving like the air on the hill. And then . . . she'd been broken too.

'You can rest when we get to the top.'

'Can't we go back please? I'd like to go back to Madame.'

'And to Umberto?'

Sonia trudged on, tears in eyes which now were full of stupid fear. He could see by her expression she wouldn't talk any more. Further questions would produce nothing, probably there was nothing more to produce. So what was he doing bringing her up here? Why here? Because there was more than just the spoken questions. There was the need to live over again. It invaded him from below, out of the dark, that was all he knew.

'We're almost there. Look.' He was ahead now, on the crest, pointing down at the sea. 'There's the calanque.' She would have to do what he said. She knew that already. She stood miserably on the skyline, shoulders rounded and panting for breath. 'The sun's going down.'

'I'm frightened.' A more experienced girl wouldn't have said that in case it was just the thing to excite him to frighten her more. But that wasn't what he wanted. On the contrary, he wanted cooperation.

Rehearsal. He wanted the next best thing to joy.

'I only want you to do what you did before,' he said.

'Not here.' She looked round at the huge empty scenery of mountain and sea, the red and gold sky. 'Not out here.' He saw what she was afraid of. Away from the microphone in the wall the part she had to play might be no longer a part but all there was, not charade but reality.

He took her hand. 'Come lower down. We'll go towards that scree.' Every stone, every bush was as strange as the surface of the moon yet familiar as his own skin. This was where his life had twisted on its base. That water in the deep cleft was what he'd swum out on, never to look back and never be free from what he'd see whether he looked or not.

She was resisting, pulling back towards the other slope and the distant safety of the Ghazakian establishment. But she must come. He'd decided on a place a short way down in the shelter of some rocks. Perhaps there, so close it might be the exact spot itself . . . maybe there, rehearsal would yield catharsis like a sacrament. He exerted the necessary force and Sonia came stumbling along at the end of his arm. But she was beginning to be noisy. She was crying out her protest, fear, refusal. They'd reached the rocks and he turned, still holding her. 'I don't want to hurt you. You must take your clothes off. I won't hurt you any more than the other time. Just do as I say and you won't be hurt.' But he was holding her too hard. Her arm was limp as if he'd broken it in a vice. 'Just do what I say.'

'If it was your daughter . . . and someone who . . .'

'Do what I said.'

She began to take her clothes off, undoing things with clumsy fingers while he held her, issuing those loud inarticulate noises that made him angry. 'Be quiet,' he said. He reached into his pocket and took out the trinket he'd brought for her. 'Here, look, this is for you. You see, there's nothing to be afraid of. It's for your work.' It was actually a better trinket than the last time, a pendant with small rose diamonds on a chain that might well be gold.

'I don't want it.' Her noisy mouthing continued when she'd said that, like a heifer in line at the abattoir. When she was naked he pulled her down in a confused series of motions so they ended up with his back to the rock and her astride him. Like the first time. But she was fighting him too soon. 'Wait,' he said. 'Not yet, it wasn't like that. I'll tell you.' She didn't listen. She fought with the despair and inefficiency of a woman attacked in the dark. 'You fool. Not yet.' No catharsis was possible with this sort of indiscipline. She was wrecking everything. She was being unprofessional to the last degree. With his free hand he slapped her arm quite hard to calm her. The arm under the impact of his hand had felt good, felt right. He was aware of a split in his mind like the effect of migraine, one part blind, the other exceptionally vivid. He took hold of her with hands in which the strength of youth seemed concentrated.

'Let me go,' she cried out. Almost a scream. 'Let go!' Her fists like twigs in the wind beat about his head. She was doing what she was paid for but doing it of her own accord. Perhaps that would work. Bernard now effected penetration, as they said in the assize courts when cases like this came up. To each profession its vocabulary, he had time to think before the blow came. She must have seen a stone within reach, and a sizeable one. It was like being hit with a mallet to the side of the head. He let go of her and in a second she was off him, standing and shouting down the slope.

'You boys! Look!' She waved her arms. An answering cry, uncertain but with bravado in voices not quite broken, came back up the hill. They must be not far from the edge. Bernard stood up with his back to them and went behind the rock. His head spun and his ears rang but he had the sense that no sound from the outside world reached them. He remembered in one of Conrad's books a man permanently deafened by a blow to each side of the head. With billiard balls.

'Get dressed,' he said. 'Suppose they come up after you.'

'They're only half-grown boys.' She began to pick up her clothes.

There were four of them, standing close together as if they'd been examining something at their feet. They were at the place. There was the rock, but it seemed pushed onto its side, the part that had been lodged in the ground was a different colour, lighter, exposed to the air.

They must have somehow discovered the hole. Had they been down it? Of course. But how far? How deep was it anyway? He remembered the sound of falling stone in the depths. But if they hadn't dared go that far others would, as soon as it was known about. Speleologists with special equipment and the mentality of ferrets would come out here and the burial place would be desecrated. The remains found. And his grandfather's Huguenot cross with 'Bernard Vipont' inscribed on the back would be stolen. Or passed to the authorities, ending up on the Public Prosecutor's desk.

'Get away from here, you boys,' he shouted in the biggest voice he could manage and they looked at him in wonderment. The sudden sight of a naked woman had stunned them. 'Clear off! *Foutez le camp!*' he roared, and after a moment they moved away at a run downhill towards the calanque, like goats.

'They think you're my husband,' said Sonia and giggled. She seemed to have quite recovered. Bernard on the contrary felt the pain at the side of his head beginning to turn into a severe migraine, a real one.

# Chapter Eight

THE INTERNAL TELEPHONE system, newly installed, was being capricious as if Juanita's influence had corrupted it. Now he heard both their voices, overlapping as if they were in the same room.

'Any man can get himself looked after. He only has to put his hand in his pocket. He can buy it.'

'It's very cynical to say that Juanita. You know he's good. And just. Not selfish at all. He's gentle, he never hurt a fly in his life.'

Juanita's scoffing laugh rang in the earpiece. He'd tried to call her to ask if Marion had indicated when he might hope to see her. It was a diffident way of approaching your own daughter but great circumspection was now necessary. In July, along the Mediterranean shore, anything can happen – it's the season when young women are easily blown off course. 'Not selfish? He's a monster of selfishness. There's no difference between men who consider themselves English and the rest. People say there is but as Christ is my witness, I know there's none. They're all pigs.'

'You don't mean that.'

'I do. As Christ—'

'—is your witness. I don't believe you. I know how you feel, it's obvious. He's going to be very upset.'

There was a click, suggesting someone had noticed the receiver off its base and replaced it. No more overlapping voices. Bernard understood that the two opinions expressed about him were really the same, but what were they talking about? Was Juanita about to hand in her notice? He didn't believe it. She wasn't going to walk out of the Villa

Vipont, he felt sure about that. Marion was the one preparing the ground prior to abandoning him, that's what it was. Dread returned. And what if that Huguenot cross found its way onto the Prosecutor's desk, after she'd gone? And the papa who'd never hurt a fly was dragged off to the sinister buildings at the Baumettes to be held for questioning? She would never forgive herself. She must be protected from her own plans. Still more urgently, a lever must be found to dislodge the Prosecutor. Bernard picked up the telephone, the one leading to the real world.

'Maître Saint Just de Tremblecourt, if you please,' he said when the number in Nancy answered. They went in for resounding territorial names up there. 'Vipont, of Marseille.'

'My dear old Bernard, what a joy to hear you,' came the voice of his colleague, suspicious and spuriously affable. 'And how can I be of service?' He'd got there already. That was the problem with brothers-at-law, they knew if you rang them after ten or fifteen years of silence it wasn't just for back-slapping.

'My dear Philibert. Tell me how are your pheasants at Tremblecourt? And your hounds? I often think of your sister, Emeline—'

'Amandine.'

'Indeed, Amandine. How is she? So charming. I was fond of her.'

'She's well and breeding healthily, like the hounds and pheasants.'

'And you?'

'Ten seemed enough. After ten the generative impulse flags.'

Caroline Ghazakian would soon sort that out with her expedients against flagging. 'Whenever I think of Amandine, I recall our adventure with the village notary at Tremblecourt . . .'

There was a short silence. Bernard had helped deprive Amandine of part of their father's inheritance, thanks to his special expertise in the succession law. The notary had been squared, Amandine had probably never even noticed and Philibert hadn't yet repaid the obligation.

'I've been waiting all these years for the occasion to—'

'Good. The occasion has arrived. I need information urgently but I've very little to go on. One Weiss, Michel, an inhabitant of your town, now holed up in a convent outside Marseille as an oblate.'

'A religious? The Church, you know, has always sheltered her children.'

'Sometimes against better judgement.'

'The Church is venerable, Bernard.'

'Listen. I want to know quickly who he is and why he left Nancy. The law's venerable too. We still put it to our own use, as the notary of Tremblecourt must remember.'

'When did he leave Nancy?'

'When his daughter who lives in the convent with him was a small child. Say fifteen years ago.'

'What's the convent called?'

'Le Couvent de la Génératrice-Immaculée.'

'It sounds like the ecclesiastical equivalent of a banana republic.' Philibert had always been quick on the uptake.

'I think it's a very minor order.' Better say nothing about the connection with the Caraman family. Philibert would back off at once. The Public Prosecutor in Nancy was probably an even less amenable figure than the one in Marseille and Philibert with his hounds and pheasants and ten children had too much to lose.

'Doesn't the girl have a mother? What's become of her?'

'She refused to follow Weiss down to the Midi. She may still be in Nancy. Or he may have done away with her.'

'Identifying features?'

'A number of gold teeth dating from quite a few years back.'

'So there was a period of prosperity.'

'Before the convent.'

'Any possessions?'

'Possessions?'

'Saved from the wreck. If he brought a daughter into sanctuary he may have brought an endowment. The convents often insist. To cover the cost.' Decidedly he was very quick, like one of his hounds after a rabbit, or whatever it was they chased.

'Nothing but a motor-bicycle that I know of.' That painting wasn't for Philibert to poke his nose into. It was still in the domain of research.

'I'll ring you tomorrow.'

'Good hunting, Philibert.'

'There's not much scent in what you've given me so far. Weiss is a common name. Perhaps you'll think of something else.' He was saying he hadn't been told the reason for Bernard's interest. Some anodyne must be offered.

'It's a banal affair – credibility of a witness.'

'You don't say so.'

\*

It was four days since he'd seen Luis. He kept a small van in the garage in town for use during operations and as it wasn't there, Luis must have been going up to the convent every day. He never used the van except for business. Bernard understood that. Luis declined the trappings of normality. But he also had a way of going out of circulation, not getting messages, not sending any. Bernard decided to wait for him in the garage at the end of the day. Meanwhile he must have a word with Albertas. As soon as he reached the office he called for him.

'Drop everything. There's some urgent work.'

'Drop everything, Monsieur Bernard? All my work is urgent. Since I do all there is.'

'This is something for your network. No one else could do it. You know how the real power in the legal profession belongs to the clerks. And not just in this office.'

'There are strata, Monsieur Bernard.'

'That's what I mean.'

'To each its proper field of activity.'

'Exactly. And yours is the one where information can be gathered.' This was because the mafia of clerks, unlike attorneys and advocates, co-operated instead of being in cut-throat competition. And because they had the detail of every file stored in their heads. That was how they'd risen to be chief clerks and members of the brotherhood. One way or another, you had to pay for what you got, but you got it, as long as you'd never double-dealt on a colleague.

Albertas sighed. That meant his protective instinct for Bernard had been called out. 'What is it you want to know? One day one of my contacts could get suspicious – information given in trust and put to doubtful uses . . .'

'Don't worry. All I'm looking for are traces of this family.' He handed Albertas a paper with Michel and Mado's names and ages. 'These people moved from their place of origin, which may have been the north-east, about fifteen years ago. Probably on the quiet and without leaving any forwarding address. They came here, without the girl's mother. She either stayed behind or disappeared altogether, I don't know which. It could be an indication – a missing woman.'

Albertas stood there looking down hard at the paper as if some of the message on it was in invisible ink. 'Any know affiliations?'

'The Church.'

'Protestant?'

'Catholic. When Protestants slip over the margin they stop being Protestant. Protestantism's an act of the will, that's implicit in the word.'

Albertas didn't argue with this. 'They could have had a different name. A name can be an act of will too,' he said.

'Yes, they could well have. And they may come from somewhere quite different. That's why we must try everywhere.' The clerks' mafia was like water – urgent enquiries spread almost instantaneously from end to end like a dye. 'And I think they had their hands on quite a bit of money at some time before they disappeared. That's all I can tell you.'

'It isn't much.' Albertas looked as pleased about that as Bernard thought he would. His network faced a challenge.

'Just one thing – there may be a history of luxurious dentistry. A good deal of background gold.'

Albertas seized on this. 'Gold is traceable. Every gram of it in France exists under state control.'

'You mean we can't call our fillings our own?'

Albertas ignored the puerile question. 'Supplies of gold, even to dentists, are officially documented.' A curious excitement had come into the expression of his eyes and mouth – a psychic alchemy was in progress. Gold – the matter of waking dreams.

*

The interior coachwork of the Bentley included a bar and Bernard sat on the back seat with a small glass of whisky in front of him. The whisky went with the walnut veneer and the leather and the pile carpet. The door of the garage was shut and only the bulb set in an alcove over the back seat lit him dimly like a chieftain of the underworld. He tried a sip. You were supposed to be able to smell the burning peat. There was a noise the other side of the doors, then the sound of the lock. But Bernard had left the doors unlocked on purpose so Luis couldn't think he was being taken by surprise. There was a pause. Luis had found that out. Then he appeared, sideways in the opening with the late evening light behind him. He slipped in and closed the door.

'Bernard?'

'Here. Come and drink this whisky.' A real chieftain shouldn't need help with a glass of whisky – he was a marginal in a man's world, not up to the image.

Luis approached, with his sidelong walk like an athlete about to hurl something or fell an opponent with a lightning strike from nowhere. But Bernard had never been afraid of him. He knew Luis had cleansed the world of some collaborationist scum but a lot of cleansing went on around that time. It didn't mean a man was a danger in normal conditions.

'Why're you here?' Luis asked.

'Why do you think? Because you've been out of touch.'

'I've been busy.'

'You sound like Albertas. I'm busy too, very busy with all sorts of things.'

'It's got complicated,' Luis said.

'You're not at life's first complication.'

'Let me try that whisky. Then I'll tell you.'

'Get in.' They sat side by side on the leather and stared ahead into the darkness. Bernard handed over the glass.

'Soames would like this. This is a good one, I can tell. They mature it for years in oak. You're supposed to be able to taste the oak.'

The mention of Soames put Bernard on his guard. 'You've seen him recently?'

'I was out there a couple of days ago.' Luis didn't sound as if he would offer more than that.

'He came in about a will. I wasn't there.'

Luis was shifting about on the leather uncomfortably. 'I have to talk to you, Bernard, about . . . but not now.' He finished off the whisky. 'I've got someone out there in the van.'

'Not Marion? You don't mean . . .'

'No, no. It's not Marion.' Luis sounded very uneasy.

'Who then?'

'Someone else.'

'Look, Luis, if this is private just say so and I'll go off with my eyes shut. You needn't worry. I won't say anything.' He knew it was a cynical calculation, but Luis's fidelity to Marion mattered less than her attachment to him. Till September anyway.

'It's nothing private. It concerns you.'

'Then tell me.'

'It's that girl from the convent – Mado.'

'You brought her down?'

'Yes.'

'Couldn't you find a place up there?'

'It's not that.' Luis was silent a moment. 'And why d'you think I'd want a place? For what?' Now he sounded angry, the anger of someone with a normally even temper. People like that are harder to stop once they get going. Bernard put a hand on his arm.

'We've got the same interests, remember.' That might no longer be true. Could it be that Luis really loved Marion with the kind of lasting love that can't be changed any more than the skin you stand up in? That it wasn't a game for a few seasons? If that was so, their interests could turn out to be at war.

'Yes. I think so.'

'Why did you bring the girl here then?'

171

'She's frightened for one thing. She thinks he'll kill her.'

'Who? Michel?'

'She says he beats her and one day he'll kill her because she doesn't obey him. It drives him mad if she disobeys.'

Bernard was shocked. 'A normal father doesn't do that.'

'I know. But I don't know which of them is normal. She's strange.'

'She may be lying. I've seen her, Luis. She might be retarded. Or deficient.' When he'd told Luis to practise charm on the girl he hadn't bargained for anything as drastic as this.

'She said if I didn't take her with me, she'd run after me. She said she could run as fast as the van along the track. I couldn't do that. She was crying all the time.' How had they got so far that soon? Had she seduced him as he came down the ladder off the roof? It can happen so quickly, and loving someone else, even if you do, doesn't prevent it. The category's not the same. 'I couldn't leave her there with him, and the fathers, and no one to understand about . . .'

'What's she doing now?'

'I told her to wait and do nothing. She won't move.'

'What are we going to do with her? I suppose you haven't thought about it. She's a juvenile too. They could alert the police.'

'They won't. He's a clandestine. She hasn't even got any papers.'

'Does she know he's a clandestine?'

'She seems to.'

'And does she know why?'

'It's just always been like that. Always in the convent. Always hiding.'

'You said she's frightened, that was one thing. What else?'

'Well, I was thinking of you, you see. Mado says that picture's hers. She says it's her dowry at the convent.'

'But it isn't a convent for brides of Christ.'

'She just believes it's hers, that's all. She's like a child with a story for children. The picture's what makes her somebody.'

'Yes I see. The little girl with no mother but a picture.'

'And now she wants it taken away.'

It was clear now that it must have been Michel who brought it to the convent, and not the Caraman family. But that didn't mean that the painting wasn't being used as a lure, not if Michel and Caraman were as closely linked as Bernard believed. And naturally the girl wanted it taken away. She wasn't part of any deep scheme. If Luis had shown interest in it then she wanted it for him, that was all. The situation was growing more complicated from hour to hour and now Luis had abducted Michel's under-age daughter . . . that would fall into the Prosecutor's province . . . and there was the gold Huguenot cross and chain . . . what else lay in wait round the next corner?

'How does she think it can be taken away?'

'I said you'd know how. By the law.'

'Good God, Luis. The law? With the Prosecutor on the other side? How long d'you think that would take? I'll tell you. A couple of generations. If she wants the picture she won't get it through the law. If she deserves the picture we'll have to take the law into our own hands.'

Luis thought about this, and while he was thinking Bernard thought too. Michel wasn't credible as the legitimate owner of such a work. His possession of it made him even more suspect than before. If the picture was as worth having as Bernard believed it was, he could give the girl something for it. A respectable figure for a copy. Authentification wouldn't come into it. When he had it safely in his attic would be the time for authentification. Luis would be satisfied, everyone would be satisfied. The painting would join the Vipont trust.

'What'll you do with the girl? I mean now?'

At that moment there was a noise at the garage door and it was pushed open by the width of a young girl's figure. She was in. She closed it behind her and stood looking at the car, its soft internal illumination and the two men watching her from the back seat. Bernard leaned forward to get a better look at her in the shadows and darkness. It was a disadvantage to be seen and not see.

'Come here please,' he said but she didn't move.

'Luis?' she said.

Luis got out of the Bentley and went over to her. She took hold of his arm at once, not putting her hand through it but clutching on above the elbow as if the feel of the muscle there was all that stood between her and annihilation. All the same there was an element of familiarity in the hold. There couldn't really be any doubt, they'd lain together, somewhere up in the convent precincts. The thought inevitably brought Marion to mind. I'm a kind of pander, Bernard told himself, I exploit my own daughter's loves. But death will part us soon enough. There's no pandering to death, it wipes out father and daughter alike whatever you do. He felt cold and his heart contracted. 'Luis,' he called, 'bring her over here.'

Luis pushed the girl along in front of him without ceremony. That showed her meaning to him was limited to pity and the few minutes of pleasure he'd taken without thinking. 'Get in. I'll follow,' Bernard heard him say, in the same kind of voice he might have said, 'Just put your legs round me. I'll do the rest.' The girl obeyed. Everyone obeyed Luis one way or another, because he stood for the elements.

'Are you thirsty?' Bernard asked the girl, seeing her fear. 'We've got some Perrier.' She shook her head. An animal let out of the cage for the first time doesn't stop to drink or eat, it flees wherever its instinct guides it. In Mado's case the Vieille Charité would be just the place. She was the stuff of the refugee populace that filled it. Luis pushed her down next to Bernard and climbed into the front of the car, turning so his face and his arm along the back of the seat were close to her. She didn't take her eyes off him but perched there on the edge of the leather. Bernard recalled the bared breast beyond the tree. This was very different. That had been a captive's fantasy, this was escape. 'Have you ever been away from the convent before, Mado?' he asked, knowing she hadn't even been to school.

'No.'

'Not even to go down to the sea in summer?'

'He doesn't let me. It's immoral, what they do by the sea.'

'Sunbathing? Immoral?'

'Other things too.' She must know now pretty well what they were. Before she'd only guessed at it, and poor Alain had been no help.

'So you've always been there in the convent, like a nun?'

'Ever since I remember.' She spoke without any accent of the south, in a voice with a slight guttural intonation like Michel's. She couldn't

174

have had much conservation in her life with anyone else. That was a thought to stop you in your tracks. The regime imposed by Michel on Mado was that of paternalism taken to the extreme, somewhere near the absolute. If he'd gone on to kill her for disobedience that would have been it. I'm a pander maybe, thought Bernard, but not a monster.

'You don't remember any time before that?'

'No.'

'Not even your mother?'

'He says I haven't got a mother.'

Bernard looked across at Luis. It didn't seem as if she had much to say about the past. That left the picture, and the only thing to do with her in the meantime was to put her where she wouldn't be found.

'Did he never tell you where you came from, before you came to the convent?' Luis asked, his voice gentle, low, enveloping. Mado seemed to stir on the seat, aroused just by the sound of it.

'We know it was Nancy,' Bernard said.

'No it wasn't,' said Mado. 'On his permit it says Lyon.'

'His permit?' Luis asked.

'For the motor-bicycle. I saw it once when he forgot. I never see anything he doesn't forget.' As if unable to restrain herself longer she put a hand on Luis's arm.

Lyon. His permit had been issued in Lyon, though it was certain from what he'd confided to Sonia in the dark of the cinema that Nancy had been his point of departure. So at Lyon he'd obtained a new permit. No doubt in a new name. Not at all an easy thing to do unless you had the complicity of the authorities. Powerful and protective friends like the Prosecutor, for example. 'Have you ever seen anything else he'd forgotten, Mado?' Bernard asked. 'Anything about the time before he came down here with you and without your mother?'

'I saw once in the box under his bed. It was when they took him to hospital for his – the time he couldn't piss anything.' For the first time a smile came onto her face and transformed it into an image of gratification.

'And what did you find in there?'

'A pistol . . . his riding whip . . . and a paper, painted with figures and coloured writing, and gold. Not a paper really, a kind of skin.'

'A parchment.'

'It has his names on it. And another one.'

'Another saint's name?'

'I don't think so.'

'Can you remember it?' There was something in this, Bernard could sense it. If the other name was in the middle then Weiss was probably the family name of his mother. The first family name would be the patronymic.

'No.'

'Try. It's important. It may be important for you.'

'I can't. But anyway this thing . . . it's to make him a member of the Knights of Something. Mother Mary or something like that. He must be very proud of it.' She smiled a second time. You could see how she hated him, from the heart. Could any daughter come to hate like that? Was it the reverse side, and the coin had only to be turned over?

'I've heard of those knights,' he said. 'They came up in some case about property. With holy men it's usually property.' Albertas could go into it. If those knights had taken Weiss on board there might be ways of identifying him by their records. The networks must run them to earth. But that was for tomorrow. Now the urgent thing was to put this girl in a place of security where she could concentrate on recalling that name. He turned to Luis.

'Would the sisters at the Vieille Charité take her and keep their mouths shut?'

'I'm not going to any sisters,' Mado said.

'If Luis tells you to?'

'I won't,' said Luis. 'I know them. They're fit for prison guards, those women.'

'I'll go with you. I'll go where you go,' Mado said, her eyes fixed on Luis.

'You'll do what I say or I'll kick you out,' Luis said in the simplest way, and Mado just nodded. 'And try to remember that other name now.' An intense concentration came over her on receiving this order, as if he'd touched the right key. Bernard watched as she scanned the sparse store of information within her.

'I can see it,' she said. 'Some of the letters in gold.' She laughed, a high-pitched laugh like a cracked bell and with no gentleness in it. 'Like his teeth. Some gold and a lot of black.'

'The gold letters would be the initial ones. So, an M and a W. What was the other? Look hard,' Bernard said.

'It's like a snake. It's an S.'

'A golden S. What did the black teeth say?'

Suddenly she cried out. 'I see it all the time, that's why I forgot. On the sewing-machine. Singer. Michel Singer Weiss. That's what it says on his parchment to make him a shining knight.'

Bernard stepped out of the car. He must get on at once to the colleague in Nancy. It was under the name Singer that Mado's mother might be traceable. There was no time to lose. Here in Marseille the Prosecutor wouldn't be losing any. If he was Michel's protector – for reasons of state dictated from on high, or because Michel had something on him personally – the disappearance of this girl would set the alarms going.

'That's useful information, Mado,' he said. 'Now Luis will take care of you. We'll arrange to get you your picture back too. If there's anything you want – clothes or things – tell Luis. He'll get them. Keep out of sight, remember that. You don't want to be taken back to the convent and the shining knight.'

'I don't want anything,' she said.

Those were the most trouble of all, the ones who started off saying they didn't want anything. All their forces were concentrated on getting the hooks in. Still, that was more Luis's problem than his. As long as Marion knew nothing about it, yet. The whole thing demanded careful timing, he thought as he drove up the steep last approach from the Corniche to the electrically operated portals of the Villa Vipont.

\*

'I've found a trace for you, Bernard.'

'Just a trace?'

'Enough, I think, to square the account you mentioned.'

'Well, let's hear the details.'

'A woman by the name of Singer disappeared about fifteen years ago leaving some small debts – rent, gas, local tax. She'd been living as an occasional prostitute, one of those women with too little income who round off their month by the quickest expedient.'

'Go on.'

'The usual searches were made. In other words, not much. Women disappear all the time leaving accounts unpaid. Sometimes I wonder if they recognise our structured world at all.'

'They recognise without subscribing. And those searches – what did they come up with?'

'Not a great deal. Not a great deal at all.' There must be something or he wouldn't spin it out like that.

'You disappoint me.'

'Wait. She was never tracked down and the debts had to be written off. It was said she'd gone to Paris but no one really knew. In Paris, a woman like that's very soon swallowed up. Just part of the diet of the capital.'

'Is that your trace then? No more?'

'Just one little detail.' Philibert held the pause as long as possible. 'A postcard sitting for years in the undelivered section of the central post office here. Sent to another woman who moved on.'

'You have an agent in the post office?'

'Naturally. Or rather my clerk has. Hasn't yours? Indispensable my dear Bernard.'

'Was it from Paris?'

'No. From a town in England. That's why it was never returned to sender. The post is a public service but it doesn't exist to serve a public of island barbarians. I have it in front of me now. I shall have to return it to the undelivered section later today.'

'Read it out.'

'It just says, "Found work in Liverpool. Good clientèle and generous and more French personnel wanted. Came over with a girl from Paris. It seems there's a contact in Marseille – old school friend of the management here. So I thought of you, case you go back there. A

Madame Ghizakin or something. She keeps a house, so you just ask."
It's signed Madeleine Singer. That's all, no address. So there you are,
Bernard. If this Madame Ghizakin who sounds Russian to me is still
around, the police public morals section will know all about her and
her house. You could send a clerk – have you a young clerk? Obviously
at your age you can't decently set foot there yourself.'

'I'll think of a way to make contact with this woman if I can run her
down, don't worry. I'm grateful, Philibert, this may be a valuable lead.
Let me hear if you learn anything else. I wish you a good season with
the pheasants.'

'You should come up and join us for a few days in September. It's a
bloodbath. Great sport.'

'Thank you, I'm not good at killing things. My daughter would tell
you I'm incapable of hurting a fly.'

'None of my ten would say that. I don't believe in over-indulgence.'

'Goodbye, Philibert.'

*

It was Umberto who answered the telephone. 'I regret, Monsieur, I
have instructions that Madame is unavailable to speak to you. And
your visit, if you made one, would be unwelcome.'

'Don't be ridiculous, Umberto. Pass her to me immediately. You
should know by now how women are capricious.'

'Madame is very angry with you, Monsieur. She's had a long talk
with that little idiot Sonia. Madame is angry with me too. I may be
dismissed. This is your fault Monsieur Bernard.' He sounded near to
tears.

'If you're fired you can come and work for me at the Villa Vipont.
Outside. The gardens . . . the olive trees . . . the car . . . the odd jobs.'

'I'm a trained indoors domestic, not a donkey for labouring your
terraces, Monsieur.'

'Well, where is she?'

'Out.'

'Do you think she means it this time?'

'I'm certain she does. Madame is a very decided woman. And to

179

make it all much worse, the little idiot Sonia has disappeared.'

'Disappeared? How could she, from under your eye?'

'She had leave to go and see her old parish priest. This afternoon, at the hour of the confessional. She hasn't come back.'

'What about her belongings – clothes and things?'

'Only what she wore. With a little bracelet some client gave her.'

'I see. Well, we can't worry about that now. I want you to do something for me, Umberto, and I'll tell you straight away what I'll pay for this service.' He named a figure to make even Umberto thoughtful.

'No more subornation will be possible. I think the women have been warned,' said Umberto. 'What was the service?'

'Something delicate which only a capable man could bring off.'

'I am a capable man, Monsieur.'

'Of course you are. I know it. Now this is what I want you to do for me. Madame has a filing cabinet in her office, I've often seen it. She's an orderly woman.'

'And very suspicious.'

'Then take great care. How long is she out for?'

'She's dining with his Eminence at the Archbishop's palace. A conference of Catholic charities. Madame is one of the Presidents of Honour.' Umberto sounded very proud about that.

'So you'll have to be quick. Go to the office – create some pretext, break a window or something that needs mending. Search in the files for one that covers dealings with sister houses. My God, it's not all been hidden away in a computer, I hope?'

'Madame hates them. She thinks well-tried methods are best for a business like hers.'

'How right. Well, Umberto, look for correspondence with a house in the English town of Liverpool.'

'Liverpool?' Umberto sounded disapproving.

'A great maritime city like Marseille. Except it gives onto the ocean, not this inland sea of yours.'

'I only think of football, and the hooligans.'

'I'm beginning to wonder how capable you really are, Umberto.

Forget football and think about the mission I'm giving you. If you're going to be sacked you'll need the money.'

Umberto made a sound like a whimper at the other end of the line. 'I'll go and do what you say, Monsieur Bernard.'

'I want the address of the house in Liverpool and the name of the Madame. And anything else you notice – names, dates, anything to do with the personnel.'

'Are you looking for someone in particular?'

'No one in particular, no. The important thing is the address.' It was a mistake to mention the personnel. It must be played down. 'The name and address are all that matter. You know my family origins are in that region of England.'

'I understand now, Monsieur Bernard. You're planning a journey to Liverpool and before you go you want the address of a good house where you'll be received as you are here. Or rather, should I say, a lot better. Because here we receive you no more. It's very sad.'

It was an interpretation that Bernard was content to let pass if it satisfied Umberto's curiosity. 'You have a natural comprehension of these things, Umberto.'

'Of course I have,' said Umberto. 'I am Italian. Wherever a man is in the world he needs a place to rest his head and refresh his spirits.'

'Quite right.'

'And rally his forces.'

'Yes, Umberto, we don't forget the forces. Now get to work please, and call me at home tonight at the latest.'

That just left Albertas and his searches. It was no good hustling Albertas and he hadn't had much time. But he was very quick once he got going, like a stoat moving in a flash through darkness. Bernard decided after all to ring him up at home, in spite of the hour. 'Albertas?'

'I am at table, Monsieur Bernard.'

'How have you got on?'

'I am at the cheese.'

'I mean with the network.'

'Is the morning too long to wait, Monsieur Bernard?'

'I have no time to lose.'

'Remember other people have other priorities. One needs patience.' Obviously, he'd found nothing, the mafia had failed him and he was looking for a loophole.

'So – no good?' In the background he could hear the clink of glass and the pouring of wine.

'On the contrary. I find that in Nancy fifteen years ago there were several families of the right formation. And one of them was lost sight of soon after.'

'How did you find it out?'

'They were people who lived on charity and one of the charitable societies kept records.'

'If they lived on charity they couldn't have afforded gold teeth.'

'No. Not then. And supplies of gold for dental purposes weren't resumed in Nancy after the war until 1950. A good colleague has searched from then until the time of disappearance and none of the patients treated at Nancy fit the case. They were all much older people.'

'Putting their savings away safely.'

'So this man's crowns were either fitted somewhere else, or earlier on in a place where gold was available. The charitable society's records go back beyond 1950 and he was an old client.'

'What sort of charitable society?'

'A minor religious order connected with some knights or other. Their affairs were wound up by a cabinet of advocates. That's how I reached the source.'

'Very good, Albertas, as far as it goes. Do you know what these people were called?'

'They sometimes went by the name you gave me. Weiss. And other times Singer. One of them may have been the woman's patronymic.'

'So if he was on charity from 1950 and there was no gold in Nancy before that, it must have been somewhere else. Where was there any gold?'

Albertas cleared his throat and there was a short silence. When he spoke the tone of his voice had changed. Now he sounded, to Bernard who knew his voice so well, as if he was aware that they stood on the edge of deep waters. 'It seems there was one place where there was abundant gold for dental purposes – if you were a person in authority.'

'Where?'

'Lyon. At the end of the Occupation.'

Yes. Of course. 'Where did the gold come from? Why was it available there and nowhere else?'

'Those are questions for journalists and historians, Monsieur Bernard, not for lawyers. Especially for you who should be careful, for reasons we know. But there were rumours on the point.'

'And what did they say?'

'I prefer not to repeat it on the telephone. It's why I thought it better to wait until the morning.'

'I can't wait until the morning. And this is not what you call my paranoia. I'll make a guess and if I'm wrong, don't ring off.' Albertas said nothing. He was waiting. 'According to rumour the gold came out of the mouths of the deported.' There was a click on the telephone, like when Marion and Juanita had noticed the receiver off its base; but this sound echoed from far down the spiral to hell.

# Chapter Nine

SOAMES HAD AGREED at a few hours' notice to accompany Bernard on this trip because, he said, he had property in the north of England that needed seeing to. Bernard thought that was probably not his only reason. He had a feeling Soames was there to keep an eye on him. 'What have you got to do about it?' he asked as they sat side by side in the aeroplane.

'Sell it,' said Soames. 'I'm looking to buy another house in the Camargue and some land.'

'Are you dissatisfied with your present residence? The mosquitoes? The German tourists?'

'It's for someone else. To get them decently set up.' Soames looked down at him from eyes so far back inside his head you'd need an excavator to unearth their meaning. Bernard, however, could guess what it was. Soames was colonising future generations. He had no children of his own and instinct was working while there was still time. Luis and Marion were to be his immortality. That remained to be seen. Some daughters stay at home out of filial love and from a sense of responsibility – as long as they have as much freedom as your income will run to. You have to be wary about it, that's all.

'How long will you need for your business?' Bernard asked.

'A day. Just a couple of people to see, then I'm yours.'

Bernard had reasonable school English, plus a few inherited sayings of his father's which he treasured like letters. He hadn't had the occasion to develop his command of the language to cover difficult affairs in the adult world. Soames was going to help.

'We'll be visiting the most reputable brothel in Liverpool,' Bernard said.

'Will we now. Reputable? I doubt the competition's very strong. It'll be interesting to see. I don't patronise brothels these days.' Bernard kept discreetly quiet about that. Maybe Soames stood in need of one of Caroline's expedients. 'I knew one in Nîmes that was good though. Years ago.'

'When you were freer?'

'Before I'd found out what I know now about love.'

'My friend Caroline Ghazakian in Marseille would be pleased to welcome you in her excellent house, I'm sure of that. In fact, the one we're going to came out of her address book. Just mention my name.' Bernard knew that even love leaves the libido elbow-room.

The aeroplane was losing height. Bernard had been to London a couple of times before, arriving by train. Now he saw the pattern of brick and oblong gardens under a grey sky, and there was no denying that the view didn't excite him as the Thames and its tides had done in the past. Townscape was for looking at from bridge level, bird's eye view was for woods and hills. Of course there was no sea here. In Liverpool the impression would be altogether different, more like Marseille. It was probably sunnier at Liverpool too, beside the blue ocean.

'I regret we can't stay a night or two in London but my business is too pressing,' he said. For some reason he always found himself addressing Soames as if he really was a general. 'Would you have wished to stay there?'

'London's a funny place,' said Soames. 'Either you feel at home there or it's a living death.'

'Which is it for you?'

'I'm a Cumbrian,' Soames said.

From London they took the train. 'This is a flat land,' said Bernard as they ploughed their way through the bourgeois Midlands.

'Where I'm from there's mountains and lakes.' He looked in two minds about setting eyes on them again. He'd been away a long time.

Mountains and lakes stay the same but exiles change and grow. Bernard felt a new spring of sympathy for him.

*

Rooms had been taken at the Adelphi Hotel. Bernard's first impression of Liverpool was that it had force but not grace. Some parts of Marseille were like that. But here you felt the town and the land behind it reaching into the middle-aged spread of flat country they'd travelled through were all one, whereas in Marseille you could never think that. Marseille was a country on its own, standing between the sea and the stony hills.

Bernard liked the Adelphi and its pillared hall. It had scale and class and made him feel that his forebears, like the Phoenician founding fathers of Marseille, had come from a place with Hellenic links. Perhaps they'd even drunk their whisky and driven bargains in the shadow of these Ionic columns. The fortunes of the Vipont had been first laid down here. He went to the bar and asked for a glass of champagne.

'There's bottles and half-bottles,' said the barman, eyeing him with due contempt.

'Then I'd like a bottle, please.'

'A full bottle?'

The man annoyed him, he wasn't a serious barman. 'I certainly don't desire that it be half empty,' Bernard said, forming the sentence carefully, and took his place at a table as far from the bar as possible so the barman would have to walk over metres of carpet to serve him. He lit a cigar and waited for Soames.

'I'll go for a whisky,' Soames said when offered champagne. How perverse. The Adelphi champagne had proved first-class.

'Some whisky,' Bernard called out in the direction of the bar, snapping the fingers of his raised hand at the same time.

'You can't do that in this country,' said Soames, quickly getting up. After a moment Bernard heard him join with the barman in a short, single laugh as if nothing here was spent unnecessarily. One laugh would do, more would be improvident. Bernard took note. He knew he was a wasteful person. He lashed around in life as if there was no bottom to his resources.

'Our friend over there took you for a South American,' said Soames on his return with a tumbler full of whisky almost as pale as the champagne. He raised it. 'Santé.'

'Santé, my dear Soames. So. I see.' He must try to seem less South American, whatever that meant. 'What made him think that?'

'He was in the Navy. He sailed in their waters. He says they always carry on like they're wearing bull-fighter's trousers. All up front.'

'I seem like that to him?'

Soames put a hand on Bernard's arm. 'Don't let it worry you. He's only the fucking barman.' Bernard could see there were nuances here that he had yet to fully grasp. 'Mind you, he said the French come on much the same way, in his experience,' Soames added.

'Were your telephone calls successful?' Bernard asked.

'I got through all right. I'll have to go up there.'

'My business can't wait very long.'

'We'll go to this cat-house you mentioned this evening, if you like, after dinner. I look forward to giving it the once over.'

The taxi drove in the direction of the docks, so Soames said. 'That there's the Cotton Exchange. Where ill-gotten fortunes change hands.' Bernard looked at the building closely for signs of Hellenic influence. His father had told him that the Vipont had been something in cotton, once. Then there'd been trouble and they'd sailed to Marseille. So that building was probably where the trouble, whatever it was, had struck. The Public Prosecutor came to mind. It was late evening now but still light, the sky orange and dark grey and swiftly mobile like a film speeded up. You could smell the ocean on the wind, Bernard thought, breathing it deeply through the open window of the taxi. 'This is the square,' Soames said.

There were trees and railings and houses of dark stone with windows jutting forward from the façade like a chin and nose grown together. The pavement was lined with big cars, some of them containing chauffeurs. The house they were making for was at the corner of the square where several streets met and crossed, and it stood back behind a couple of trees and a short garden. No doubt there were other entrances so no one need ever feel cornered. They were shown into a sitting room which had none of the stagey elegance of Caroline's boudoir. It was small, dark and panelled like an anteroom anywhere, suggestive of painful experience in store. The suggestion was belied from time to time by muffled thumps and laughter, quickly cut short, from the floor above.

'They know how to let themselves go, in Liverpool,' Soames said. At last the door opened and a woman of about Caroline's age came in, preceded, surrounded and followed by a rush of perfume.

'I am Mrs Molyneux,' she said. She was strikingly handsome with a high colour and seemed overpoweringly energetic for her age, like a racehorse perhaps no longer up to the jumps but still capable of churning a great deal of turf as it pounded along. 'And how is my dear old friend Caroline? We worked together as young women,' she charged on without waiting for an answer, 'of course, Caroline's a few years older than me – and before that we were at the same convent. Poor Caroline was one of those French girls sent to a convent in England so she'd always have friends in two countries. Just in case. Not that she ever picked up much English. We were the liveliest girls in the school, I can tell you, and then later at work.' She laughed exuberantly. 'We were terribly lively then, I promise you that. And is Caroline still just as lively as ever?' She paused at last. Surely these silent visitors must be able to report on poor Caroline's liveliness?

'Mr Vipont speaks some English but he doesn't get a lot of practice,' said Soames.

Mrs Molyneux switched her attention to him. Bernard could see at once what she was thinking. Soames didn't come from the world where her clientèle was mainly drawn. She turned on an extra voltage of charm to make him feel at home for the short time he would be here. 'Then you'll be so kind as to explain his requirements to me,' she said, dropping Caroline. 'I like to know just what a gentleman wants before I say if I can provide it and on what terms. Is Mr Vipont a business acquaintance?'

'Kind of,' said Soames.

Mrs Molyneux seemed to think she wouldn't get much more out of him and she turned back to Bernard, speaking slowly and distinctly, eyes and teeth flashing on and off like the illuminations he'd seen in Piccadilly Circus. 'Tell me just what we can do to please you, my dear, in your own way. I can't have you going back to France and complaining to Caroline I disappointed you. She'd think I'd lost my touch altogether. If there's anything you can't explain, I haven't forgotten all my convent French, not yet. But of course I have no specialised vocabulary.' She was certainly putting herself out. She was much better looking than Caroline and grand as a corrupted duchess, with an aquiline nose and a dark gold streak in her black hair like a heraldic device.

'All I desire this evening, Madame, is a little information. Naturally I expect to pay two times your most elevated tariff.'

'But you speak English beautifully.' She put a hand on his knee. It felt quite heavy, due to the number of rings. 'Quite beautifully. What do you want to know?'

While he haltingly explained he watched her. Once the illuminations went down she looked a lot older, eyes hard and dead as flints, the gold in her hair turned to brass.

'I see,' she said. 'I remember Madeleine Singer though it was a long time ago. Bit of a shrinking violet, was Madeleine. Why I remember her so well is she's the only one of my staff who ever dropped out of the profession. She went civilian. So I don't see how I can very well tell you what you want to know. If she'd gone to another house or into freelancing that would be different, dear.'

Bernard had foreseen difficulties, if not this one. 'I am a lawyer, Madame,' he said. 'Madeleine Singer may have rights in an inheritance I administer.' It was the story he'd spun to Soames and it was one that always worked. People had a pious reaction about inheritances in case they ever got one themselves.

'Perhaps I should ask Caroline her advice. You have her telephone number? I'm sure I don't know what's best.'

'Madeleine Singer didn't come to you from Caroline. She was what you call it – freelance. Caroline knows nothing about her. I never confuse professional and private life.' That was another sentence prepared in advance. He couldn't have delivered it in English off the cuff. Soames knew that and was looking at him in a sceptical manner.

'That's quite true. She was recruited for me in Paris. Poor Madeleine turned out to be not quite what the customers expected. Not exactly the Moulin Rouge. All the same there were some who liked her – the quiet ones you know. I suppose if it's a legacy . . . but you have to promise to be discreet, extremely discreet about where she is now.'

'Madame, as I said I am a man of the law. More discreet than a priest.'

Mrs Molyneux laughed again, her lights switched back on. 'I know a few of them here who—' she began, and left the sentence in the air. 'For you, dear, and being a legal matter, I'll do it. I'll go upstairs and look up my records.' She opened a cupboard and took out tumblers and the sacred whisky bottle; then she turned to Soames. 'If you like, while you wait, I'll send down one of the . . .'

'Love's by way of being my handicap there, Mrs Molyneux,' Soames said, and she bowed her head in respect and left them to it. All this was a long way from Umberto and the champagne bucket and for the first time Bernard felt grateful to his ancestor for sailing away to the regions of the vine, to Marseille and its commodious tolerances.

*

At about the same time of the same evening, Sonia waits in the shadows at the back of what was her parish church before she became an inmate at Madame Ghazakian's, up there in the safe, prosperous quarter. The parish priest, who found her a bed for last night, has now heard her general confession but she isn't quite shriven on account of the firm purpose of amendment, which Sonia's circumstances preclude her from signing up to.

'A devoted heart is really more important,' the priest says in the end, sketching the gesture of absolution and hoping the poor child will some time find a husband among the clients. Or at least a protector – then her transgressions will fit within the limits of the tolerated.

Anyway, there's a difference between selfish sin and earning a liveli-
hood in the only way nature fits you for.

Now the church is empty, except for her. Soon someone will turn
the last lights out and lock the doors. Sonia waits for the person she's
agreed to meet here. A slight sound near the door behind her makes
her turn her head and there he is, in his monk's gown under a coat, not
looking out of place here in the church as she does, a whore anyone
would recognise as such. He approaches with the silent walk she
remembers from before, in the dark of the cinema. Perhaps it wasn't
very wise to tell no one at all about this rendezvous. She'd half hoped
he wouldn't turn up for it, and now that he's there beside her, standing
over her, Sonia feels afraid.

'Come,' he whispers, and takes her by the hand. He's certainly very
handsome in his black coat, very refined – he looks like a desert prince
with his dark skin. Compared to him, Bernard in her memory is
clumsy, blurred at the edges, overweight.

'Where are we going?' she whispers back, though they're already in
the unlit street in the summer rain, with the church door closed
behind them.

'To the cinema.'

'Don't you want to . . .?'

'Afterwards, perhaps.' He's pulling her along, walking quickly with
head down and half his face buried in the collar of his coat. Not that
anyone in this quarter of the town would wonder much about a curé
still in the vigour of his years, going with a whore.

'There aren't any cinemas near here.'

'My motor-bicycle's in a yard in the next street.'

'What film will we see?' Sonia doesn't often get as far as a cinema.
He doesn't answer. His hand is hard and cold in hers, full of bones
near the surface and muscles like cables in the fingers and wrist. It
frightens and excites her. Sonia has never been excited like this, not
with a man. Among the girls there's sometimes what she thinks of as a
comforting, a consoling – between two or three of them at a time –
but with the customers it's work, no more. She imagines those dark
hands – between her legs, forcing . . . and she feels ashamed. But the

thought persists, it caresses her in waves . . . amazing, a thought as hard as a hand in there.

'This way,' he says, leading her into an unused back yard where she can just see the motor-bicycle against the wall. Then her own back is pushed to the wall and he's standing against her. 'I want you to tell me something,' he says.

She can feel that what was wrong with him the other time isn't wrong any more. Probably he needs a junk yard and a woman to be afraid of him. Fear doesn't seem to stem her own excitement however, in fact she doesn't know which feeling is which in the current of her sensations. 'Tell you what?'

'Has anyone asked you about the last time we met?' His hands are about her breasts, and there's nothing gentle in them. Sonia wouldn't want them gentle, it isn't what they promised.

'Monsieur Bernard – that lawyer who's a friend of Madame Ghazakian.' Her own voice sounds breathless to her.

'Vipont? A sort of English fool with glasses?'

'He's quite rich, I think. He gave me this.' She holds up her wrist and he feels the bracelet in the dark. 'It's got rubies on it. I think they're rubies – they're blood-red.'

'What did you tell him?'

'He asked questions about you.' She isn't sure what it's wise to tell – perhaps if she seems to answer honestly he'll be good to her. His knee is between her legs.

'What questions?'

'About where you came from.'

'And did you say what I told you, that time?' Now the knee is like a hammer, and all careful judgement about what to say and what to keep quiet is impossible. Sonia is near to climax.

'I told him what you told me. Everything you told me.'

'Did you? You fool.' Now the hands move up, they're on her shoulders, on her neck. 'You said I came from Nancy?'

'I think so.' One hand drops down, fumbles below there, a rapid, steel-fingered hand.

'Sit on the ground.' Sonia has time to feel glad the man isn't

humiliated any more by failure. Her thought, such as it is, is like a
strand of seaweed in the waves of her own pleasure, back and forth.
She knows his hands are about her throat, she can feel the tidal
strength in them, the sensation of his terrible strength . . . of a desert
prince, dark like the darkness flooding all the scene behind her eyes.

*

'We'll hire a car and a chauffeur,' said Bernard. 'The best way to see
any country is from the back seat of a car. One can concentrate.'

'There's not a lot to concentrate on, over on the moors,' Soames
said, but it was obvious he felt a deep, reluctant excitement.

'You look forward to seeing your native place,' said Bernard. 'Your
home ground.'

'The Camargue's home to me.'

'Because that's where you live with the beloved.'

Apparently, Madeleine Singer had set up in civilian life with a client
from a country town a good deal further north. Mrs Molyneux
believed they'd married and ever since formed a worthy couple. The
only problem, for Bernard, was that the client was a solicitor. Or
rather, that seemed a problem when he first heard about it, the only
method he knew well for dealing with fellow lawyers being to have
some hold over them. And of course, on reflection, he had the firmest
possible hold over this solicitor. Madeleine was already married to
someone else.

'So where are these lakes?' he asked. 'All I can see here are sheep,
grass and quarries.'

'Just wait,' said Soames. 'Our lakes don't show themselves on the
street like freelancers.'

It wasn't cold but veils of rain swept across the windscreen, the
windows and the landscape, followed by brief episodes of sunshine as
hot through the glass as rays in a lens. 'It's a climate of contrasts,' said
Bernard.

'It's a real bugger of a climate,' Soames said.

It was arranged that Soames would go on to his home town in the car,
leaving Bernard to see Madeleine Singer on his own. No intermediary

was needed, they could communicate in French and Soames would know no more than what he'd already been told about the mission. Luis would very likely tell him later but by then it wouldn't matter.

'I'll have to ask my husband if I can talk to you,' said Madeleine on her doorstep. She looked frightened. This country town was her bolt-hole but behind her surface of bourgeois credit was the same marked humanity as Sonia's. 'He's at his offices until six.'

It was raining and Bernard had no hat. 'I'd like to come inside for a minute. I have a message for you from Mado.'

Now she looked terrified. 'Mado? She couldn't send a message. She doesn't know me.'

'Can I come in please?' He didn't wait but stepped forward into the doorway of this square house of red stone, up a flight of steps from a gravelled forecourt. 'I told her I'd be looking for you.'

'We'd better go in here,' Madeleine said, and led the way into a small room off the entrance hall where, like a good Frenchwoman, she did her sewing and kept her accounts, as he could see. There were a couple of chairs with straight backs, and she at once fell into one of them as if her legs would scarcely hold her. 'What do you want? Why did you tell her you were going to find me? I've no right to any messages from her.'

'Right? You brought her into the world.'

'I never wanted to. He . . . wouldn't let me go to the woman who took care of that.'

'In Nancy?'

'We were in Lyon then.'

'When were you in Nancy?'

'I come from Nancy. He was sent there to work – before the end of the war. Then we went to Lyon because . . . and then later we went back to Nancy. There were other places too, in between.'

'You moved about a lot.'

'We moved when the fathers told us to move.' She looked ill, grey, destroyed. Her eyes slid across the room towards a cupboard in the wall, then back to him, then the cupboard again. He knew what must be in it. He leaned forward and touched her arm.

'I believe you need a little reinforcement, Madame Madeleine,' he said. A whisky would loosen her tongue and then he would perhaps feel less of a scoundrel himself.

'Would you like something, Monsieur?'

'I can't drink whisky.'

She smiled for the first time, a brief, small smile showing the stealthy charm that must have attracted the solicitor. 'It isn't whisky. I keep a little champagne . . . stoppered of course . . . an occasional sip . . . my husband thinks it helps me feel not so much a fish out of water. He's a kind man.'

'He's not like the other, then.'

She had her back to him and was taking the stoppered bottle and two small glasses from the cupboard. 'The other?' She drank some wine and poured more into her glass and then drank that. 'You want to know about the other? Is that why you've come? Only to ask about the other?'

A former whore doesn't lose the knack of cutting through pretext almost at once, he should have known that in advance. It made it easier, really. The other thing to remember about them was that you must expect to pay your way. 'Did you know he went back to Lyon?'

'I knew he would. He knew things about important people there.'

'In the administration? Politicians?'

'And lawyers. Judges, I think.'

'Did you leave him first?'

'I hid and waited till he went.'

'With Mado?'

'Yes. He was the one who had to have her.'

'You didn't want to? Or you were too frightened to stop him?'

'He'd never loved anything else. The whole world – he hated it, hated it all. Only her.'

'Are you so sure? She must be called Mado after you.'

'You don't know him. That was his way of telling me to go. I was finished – I'd done what he needed. He gave my name away like ripping a ring off my finger and I didn't exist after that.'

'What if it had been a boy?'

'I'd be sorry for it.'

'I think you can be sorry for Mado too.'

'Yes.' She was shaking as if the attack on her identity had never stopped. Some of the wine had spilled on her skirt and she wiped it with the back of her hand.

'But she isn't with him any more. She's safe somewhere else.'

'Have you taken her, Monsieur Vipont?'

'Friends of mine are looking after her.'

'And him?'

'He doesn't know where she is.'

'He'll find her . . . with his powerful friends . . .'

Bernard reached into his breast pocket and took out his cheque book. 'Listen, Madame Madeleine. Allow me to ask if you have a French bank account?'

'I've a little annuity in France. My husband here – he gave it to me.'

'So you need never feel like a fish out of the water. He certainly is a thoughtful man for a lawyer. *Un gentleman*. Well listen, I'd like to add a little to that annuity. He needn't know. I think you're a brave woman and your secrets are safe with me. I have some of my own so I know about that. In return you can help me, if you like.'

'You want to know about his friends.'

'Yes.'

'They're your enemies, perhaps?'

'I suspect they're people who don't like my associates, that's the way I'd put it.'

'The ones who are looking after Mado?'

'Exactly.'

'I understand.' This woman was as quick on the uptake as Philibert. Maybe is was a characteristic of the people of Lorraine, this ability to light up dark places. There was that painter from Lorraine – a flash was released in Bernard's mind like a firework in the night sky. But of course. La Forest, the Caravaggist – a Luminist, they called him – that was his name. The painting in the Cardinal's room at Luminy. Most of La Forest's work had been destroyed in a fire at Nancy . . . was it? Some survived – perhaps in the household of a departed victim. A panel of La Forest the Luminist to end up in hiding at Luminy. It would be a fair investment for a trustee. 'You think because of what I was, I can't understand?' Madeleine said.

'No, dear Madame, I believe you understand perfectly. Tell me how he has these powerful friends.'

'It's because he knew so much. He never forgets anything. His mind's a locked dossier. And that was his work. Getting to know things about people. Weak people – powerful ones too.'

'So now the powerful ones protect him.'

'Yes.'

'From what?'

She looked as if she'd been tricked. 'If I'd thought you didn't know that already . . .'

'I may know. I'm not sure.' He could say he did know, but then she would never put it into words. It was a thing you didn't put into words if there was any way out. He must make sure she saw none. 'I want you to tell me – between these walls – so I know I'm right. I think it'll do you good. It's what my contribution to that annuity is for. I know it's difficult because it's your past too. But I meant what I said, you're a brave woman.'

Madeleine sat in silence for a minute. 'He was condemned by the court in Nancy, after the Liberation,' she said at last.

'Prison?'

'No. The other. What the General, what De Gaulle called it – a dozen bullet-holes in the hide. But they never caught him to put them there. His friends looked after him.'

'I wonder they didn't send him to Argentina, or Paraguay, like lots of others.'

'He wouldn't go. He said he would never leave the *patrie* he'd served. France owed him shelter, he said. And because he knew so much . . .'

'He was an officer in the Milice?'

'Quite high up. People were still afraid of him. He liked that. It helped him with his . . . sex.' She said it almost prudishly. That, of course, was because the man's fantasies would be hidden in his head, not under his clothing.

Bernard stood up. 'One more detail. Why did he go to Lyon to be looked after?'

Madeleine smiled, then her smile of stealthy charm turned to a laugh, different in kind. 'It's where the fathers were, the ones he knew about, so they'd hide him. They all turned into bishops and priors and things. Like caterpillars into butterflies.' Her laughter was convulsive now. Soon it might turn hysterical.

Bernard took her arm in a firm hold. 'In those last days before he went into hiding – did he collect money as well as information?'

'He never had anything. Nothing. Without the fathers, we starved. Just information and that wrapped up picture we had to carry everywhere. He said it was his fortune.' She laughed again but more quietly. 'Fortune from the Pharisee trained into darkness, that's what he liked to say.'

'Did you know the names of any of the fathers?'

'No. They're very secret. Never a real family name to get hold of.'

'You've helped me, Madame Madeleine, and I'm grateful. As soon as I get back to Marseille I'll send to your bank. Give me the address.' A film of disappointment misted her features. 'No, of course, you want it in your hand.' He drew his cheque book out again and sat down. As he wrote, something else struck him. 'The condemnation in Nancy – that was 1945?'

'I don't know. I wasn't with him then. I was a young girl in 1945. But it was just after the Liberation, I told you.'

'In that case the sentence would be prescribed in '67. Finished. Society wiped the slate clean, good as an amnesty. Eight years ago he could come out with nothing to fear.'

'Come out? Nothing to fear? Monsieur Vipont, I don't think you know everything I'd expect a lawyer to know about our country. It'll never be safe for someone like him.'

'The people who arrange their own justice are well-informed?'

'All I know is, he lives in fear of them. Sons, grandsons of the men and women he . . . questioned.'

'There were ugly things?'

'It's what some of the other women heard.' So the Prosecutor – or the higher authority behind him, powers opposed to reopening old French wounds – they were Michel's only protection. 'But you could never say he was ugly himself. He was very handsome. On the outside.' There was a sound from the entrance hall, a door closing, footsteps. 'My husband sometimes comes home to *déjeuner*, like a Frenchman.' Madeleine looked happy, holding the cheque up before her. 'I'll show him the legacy you brought.'

*

Bernard returned to the Veteripont Arms to wait for Soames. As soon as he saw the inn sign he grasped the origin of his name. It meant old bridge and had been corrupted to Vipont. He enquired about the Veteriponts.

'Come over with the Conqueror, did the Vyponts,' said the barman. 'Built that cassel up on the hill. Caesar's tower, that's the oldest bit, open to public these days. Only way to stop it falling down.'

'Who does the castle belong to, without indiscretion?'

'Used to belong to Lord Haweswater, did cassel. Coal money. Sold it to a businessman from London. Chap went out shooting with a duck's wing in his hat and gaiters on.' There was mirth from other parts of the bar.

'And this elegant Nimrod, this London sportsman – is he still the proprietor?'

'Went and shot hisself one day up on the moors. They say it was the one straight hit he ever did manage.' There was more laughter but Bernard didn't join in, thinking this reaction rather callous. 'Can't settle to live in a cassel if you're not born to it. Maybe one day Vyponts will come back again.'

Bernard walked up the steep cobbled street between old lime trees, to the gate pillars of red stone at the top. There was a kiosk for tourist material and a window for tickets of entry. Faded brown photographs of the interior of the castle showed big rooms full of enormous furniture of many periods. There was, to Bernard's eye, a lack of homogeneity in the ensemble which you wouldn't have seen in a French château of the same importance. It was as if the décor and effects of one generation were piled up on those of the last, and so on down to the original skeletons.

'Are the furnishings of the castle still in place?' he asked through the window.

'Oh no, that's all gone, that old rubbish,' said the young girl on the other side. 'Inside of the castle's used for films, mostly, now. They bring their own stuff. Ticket for the garden? *Le jardin*?'

Bernard decided not to go in. If the first Viponts' bones had been thrown out with the furniture it wasn't for the last of them to pay a derisory sum to march around the native place like a tourist with his mouth open. All the same, this was something to tell Marion about. Caesar's tower. Their point of origin. Something for Juanita to chew on as well. He could be as Roman as Pontius Pilate.

When he got back to the Veteripont Arms Soames was there. He'd worked out about the name also. 'How does it feel to be called after a pub?' he asked.

'I think it's called after us,' said Bernard, and Soames laughed.

'Very likely,' he said.

'Has your business gone well?'

'It went okay. Property's risen. Funds to invest in Camargue land. And yours? That legatee open up like you hoped?' Evidently Soames knew something more than he'd supposed. He must have talked to Luis before they set out, though Bernard had done what he could to prevent it. What was Soames's calculation? Surprise?

'It was interesting.'

'How much of the interesting answers will you be passing on to Luis?'

'Luis and I are in each other's confidence. Why?'

'Because I know a lot about his likes and dislikes. And that's putting it mildly. Let's us go and have a drink.'

They settled in a corner of the bar beside a window through which one saw the rain and the trees and the red stone turning almost black as the water ran down it. It was a dying scene. The barman, noticing Soames's leg, came across to them.

'This gentleman here, he's a Vypont by birth,' Soames said, 'and he

201

never touches a drop but it's champagne.'

'Right away then,' said the barman.

'Look,' said Soames. 'Luis, he's an idealist. You and me, we aren't. It's a big difference. We can love a woman, or a horse, or a bit of country. A picture or a poem maybe. But Luis, he has this passion for his idea. It can run him up a dangerous street.'

'Intellectual passion is very French,' said Bernard who was already beginning to feel less English now he was here. 'It's something not well understood on this side of the Channel. But you underestimate me. I work for a dangerous idea too.'

'And what is it, this dangerous idea of yours?'

'Finding the people who did away with my father when I was nineteen. And doing something to them that hurts.'

Soames didn't speak for a time. 'I can respect that,' he said in the end. 'Every generation owes it to pay off the scores of the one before. The Romanies call that appeasing the spirits. But still I don't think we're saying just the same thing. This town has the biggest Romany gathering in Europe every year – thousands of caravans and horses. Intellectual passion isn't what fires those people up. It's the idea of the race, the road, it's fair deals for Romanies living, dead and to come. Same with Luis, in his way.'

'I don't believe Luis would be happy in a caravan.'

Soames made an impatient sound. 'I just wonder how long it took those first Vyponts after they came over from France to develop a bit of imagination,' he said.

'So you're saying Luis's passion isn't so much personal. It's righting the wrongs of his ethnic kin? I don't think he knows them.'

'Something more like that all the same,' said Soames. The barman arrived with a champagne bottle in a bucket. He looked pleased with himself.

'Bubbly coming up for Mr Vypont,' he announced loudly, and everyone in the bar looked their way. 'And I hope you've come over from France to let those poor sods out of the dungeon up in yon tower of yours. I've brought you crisps and peanuts, gentlemen. Anything else you want, just blow a blast on your trumpet.'

'A simple soul,' said Bernard when he'd gone.

'There's not a big lot of variety to the custom of a pub like this,' Soames said.

'Except when Romanies gather.'

Soames considered him almost with approval. 'That's right. Only, with them, you have to look out. Once roused, there's no stopping them.'

'I've noticed it in Luis.'

'Love and hate, they're things that take them round the far side of the hill. Where the sun never sets on them and their idea, whatever they've taken in their head.' Soames drank some of his champagne. 'You know that, you've used it in Luis. And it turns out you're similar. I'm more philosophical maybe, I have it from the poets. But to go back to Luis – now that Ida's soon going to lose what she saved out of Birkenau . . . well, that makes him angry. And when Luis is angry, he's a big danger to himself.'

'I'm sorry about it,' said Bernard.

'So am I.'

'I've never forgotten her. You couldn't, if you wanted to.'

'That's right.'

This brought Bernard to one of his theories. 'I'd like to tell you how I think about mortality, how I see it.' A wooden look came onto Soames's face and into his buried eyes. He'd spotted a hobby-horse. Bernard had seen the look before on other faces, but he was mounted, and he rode on. 'I don't believe in after-life, of course. Only in the perennity of essence. Which is something more complex than we think it is, because we're trapped in time. And snared by love and grief.' He thought that rather good, and refilled his glass. Soames did the same. 'Essence is less coherent, but more enduring, than it feels to us *in time*. So we die, and our essence disperses. A musician, let's say, comes to the end of his road. All the essential part of him – all he really was – is resumed into the parent essence of music, where it came from. Do you see what I mean? He hasn't disappeared at all. It would be the same with beauty. Resumed, not lost. That's what I wanted to tell you.'

'It's poetic, your thought. Quite surprising. I'll hang on to it,' Soames said.

'It's more than just poetic. It's the way out of a blind alley. A misunderstanding.'

'Nothing's more than poetry,' Soames said decisively. They sat silently for a minute or two with the champagne glasses emptying and the rain now streaming down the window-panes. 'How soon my Lucy's race was run,' said Soames at last in a voice of sorrow out of reach. 'But if what you say's right, she'll lean her ear in many a secret place.' Bernard supposed these remarks were poetic in origin and therefore, like the sorrow, to be received with all respect. Soames straightened himself in his chair. 'We were talking about Luis. You've maybe heard how he once did in a villain from the Milice. That was when there were still plenty left and no one asked too many questions about what happened to them.'

'We're near the end of this bottle.'

'We'll send that joker for another.'

'I'm afraid we may become drunk,' said Bernard.

'I could do with it. It's not every day you come back to your starting point. Same for you. Where were we?'

'On Luis's past.'

'Right. Well, it's different now. Vengeance is the State's but the State doesn't repay. That's the big difference between the Republic and the Lord. The Republic likes a veil over indecencies in the past. You never know who may be caught exposing himself. Now, if someone like Luis comes on another villain – a real one, not small fry – and reacts how Luis reacted the other time – he's going to end up in the Baumettes. The courtyard at dawn. For the chop. So there are things he mustn't know.'

'Luis suspects he knows already.'

'Tell him he's mistaken.'

'He wouldn't believe me.'

'Your Marion must tell him then. She won't want to lose him so soon. And now she mustn't. He'll listen to her. We must get him out of where he is. I've reason to think you'd do yourself a favour by taking cover too. Leave your poor father to be resumed into the spirit of the laws, or whatever it is.'

Mentally, Bernard swept these remarks aside. What interested him was why Marion mustn't lose Luis so soon, in Soames's calculation. Did Soames know something he didn't, or was it just that he spoke already in the shadow of his coming loss? 'I'll have to think about that. I'm a modern parent. I don't interfere. Young women nowadays – you can't tell them what to do, you know.'

'Oh?' said Soames. 'Things gone that far?'

'But I note what you say. Luis mustn't be dangerously inflamed. I'll tell him nothing about what I've discovered here. You have my word. He'll probably forget all about it.'

'I told you, he doesn't forget.'

The barman arrived with a new bottle. 'Compliments to Mr Vypont from Messrs Grimstones, solicitors of this town,' he said, obviously impressed.

'To screw a bottle of champagne from a north country solicitor you must have been godalmighty diplomatic with your words,' Soames said. 'I hope you're as good as the one you've just given me. If not we're in the shit, every one of us.'

*

The returning aircraft circled the approaches, the grey and pink limestone hills and the blue roadstead with the town spread like a stain between them, then headed northward to land, nose into the Mistral. The view of the town from the air was a shock to Bernard, like a new insight into the id. He felt himself part once and for all of this scene in the moment he saw it, so splendid and so careless of splendour. The reputation of Marseille – cross-bred, separate, shady – seemed to match him exactly, like a fingerprint. The visit to Liverpool had taught him where he belonged. He could imagine a nostalgia for moors and lakes but he doubted if he would put it to the test again. This outpost of land, not quite France, not quite any of the lands of origin of its mixed population, an island ringed by islands of rock, this was his place.

# Chapter Ten

LUIS SHOULD HAVE seen this coming. Marion had never been inside the Vieille Charité because her father forbade it and, mysteriously, she seemed to respect this rule. But now he was away for several days. Paternal authority had been shelved and here she was. The problem for Luis was that Mado was back there in the kitchen. Mado liked cooking and attacked it with experimental energy. Apart from enjoying the meals she prepared, he'd been careful to keep away from Mado ever since he brought her here, and at night he locked her in the room where he'd told her to sleep so she couldn't sneak into his bed. He knew if that happened he would fail to throw her out. Nevertheless she was under his roof and that was a situation not easy to talk oneself out of, Luis thought.

As he and Marion stood there looking into each other's eyes, he saw her expression slowly change. She was suspicious. Perhaps that was because he hadn't yet put his arms round her. He did so now, pressing her against him.

'What's the matter, Luis?'

'There's someone here.'

'Who? Not old Albertas?'

'No. A girl.' He knew it would be much worse if he tried to hide it or put off the bad moment. Her reaction surprised him.

'That doesn't matter. You've done without for a week. Now I'm here you can send her away.' She really was more gitan than he was. She put a hand in the pocket of his trousers and passed it round the front as if her wrist was made of rubber.

'I can't. I'll explain. I'm looking after her.'

'Explain then.' Marion tightened her hold.

'She's very young. She ran away from her father who beat her.'

That proved to be the right thing to tell her. For a spoiled only child she was very quickly roused to indignation at the tyranny of fathers. Luis imagined that being spoiled was a tyranny in itself, in a way. Marion was so indignant she took her hand out of his pocket as though what she'd found there was responsible for the oppression of daughters down the ages.

'Beat her? How horrible. Where did you find her?'

'Up at Luminy, in a convent in the woods there.'

'Did she escape and hide in the convent?'

'That's where her father is. He's an oblate.'

'It's too complicated. A father who beats her and lives in a convent. I don't understand. Never mind. Where is she?' Marion pushed past him and entered the big room under the roof which served Luis for everything. 'It's hot here. Is that your bed?'

'Yes.'

'Does she sleep here?'

'Yes, Marion, she does at the moment.'

'Where?'

'I lock her in that little room there. I haven't touched her since she's been here.'

'You lock her in? You're as bad as the father who beats her.' It looked as if there would be trouble whatever he said or did.

'Mado!' he shouted. 'Come here.'

'She isn't a dog. You're a bully. Juanita says all men are and she's right.'

If he hadn't been in love with her, Luis would have thought Marion was being rather unreasonable, and he'd have known how to deal with that. As it was, he stood there stupidly while Mado slid round the door from the kitchen. She didn't look beaten, she looked like a poor ignorant girl longing to put temptation someone's way. Luis believed almost anyone would do, now that he treated her so strictly. If she resented being locked out of his bed she was that much less likely to make any mention of the one occasion – up at the Couvent de la Génératrice-Immaculée – when he'd been caught off guard. Anyway he hadn't expected her to be a virgin, coming on as she did, and when he found out it was too late to go back. He was sorry about it because he believed Mado was a romantic and should have had her first chance with someone not tied up fast elsewhere. Not that any of it really mattered. There was too much fuss about the dignity of human life and the rights of men and women. A girl, a dog, a man, a horse, they were the same in one important respect. No god made them. They were only what another of Soames's poets called them, the clay grown tall. Who worried about the virginity of a dog?

'This is Mademoiselle Vipont,' he said, surprising himself with his own formality. For the first time it struck him that perhaps he looked up to Marion too much. She seemed to expect it and get it. Even her own father looked up to her. Was that good for her? He wasn't sure it was. She might even prefer a different sort of treatment. He'd have to think about it, between now and the day they set up permanently together.

'Hallo Mado,' said Marion. 'Is that the kitchen? Let's go in there.' The two of them disappeared through the door and shut it behind them.

'*Putain*,' said Luis, and kicked the foot of the bed. There was a tapping on the door behind him. 'What?' he shouted, but no one answered and after a moment the tapping was renewed. It was Pierrot. 'What do you want, little *emmerdeur*?' he said, and then remembered that Soames had never called him that. 'I'm sorry. I've got troubles. I didn't mean it.'

'I don't mind much, Monsieur Luis,' said Pierrot, accepting the apology with reserve. 'I've got something to tell you.' There was a light in his eye which seemed to Luis to have a sexual origin.

'Was it you who told my friend the way up here?'

'Yes. I didn't like to see her wandering about alone down there all lost. There's a lot of rape in the Vieille Charité. And she's very beautiful.'

'No. She isn't beautiful. That's a trap. She's everything, but not that.'

'She is to me.' It was hopeless. He wished Pierrot well and he could see it was a lost cause. Beauty, the betrayer.

'Try and see it differently. You can still love a girl without filling your head with dreams of beauty.' Pierrot wasn't listening. He was too young and Luis was too old. 'Anyway, what have you come to tell me?'

'The boys – they've been back to the hole. They've been down.'

'How far down?'

'Not too far – twice the height of a man, about. Then it's nearly blocked. There's an opening they say they could get through if they just had enough ropes. That's what they say. I think they were afraid. They did have a torch.'

'They could see into the opening?'

'Yes.' Pierrot looked wide-eyed at the wonder of what he was about to tell.

'So?'

'It's like a chimney with ledges. At the bottom they think there must be the big cave under water, deep, like the crypt of Saint-Victor. Do you know the crypt of Saint-Victor, Monsieur Luis?'

'I do. Not many know it better.'

'Well, the torch wasn't strong enough. But . . .' he stopped, whether by story-teller's method or some fear like a superstition, Luis wasn't sure. He was only a child after all.

'Go on, Pierre. There's nothing to be afraid of here.'

'One of the boys went down to the first ledge.' He shuddered at the terror of the thought. 'In the dark. Squeezed between the stones. He went down because of what they could see there.'

Luis began to feel he was being manipulated. 'I can guess what it was,' he said, then relented. 'All right, Pierrot, I don't know. You tell me. It had better be good. A dinosaur?'

'A body,' said Pierrot.

'Is that what frightened them before?'

'No, what they saw the first time was just clothes – rags and a bit of shoe. The body was lower down the shaft. Not so much a body. Bones, Hair. Dust.'

'When it was thrown in it went further than the clothes because it was heavy. The weight took it down the shaft.'

'Yes. Clothes don't go far when you throw them.'

'So the body was naked and the clothes were thrown after.'

'I think so,' Pierrot said judiciously.

'Man or woman?'

'By the shoe they say it's a woman.'

'They'll keep their mouths shut?'

'If you pay them.'

'I'll pay them well to keep away from that hole from now till I've seen it for myself. How do they go there?'

'With the money you've given them they take the bus to Luminy.'

'Tell them to take the bus tomorrow morning again. I'll wait for them by the University gates at eight. They must show me where the hole is.' Luis went to the cupboard in the wall where he kept tools and cash. 'This is for them. More when I know they haven't talked to anyone else. And this is for you. Don't tell them what I pay you.'

'They just think you give me cigarettes.'

'That's right. Now you'd better go away and do what I told you.'

'There's something else.' Pierrot looked secretly very pleased, all his intelligence bearing fruit.

'Is there. I can see it's something you think you've been clever about. Come on then.'

Pierrot reached into his pocket and brought it out curled up into a fist. 'They said they'd found something. The one who went down with a torch between his teeth, he found it. They didn't want to show me. I said whatever it was I must give it to you, otherwise you and your friends would do what you said . . . last time. What you promised to do to them.'

'It was a joke between you and me.'

'They believed it. People think you're the head of a clan, that's why. You can do anything you want.'

'Let's see what you've got there.'

'They're not bad, the boys. They haven't been bad to me.'

'I'll remember it. I'll tell the clan. Now hand it over.'

'I said they could keep the rusty old knife. But not this.' Pierrot slowly unfurled his fist. In his palm was a fine gold chain with a Huguenot cross linked on it. Luis took it and turned it round in his hand. 'Was this on the body? On the bones? Or with the rags and shoes?'

'It was mixed up in the hair.' There was one reddish-brown strand still attached to the chain, and when Luis pulled it, it broke at once. He crossed to the window to inspect this item in the light, turning it over. Astonishment like knowledge of a new world filled his mind as he read the name inscribed on the reverse side. Bernard Vipont. He put the cross and chain into his pocket at once and turned back to Pierrot.

'If you or the other boys, any of them looked closely at this, that could be dangerous for all of you.'

'It's something for the clan?'

'That's it.'

'Then no one knows anything. No one's seen anything.'

'You were right to feel clever Pierrot. You've done very well. Now you can come and see the two girls I've got here. If you're polite I expect they'll be nice to you. D'you know how to kiss their hand?'

'I can think how to kiss them anywhere,' said Pierrot, raising his good arm to wipe his mouth on the back of his sleeve.

\*

When Luis and Marion left to book into their usual hotel, Mado watched them go with wounded eyes. Despite believing, in theory, in sexual relations without emotional waste, Luis felt more brutal about this than he liked. He recognised that as a beginning of tenderness. Marion must have seen it for herself.

'Somewhere must be found for her,' she said.

'I promised your father to keep her till he gets back.'

'And what do you suppose he'll do with her then?'

'He always seems to think of something,' said Luis. 'And now he'll have to.'

'Don't let's go to the usual place.'

'Where then?'

'Out of Marseille. Somewhere on the coast.'

'Marseille is on the coast.'

'Don't be a fool, Luis. I mean the coast beyond the town.'

'All the most beautiful coast is part of the town.'

In the end they lay side by side in the back of the van in Bernard's garage and then invented positions to avoid discomfort by being crushed to the metal floor.

'It wasn't exactly relaxing but it wasn't bad,' Marion said afterwards.

'It's not meant to be relaxing.'

'That's the macho point of view.'

'I didn't go to the University. My point of view is what it has to be, not what it would be, probably, if I was better educated.'

Marion considered this, still entangled with him as if the complexity of their connection would take some time to undo. 'Your point of view's okay, Luis. Don't change it. Whose van is this?' she asked suddenly.

'It's your father's.'

'What does he want a van for?' She'd worked herself free and was sitting with her legs hanging out of the back, feet swinging.

'For me. Odd jobs. This and that. Here, put this on. There's sand on the floor.' When she stood up he saw that there was indeed sand on her and with care he brushed it away. Marion had the trick of dressing or undressing as quick as lightning. While Luis was still fiddling with his shirt buttons she stood and watched him, like a bird whose feathers are restored to place in a single flourish.

'If it's yours why don't you use it?'

'We just have.'

'You're not giving straight answers to simple questions.'

'Because I'm older than you and I'm a man. It's not suitable for you to ask me a lot of questions.'

Marion looked hard at him, suspicious of some attempt at a joke, but he was scowling at his shoe laces. 'You won't be able to treat me like that when we live together and I'm in charge of the house,' she said.

213

There was something pathetic in this remark but Luis had decided not to give way to devices. The Huguenot cross in his pocket seemed to put everything in the world into a new light. 'You're wrong. I'll be much more brutal then.'

'If you are, I'll go back to Juanita.'

'If you want to know what I think, when you leave the Villa Vipont, I reckon your Juanita will have ideas of her own. I think she'll surprise you.'

'She promised she'd never leave papa without someone to look after him.'

'Did she so.'

*

They walked with arms about each other among the crowd of people on the Vieux Port, under the stars and the dying moon, razor-edged in the west marking where the sun had gone first. There were always plenty of people here, day or night, you could never be alone. There were those who were idle, motionless as if they hadn't stirred for years, and the others darting about like fish in a shoal, this way that way, back and forth. Luis always felt good here. It seemed a place where freedom began and ended with the sea, the town, boats.

'Mado told me about her picture,' Marion said when they were standing between the quayside and the Hôtel de Ville.

'What did she say?'

'She said you're going to get it back for her. She's got nothing else.' He wondered what other stories Mado had brought out for Marion. He would never know.

'Yes. Well, I will.'

'When?'

'Soon.'

'So she can sell it and she won't need looking after any more.' That sounded like a good, easy solution. Only a pampered daughter would see things in such simple terms. What you want is what good organisation will put immediately in your lap. He leaned down, put his mouth to her ear and passed his tongue round the contours. It was

214

almost sad to think that when he took her away to live with him in the Camargue, her days of being spoiled would be numbered. It was like a kind of murder. 'Because you see, Luis, I don't want you looking after her. I think she's mixed-up. She's trouble.'

'Shall we go back to the van?'

'No. I've read about girls like that. Haven't you noticed how she pulls at her hair? She twists it into rats' tails and then she pulls it as if she's tightening a knot. That's sick. Tightening knots on herself instead of tightening them on someone else. You. That's what'll come next.'

'Perhaps I'd better give her to the nuns after all.'

'She isn't yours to give. Just get her picture, that's what you can do for her.'

'I must wait for your father.'

'Is that the sort of business you do together?' Luis didn't answer. 'As soon as papa comes back from England I'm going to tell him.'

'Tell him what?'

'About me and you. I'll say we're going away as soon as you've got that girl her picture. Perhaps he'll buy it. Perhaps he'll let her stay on in the Vieille Charité. You won't need that attic any more when you're with me in the Camargue.'

'No, Marion.'

'I can't wait any longer, Luis.'

Suddenly Luis knew what had been in the back of his mind this last half hour. Marion didn't trust the pill. She used a cap and usually he could feel it. Not this time. Nor the last. Probably that was why she said she felt him coming inside. There was nothing in there between her and him. He decided not to say anything about it, as if there was an unspoken understanding. 'I mean, you won't tell him. I'll tell him,' he said.

'Then he'll pretend I'm a minor – long enough to threaten you with the law against older men who steal girls from their fathers. Mado's father could do the same. You'd have two fathers on your back. If I talk to him I can tell him a lot of lies he won't dare test out.' She laughed, a laughter that had sadness and a kind of bitterness in it too.

215

'You can't guess how easy a father is, if you know how.'

'I forbid it,' said Luis, as if they were already under the same roof. He felt as he had earlier on, lord of a world in a new light. 'I don't want any lies. When I talk to him he'll back down and we won't hear anything about the law, I can promise you that. So I forbid you.'

Marion looked up at him with wonder and said nothing. It made him see how much he'd been subsidiary to the Vipont will in various ways. He respected them for making use of him, and now he would do as much for them.

'Why are you so sure? It isn't like you.'

'I know him better than he thinks I do, that's all. Better than anyone.'

'Don't hurt him, Luis.' Marion paused and when she spoke again it was with a hesitation like a reluctance. 'The police came to the house today.'

'What for?'

'They wanted to know where papa was these last two days.'

'He's in England.'

'Yes. Luckily.'

'What do you mean?'

'They had a bracelet he'd given to a . . . girl. She was found on a building site. She'd been strangled. You wouldn't hurt a poor prostitute would you, Luis?'

'Nor would your father.' Luis turned the gold cross over in his pocket, feeling its polished smoothness.

'No, of course not,' Marion said, and taking from her own shirt pocket a coin that would have covered the needs of a mendicant for a whole day or two, she threw it far out into the waters of the Vieux Port. 'Gyptis and Protis, send us luck,' she said in a troubled voice.

\*

The van was out of sight among the trees lower down and Luis was having a coffee at the mobile buvette stationed at the gate of the faculty. He was round the side of it, leaning against one corner, his body in the slumped pose he adopted when he didn't want to be remembered. The bus came up the hill, swung round, and stopped in the blazing unshaded light as if the idea was to roast everyone inside. Four boys got off and made at once for the nearest pines for cover. When the bus pulled away Luis went across.

'How many of you found this place we're going to?' he asked.

'Only us four.'

Luis put on his most threatening aspect. 'And no one else but Pierrot knows? Be careful how you answer. I want the truth. If you've told anyone else, better say so now than leave us to find out later.' Did they know what truth was? Did anyone?

'No one else. And Pierrot won't say anything.'

'I know. It wouldn't be worth his while. Nor yours.'

'We understand, Monsieur Luis, you can count on us.' One day they might want revenge for this obedience, but he wouldn't be around by then.

'Which way?' They started off up the hill towards the crest. 'Keep under the trees.' The four of them scuttled silently along among the pines with Luis following behind like a warder. Actually, he would have liked some conversation but they couldn't be expected to know that. He would have liked to know what their pleasures were, the first thing you always want to know about anyone. One of their pleasures must be what they came up here to look for – exploring, fishing with a bamboo pole stolen from some garden, watching girls far off with their lovers from the University? Probably all that. 'Is it under the mountain or towards the calanque?' He knew which way the cave must be because it went down, so Pierrot said, to sea level and at the foot of the Mont Puget there was a high cliff falling straight to the water, so it couldn't be there. But he just wished one of them would speak. He thought of Pierrot and his intelligence. This was a bunch of little brutes by comparison. Then he thought for the first time of Pierrot's future. He ought to do something about that, the boy shouldn't be left to rot in a world with no mercy for the weak. But what was he good for, apart from intelligence work? He wouldn't be any use with horses. It was sad, but there's only enough space in any life for a limited amount of compassion. It depends on how free the rest of your space is.

'Thank you for the money, Monsieur. We never had money like that,' said one of them. Perhaps he realised Luis felt lonely and was hoping for signs of fellow life. It was something.

'You'll have more when I know I can trust you.'

'We're silent like the grave,' said the same boy.

'For all of you, it's silence or the grave,' said Luis when they paused near the crest. The heat was violent, you were naked under it like a worm in a fire. From here you could see the storm gathering over the horizon above the Corsican mountains, ready to launch itself north-wards on the continent, a Napoleon of a storm full of sound and fury and will. Luis was out of sympathy with the will and its manifestations. Impulse of the moment was what he went by.

'It's coming. It won't be long,' said another boy. There was a silent forked flash at the far end of the sky as if Gyptis and Protis had spoken. In the heat it made your heart miss a beat.

'The place is further down, it's where those rocks are in the bushes there, near the edge. The sea's just below, the height of a house,' said the brightest of the boys. Luis wondered how long they had. Exposed here, the storm could wipe them from the face of the earth. For a moment he had a feeling as strange as when he'd examined the back of the Huguenot cross.

'We'd better be quick,' he said, and made off fast for the rocks with the boys following at first, then running on ahead. This hole was their discovery, it was theirs to give up for reward and formalities of priority were to be observed here, among the scree and the shrubs. The sea, still flat calm from above, appeared darker near the horizon, darkness spreading through it as if the water felt the storm coming. It must be the first motion of the wind over the distant surface, turning the face of the sea.

'Here it is,' said the boy. They'd stopped among the rocks a short way in front of him. Luis looked around. Nothing but rocks, fixed as the mountain behind. The boys were standing round one of these and looking down at it as if it was something they'd managed to track and kill. Were they trying to hoodwink him? There was nothing here. Then from the blue above there was a flash and almost in the same moment a crack that made the ground leap under your feet. In the minutes they'd taken to get down here, the furnace in the sky had created its own storm ahead of the one from Corsica. A single tower of clouds stood over the Mont Puget. A rush of wind was followed by rain, falling warm and dense from nowhere. The same thing could happen in town in a heatwave but out here, between sea and mountain, it was all the more brutal and naked.

'That's the way we first found it,' said the boy. He was pointing down to a shelf of flat stone. Rainwater was now pouring over this smooth surface from the ground above, gathering into a natural gully in the stone, washing onward, and there vanishing under the rock while they stood about it. 'It rained like this and the water just goes into the ground. You don't see it any more. We knew there must be a hole.'

'How did you move the rock?' They were only four boys and the rock was big, quite a bit bigger than a new-born foal curled up.

'We came back with some bars. How that rock's balanced over the hole, it's not so hard to tip over, not with bars. And four of you.'

'So when did you put it back?'

'After we'd been down. We saw a monsieur up there.' The boy pointed. 'He was with a woman. They were—'

'They were what? Watching?'

'No. They were fucking. The woman saw us and shouted. Like she wanted help. We were frightened. But we came back and tipped the rock again. We put it back in case he'd seen. We knew you didn't want anyone else coming round here to put their nose into that hole.' Like all organised workers they'd feared for their subsidy. But they hadn't done badly for four brutes only on the threshold of adolescence, which Luis remembered was not a judicious time of life.

'Can you describe the man you saw?'

'He had his clothes on. She didn't, not a stitch. He'd just opened his trousers to get on with the work.'

'Never mind that, that's not our business. What about his face – his build?'

'His back was to us and then he went behind the rock when she screamed and got up. But he was quite big – not dark either, with glasses.'

'And clumsy at it like an Anglais. It's why she screamed,' said one of the others, well up in folklore. They all four laughed, as the thunder rolled over sea and mountain.

'Which one of you found the bones?'

'It was him,' said two of them, indicating the smallest, a thin, wiry weasel of a boy who hadn't yet spoken at all.

'How wide is the gap you went down?'

'Don't know,' mumbled the boy.

'Would I get down it?' There was a long pause. The rain had stopped and the great storm could be seen charging across the sea to the mainland while the local one passed beyond the Mont Puget to strike on the hills behind. 'Come on.' But perhaps this boy was half-witted. There were a lot of syphilitics in the Vieille Charité. It might account for his having been less afraid than the others. Wriggling down a crevice in the dark meant nothing if your imagination was stillborn.

'You need lights, but you could do it,' said the boy. 'And ropes. And a pick if you want to get right down, for footholds.' So he'd been thinking and he was far from dumb. He was one of those rare useful people who say nothing till they have something to say. Luis patted him on the shoulder.

'Thanks,' he said, then thought of something else. 'Your torch didn't show down to the bottom, I expect?'

'Not nearly. I just saw rock and then dark.' That was all right then. The cave at the end of the shaft was virgin, with whatever secrets it held. The sun was beating down again on the wet hillside, the rocks and cliffs glistening as they dried in the heat. To the south the sky was black, the blackness approaching in a line from horizon to horizon like an army on a desert.

'Let's get out of here,' said Luis. What if one of these boys was struck down? Questions would be put about what they were all doing here together and secrecy lost for good. 'Run.'

By the time they reached the van the storm was on them. Luis put the boys in the back and dropped them on the outskirts of the town.

'Until I'm finished with that hole, you'll get the same money every week from Pierrot, like I promised. I don't want anyone near it again till you're told. Then you can have it back.'

'Yes, Monsieur Luis,' they all said, even the weasly one speaking up for this important message. They must be longing to ask how many weeks' money they could count on, but audacity didn't go that far. Luis didn't want them to know it was a matter of days. The longer the perspective of gain the surer obedience would be.

'In a month I'll know a bit more,' he said, and their expressions lifted. Before leaving for his new life he would see about them. Like with Pierrot, a small sum was a fortune going a long way.

*

The stone-work at the Couvent de la Génératrice-Immaculée was done. The Prior expressed the appreciation of the assembled community and presented Luis with a history of the gypsy martyrs of Stefan the Great, Athlete of Christ. He had, apparently, slaughtered thousands of them of all ages as an offering to the success of some Crusade of which he was the hero. Luis thanked the Prior politely, shook hands with those of the community he knew, and said he must go a last time up to the roof to make sure he'd left none of his special chisels behind. The Prior took him on one side and signalled the brethren to disperse.

'Mon cher Karoly,' he said, using a paternal tone which would have put Luis on his guard if he hadn't been on it already. 'I think you're a man living in touch with your instincts, in the Freudian sense.' Luis wasn't at all clear what the Prior meant. He'd heard of Freud, certainly, but in connection with Oedipus, not convents.

'I pay attention to them,' he said cautiously.

'I mean with regard to our sisters . . . to women.'

'That's what I mean too.'

'We here – we don't administer the sacrament of penance in the lay world, only in our own.'

'You don't get girls in your confessionals?'

'We're a celibate household.'

'How can I help? You want to know how their minds work?' Luis didn't think himself at all expert on this but he must know more than these men, shut away from half humanity.

'All minds work as one in Christ our Lord. It's not that. Michel – you know him I think, the oblate – poor man, he's distraught. That's why you didn't see him just now. Oblates, you understand, are not bound to lifelong celibacy – he had – has – a daughter living here under our protection.'

'Yes, I've noticed a girl about.'

'She's disappeared.' Luis said nothing. The disappearance of this girl was no business of his until it was clear what the purpose of the conversation was. 'She's at an age when a young girl – a virgin in shelter – could become infatuated with an older man.'

'You think she's fallen for one of the monks? Have any of them disappeared too?'

'Certainly not, Karoly. Speak with more respect of these unshake-able soldiers of Christ. But I thought you might have some light to throw on the girl's movements? You, an instinctive man feeling a natural interest? There's no shame in that.' The Prior's voice trembled as he spoke. It must be the old, the natural undertow.

'I know nothing about her.'

'Michel fears she could have been taken away by road.'

'Maybe one of your suppliers in a delivery truck.'

'We're self-supporting. Flour and salt and cleaning materials come once a month. Not in the last few days.'

'Then it looks as if Brother Michel's mistaken.'

'It leaves your van.'

'How old is the girl?'

'Sixteen.'

'I'm not a thief of minors. For our people, children belong to the father.'

'However, it is known that your girls are taken very young. As children almost.'

'I don't know this daughter of Michel's.'

'One of my brethren saw you talking with her, when you were mending the roof.'

Luis smacked his right fist into the open palm of his left hand, loudly. 'I'm an artisan, not a monk, Prior Caraman. I don't answer to anyone for my conversations with women or men. If Michel's girl ran away and she's sixteen he can complain to the Gendarmerie.'

'We prefer to keep our affairs discreet and deal with them in our own way. No one wants the gendarmes in this place of prayer.' The Prior had taken a step backward.

'And if an offence is committed? What's your way with that?'

'Our rule provides for modes of correction.'

'Michel probably knows all about them.' As soon as he'd said it, Luis felt this was a mistake.

'Why should you think so?'

'Something Alain . . . something he said.'

'Little Alain – he's a child himself in his own way. An anal-regressive.' The Prior smiled. When he did this his mouth, usually thin and flattened out like a crushed lizard, seemed to swell up. 'Children sometimes babble too much. It's their prerogative but when a child becomes a man it's a prerogative he must learn to lose.'

'Alain needs care. He had no mother.'

'That's my business,' said the Prior. The smile had gone and the tone was sharp. 'He needs spiritual care and I give it.'

Luis didn't want to seem too interested in Alain, because he was soon going to need him. He shrugged, and raised his hands in a gesture of indifference. 'Of course,' he said. He opened the book he'd been given and turned over some of the pages as if searching his mind for the right phrase of appreciation. There were some plates, nineteenth century reconstitutions of Romany costume of the heroic age of Stefan. 'These were Kalderash,' said Luis. 'They were noble Romanies who wore all their fortune in buttons and gold coins round their necks.' He turned a few more pages. 'This slaughter of these martyrs – that was what they call a devouring. *Porraimos*, that's the Romani word. There was another devouring not so long ago. When I was a boy and you were a young man. That was a sort of crusade too. Before Alain was born to an orphanage. I wonder where Michel was then?'

It was a shot in the dark, intuitive, unpremeditated. The Prior made a sound of clearing his throat and drawing in his breath at the same time. He was afraid. Then the sound of a motor-bicycle approaching through the wood interrupted them.

'There he is now,' said the Prior, and stepped forward to speak to Michel as the motor-bicycle halted on the gravel forecourt. Luis didn't hear what either of them said, the words were drowned by the engine. He looked hard at Michel for signs of distress but saw only what he recognised as rage. Now the engine stopped, Michel swung his leg over, propped the motor-bicycle on its stand and came towards him. As he approached, Luis noted something behind the rage, something that looked like despair. The eyes were wider open than before, they were a wound on the world. You can only gaze so long into that. Luis looked away.

'Did you see my girl yesterday?' It wasn't a question, it was a charge. It was three days since Mado left the Couvent. Either Michel was trying to trap him or he'd lost touch with time. Luis remained impassive and watched. 'I know you and your people. I know how you move in the dark . . . degenerates . . .' He made an unfamiliar sign in front of his face, a downward movement, driving a stake, not a cross, into the ground.

'I'll report her missing on my way back into town if you want,' Luis said, and turned away. He heard a shout behind him, the voice of the Prior. Looking back he saw Michel advance on him with a riding whip in his hand. He must have had it with him on the motor-cycle. Luis raised his arm and the blow fell on the History of the Romany Martyrs in front of his face. He felt cold, in control – there was time . . .

'Brethren, please,' said the Prior in the excited voice of a stranger to violence. 'Not at the door of our Mother's house,' he pointed upward to the roof where the blue and gold flag of la Génératrice-Immaculée flew on a white pole. 'Michel, reflect and put your whip away. I will hear your confession later. Karoly, it's time you left us to our peaceful life. Like Maître Vipont, you're a disturbing presence here.'

'I'll leave you in peace when I've been up to the roof,' said Luis.

'Be quick then,' said the Prior. 'And on no account report the girl missing. We'll find her. Now go away and stay away.'

*

Alain was waiting near the foot of the ladder, where Luis knew he would be. Alain had adopted a much more cavalier attitude to his duties as door-keeper, and when Luis was around he was never far away. 'Doesn't the Prior punish you for neglect?'

'Since you and Maître Vipont came the discipline in the Couvent hasn't been the same. Some of the monks think it's because you're aliens to God.'

'Perhaps we are. God knows. Come up onto the roof with me,' Luis said, and Alain followed him up the ladder. The usual twinge of shame entered Luis's mind. In a way, he was acting like the worst sort of woman. Nevertheless, he had to go on. The painting in the Cardinal's bedroom was indispensable. He already had the means to buy Marion's freedom from her father, he needed other means to buy his own. He considered himself bound to Bernard by obligations that only some form of redemption would undo. He wasn't a thief, he paid for what he took. He would find a way to repay Alain too. In fact, he already was repaying him by forcing him on the road to independence. Later he would try and teach him to want women. Nothing could be worth more than that – provided you could get them when you needed to. Standing back from the balustrade and well out of sight from below, they looked over the crowns of the plane trees, the fields where the monks made their living, the forest, the jagged crests above the calanques and the sea.

'Did you take Mado away?' Alain asked. He sounded sad. Was that because Mado had gone, or because it wasn't him Luis had taken?

'You didn't want her for yourself, did you?'

'Is she all right where she is?'

'She's safe. I don't know about all right.' Perhaps this sadness of Alain's was the first sign of more normal tendencies. If that was so, Luis could feel less of an exploiter. 'She wants her painting and I'm going to get it for her,' he said.

'Yes. Good.'

'You'll have to help me.'

'You know I'll do anything for you, Luis.'

'Don't talk like that. It's for Mado, think of her for when you get out of here.'

'Yes, I will.'

'So is there a way in, at night?'

'Everything's locked up and all the keys are put in Father Prior's study.'

'Who puts them there? You? Is it part of your duties?'

'Yes. But if you tell me to, I'll—'

'No. Of course not. They'd know at once. It may mean climbing in and out. That's more difficult.'

Alain began to speak excitedly, raising his voice until Luis gestured to him to be quiet. 'There's the cellar – the trap to the cellar. It's only bolted on the inside.'

'Isn't the cellar locked?'

'It used to be and then someone said that showed we didn't trust each other. Since then it isn't locked any more. There's a string on the door so the Prior can tell if anyone's been down there but I know how that works.'

'Where's this trap?'

'Under the west wall. There are two big Anduze vases with lemon trees standing on it. It takes two of the brothers to move them.'

'You can move something heavy with rollers. Broom handles. I'll bring some.'

'When will you come?' Alain's eyes were sharpened to pinpoints.

'Not tonight. I'll have to borrow a horse to come through the woods. Tomorrow after midnight. I'll be here at two. Can you be sure of being there in the cellar at two, Alain?'

'Oh yes, yes,' said Alain and Luis felt the shame again.

'Don't try and open the trap till you hear me. Is there gravel at the side of those pots?'

'Yes.'

'Find a time tomorrow to scrape it away, just a width like this for the rollers. There'll be less noise. And if I come and you haven't done it, I'll know something's gone wrong. Now I must go. I'll go down first, you follow in a minute. If you don't see me at the bottom of the ladder the way's clear.'

Alain nodded. Then, as Luis turned away towards the ladder, he suddenly took a step forward, put his arms round Luis's neck and for an instant pressed himself against him like a dog that jumps into your arms. Luis flinched but accepted it. What else could he do? He patted Alain's shoulder and put his foot on the first rung of the ladder, descending quickly. Glancing up at the last moment, he saw on the face watching him from above a mixture of emotions as clearly marked as notes on a page – excitement, gratitude, shame and sorrow. Sorrow at the end, the last note.

\*

Luis had never before involved Soames in anything doubtful but they were nearing the end of their story so it was different now. Sometimes Luis thought he would live for ever but that this wasn't so for everyone. Other times he felt death not so far away. Whichever it was, death would separate them all, iron though their links might be. But it wasn't Soames who answered the telephone. Luis had forgotten. 'I need a horse here in Marseille, tomorrow night. Where's Soames?'

'An Arab?'

'A *camargue*. Quiet and sure-footed in the dark. There's no moon.'

'How long for?'

'Just the night. It can't wait.'

'You'll have to come, Luis. He won't be back.'

'I'll take a taxi at Arles.' She'd never learned to drive. Even the telephone she held at arm's length as if it was a snake.

'What do you want it for?'

'That's my business.' He remembered her answer when he'd asked about her health; he'd always returned a hard word for a hard word with her. Like that, they need never speak the softer words that can tear like a thorn.

'If it's dirty business I don't want Soames in it.'

'He's away in England. By the time he gets back the horse will be in his field again.'

'If you play a bad trick on him and the gendarmes come I'll take your eyes out with my own fingers.'

'You can do that,' Luis said and rang off without saying goodbye. He never said goodbye to her and never would.

She was standing against the pillar in front of the *mas* like last time, when the taxi drew up. It seemed to Luis she looked older and thinner than a couple of weeks before. It felt as if his vision of the world was shrinking, dying in front of his eyes. While he paid the driver he felt the anger rise in him. She was stealing herself and his vision from him.

'Why don't you get out in the sun more? You look white. Not like a Gitane, you look like a German woman. But there's nothing of you. You look like you did when you came out of Birkenau.' Nothing would have been too hard for him to say it, he felt so angry and sad. She knew, and put a hand to his face.

'Be quiet, be quiet now. I'll come out in the sun with you to choose the horse.' They crossed the dried grass and sandy earth and walked a little way under the plane trees towards the nearest field where the *camargues* grazed. She stopped and put her hand against a tree trunk as if for support. 'I can't go any further. I'll wait here. Don't be angry, Luis.' Luis walked on by himself, marched on towards the horses like a soldier still marching after a defeat, a survivor, marching obstinately, by habit, by training. He raised a hand and wiped his face with the back of it.

When he came back with the horse on the end of a rope she was smiling at him. 'You know you're at the age when a man's best,' she said. 'Not too young when they're still just beasts. When Soames was your age he was magnificent.'

'Tell him that and he'd laugh at you.'

'I have, it's what he did.'

'I expect he believed you though. The English are very vain.'

'Of course. Their jokes are to hide it.'

They stood side by side in the shade of the tree, she leaning against it now, her arms hanging, taking force from it – from the roots in hot earth.

'Do you know the right way to grieve, Luis?' she asked, in a stronger voice.

'I don't know anything about it.'

'It's by looking into the sea. How all the water goes there, and carries everything, in the end. Even trees. And then it's by having your own children to look at. In their eyes, like I look at you.' It was the nearest she'd ever come to admitting that he wasn't just her young brother. And it was all right now, the anger was gone. She took his arm, and with the gentle compliant animal they slowly walked back to the house, not talking at all, breathing the air of the Camargue that had always sustained them. Before he started up the engine of the horse box he heard her singing somewhere inside, the voice low and rough as always. It was her way of sending him off without words.

*

He'd been wrong about the moon. It was in the dying phase, but by one in the morning when darkness should have been complete, it threw enough light so he could see the path climbing among the oaks and pines. The *camargue* followed it as if this was a lifelong familiar track, apparently knowing at every fork which one Luis wanted before he knew it himself. Quiet and steady, horse and rider one as they progressed through the wood, under the moon.

'Stay here,' Luis murmured, circling the halter round a tree trunk. He laid his face along the animal's muzzle. 'I'll be back.' A horse you rode in the dark wasn't so different from a woman.

The Anduze vases had been cracked by frost and were bound with wires, like a strait-jacket on a madman. It was necessary to raise the foot of the vase so it rested on a roller, then lift the other side to rest on another. That was easy. But after the move the first vase must be restored to the ground, freeing the rollers for the second one. He should have brought more. During this operation the side of the first vase split open and spilt its contents onto the ground. The lemon tree, with its root-ball dry as a hedgehog, now lay on the pile of gravel scraped aside by Alain. If it had been kept properly watered this wouldn't have happened. Luis heard a knocking on the underside of the trap. Alain must have heard the lemon tree fall. If he was kept waiting in the dark while Luis cleared up the earth and tried to restore the tree he'd get nervous and make some mistake. Luis crossed to the other vase and quickly repeated the manoeuvre, then levered up one half of the trap with the bar he'd brought. There was no light down there but you could see the first steps of a narrow stair. Alain's head suddenly popped up into the moonlight. He was an unlikely accomplice, pale, undersized, unskilled but not afraid, so Luis believed.

'Where's the horse?' Alain whispered.

'Back in the trees. Why?'

'I love horses. There aren't any here. I miss them.' He had the build of a jockey and perhaps the heart of one. Maybe there was a future for him somewhere in there.

'No time for that. I won't forget. Let's go.'

The painting was in the same place in the Cardinal's bedroom. Luis hesitated over the frame. It would be cumbersome on horseback. He decided to take the painting out and push the frame under the bed. He signalled to Alain to hold it upright while he examined the bent nails securing the stretchers from the back. The house was still. As Luis straightened up and stood with the canvas in his hand he felt the stone and wood, the body of the building breathe around him. The monks worked hard and slept sound – Alain said the Prior took a sleeping pill every night. Only Michel would sleep badly. There was no time to waste.

Outside the trap, Luis showed Alain the ruins of the vase. 'I'll put it together roughly. You'll have to look in the daylight when you can. Scatter a lot of leaves around.' Alain nodded but Luis doubted if he was really listening.

'Can I see the horse?'

'Come on then.'

As they came through the trees the *camargue* raised and lowered its head in welcome. Luis held his hands about its muzzle to keep it silent. 'There is it, a simple brute and a good servant.'

'It's beautiful . . . beautiful.' Alain raised his hand to touch the white shoulder, still and warm in wan moonlight.

'They're only like *femmes de ménage*,' said Luis.

'I don't think a woman could feel like that.'

'You don't know anything about it.' When Luis turned back he felt a hand on his sleeve, holding it tight.

'They'll find out. Don't leave me here . . .'

'You're free. You can walk out when you want.'

'They'd catch me. Michel . . . I'm afraid now.'

Luis shook his arm free, knowing he couldn't shake off the pity. 'Don't be a fool.'

'You took Mado.'

'She ran after the van. She's a girl.'

'I'll run after the horse.'

Luis knew this situation called for some outgoing gesture. But he didn't have an outgoing character, he had the character of a Gitan. He didn't even make any music like other Gitans. Now he must do something to save a dangerous crisis. He turned to Alain and put both hands on his shoulders. 'I'll come back for you. You know you can't stay with me but I'll help you. You should work with horses.' He felt the little arms embrace him like the wires on the Anduze pot. 'Trust me. Stay here now and be – brave as a man.' It was only an idea, most men aren't brave and Luis knew it. But it was the idea Alain wanted, it was the right one for him at the moment.

'When will you come?'

'When Maître Vipont gets back. Soon. I can't do it without him. Stay here and keep your eyes open and your mouth shut. Is there a way to let me know if anything goes wrong?' Because Luis had a feeling something would go wrong.

Alain thought quickly and when he spoke he sounded calmer. 'There's the flag,' he said. 'The flag of la Génératrice-Immaculée. I take it down every evening and put it up in the morning. When the Cardinal's here I put his flag up.'

'No one but you does it?'

'It's one of the things the Prior thought of to keep me busy. No one else has the time. I'm not strong enough to work the fields.'

'So what about this flag?'

'Michel says you see it over the top of the trees from Mazargues, coming out of the town.'

'Well?'

'If I don't put it up, you'll know there's something wrong.'

'And if something went wrong after you put it up?'

'I take it down at eight o'clock. It's still light for hours.'

'So I have to go to Mazargues twice a day to see if you're all right?'

'You can always come and take me away. I'll be waiting.'

But Alain was a problem for Bernard to solve, not Luis. Luis couldn't set himself up against the Prosecutor, the Prior and the Archbishop all at once. They were powers, and only a power could play them. He fetched the painting wrapped in a blanket, closed the trap on Alain and moved the vases back. They'd taken too long back there with the horse. Out of the moonlight, in the shadow of the high wall of the house, Luis had a feeling he was being watched. It was very unlikely, the wall was blank and the shutters closed. But the intuition persisted. There was a dangerous man in this building, his discipline lost along with his stolen daughter. Both vases were in place and only the spilt earth in the gravel was there as evidence. That must be left for Alain. If Michel was watching he would be armed, Mado said he had a pistol, and householders who gunned down intruders in the night always got off. Society encouraged them to fire on the minor delinquent for whom there was no amnesty. Amnesty was for the people who'd sent the trains to Birkenau. Luis made his way back to the horse, a shadow moving among the shadows of trees.

# Chapter Eleven

---

MARION AROUSED HER father's suspicions by coming to meet him at the airport on his return from London. She looked lovely in a short, loose cotton dress which propelled the image of nakedness into even a father's mind. *Even* a father's? There she was, barely covered, that's what it came down to, whoever you were. But why was she there? Her presence was nice but unnecessary, and Marion didn't do unnecessary things at the expense of her own time. He kissed her warmly and held on afterwards as if the feel of her would somehow reveal the motives.

'Did you like England?' she asked.

'I saw the castle where our forefathers came from.'

'I expect it's terribly primitive.'

'Certainly not. A very fine castle, on a hill. The tower of César, that's the name of the dungeon.'

Marion laughed with the laughter that hides something. He saw her looking at Soames, who was standing behind him, and by the expression in her eyes, bland but affirmative, he knew that some message had been exchanged – and not just a passing item of intelligence. Her expression wasn't as bland as he'd first thought. Now her eyes were lowered. This was something close to home. 'Sounds a bit Pagnol,' she said. Pagnol was not approved in university circles because of his folklore side. 'Which César, I wonder? Did a sailor from Marseille go all that way to build a dungeon?'

'Don't be absurd, Marion. You are a descendant through me of Gaius Jules César who invaded the British Isles to take civilisation from France to there. If I'd known it in time I'd have called you Gaia.

Now hold my briefcase, I see my suitcases arriving.'

Soames had left his Jaguar in the car park and said goodbye to them at the taxi rank. Because naturally Marion had come by taxi. Economising effort was a speciality inherited from her mother and a lineage of Iberian loafers, as Bernard liked to say when irritated. But he wasn't irritated now, he was curious. Besides, she looked so fresh and full to the brim like the first glass of champagne of the day. In the taxi she seemed unusually quiet.

'Well, Marion. In less than a month you start at Luminy. Are you ready? Have you been studying hard?'

'It's not the law, papa, I don't have to go to court. Anyway you know as well as I do I'll only be a dogsbody. Female workers are all dogsbodies here.'

'Nonsense. You have a good degree.'

'In the Midi a girl with a good degree just makes them worse than ever.' She was probably right. It was deplorable in the abstract but not such a bad thing from the practical point of view. The Vipont fortune under his control would keep its magnetism. Expensive tastes were to be encouraged.

'I brought you a little present from London.' She looked at him rather mournfully, he thought. Perhaps he'd been too obvious. He should have used a gradual approach and kept it for later. But it was too late now. 'We stayed one night there. In quite a good hotel – the Savoy, it was called. From the windows of my bedroom you could see the Thames where Gaius Jules César sailed in on his civilising mission. To which we owe our being.' He was babbling, and he knew it. It was because she made him feel the gift was a solecism in some way. Yet one can surely offer one's daughter a pair of pearl earrings without such fuss? He took the blue leather case from his pocket. 'I bought them in Bond Street which is the most chic in all London. Even Cartier has a boutique there.'

'They're beautiful,' Marion said, and so they were. The pearls were fat and asymmetrical and seemed to drink in the light around them. 'Are they real?'

'But of course they're real, Marion. Do you think I'd offer you something fake without saying so? The love you've always had, wasn't it the real thing?' He knew why he spoke like that. It was because Marion, for reasons he didn't understand, wanted neither the pearls nor the so-authentic love. She would take them, but they were devalued as they passed into her possession. Something had happened to move her further from him. He felt a painful constriction of the throat. 'If you think they're not your style you can sell them, I don't mind.' Marion took his hand but didn't say anything, so they sat in silence as the taxi darted through the traffic round the Vieux Port on its way out to the Corniche. 'Why did you come?' he asked in the end.

'To say – it was to tell you . . .' Whatever it was, it refused to come out. 'Just to welcome you back. You don't often go away. And look how glad you were to see me. You were able to tell me all about the dungeon of César.' Their communication was entering a phase of more considerate, more distant lies, it seemed. 'And it's lucky you were away for those days.'

'Lucky? Why?'

'A police inspector came asking for you.'

Bernard's nervous system lurched unpleasantly. Had the Prosecutor Caraman set something up to take advantage of his absence? No – he couldn't have known about it. 'What did he want?'

'A poor prostitute was found dead in a builder's skip near here. Not much more than a child, really.' They were on the Corniche, the Villa Vipont was round the next bend, above them on the steep slope.

'It often happens, but usually in the old town, not here.'

The taxi was one with a partition but Marion spoke very low, her head near his, just in case. 'She had something the Inspector said came from you. A little bracelet.' She paused, and moved away a little. 'I wish it was someone else who had to tell you, not me.' There were tears in her eyes and her face was flushed. She held the little box with the earrings away from her, as if it contained some creature like a scorpion with a sting in the tail.

'That's terrible,' said Bernard, tears in his eyes too. 'The poor girl. She'd done no harm in the world. But you must know, Marion . . . a man has—'

'I do know. Juanita told the Inspector you left four days ago.'

'It was three days.'

'She wanted to make sure.'

'Surely she didn't think I could—'

'She thought of protecting you, that's all.'

They were climbing the last short winding stretch of road to the gate. Found near here? And whoever it was put the remains in a skip, knowing the bracelet would soon be traced? Was it the paranoia again or did this carry the hallmarks of a dirty trick? Had someone else bought information from Umberto just as he had? Bernard could hear in his head the sound of protest mouthed by Sonia out there high above the calanque – and the other sound, unexplained, of the goatherd in the same place long ago, like an anguished yawn. They were at the gates. He must seem to be in control, especially of himself. At least he knew the way now to put Caraman out of action, he thought, after the visit to Madeleine in her rainy northern valley.

'Here we are, Marion. Remember, whatever happens, I'll always be the same.'

'Yes, I'll remember.'

Juanita was on the doorstep, standing with one foot forward and hands spread out on her skirt, eyes flashing with indignation. 'The *gitano* is here,' she said, looking from one to the other of them, unsure who to blame for this social calamity. 'He's in the *salle à manger*. He demanded a glass and poured himself a lot of your whisky.'

'That's all right, Juanita. He's welcome to it,' said Bernard. At least now he understood better how his true place was here, he need feel under no pressure to drink like a gentleman.

'You leave me to deal with crisis which is the role of a man.'

'I can't see any crisis.' As he spoke, Marion slipped past Juanita and into the house. Juanita remained foursquare in front of the entrance. 'Let me pass into my own house with my luggage.' Juanita moved grudgingly aside to let him through, but then took hold of his arm as soon as they were standing in the vestibule, as she called it.

'Did it rain all the time you were in England?' she asked fiercely, as if any denial of this received idea could only be proof of bad faith.

'We were in brilliant sunshine almost all the time,' Bernard lied.

'I don't believe you.' She threw her head back and laughed, showing an array of strong white teeth.

'I don't care if you believe me or not. I don't pay you to believe me.' She still held his arm and now she came a little closer. There was a faint, heady aroma of scented soap and fresh perspiration. He must be careful or he'd find too late that he'd compromised his liberty. 'I have two suitcases and my briefcase. Please either take the briefcase to my study or the smaller suitcase to my bedroom.'

Juanita took the smaller suitcase and followed him upstairs. When he came out of his bathroom she was still there. 'What is it?' he asked, knowing what it must be – the Inspector. But it wasn't that.

'That man, he's never come here before. What does he want?'

'He's a friend of mine, you know that. And of Marion's.'

'I've heard something about him you don't know.'

'Who did you hear this something from?'

'An old Gitane at the church yesterday, on the feast of the Assumption. Some of them are good Catholics. In their superstitious way.'

'I thought that was the only way there is.'

'What she told me is something you should hear.'

'It'll all be lies.'

'She didn't take any money. I offered it but she shook her head. She said this was a question of Romany law. You should be interested in that.'

There, Juanita was right. Any inference from law was interesting, and perhaps important.

'Well, go on. What did she tell you?'

'His mother was a whore.'

Bernard was disappointed. 'Is that all? They're a class of worker I don't hold in such low esteem as you do.'

'I know.' Some modesty, or kindness, held Juanita back from mentioning the dead girl and the bracelet. They must have arranged between them that Marion would tell him. Bernard saw that he was better looked after than he deserved, maybe. 'But that's not all. The

Gitans turned the mother away, she was condemned by the *stabor*. Their tribunal, she said.'

'What for? Anyway, if she's who I think she is, she lives happily in the Camargue with an Englishman.'

'It was because she went with her own brother. That makes a woman unclean all her life in their law. *Mahrime*, she called it. And this friend, this Luis, he's *mahrime* too, because he's the result.'

'Why did the old woman tell you this?'

'Because he's been seen with Marion. When one of their own people is condemned, they watch them always, they keep an eye on them. She told me about it because a man born like that mustn't have children.'

'You mean they'd be under some Romany curse from the day they were born?'

'They'd be deformed or half-witted. That's what you ought to know about it.'

Juanita no longer looked as if this was part of some game to torment him. 'Is that so?' he asked.

'My mother was a midwife. She always said it was so. It happens quite often with peasants in the mountains.'

'I don't think there's anything to worry about,' Bernard said, though he was far from sure. Passion made people careless and young women in love were perverse and headstrong.

'Then you're a very simple man to be a father of girls, Monsieur Bernard. But I can see it's not what you really think.'

'If they keep their eye on these ... condemned people – what's it for? If a man like that shouldn't have children, what can they do about it by keeping an eye on him? It sounds more myth than law.'

'She said to tell you. If they thought he was planning something they'd catch him one day and geld him. That's the law.'

For the first time, Bernard took Juanita's hand in his and held it a moment, till she withdrew it. 'I'm sure the Inspector won't come back,' he said.

'He won't, if there's no reason,' said Juanita.

Bernard went downstairs to the dining room with new avenues of anxiety opened up in his mind. Luis was standing in the window onto the terrace, looking out at the sea. There was no sign of Marion. When Luis turned, he was smiling, an Apollonian figure with the dying light of sunset behind him. 'Salut, Luis.'

'Salut, Bernard.'

The sight of him put Bernard in mind of his great discovery regarding the picture at Luminy. 'You have an empty glass? Let me fill it for you. I've renounced whisky for ever. I count on you to finish the bottle.'

'Marion finished it.'

'That's all wrong – but never mind now. I have something important to tell you. That painting at Luminy.' He lowered his voice and drew Luis away from the window. 'We must get it at all costs. We'll go to my study and make a foolproof plan. Wait while I fetch a bottle of champagne.'

'I have it already. It's one of the things I came to tell you.'

'How? It's in the cellar.'

Luis laughed. 'Not the champagne. The picture.'

'Wait here, Luis.' On the way to the cellar and back Bernard reassessed the situation. Luis had taken the initiative and the painting was in his possession. That was exciting but there were two accessory implications. The picture was in Luis's possession and not in his. And the operation at Luminy, which he'd been counting on to keep Luis busy until the start of the University term, was now apparently cleaned up with a couple of weeks still to go. 'Where is it?' he asked Luis when he got back with the bottle.

'Locked up in the van.'

'Here? I didn't see it.'

'No. In the garage. The safest place.' So in a sense, the painting was in their joint possession. That was better.

'How did you do it?'

'With help from Alain. I went up on horseback. There's a way in through the cellar.'

'Alain will be all right?'

'He won't ever talk, don't worry.'

'What I meant was, is he in any danger?' It was sad when one wasn't credited with any capacity for unselfish thought.

'If he gets into trouble I've agreed a signal. But I had to promise you'd get him out of there – see him safe.'

'Did you.' Bernard reflected on this before speaking again. What was Luis up to? These initiatives in his absence were a way of driving him into a corner. They were unlike their past dealings together. On the other hand, it didn't much matter about Alain. With the information he now had, Bernard felt sure that not Michel, not the Caraman brothers, not even the Cardinal would dare make much fuss about the missing picture. Not once they knew what he knew. The Couvent de la Génératrice-Immaculée was in a weak position. There was a difference between sanctuary to a sinner and succour to a war criminal who had to be hidden because he knew a lot about people in power and refused to leave the *patrie*. The Prosecutor would pass the message. 'I wonder why you didn't take him away then and there on the back of the horse. He's a featherweight. And he's not a minor. You took the girl.'

'That's because I'm not staying in Marseille any longer. That's another thing I have to talk to you about.'

Luis sounded worked-up and excited. He wasn't usually excitable in talk. Perhaps he'd somehow learned of the threat hanging over him. Bernard would have liked to mention this, in an oblique manner, but the background was too sensitive for anything he could think of saying at the moment. When it came to a man's mother and her past as a whore you had to proceed with diplomacy, if at all. 'We'll take this bottle of champagne into the study. This'll do you more good than all the whisky in Scotland.'

Bernard's study was a comfortable small room with a glazed door onto a courtyard containing a Phoenix palm, and a fountain in one corner. There were no other plants because he didn't want the man who tended the garden peering in at the window. The study was a sanctuary. Luis paced about with his champagne glass in one hand and the other in his pocket. Hot air from the sea blew in through the open window and Bernard closed it, turning on an air-conditioner which made a deep, calm, pervasive throbbing sound like the motors of an ocean-going liner. He found this noise soothing and an aid to detachment.

Luis came to a halt in the middle of the room, facing him in his armchair. 'I'm going away tomorrow and taking Marion with me,' he said, sounding as if he'd run up a hill. 'It's best for her and you mustn't make it hard. She wouldn't be happy if you did that. I know how to make her happy whatever you do. We'll have children. But I don't want you to be difficult with her. It would make you unhappy too.' This was a long speech for Luis. He emptied his glass and took a deep breath. He must have spent a lot of energy working himself up to this pitch. Through all the years they'd worked together, Luis had never made any real resistance to Bernard's plan for all their lives.

It shouldn't be too hard to counter. Neither Luis, nor above all Marion, was accustomed to living without access to appreciable sums of money. Money was nothing – but it was like a master-code without which you became a victim of the Vieille Charité, not one of its rulers. 'We've never quarrelled, you and me, Luis, and we won't now. But I'm not going to buy that painting from you. I'll pay a reasonable price for a good copy to someone appointed as the young girl's guardian – have you still got her safe?'

'She's at the Vieille Charité.'

'Doing what?'

'Lying low like I told her. Waiting. But not for much longer.'

'The Prosecutor will see about a guardian with the judge for minors. There'll be no trouble in that quarter, I can guarantee it.'

'None of all that matters, it's got nothing to do with it. I promised Marion I'd tell you. You must let her go.'

'The girl? Let her go?' Bernard felt confused. Luis's ideas seemed to fall over one another in his excitement.

'No. Marion.'

'Marion hasn't asked me.'

'Sometimes we have to think and act for them.'

'That doesn't sound like Marion to me. I'm not sure you understand her properly.'

'You've been indulgent. They don't always thank you.' Bernard thought Luis was right about that. Indulgence had been the safety valve of love. Everyone in the world with a message to give – poets, priests, gurus – they preached love. 'Greater love than this hath no man . . .' Bernard disagreed. Love of a daughter could crucify you on its own. Just on its own.

'I won't let you go. I'll telephone the Prosecutor here and now. There's a painting in the van and you've got a record.'

'A record? I shot a collaborator. No one wants to question me about a strangled whore.' So Marion had told him. It seemed to Bernard that Luis knew a lot. Too much perhaps.

'You'd be safer in the Baumettes, your own people are after you – you're *mahrime*. Believe me, Luis, I know what's best for all of us.'

Luis had been pouring champagne into his glass but now he put down both glass and bottle. '*Mahrime*? You shouldn't say things you don't understand, even if you're angry. I wanted to make it easy but it's never easy. When I have girls from Marion and they grow up, it'll be the same. I won't give them. There'll have to be a price. Well, I can pay for Marion now.' He drew his fist from his pocket, curled in on itself.

'Pay for Marion? My daughter isn't for sale, Luis. And if she was, she'd be a long, long way out of your reach.'

'I've got you both here in the hollow of my hand,' Luis said slowly, opening it out.

A Huguenot cross on a gold chain is a common enough item. How had Luis guessed that he once had one and had it no longer? Not for the first time Bernard wondered if the Romany intuition could be a reality. If that was so then Luis knew that for him a gold cross and chain like that one had an ominous significance. Bernard had read reports of extrasensory perception experiments, thought-transference of more or less distinct impressions from one mind to another. It must be something like that. 'Take it. It's yours,' Luis said, holding his open hand towards him. Bernard took the cross between thumb and forefinger and turned it over. It was the same lettering, more rubbed than he remembered, but the same. What Luis said was true. This cross was his.

'How did . . .?' His thought, rebounding from shock, sped forward.

Actually this was one worry less. Now the cross would never end up on the Prosecutor's desk. But the information still could. 'Those boys, of course . . .'

'They know nothing. It's just pocket-money for them, that's all. They didn't see your face.' So Luis knew about that too.

'And Marion?'

'She'll never know from me. But Soames will come for her tomorrow in his Jaguar. It's only an hour or so to the Camargue. You'll still see her.'

In Bernard's chest the tears welled up like a pleurisy. He felt he'd drown in them. He was still looking down at the cross. Luis was right about the bride-price, there it was, paid up into his hand. He tried, even now, to think forward. 'That hole – it must be blocked up. The boys will go back. And the remains covered – interred.' He couldn't think of another way of putting it.

'I'll go tomorrow. I'll be up there by dawn.'

'Alone?'

'It's the last work I do for you except making grandchildren. Only remember then who gives the orders. *Papys* are for the décor.' Luis laughed, the free laugh of a man on the threshold of his kingdom of desires.

'Has Marion gone to telephone Soames?' It was by guessing what they'd do before they did it, that you had a chance of staying ahead. And you must fight back, always fight back.

'He may not be home yet.'

So she had. 'In that case she'll leave a message.' Luis didn't answer. Madame Soames was his secret. 'A message with your—'

'Perhaps.'

'Travelling around with Soames I got to know him better, and I can see he's a good friend. A bad enemy, I think.'

'Soames doesn't have enemies, he has targets for jokes. Not like me. I can have real enemies.'

Bernard saw now what must be done. The mention of Soames and what Luis had just said about himself brought the solution fully formed to mind. 'I made a very interesting discovery when I was in England.

243

When you hear it, you may not be in such a hurry to leave Marseille.'

'I'm going, whatever you found out in England.'

'Perhaps not at once. You've got time. Marion's young.'

Luis laughed again, the same way. 'There's nothing you can say would make any difference. I'll fetch Marion now and you'll tell her it's going to be all right. That's what she wants to hear.'

'Wait, Luis. Not yet. Listen. Sit down and listen. That man, Michel – I saw his wife, Mado's mother. She's a respectable woman living in the north of England. She drinks champagne.'

'When you pay Mado for the picture she can go and find her. I expect it's the only way to stop her going for a whore. Or her father killing her. Since she disappeared, he's what they call it – mad from grief.'

Bernard could understand that. He nodded. 'We'll come to the picture in a minute. What's going to interest you is what the woman told me.'

'Well?'

'This Michel was a high officer in the Milice. He was tried and condemned at the Liberation but they never found him. He's been hidden in the convent network.'

'Well, that's good. Now you can denounce him and make the Prosecutor have him arrested for all his old crimes.' Luis sounded as if that was as simple to put into effect as it was to say. Sometimes he was like Marion, sharing her instant belief in Bernard's powers. What chance had these children of managing without him, to shelter, rule and support them?

'Even if I could, it's too late. Some of the crimes were amnestied in '52 and the rest lapsed in '67. Society wiped the slate clean. Michel has nothing to fear from the courts.'

'What did he do?'

'Gathered information. Extracted it. The way you can imagine.'

'There are still some around who'll take care of him for that.'

'He's protected from too high up by too many people. But that's not all he did, Luis.'

'What else?'

Bernard hesitated. This was the point of decision, ethically and practically. It involved the line between useful truth and sworn truth – a nice legal distinction. If he said any more he'd break his word to Soames and have him as an enemy, and he didn't think the enmity would be limited to jokes. But he had no choice. What would Marion's life be like in a hut in the Camargue with a handicapped child or a gelded man – or both? 'She said he was one of those who sent people away. Ethnic groups, they called them. He organised rounding up and entrainment to places like Auschwitz. Birkenau . . .' They were names on the map, Bernard wasn't even sure on which side of the Polish frontier they stood. But it was enough for Luis. The work was done. It was dirty work, but necessity can drive you to dirty work in the interests of . . . those you love.

'Ethnic groups?'

'Jews. Also—'

'Gitans.'

'Yes.'

'She told you that?'

'She did.'

'And no one can touch him? The judges, the State, the Republic – they've let him go?'

'Yes. He only lives in the convent to be safe from fanatics. That's what they call them.'

'Fanatics . . . we'll see about fanatics.' It was like watching a chemical experiment. Luis was changing visibly from gatherer to hunter. The pupils of his eyes dilated to meet the darkness as it fell on his mind.

'There's not much time, Luis. As soon as the Prosecutor or the Cardinal thinks he's a danger they'll try to move him on. To Rome. Argentina. He wouldn't go before but he's older now. He's lost his daughter. He may be longing for safety after all these years. Like any ageing man.' Bernard let himself think only a certain way ahead. Far enough to make sure something would soon befall Michel, not to see what must then become of Luis. He only knew he was setting in motion a strategy to keep Marion safe in the end, in the security that was all she'd ever known, the paternal cover, always.

'I'll tell Marion she must wait a bit longer.'

Bernard picked up the house telephone and she answered at once. 'Marion, please join us in my study for a glass of champagne.'

'Does this mean you're being reasonable, papa?'

'You know how I always am.'

'Yes, I know how you are.' She might take it as a conspiracy and turn on both of them. There could be a painful scene. Now there she was in the doorway. As always Bernard's heart opened out at the sight of her. What life would there be, the day she wasn't there to give him this opening-out heart? It would atrophy and shrink like a dead bird in a cage. She looked at them hard, each in turn.

'You've planned something,' she said.

Bernard gave her a glass filled to the brim. 'Look – the meniscus.'

'You've told me about it hundreds of times before.' She turned to Luis and raised the glass. 'To the beginning of everything,' she said, and added, 'the telephone didn't answer.'

'Don't try again. I'll go and see Soames, I have to see him now. It's all right, Marion, remember that whatever happens.'

'But he was to come here—'

'Not yet. I'll tell you everything. Just wait a day or two and don't ask any questions.' Bernard thought this could have been communicated in a more roundabout way to avoid immediate trouble. To his surprise, Marion accepted it.

'All right, Luis. I'll do what you say.'

How extraordinary. Women never said that to Bernard. They did it, after prevarication and protest. 'Bravo,' he said. 'Joy postponed accumulates at compound interest.' Neither of them would suppose he thought this, it was only to cushion reality.

Marion now turned to him. She emptied her glass and put it down on his writing table. 'But if anything goes wrong, I'll drive you into the desert – all the rest of my life,' she said. His heart shrank like a touched ulcer. That was what she meant. She would drive his heart into the desert as a sheep covered in sores.

When she'd gone, Luis put a hand on his arm. 'Nothing will go wrong, Bernard,' he said. 'Now we'll go out in your car. I haven't looked for Alain's signal today and we must go to Mazargues, it's only ten minutes from here. Afterwards we'll look at that picture and you can say what you'll pay.'

At Mazargues they drew up under the trees. It was late now and the light was fading, a bruised red on the skyline behind them, grey over the woods of Luminy half a kilometre ahead. Luis was staring hard at the distant crown of trees. 'The flag's still up,' he said.

'What does that mean?'

'He hasn't taken it down – it's the signal.'

'Couldn't he have forgotten or been prevented?'

'He's been prevented all right. He's like clockwork.'

'How would they prevent him?'

'They'd lock him up. They've got their own law in there, the Prior told me. And there's Michel. A specialist. Once the picture was missed they'd start on Alain to find out what he knew about it.'

'They can't lock anyone up without a judge. Only a judge can put you away without trial under the law.'

'You must get him out, Bernard. He's not a monk, just a sort of servant. They probably bought him for nothing from the orphanage. You must go to the Prosecutor and make them release him.' The usual blind faith. As it happened, this time it was justified. The Prosecutor could be forced into line and it must be done at once. If the alarm was given and they had time to push Michel on to the road to Rome, Bernard's hold would be lost. He would be exposed on all fronts.

'I'll see him tonight.'

'What about the picture?'

'We'll look at it tomorrow. It's safe where it is.'

'No. In two days I want to be in the Camargue with Marion. I won't sleep till then. I want to see about the picture now. Then you can fix the Prosecutor while I go to see Soames.' A lot could happen in two days. Bernard turned the Bentley and headed back into the centre of town.

There was lighting in the garage for the purpose. Luis took the canvas from the van and placed it on a wooden stand. They both stood back in silence and gazed for a long minute at the darkened surface.

'The great Luminist. Maybe,' Bernard said finally.

'You said Tenebrist the other day.'

'We'll call him a French Luminist, for Luminy.'

'Caravaggio was Italian.'

'This isn't Caravaggio. Look at the figures, how the carnality's in the mind – formalised. No Italian would do that. This is the work of a Frenchman.' The painting might be a study for a larger work, the canvas could be reduced. It concentrated your attention on what was left – that eyeball more enamelled, less liquid than the pearls round that neck – and the Romany soothsayer, typified to abstraction. French, only French.

'The old prejudice,' said Luis.

'Artistic stereotype, not judgement.'

'I judge it. It's racism, like always.'

'But maybe a masterpiece. Or a copy of one. Probably that.'

'If you like it, it's yours. And you'll look after the girl the way you said.'

'Yes.' He would acquire this picture as a trust speculation. To the girl it would mean a fortune and he'd tell Albertas in the morning to apply at once to the court for a guardian.

'I'll take the van to the Camargue,' Luis said.

Bernard put a hand through the crook of Luis's arm. 'Listen a moment. A warning, Luis. I'm sorry it's a painful one. Soames told me your . . . Ida . . . is mortally sick. He knows I saw Michel's wife but I didn't tell him what I told you about Birkenau. It wasn't the moment. If it's near the end of her time – Ida's time – better if you didn't tell him either.'

'I won't. Not now.'

Luis went off in the van first. Bernard followed ten minutes later in the Bentley with the painting on the seat next to him. He had nothing to hide.

*

'I expected you, Vipont, but not on the telephone at this time of night. I have a report in my office on the murder of a prostitute, possibly under age. And a piece of cheap jewellery apparently bought by you near the Palais de Justice. I'll send for you tomorrow to hear your explanations.' Caraman sounded pleased about all that, scenting a victory.

But it was enough for Bernard to say that he'd met Madame Singer in England. The silence following repaid him for the humiliations, the snubs and hubristic condescension he'd suffered from the Prosecutor over the years. 'A most respectable lady, living as the wife of an influential country lawyer. Her memory's excellent. I need only give her the address of Singer-Weiss for her to start divorce proceedings. She has plenty of money, it would be to regularise her situation and bring him and his associates into the light. I'll advise her to start with the English press.'

'That's enough, Vipont. If you've rung me now you must want something in a hurry. What is it?'

'An oblate is being detained at the convent against his will. I'll pick you up at your house in my car in fifteen minutes and we'll run up to Luminy and order your brother to release him.'

'This is France, not England. We haven't the so-called habeas corpus they're so proud of. We have the Rights of Man.'

'There's something else for the English press to get their teeth into. A private prison and the wrong man in it.'

'I'll be waiting for you, Vipont. But let me warn you—' Bernard didn't wait to hear the warning. He rang off and hurried out to his car.

On the way, with Caraman silent beside him, he thought again about poor Sonia. There must be a reason why her body was found so near the Villa Vipont – a well-lit residential quarter. It had been brought there. But who could connect him with the girl? Unless she'd talked – to an oblate crazed with grief, for example, looking for solace.

'There's another thing about your protégé, Singer-Weiss. I've learned that he knew that girl they found. The Inspector will be interested to hear it.' That should delay any plan to remove Michel to Rome and Luis would have more time. The Prosecutor said nothing. He must be reviewing his powers and options and his silence made Bernard wonder if he'd made a mistake. That Inspector was only a man under orders – the Prosecutor's orders. Far from delaying the plan, what he'd just said might hasten it. As they came to a halt on the gravel under the lightless windows of the bastide, Caraman spoke for the first time.

'Sound the horn. Otherwise they'll never wake up. In my father's time there was a concierge at the gate but these troglodytes exhaust themselves turning over the earth every day. They sleep like hogs.' The double horns of the Bentley rang out, a euphonious chord startlingly loud in this enclosure of walls and trees. The Prosecutor stepped out onto the gravel and walked to the perron. Half a shutter eased open at the level of the Prior's rooms on the first floor.

'Jean-Marie, come down at once.'

'Is it you, Alexandre?'

'Of course it is, you fool. Hurry up.'

As soon as they were in the Prior's study, the Prosecutor turned on his brother and spoke again. 'Don't ask questions, Jean-Marie, get a bottle of Armagnac and some decent glasses. At least we can do what we have to like civilised men.' He rose slightly in Bernard's esteem. The Prior did as he was told. Maître Vipont has informed himself about the personnel of the convent. Where is the oblate Alain?'

'In his cell, Alexandre, like the other members of our community.'

'Voluntarily?'

'Can a sleeping man be a volunteer, or anything else?'

'Don't be a Jesuit with me, Jean-Marie. Go and get him.' There was something to be said for the habit of authority. The Prior hesitated.

'Alain is in penitence,' he said at last.

'You mean he's locked up?'

'He's under surveillance.' The brothers exchanged a glance which Bernard had no trouble interpreting.

'Surveillance by Michel?' he asked.

'Michel sleeps in the cell adjoining Alain's.'

'And has the key?'

'His duties require it.'

'Come, Father Prior. Michel has no duties. He's in asylum. And

250

Alain isn't under vows. Even if he was, you can't hold your sons in Christ prisoner in the walls.'

'We observe the Carthusian rule. Every charterhouse had its prison, for penance.'

'Until the Revolution.'

'Our order outlives revolutions.'

'What restraint is Michel authorised to impose?'

'I was most loth . . . to authorise anything.' The Prior removed his glasses and peered at Bernard with distress in his eyes as he wiped them. 'You know, Maître Vipont, how dear to me Alain is. You've seen him with me. But he's changed. I thought it necessary he be disciplined. Particularly since the disappearance of an item of value.'

'What item?' asked the Prosecutor.

'A painting in his Eminence's apartment. Only the frame was found. Alain has access there for domestic purposes. And there were signs of entry by the cellar.'

Bernard turned to the Prosecutor with a smile. 'I think that falls in your domain. The police judiciaire,' he said.

'*Passons*,' the Prosecutor said simply, with a movement of the hand that swept the painting and the Cardinal and the police judiciaire under the carpet all together. What's under the carpet can be fished out another day, the gesture implied.

Bernard turned back to the Prior, still standing behind his desk. 'I'm instructed to act for Alain by his friends. The Code provides for it. How has he been treated?'

'He has been sequestered according to the rule. Surely you can't imagine he's been abused physically? Moral pressure only has been put on him, to confess frankly.'

'Do you mean sacramentally, or in the police sense?'

The Prior sat down heavily in his carved throne and put his face in his hands. 'I knew wrong must come of it in the end. To our peaceful, laborious house . . .' He turned to his brother. 'It was you who brought them, Alexandre. Michel and the girl with that wretched painting. I told you then it would be better they leave France. We have too many wounds to heal.'

'Be silent, Jean-Marie. You're drivelling. Vipont, we're not here for an inquisition. As far as Michel is concerned, the Concordat allows the Church a power of sanctuary. He's in sanctuary, that's all. A guest.'

'You know his past from the confessional, Father Prior?' Bernard asked.

'In the secrecy—'

'He was a Milice interrogator. You know what that means?'

'He's a son of God seeking redemption, as we all ... and he has a daughter.'

'He's one of the men who sent children with their mothers to the camps.'

'Holy Mother Church has the right and the mission to forgive on earth. In the end, God must judge.' Bernard doubted if this was theologically orthodox. In another age the Prior would probably have been burned alive for such a feeble doctrine. All the same, it claimed a power of general pardon. The Code didn't acquiesce in that.

'The prerogative of pardon belongs to the President of the Republic. Whatever Michel's crimes were, they're amnestied. What's left is an ethical question.'

'We give sanctuary to penitents who deplore sin and resolve to amend.'

'Can a man like that make amends? Don't you put temptation his way with the key to Alain's cell? Don't you know about the compulsion to repeat, Father Caraman? The erotic component in ... extracting confessions? Karoly tells me you cite Freud.'

The Prosecutor banged his fist loudly twice on the corner of the desk near to him. 'Enough of this filth. Fetch both men here, Jean-Marie,' he said.

'And I'll come with you,' Bernard said as the Prior got up. At the door Bernard looked back to see the Prosecutor raise his Armagnac glass to his nose and inhale the perfume.

Bernard followed the Prior up the service stair to the top of the building. Each time a light was switched on its predecessor went off, gloom following them as they went up and along. It was hot here under the roof, like an oven. At the end of the corridor in the half darkness was a heavy door. The Prior knocked on it softly, a series of spaced taps.

'Don't you have a key?' The Prior shook his head. There was the sound of a bolt drawn and a key turned. Michel appeared in the doorway, dressed in grey trousers and a cotton shirt open at the neck. He looked like an eminent civil servant near the age of retirement but with the light of mania in his eye.

'Father Prior? What is it? Who . . .? Ah, I see. The curious lawyer.'

'You must have heard my car and seen it from your window,' said Bernard and pushed past him.

'My cell looks onto the back.' Beyond was a narrow passage, dark and smelling of urine and fear.

'Turn on a light,' said Bernard. The walls were bare except for a crucifix. 'Where's Alain? Open these doors. Alain!'

'He's asleep. No need for such noise,' Michel said, and taking a key from his pocket he opened a door at the end of the passage. 'Wake up, my boy! You have a visitor, Brother Alain.'

Bernard entered Alain's cell. This was where the smell came from, it was very strong in here. Alain was in a corner with his back to the wall. It was impossible to know how much of the terror he showed was performance. Bernard suspected it was quite a bit but now wasn't the time to think about that. He was here to take him away and questions could come later. 'You're coming with me to my house tonight and my housekeeper will look after you. Bring anything you want to keep with you. I don't think you'll be coming back.'

'I've nothing that belongs to me,' said Alain in his precise, deep voice.

'Well get dressed for God's sake.' Because he was naked, holding his hands crossed in front of his groin. Bernard looked away. If there were marks on him he didn't want to see them when he turned round, he'd rather not know. 'Be quick. We'll get you proper clothes tomorrow.'

'Where's Luis?' Alain asked.

'He's gone away.'

'Will he come back?'

Bernard was already out in the corridor and heard the question behind him. He didn't answer. The mention of Luis was unfortunate. It would go to confirm suspicions about the picture, linking it with Luis, Alain, and the disappearance of Mado. The Caraman brothers could do nothing about these disappearances, but they might hasten the removal of Michel to another sanctuary, another country. Before Michel had time to disappear Luis must catch him as he'd caught the Milice villain years ago, in those days when much summary private justice passed under the bridges of France to be washed out to sea. Now it was different. Summary private justice was no longer allowed to pass under the bridge.

'Au revoir, Brother Alain,' said Michel. Bernard turned to see Alain facing Michel for the last time.

'God forgive you, Brother Michel.' Alain raised his face towards Michel's as if to offer the kiss of peace and when Michel lowered his own by reflex, Alain spat like a camel.

'We'll go down to my study,' said the Prior. He sounded done for. 'My brother will tell us what to do. Come with us, Michel.'

The Prosecutor had put himself in the Prior's carved chair and made no move when they filed in. 'So you have your prize, Vipont,' he said. 'Dispose of it, it's worthless. I shall remain here tonight with my brother. Call my office first thing in the morning and tell them to send a car for me. I think we have no more to say to each other.' He looked hard at Alain as if to be sure of recognising him the day he got picked up and brought to court for some misdeed on the streets of the old town. 'As for you, you owe everything to the Couvent de la Génératrice-Immaculée. You were an orphan and better for you if you hadn't been—'

'Please, Alexandre,' the Prior protested. 'Be less harsh. Alain has always been devoted to me.'

'What sickly nonsense. You choose disciples from the botched and bungled. Why are you still here, Vipont?'

Bernard was still there because bait must be laid for Michel. If the Prosecutor was staying the night it meant he planned his urgent removal. That would take at least a day, from a place without a telephone and no car. All the same, Luis would need more than a day. Michel must be induced to dig his heels in as he'd always done. Bernard swallowed his revulsion and turned to him. 'Father Prior said you'd lost your daughter. You know I have a daughter too. I may be able—'

'No, no,' said Alain.

Standing beside him, Bernard took his arm. 'Marseille's too dangerous for a young girl to be lost in. My chief clerk has access to networks in the town . . . lines of enquiry. I'll call him tonight.' He could see that Michel neither believed, nor dared disbelieve, and when he spoke stumblingly in the end it was with hope over reason.

'I'd be grateful . . . from the heart . . .' The words wouldn't quite come out but the sense was clear.

'We'll notify the results to Monsieur Caraman. I know you keep in touch with him. Though perhaps now, it would be safer for you to send one of the other monks into town on the motor-bicycle. Your past . . . word gets about. I advise you to go no further than the shrine, to collect the offerings of the poor.' Still holding Alain's arm, Bernard turned to go. He stopped at the door and turned back. 'My advice on the legal matter is that the Couvent hasn't a leg to stand on. You'll have my written opinion after the usual delay – a month or so.' No one said anything, but as they reached the head of the staircase there was a step behind them and the Prior took hold of Alain with both hands and turned him round.

'Bonne chance, mon enfant,' he murmured and in the dark inclined his head to place a kiss on Alain's forehead. It was a farewell without blessing.

In the car, Alain sat leaning forward with fists clenched and eyes fixed on the zone ahead lit by the headlamps. He didn't seem interested in the Bentley any more. He was thinking of Luis and everything to do with him with an intensity that transmitted itself even to Bernard.

'You want Michel to stay,' he said.

'Yes. For a time.'

'Why?'

'Because they want to move him on.'

'You mean he's valuable because of that?'

'For a few days.'

'Valuable to Luis?'

'Very valuable to Luis.'

They finished the journey in silence. At the Villa Vipont, Bernard rang for Juanita and presented her with Alain. 'This is a young religious who has had the luck to escape from tyranny. Please look after him properly until—'

'Until you decide what to do with him. Like any tyrant.' Juanita inspected Alain with evident disapproval. Bernard guessed the reason for this was that she didn't consider him a proper man. He was neither a curé nor a normal male sinner.

'I expect he's hungry,' Bernard said.

'I have some steaks of *toro*, we'll see if that puts anything into him. Follow me,' said Juanita and sailed away, towing Alain in her wake like a dinghy.

# Chapter Twelve

LUIS CHANGED HIS mind about going straight out to the Camargue to see Soames. Instead, he went to the Vieille Charité. There were loose ends to be tied up and the first of them was Mado. Since Marion's visit she was withdrawn in her manner but secretly resentful, Luis thought. When she looked at him, which was seldom, it was with a vengeful expression she may have been unconscious of. Luis had seen it before. You couldn't satisfy everyone who sought satisfaction from you, and that was how it was this time.

'Collect your things, whatever you've got,' he told her. 'Maître Vipont is going to look after you. He has the painting and he'll be fair with you, I can promise that. But you can't stay here now.'

'Where must I go?' She spoke in a voice unlike her usual one, lower and harder.

'To the nuns downstairs. Only until Maître Vipont sends for you. I have to go away.'

'I could stay here and wait for you.'

'I won't be coming back.'

'So you kick me out on the rubbish.' Luis knew some sort of explosion wasn't far away – rage, tears, desperate proposition, probably all three. She must be moved on at once.

'Come on. You're a good girl, Mado, but I'm no use to you. Get your stuff.' She didn't stir and he took a step towards her as if to offer force if necessary. It was a wrong move. She charged at him like a maddened animal. But this wasn't an attack, it was for comfort. Luis found himself holding her against him as he hadn't intended, because he didn't want trouble. But trouble was a normal part of life, as he knew. She wore a thin dress and by the feel of it, nothing underneath. Her hands were on his back. The situation was hopeless. The dress had buttons below the neck and Luis quickly undid them and let it drop to the floor. It's hard to stand by and see unhappiness when you're the cause and do nothing at all. Naked, she seemed justification enough in herself. The force at work was impersonal, it was right because you owed it a natural obedience, and you paid up. Besides, you must respect the desires of others if you can. He lifted Mado onto the side of the table and gently edged her forward onto him. It was good. Not like with Marion – with Marion it was sublime – but still very good. The girl's head was thrown back and her eyes shut. Luis lent himself to her rhythm and ensured the right timing. It came easily enough.

'You're a proper woman, Mado, and I never forget that. Look out for someone who deserves you,' Luis said afterwards. 'Now we'll go down to the nuns.'

The nuns, naturally, treated him as a paedophile rapist but that didn't matter. Their job was to house the girl and await Bernard's instructions and they wouldn't dare do anything else. 'Maître Vipont's chief clerk will tell you what you're to do,' he told them and they inclined their heads in furious submission. He shook Mado's hand, squeezing it slightly so she'd know this was by way of being a joke.

'Goodbye now, Mado,' he said. 'And the *baxt* be with you.' It was the highest wish he knew.

'Goodbye, Luis. Remember me.' He turned away quickly. The pain for her was only temporary, she was young. But in a sense it was permanent for him. This was the end of his youth. With surprise, he noticed something in his hand. It was a little piece of jade, like a tooth. He recalled seeing it hung round her neck on a shoelace.

Upstairs, he went through his supply of ropes and tackle for climbing. Over the years he'd accumulated quite a lot of that on missions for Bernard. And he had a light miner's helmet with a torch in it. The batteries were past their best but probably had two or three hours' life left in them. The boys hadn't told him much about the gradient of the shaft or the character of the surface, because they hadn't seen much of it; it was the act of penetrating the unknown that held their attention. He found a pair of studded boots and some denim overalls, a bar of chocolate and a loaf of bread. He was ready. He lay down on his bed fully dressed and waited for the hour before dawn, thinking about Marion and about Ida's sickness, advancing without pause; another impersonal force, possessing and destroying. Luis was usually good at short episodes of sleep, waking when he wanted to, refreshed and ready. But now sleep wouldn't come. Instead there came echoes of sickness like a buzzing in the ears. Perhaps a drink of whisky would help. It was a remedy he'd learned from Soames and kept for rare occasions.

He fetched Soames's glass from the cupboard where it stood in a protected place like a precious vessel, which it was, in a way. The glass of *baxt*. He poured a dose of whisky and went through to the kitchen for the water bottle. Then he thought he heard a stealthy sound behind him, as if Mado had escaped and returned. He swung round sharply, his elbow catching the glass of *baxt* which he'd put on the table beside the sink. It lurched across the wooden surface like an animal with a will of its own; Luis put out his free hand to catch it, and instead, knocked it to the tiled floor where it smashed into a hundred pieces. He looked down at it in grief. It was gone for ever, his glass from Soames. Luis didn't wholeheartedly believe in the *baxt* except as another word for the inevitable, and still less in the power of a drinking glass to imprison it, hold it, disperse it if broken. All the same, this was something that made him feel bad. He knelt down and gathered the fragments, washed them and placed them carefully in a wooden box where he kept the few brief notes he'd ever had from Marion. His eye caught something on the floor by the door, a sheet of scrap paper.

It was a crude drawing in pencil. There was the figure of a man, apparently naked but without genitals. These were depicted beside him and lower down the paper as if torn off and thrown to the floor. Luis crumpled the sheet with a feeling of slight, not very particular disgust. The Vieille Charité was a nest of informers, denouncers, anonymous makers of menace and insult. There was nothing special about this one, except its arrival coinciding with the smashing of the glass of *baxt*. He opened the shutter and threw the paper out into the night and when he went back to bed he slept at once, even without the whisky.

\*

At first grey light he was already at Luminy, the van parked under the pines along a track overgrown with cistus and honeysuckle. The dawn was silent. The swifts had gone, the nightingales long since worn themselves out. The cicadas hung fire till the temperature rose. Luis looked over at the cranes and building works of the faculty behind its high fences. He wondered if he was doing wrong to take Marion away from a career with her own kind – if in the end she would be unhappy with him. When passion turned to just habitual appetite. But this wasn't the moment to worry about it. Under the broken cover of the trees he made for the crest above the calanque, ropes and helmet and crow-bar over his shoulder, stopping from time to time to scan the scenery for signs of other human life. There were none. In this heat, people did most of their sleeping in the early hours. From the crest, the coming sunrise could be sensed behind the Mont Puget rising sheer from the sea on the eastern side; to the south, the light was velvet on a surface of sea still as death. He made for the place among the tall rosemary bushes and the scree.

Shifting the rock was hard and long. He'd thought that what four boys had done with bars he could easily do on his own. It showed he was ageing. At last the rock moved the first few centimetres and he wedged it, moved it again, bedded it on the prepared ledge of smaller stones. It would have to go back again before he left and the stones scattered. He was pouring with sweat in the cool dawn air and sat for a minute watching the sea. Below it and almost to the horizon lay what had been the land, before the ice floes melted. Forest, inhabited by men and women, had once stretched as far as the drowned coastline. Lions, perhaps, and bison, and primitive ancestors with stone weapons, resembling himself, hunting and gathering. It was hard to imagine, with the faculty of science rising from the concrete a kilometre beyond the crest. In the Camargue, a long way from any university, imagination was freer. But what needed no effort of imagination was the fantastic beauty, the sea and bare limestone mountain and empty sky turning pink at the eastern edge.

Luis stood up and approached the hole with its secrets. The opening was tight but negotiable, if you drew in your shoulders and thought yourself a boy. He shone the light in and saw, as they'd said, a chute of scree narrowing down to a shaft a couple of metres below. There was nothing to attach a rope to. He must take a risk and tie up to the rock at the surface, passing the head of the rope round another rock higher up. Did he take that much precaution because of breaking the glass? Luis felt impatient with himself. Those things were for women – to each sex its domain. His was the domain of sea and stone, ropes and rocks. He slithered down the scree with his coils about his neck.

Looking into the shaft by the light of the torch he could see the remains huddled on the first shelf down. Bones . . . a skull. He ought to feel something but he didn't. What he saw was the evidence of a comrade's private act in circumstances he knew nothing about. After this first shelf was the zone the boys hadn't seen, dropping, so Pierrot claimed, to below sea level. He could just throw the skeleton in, close up the shaft, and his mission for Bernard would be done. It would be found sooner or later but there would be nothing to identify it or link it with anyone at all. But Luis didn't seriously consider this possibility. He was here to explore an intuition.

He knew it was better not to try this on his own, too much could go wrong down there in the dark. So he'd be very cautious, and if it looked too difficult, climb back and dispose of the bones. He put on his helmet, fed the rope into the shaft and started down. When he reached the remains, spilt like a box of matches on the stone, he inclined his head out of respect. Whatever Bernard had done, it was a long time ago and concerned him, not Luis. All the same it was puzzling, he'd never seemed to Luis a man of violence. There must have been some kind of accident and then Bernard had been afraid. That was more likely, and it explained quite a bit about him, too. The hard and soft in him, the straight and the bent.

261

After the first shelf, the shaft was much narrower. The stone, pale grey and pink at the surface, here seemed almost black. Looking up, the light from the sky was now no more than a shadow less opaque than the rest. There's always a moment, underground, when you want to go back. He could see that the first stage wasn't long, it took a bend leftwards about four metres down. Luis entrusted himself to the rope, inserted the lower part of his body, and with arms above his head eased his way through the opening. It was easier than he'd expected, as if the entrails stretched to digest him. When he reached the bend he could stand and crouch, moving his head so the torch played on the surfaces beyond. Here the passage became higher and less steep. He was near the end of his first rope, with four metres outside in the dawn. So he must be nearly halfway to sea level. He unwound the second rope and looked for a point of attachment. There was nothing but smooth black stone. A practised speleologist would have cramp-irons and a hammer and a pick but Luis didn't practise speleology. He tied the second rope to the end of the first. He could only try his luck or turn back. This wasn't a vertical chimney any more, it was more like a cleft between rock faces. The going was easy but further on there could be another drop. There was a faint odour, not cold and musty as you'd expect, but fresh, reminding him of something. Then from below him he felt a draught of air. The odour was the sea and the life in it.

He'd reached a drop. A stone, dislodged by his boot, fell and clattered a long way below. The torch showed thickening darkness and then, just discernible, what might be an area of uneven stone floor. He threw down the remaining coils of rope. Now the *baxt* must be with him or against him. If the rope gave, or some psychopath out on the hillside untied it, he would never get out alive. He chased the thought from his mind and began the descent, the rope turning him slowly anti-clockwise with his own weight. The beam as he revolved threw a wandering disk of light on the walls of the cave and here and there on a stalactite hung like a swarm of sea-snails. Suddenly his feet lost the rope under him. He'd come to the end. So Pierrot was right and the floor of this cave was below sea level. How far below? He could jump, but would he get back? With his feet swinging in the void, Luis went down hand over hand. Hanging at arms' length he called on the *baxt* and let go.

He lay on his back in the dark. Probably the helmet had saved him. The torch was out, and for the first time he felt afraid. He fiddled blindly with the torch – the wires, the bulb, the terminals. Then he remembered a spare bulb fixed in a slot near the buckle of the helmet. With eyes closed and senses concentrated in his fingers he changed the bulbs. The new beam was stronger, and looking upward he saw the end of his rope, swinging and turning. It was well out of reach from the ground. Luis postponed the search for a solution, giving the *baxt* time to come into play. It was the *baxt* that had made sure of the spare bulb. He stood up.

The silence here was deeper than anything he'd ever known. There was no movement of air. The air must enter higher up in the chimney, where the dye poured in by the boys ran out into the sea. If this cave was below sea level there couldn't be any kind of opening at all or it would fill. There was some water in pools on the floor and Luis put in a finger and tasted it. It was salt, so probably it blew in the same way as the air, higher up when there was a storm and the sea moved.

The cave was the size and height of the atrium in the crypt of Saint-Victor, dug deep into the rock; at the far end was a low arch and, beyond it, a hollow like the cavity called the confessional of Lazarus. Luis studied this cell and its entrance for a long time before turning away to inspect the rest of the cave. What you noticed first was the dry air and the jagged roughness of the walls, like teeth ground for crushing bones. They were as dry to the touch as you would expect bones or teeth to be. Yet the sea was sleeping beyond the stone at the height of the rope's end above his head.

But he wasn't here to exercise his imagination. He continued his examination of the walls and the roof, just visible. Then he seemed to sense a light pressure on his shoulder, maybe the encouraging hand of *baxt* urging him forward. It urged him towards the farthest corner of the cave, where the vault sloped down to the floor like the fall of a dome. Here the surface of the stone was smoother, undulating. He stood still and let the torch light up the segment of rock facing him.

The hand seemed to have left his shoulder and planted itself on the rock. There could be no mistake. There was a hand on the rock, reddish brown and spread out, a woman's hand by the size, the fingers open like Mado's on his back a short time ago. Luis moved his head and saw other roving hands, male and female, painted on the different faces of the rock – behind, before, above, between, below. He'd found what he came for. Heredity had guided him, intuition proved itself. Further up the wall were animals. Horses. Luis's heart leapt at the sight of them. They were exactly like the *camargue* he'd ridden up to the convent in the night. This was a place where his own predecessors had come, when it was halfway up the mountainside and not under water, to celebrate what he and Soames celebrated to this day, horses and the hands of women on your back. He was the discoverer of a treasure that would one day be called after him – *la grotte Karoly*.

Luis felt too excited to stay any longer. He must get out of here or the wonder might drown the plan forming in his head. He looked about for stones for a mounting block but there was nothing, all was fixed as if the sea washed in and out of here. The end of the rope dangled three metres beyond reach. The only way was from the wall – child's play with cramp-irons, but all he had was his own invention. There were fissures in the rock near the rope, like a wall in the countryside. In those cracks, stones could be wedged for a foothold. Stones broken out of the wall using a big one for a pickaxe. He returned to the confessional of Lazarus where there was an overhang of rock. Luis always carried a heavy screwdriver, a tool with many uses. He took it out, removed one of his boots for a hammer and looked for a fault in the rock. He was surprised how easily it came away, as if the dryness of ages had made the stone as brittle as dead wood. There it lay on the ground, a piece weighing a couple of kilos and with one end sharpened where it had broken off. Looking up at the horses and the hands fixed there, that made you think. The place was like a quarry, one good charge in a crack – but this wasn't the moment for thinking it through.

Luis took his stone weapon in both hands and attacked the wall. Soon he'd placed wedges in crevices as far as he could reach. Not far enough. He would have to leap from the wall and for that he must be above the end of the rope, because of gravity. He climbed with more stones in his pocket. Reaching up, you had to insert a stone in a crack and entrust yourself to it. You had to lean into the wall, trusting to your last foothold – and the *baxt*. In the end he grew tired, he was getting past it. When his head was a bit higher than the rope's end he found a shallow recess to plant a foot and kick himself up and forward. He gave thought to Marion – then with all the force of the leg bent behind him, launched himself out.

He had the knot in his hands. Climbing hand over hand to get his feet to it was an exploit of strength. You must get there, or drop. Luis wished he was lighter. He carried more muscle and bone than he needed – another sign of age. At last he had the knot between his feet as he swung like a bird in a cage, back and forth in the dark. He could hear the rope high up, sawing against the edge of stone as he swung. He was sweating heavily in the cold dry air. He must reach the chute of scree while the rope held. Not because Luis feared death, the other side of belief in his immortality was a sense that he couldn't long outlive the source he sprang from, any more than a jet of water when the fountain dries. But there was important work first.

Part of that was gathering up the skeleton. Luis hadn't given this any thought but now, when he saw it there in the light of his lamp, he felt a revulsion. For the remains of a man he might have been less fastidious, but this had been a woman. Perhaps he'd already overspent himself on the climb. His aching body refused the order to get on with it and he stood there, paralysed, staring at his feet and the remains beside them. Soon enough, Ida would be like this. He couldn't do it. When he returned to carry out the project forming in his mind – put the confessional of Lazarus to just use – then he'd be more prepared. That's when he would take care of these dried sticks.

\*

The midday sun was strong. Luis left the van in the shade of the plane trees and walked the last part. He hadn't rung to say he was coming. Soames was probably out on the land, testing the purity of the water for his Arabs, those jewels of the prairie. Now, as he approached the house, he wished he had rung, so Soames would be here to meet him. He was afraid, a feeling he was untrained by practice to deal with. Approaching death was an opponent you could only lose against, and Soames would have shouldered his share of the defeat. The *mas* lay there in the burning sun with shutters closed, solitary on the dusty land. From all the plane trees around came the noise of cicadas, a sound Luis loved. When he reached the terrace he heard another sound, coming from the other side of the house.

On this side were only the living room with long windows down to the ground and Soames's office, where he pretended to do his accounts. Luis suspected that these accounts were mythical and that what he really went in there for was to smoke his black cigars and read his poetry books and ruminate on the spent time that makes everyone sad, even those with an ironical outlook on life.

Luis knew what this new sound was and he'd been putting off the moment of acknowledging it. It was the singing of a voice wrecked by sickness. At first, he knew the words and the melody, he could hear in memory the voice singing them when she was a girl and he was a child, the voice of a lost world before Birkenau. Now the vocal chords were like the strings of a smashed instrument, toneless, a parody. Without any pause, the words he knew changed for another, a different broken song.

> No one understands
> Only the forest and the river.
> What I speak of
> Has all passed away.
> Everything gone with it –
> The silent snow
> And those years of youth . . .
> Buried . . .

She must have learned it in Birkenau, from one of the other women. She didn't come from a land of forests and rivers and snow, she came from here. She was deliberately singing a Birkenau song, to cry out against the dead sound of her own voice. Luis banged angrily on the first shutter to hand, then on the door. He was still banging when he heard Soames's voice behind him.

'Let her be, Luis.'

'It's not good, like that . . . with no voice.' Luis sat on the tiled floor of the terrace, his feet out on the dusty track in the sun.

'It won't be long now, I think.' Luis said nothing to this, and Soames put a hand on his shoulder as if, of the two of them, he was always the stronger. Maybe he was. 'She's doing things the way she knows.'

'I've come to tell you you must come into Marseille.'

Soames considered this command for a moment as if wondering whether or not to obey. But he always did what Luis wanted, in the end, because being the stronger he could give way. He oversaw Luis's life from afar and was there when he was needed – and that was how it had always been.

'When?' he asked.

'Tomorrow. I'll telephone. You must bring your pistol.' Luis kept no gun, he never had, not since that early time . . . guns were for a closed order of men. Soames belonged to it, but not him. He was an artisan, not a soldier.

'What for?'

'Because I'm going to need it. It can be unloaded, if you like, but bring some bullets. I won't be shooting at anyone. I couldn't hit them if I tried.'

Soames laughed. 'It's not so hard. You did it before. Depends how far off you stand. So you just want to lean on a person, do you?'

'Yes.'

'Who is it? Would it be your future father-in-law? Deserves it, to my way of thinking.'

'No, it's not him,' said Luis. Soames often told him he had no sense of humour and that was another reason he needed overseeing.

'But he's told you something that makes you want to lean on this other fellow, that's it, is it?'

'Yes, that's it.'

'I thought he would, sooner or later.'

'So you know about it.'

'All I need to.'

'Then you know why you've got to help.'

'You tell me why.'

Luis gestured behind him at the house. 'That singing. It's stopped. The Birkenau song's stopped. That's why.' They stood in the silence, in the hot shade of the trees with the horses peacefully about the land behind them. 'There's one of the worst of the swine in a convent up in the hills near Marseille. I told you,' Luis went on in a low voice. 'He must pay for what he did. If he was a Gitan who'd done a tenth of it, he'd have paid long ago. For a real Christian it's not the same rules.' Luis checked himself. He despised factionalism. 'If we can deliver him, I know some lads who'll take care of it.'

'Who?'

'Old Resistants who haven't given up, amnesty or not. They keep quiet, the ones in Marseille. Since the amnesty. No meeting in the best restaurants like your pals in Nîmes. This lot stay underground. They meet and do what they have to do in a cave near the sea.'

'How do you come to know them, Luis?'

'Through contacts. There's a lot of underground contact at the Vieille Charité. I told you, it's the shithouse of the world.'

'Okay. I'll bring the gun when you tell me – just to make sure it's not you does any shooting. Have you got that, Luis? It's an order. No shooting. You and me, we'll both get back here safe and sound, and what those others do . . . what happens after . . .' Soames passed his hand across the top of his head as though he could already feel the wound that would mark the afterwards he talked about. 'What happens to me then doesn't matter. But you'll be here with Marion and your child . . .' He spoke as if it was already conceived. The door from the house opened and Soames stopped.

'Luis?' The voice wasn't much above a whisper, it hurt as much to hear it as if the throat it came from was your own.

Luis stood up. He wanted to say something hard to show how he hated the sickness and the song. But he could find nothing to say. It wasn't the time for anger any more. He folded his arms about her, it was like holding a bird's nest from last season.

'Soon there'll be children here,' she said.

'Yes. For you.'

'For all of us.'

He turned away to walk back to his van under the planes.

'Goodbye, Luis.' She'd lifted her voice almost to its old sound for the two words. But he couldn't say goodbye to her now any more than he ever had. A gitan spirit marches on, along the tracks of the world, by crossroads and paths. When he reached the van he looked back and lifted an arm. 'Until tomorrow.'

'Mind what I said, Luis . . .' Soames called as the van started up.

*

In a street behind the Vieux Port, where ships' ropemakers had worked for centuries, was a shop called La Corderie, specialised now in tennis nets and sporting gear for climbers and speleologists. Luis knew that the first essential of a properly planned operation was correct equipment and he went in to La Corderie armed with plenty of cash.

'I'm taking a party of Englishmen into the mountain to explore a system of karstic galleries,' he told the assistant in the shop, a young man of immigrant extraction. 'I've been down with ropes on my own but they're ignorant and they aren't young. I need plenty of gear to make it safe.'

The assistant eyed him with suspicion containing, Luis thought, a good deal of contempt. A Gitan doesn't have credible skills except with horses and this cock and bull story of Englishmen cut no ice with a salesman who knew his way around. Clearly, the moment his back was turned, Luis would steal something trivial, as Gitans were known to do, and run for it. Luis took hold of the assistant's upper arm in a grip like a vice.

'I had to break up a rock with my hands to get out and I want this expedition to be easier.' He tightened his hold and the assistant let out a grunt of pain. 'I've plenty of money on me, so there's a commission for you if you look sharp. A lot better than getting a broken arm.'

'It will be a pleasure to serve Monsieur immediately,' the assistant said, and fetched a steel-and-leather chair for Luis to sit on while he brought out the goods for inspection.

The ladder was the most important item, for the last stage of the descent. Rope ladders are difficult for the inexperienced. 'I must have a ladder with some kind of rigid element but not too bulky to pass through a narrow opening.'

'We have one with telescopic aluminium rungs and risers, Monsieur, but it's very expensive. It's for rich amateurs.'

'The English are generous when it's their pleasures.'

The assistant allowed himself a small laugh, ingratiating for Luis, insolent for his English clients. 'I thought they didn't practise pleasure, Monsieur.'

'They're polite, that's why you thought that. Their politeness and jokes are to hide private things from idiots.'

'Of course, Monsieur,' the assistant said, and went away to fetch the telescopic aluminium apparatus for the use of these secretive Englishmen.

Luis also bought helmets, a pick and hammer and irons to fix in the rock, and nylon rope already knotted at half-metre intervals. With all this he could imagine taking even a party of nuns down the limestone chimney on the maritime hillside, not just a couple of oblates. Then he telephoned Marion.

'I'm coming up to the Villa Vipont but it isn't to see you,' he said in a firm voice.

'You sound like an English sergeant-major.'

'You don't know any English soldiers except Soames.'

'I've seen them on funny films. You know. English films.' Marion sounded anxious and defenceless as if she didn't know which way the wind was blowing. It would have to stay like that a bit longer.

'I want to speak to your father.'

'Now you sound like Albertas.'

'Is he there?'

'Why do you want to talk to him again? What else have you got to talk about?'

'Do what I tell you, Marion. Go and fetch your father, please.'

There was a silence. When her father wanted something from her, he either bribed or wheedled. She would have to learn how to be more like a Romany woman, that is to say, make as much fuss as she liked but obey. If he'd allowed himself, Luis would have felt sorry for her.

'All right.'

'Whatever happens, always remember I love you, Marion.'

'Yes, I will.'

After a time Bernard's voice came down the line, high and nervous, as if retribution was on his heels. 'Luis?'

'Where are you speaking from?'

'I'm in my study.'

'Is there a separate line?'

Bernard gave him another number and he rang again. 'I'm coming over with the van. Have you got Alain at the Villa Vipont?'

'Yes.'

'I must see him.'

'I'm very relieved to hear it. He hangs about the gate looking miserable and Juanita says he doesn't eat anything. It's like having a lost dog.'

'I've got something for him to do.'

'Good. He's used to being told what to do. Take him off my hands, it's all I ask.'

'I'll be there in fifteen minutes. Tell him to wait by the gate and I won't have to come in.'

'He's there already. Will you take him away?'

'Yes. We'll see about afterwards. I'm going to need you too, tomorrow morning. Very early. Juanita'll have to get you up. Tell Marion it's only a day and a night more. Say it's nearly over now.'

'What do you want me for?'

'Don't worry. You're just a last resort.' Luis was laughing, excitement made him laugh. 'I'll let you home as soon as the trap's sprung.'

271

'I won't ask questions, Luis. I believe you know what you're doing. And it's for the best – whatever comes of it.'

*

Alain was wearing ordinary clothes, blue cotton trousers and a blue shirt. He looked like a student, one of those ageing ones who go on for years failing their examinations. Dedicated but incapable. Still, his face was happier than Luis had seen it before.

'Maître Vipont says you need me,' he said.

'Jump in the van.'

He didn't ask where they were going or what they were going to do. His happiness lay in being needed by Luis and that was enough. Luis drove along the Corniche and then continued on the coast road until it became a track and they were among the rocks overlooking the sea and the nearby islands where wild goats grazed, and the wrecks of Greek and Roman ships lay deep on the bottom.

'I'm going to ask you to do something that needs a lot of courage,' Luis said.

'I'll do anything,' said Alain.

'I know you will. But you've got to be careful or it could go wrong. It's not enough to be brave. You'll have to be clever too.'

'You know I'm not stupid even if I'm out of a convent.'

'That was the best thing you've done, getting out. Now you've got to go back there.'

'What will they do with me?' Alain already accepted that he must do what Luis said without question. But he sounded afraid. Luis hadn't meant that, he'd expressed himself clumsily.

'Don't worry, we won't let them catch you. I won't be far off.' His instinct was to put a reassuring hand on Alain's arm as he would have done for a normal person. But he knew it would be wrong. It would be like seeming to offer comfort of a kind he'd never deliver. He wondered if it often happened to a man with Alain's leanings, to have to do without support freely offered to people who don't need it so much.

'Do you want me to steal something?'

'No. I'll tell you.' Luis walked up a path among the rocks towards a small concrete ruin on the brow, probably something left over from the war. From here the view extended eastward along the calanques and northward to Marseille itself, Nôtre Dame de la Garde on the hill dominating the sea approaches. Far below you could see holiday-makers swimming off the rocks or rowing over the still water to the island to look at the wild goats – it was a carefree August scene. A light breeze blew off the sea, tempering the heat of the afternoon. Alain followed closely. Looking back at him, Luis saw the devoted expression of his eyes. 'Do you know any way to get a message to Michel?' he said.

'Only the post,' Alain said, after a pause.

'The post takes too long. I mean tonight.'

'There isn't another way.'

'It's what I thought. You'll have to go there.' Luis looked down into the devoted eyes with a hard expression in his own. The fear, like a child, must be overruled.

'Do I have to see him to give him the message?'

'Better not but you must be ready for it. Is there somewhere he's sure to go? Where you can leave a note and not be seen?'

'There's his motor-bicycle, he keeps that in the stables.'

'He might not go there for days. He might think it safer not to go anywhere, now.'

'Oh no, he'll go. He loves his motor-bicycle. And now it's all he's got. Every morning before light he goes to fetch the post from the day before. They leave it in the shrine by the entrance near the Baumettes. And Michel isn't afraid of anything.'

'That's it then. I'll take you up to Luminy tonight and we'll walk through the woods. You'll slip into the stables and leave the note fixed to the saddle of his motor-bicycle. I'll be in the trees, not far away.'

'Where will we go then?'

'You'll have to spend the rest of the night near that shrine and wait for him. I need to get my friends ready. I'll give you a rendezvous in Marseille and he must take you on his motor-bicycle.'

'What will be on the message, Luis? You know Michel, I think he's a dangerous man. What do you want to tell him?'

273

'You've got to tell him something. You're going to write the message and sign it. Say you've found out where his daughter is and you'll take him to her. It's the only way to catch him.'

'Where is she, Luis? Have you got her?'

'She's safe with some nuns. He won't see her ever again.'

'Did you keep her for a bit and then give her to the nuns?'

'Yes, Alain, that's what I did.' Put like that it sounded brutal, and in some ways it had been. Alain looked sad and at the same time strangely gratified. Luis had the feeling that somewhere in his lonely imagination he was putting himself in Mado's place. Probably when Alain had been in the world a bit longer, and seen something of the women there, he would change, and be happier while he still had time.

'Where must Michel take me on his motor-cycle? It'll have to be a story he believes in. He's very suspicious.'

'At the bottom of Maître Vipont's garden on the Corniche, there's a small door behind some trees. There won't be anyone around at that time, no one will see him. Bring him there. Now we'll go and you'll see where it is and I'll get you the key. When you come soon after dawn I'll be waiting just inside with my friends. Tell him Mado's in a pavilion in the garden. Say you found her and she's locked up there and she's had a change of heart. She wants to go back to her papa. That's what to tell him. And give him this.' Luis took from his pocket Mado's jade tooth and handed it over. 'He'll recognise it.'

'Do you think it's right in the eyes of God to do that, Luis?'

'Listen to me. I don't have any of your religion. Maybe our ideas of what's wrong aren't the same. To me, you can't do wrong to a man like that. What's wrong is leaving what he's done unpunished. That's what religion and society and the law do – they invent a pardon to hand out for nothing. A free grace for what the victims can't forgive if they're dead, and never will as long as they live. That's the crime. So don't ask me if I think it's right to do what I'm doing. I only know I must do it, that's enough for me.'

'Yes, Luis,' said Alain, watching him with wide eyes. 'I understand now. What you know you must do, must be right. Perhaps it's God who tells you to do it.'

'Let's get on then,' said Luis, leaving aside the question of God, and he strode back downhill to the van. Halfway he thought of something else important and stopped. Alain caught up. 'One more thing. You'll meet an Englishman, Soames. He's a man I've never lied to before. Perhaps, like you say, it's God who tells me to do it now. Soames has to think you're a contact – no, better a guide – with a gang of old Resistants to take care of Michel. We're meeting them in a cave where Soames can't go down because the Germans blew his leg off. You're supposed to know the way. Watch for the signs I give you and keep your mouth shut. Have you got that, Alain?'

'Yes. Luis, I've got it all. I don't understand, but I've got it.'

It seemed to Luis that now everything was in place and nothing overlooked. He'd come out here to be sure of it, the sight of the sea and the islands and the normal people enjoying themselves would clear his mind of doubts, if he had any. He thought for the last time of the broken glass. What nonsense that was, even if according to Soames some poet had written about a glass somewhere in England which must never be broken and was kept down a well to protect it. It was a German poet, anyway. Another reason to put it from his mind.

# Chapter Thirteen

'You're going to sea in a fishing-boat?' said Juanita. 'At your age, with a stomach like that? I don't believe you. I believe you're taking the hydroplane to Porquerolles for the sight of the naked women all over the beaches. The society whores.'

'If you were right, I'd still be going to sea. Therefore you do believe me.'

'But not fishing. So you don't need your coffee at five in the morning.'

'Do as I say, Juanita. Or I'll have to dismiss you.'

'Dismiss me as much as you like. I've heard Monsieur Caraman's looking for a woman of authority for his household, and he's a man of clean life.'

'He's a eunuch, and I wouldn't give you a reference.'

'With a reference from you, he wouldn't give me the job,' Juanita said, and banged the door behind her. An element of frustration had seeped into their relationship and these quarrels were the sign.

That was last night. Now Bernard stood with Luis and Soames at the bottom of the garden near the door out onto the Corniche, in the first hint of light. There was the high wall of the domain in front of them shutting off the westward view over the sea, still almost black with the morning star brazen and unblinking as the women on Porquerolles; and behind them the hill covered in villas of the prosperous, shutters closed. If he'd known Soames would be here, he'd have just handed over the key of the gate and left them to it. Bernard was afraid of Soames, now. And there he was, waiting in the dark with a pistol in his hand.

Was there going to be a struggle, here in the garden? What did Luis mean when he said he might be needed as a last resort? To clean up after them? Bernard believed Michel was a man familiar in the ways of violence, where he himself was a complete stranger. Even as a boy in the Resistance he'd only been used for running errands, though often enough in danger. He'd never worked on the brutal side of things and from what he knew of himself he didn't think he'd be good at it. 'He may come armed,' Soames pointed out while they waited in the dark. 'Probably will.'

'Lèt him come right in. I'll fall on him from that ledge when he's on the second step,' Luis said. 'Stay still and leave it to me.'

'I'll cover your left,' said Soames.

'Look out for the little fellow. We need him. He knows the way.'

What did Luis mean? His announcement of what went on in his head was often elliptical and left you working it out. Bernard didn't ask. This sounded to him like something intended for Soames's ears, not his. Soames was being hoodwinked to neutralise him, that must be it. 'For God's sake don't pull the trigger on either of them in here,' he said and Soames laughed, but not with humour, it seemed to Bernard.

'Keep behind that tree,' Luis said. He climbed onto the ledge protruding from the architrave of the doorway, his back to the wall. From the distance came the low sound of an engine. 'Taking it slow.' The gentle mutter of the engine came and went as it rounded bends and inlets on the Corniche road, walls of rock or rising gardens to one side, the black mass of the night sea on the other.

Was Juanita still of child-bearing age? What an absurd question to ask yourself at this time of morning in these circumstances. She might just be. Bernard closed his eyes and leaned against the wall behind him. In front of him was an ancient cypress with a trunk massive enough to hide him even in daylight. These cypresses of his were visible for miles across the sea, a monument of nature familiar to fishermen and coastal navigators. They had been one of the prides of his father who before the war kept a yacht in the Vieux Port, something Bernard had never presumed to do. It was enough for him to watch the sea from his terrace. The sea was a marvellous element but no respecter of persons. He never rose as early as this, and in spite of Juanita's strong coffee he was still only half awake. The sound of the motor-bicycle was close now, its headlight flashing in the branches above, then it rounded the last bend on the approach from the south with the light cut out. Bernard knew the road very well and could tell by the silence that the machine had stopped a hundred metres away. Michel was wary in his violence.

Bernard tried to reduce his breathing, conscious of the bulk mentioned by Juanita last night. In the south, a thin man doesn't count as a man, that's one reason she'd never go and work for Caraman. Straining his ears, he could hear steps approaching, quiet like paws along the stone of the pavement. You can't walk silently on anything but grass. Then, silence. Between his wall and the pavement there was a stretch of earth green after rain, the grass bone dry now. Bernard raised his hand and pointed at the door, and at the same moment came the sound of a key in the lock.

Luis must have oiled the hinges. The heavy iron door opened silently. That could be a mistake, Bernard thought, a suspicious circumstance. It seemed that Michel was hesitating. Then after a long pause Alain appeared, an arm held tightly about his neck from behind. He took a half-step forward, clumsily, as if pushed by a knee in the small of his back. Michel seemed almost mounted on him like a dog, his other arm stuck in Alain's side. If he had a weapon that was the fist holding it. Raising a foot behind him, Michel eased the door shut, then they stood still while he looked about him into the half-dark. Surely he must sense other bodies so close?

'Look. Her light's on up there,' whispered Alain. Keeps his head better than me, Bernard thought. Now the two of them advanced to the stair rising between olive trees and vines. Luis had said the second step. Bernard could just see Alain reach it with Michel behind him on the first. Then Alain seemed to trip, he must have known it was the place. At the same moment, Luis sprang out from his ledge by the door and as he fell on Michel, he clubbed him with something in his hand, a heavy stone. All three were on the ground as Soames took Michel's free arm,

pulling it towards him and turning the wrist in the same movement.
Something metal fell on the stone of the stair. It was over in an instant
with Bernard, still behind his cypress, hoping no blood would be shed
on the paving stones for the gardener to wonder about.

'Give your gun to Alain and fetch the van.' Luis told Soames. It was
a relief to Bernard not to be entrusted with the gun. He'd never been
able to aim one at anything, not even Philibert's pheasants. As Soames
went out into the road, he emerged from behind the cypress and
shone his torch.

Alain was standing over Michel with Soames's gun in his hand as if
this came naturally to him. Convent life hadn't given enough scope to
his abilities. Perhaps he should be in the police. In the light of the
torch he looked quite dangerous, a starved ferret. Michel's eyes were
open, staring into the beam. After watching them for a moment,
Bernard looked away and switched the torch off. Any captive becomes
a victim, and for Michel this was love and freedom lost in the same
moment. Mado wasn't waiting for him in a pavilion with a light left on
in the pre-dawn dark to show him the way. Bernard knew the thought
in Michel's mind. She didn't want me after all, that's what he was
thinking. The hatred he hadn't known about or even suspected was
reaching out to him. If there was a heart in there, it was probably
breaking.

The van came round the bend of the road and stopped at the gate.
'Get up,' said Luis, holding Michel's arms locked behind him. 'Shine
the torch this way.' In the light Luis passed a rope with one hand
round Michel's wrists and looped it twice, tightening it roughly to
make a knot. 'Get going,' he said, and added in a voice Bernard didn't
know – 'the degenerate gives the orders now. No, wait.' He pulled
back sharply on the rope and turned to Bernard.

'You can go back to bed,' he said. 'We won't need you. Tell Juanita
the boat sprang a leak.' He laughed again, in the excited, not very
reliable way he'd taken to laughing recently. Then he put a hand on
Bernard's shoulder, a rare gesture for Luis who wasn't demonstrative.
It was almost as if he was drunk, a dawn drunkenness. 'That woman's a
jewel. You don't value her right. When Marion's gone she'll take care

of you, I mean your needs – that's why I don't feel so bad.'

Bernard waited patiently. They would soon be gone and he had a strong presentiment that this was Luis's farewell and they wouldn't meet again. It wasn't the moment to argue with him about anything. 'We'll be handing over to the gang who clean up behind the judges and priests,' Luis said more loudly, giving another jerk on the rope, as if there was an animal on the other end which he had a right to torment. 'You can tell Marion I'll be back before midi. To fetch her away. Home.'

Bernard knew Luis wasn't going to hand Michel over to anyone. It wasn't in his nature to hand anyone over. Luis felt within himself a prerogative to judge. It was one of the things that made him most interesting as a man. Citizens of the Republic might feel that judgement belonged to those appointed to judge. For Luis, any man who knew the law in his bones and blood was appointed. 'Goodbye, Luis,' Bernard said and turned back to the gate, into the garden of orange trees and illusion. As always with him at these critical moments, his throat was constricted and there were tears in his eyes, ready to shame him for something perhaps imaginary.

'Fetch the motor-bicycle into the garden. And find what it was he dropped. Probably a weapon,' Luis called just before the van drew away. So that's what he'd been needed for. Humble non-combatant duties, as in the Resistance.

*

Soames drove, with the little fellow who supposedly knew the way sitting beside him. Luis in the back of the van with the prisoner, still as a statue. If the rope was eating into his wrists he gave no sign.

'We're heading for Luminy. You know the road that far,' Luis said.

'Where the University's going up?'

'Yes.'

That brought Marion to Soames's mind. To Luis's probably too, but you wouldn't know it by his voice. Level and hard as the voices of army men Soames had known, issuing orders like numbers. Sounded strange, from Luis. Well, Marion wouldn't be going to Luminy to a job in the science faculty after all. She'd soon be doing the work only a woman can do.

'Funny place to choose.'

'It's the vacation. No one around. There's a track over the hill.'

'To where?'

'This cave near the sea. They say they used it in the war. When they were young.'

'You've been there?'

'No.'

'But you brought a rope ladder.'

'Alain knew what we'd need.'

Luis's voice had returned to normal, a tone Soames believed he could read. Luis wasn't hiding anything, he was the straight man Soames knew, open as a book. This Alain was the silent sort. You could see he'd have no trouble easing his way down a cave. On a quiet bit of road Soames turned to give him a longer look. Never had a woman. Something about the hollows under the eyes told you that. Either too timid or secret tastes the other way. Unhappy, always. 'This cave,' Soames said. 'What's the access?'

'Vertical, most of the way. A long drop at the end, Alain says.'

'Near the sea, you said?'

'Yes.'

'How far down then?'

'How do I know? How far down, Alain?'

'The height of a house,' said Alain in a deep, sing-song voice, like someone in a choir. Plenty of weird ones in those. 'Two storeys or so.'

'A long way for a man with one working leg,' Soames said.

'You just drive with it and don't worry,' said Luis, and put a hand on his shoulder from the back of the van.

They'd turned into the Luminy road, through oak woods. Truffles in there, between those oaks. No lights anywhere. Not a soul, not that you'd expect souls around the science faculty. 'Go in there, under the trees,' Luis said. 'As far as you can get. Push in through the branches, that'll hide the van.'

'Christ have mercy on you for whatever you do,' the prisoner said suddenly, as if aware that hiding the van sealed his fate. He sounded more like a judge than a prisoner. A judge taken hostage and still judging. What was that dirge . . . from Yorkshire, was it? 'Fire burn' – was that it? – 'to the bare bone' – yes. 'And Christ redeem thy soul.' No, not redeem, sounded like an option. Receive. That was the word. Receive.

'And you,' Luis said fiercely. 'When it was time to shut the doors on the trains to Birkenau. Did you remember your Christ then?'

'I was never . . .' the prisoner's words ended there. Had Luis put a fist in his mouth to stop him talking? Not here to criticise Luis or what he did. When you first wake to the world, it's beautiful, it's the fountains, meadows, hills and groves and that. Later on in life it's very largely a world of shit and you don't ask too many questions. You look to the few people close to you and don't pass judgements. But Luis, he hadn't got that far, not yet. A case of retarded disillusionment. Soames nudged the van in among the branches where he was told, and turned the engine off.

'We'll follow you up the track,' said Luis to Alain. 'Take the helmets.'

'Give me the rope-ladder here,' said Soames. If the ladder was essential, whoever carried it had some control of the situation.

'No,' said Luis. 'Take the gun and come behind me.' His eyes looked too large and too brilliant, because the skin of his face was white and stretched by tiredness. Close to exhaustion, in fact. You'd think he hadn't slept for weeks, due to whatever was going on in his head.

'You all right, Luis?'

'I'm all right.'

Alain went just ahead and kept looking back at Luis, without speaking. Like a dog looking for signals. The expression was subservient and intuitive, more like a bitch. That was it, of course. This little fellow, he was under the Karoly spell. Soames had been under it with Ida for thirty years and he could see the signs. He felt sorry for Alain, but anxious too. If Alain was a guide, how good was he going to be if homoerotic emotions were boiling over? How dependable? How truthful? In the army, thought Soames with ironical hindsight, you put them in the cookhouse, or sent them home to their mothers, or shot them quietly if it was an emergency and that was the only thing to do.

The growing light behind the Mont Puget made the mountain look black and flat as an outline painted on a wall. In about an hour the rock face would spring out into the day. The Cumbrian mountains creep into growing daylight, dim colours – mist, cloud, grass, bracken. Here it was brutal awakening to bare sky. Soames never regretted the obsession that kept him away from his native place, not for a moment. The night temperature here hardly dropped and it was hot work already, going uphill. There was sweat between the palm of his hand and the metal of the revolver. They were on the crest. The sea, far down, dark but restless between legs of limestone. Calling, calling. They started the steep descent, difficult on loose stones with no knee to speak of.

'Is this it?' Luis asked. Alain said nothing. He was standing near a hole in the hillside, where a rock had been moved to one side. For a guide, he looked oddly disoriented. Poor bugger, it was his obsession. One thing was sure, it wasn't him who'd shifted that rock.

'Yes, Luis,' he said, like in a playground.

'You see, Soames,' Luis said, 'there's a shaft down there four, five metres long, an elbow, then the long drop, that's what Alain says. What do you think? The shaft's narrow, you can see. The ladder's for the drop.'

'You know as well as I do, Luis, I'd never make it back, not out of that.'

'You might.'

'You need working joints. I'd be a dead weight to haul.'

'We'll be about half an hour.'

'You'll be an hour.'

'The sun's soon coming up. I've got a bottle of wine here. You'll be the only dawn drinker around.' Luis laughed again, his unreliable laugh.

Soames took hold of Luis's free arm, the one not holding the prisoner's halter. 'What're you up to, Luis? No fucking about. I've your word for it.'

'My word.'

You can't go further than that if you have relations of trust with a man. When he's a sort of son, in a way. Still, if it wasn't for the leg . . . just to make sure . . . for Luis's own sake. Even a sort of adopted son can tell you a lie, though you don't like to think it. 'Then I'll have to take you for as good as your word.' Soames turned his attention for the first time to the prisoner. Till now he'd just thought of him as a captive, not a fellow being with feelings. He was staring down at the hole in the ground, his bound hands in front of him. Just a man. What do you know about what someone's done, by looking at them? This chap could be a doctor, or a clergyman – a fancy one, admittedly; one for the women, a well-hung parson like in the poem. Funny how some women go for the cloth – stand-in for the heavenly father, no doubt. The fools. Had this man really put people like Ida onto the train for places like Birkenau? Your imagination couldn't take hold of it. There he was, looking at the ground, a frightened man under the skin and bone and hair of someone who'd done a frightful thing, so Luis had been told. And Luis believed it. Not so sure. You couldn't know. And you didn't need to know. That was for the ones waiting down in the cave to decide. They'd hold some sort of trial, that's what they do – while our job is getting away from this safely, as sharp as possible.

'Be quick about it, Luis.'

'Tonight we'll be in the Camargue. Marion too.'

'Plus what she's carrying.'

'Yes,' Luis said seriously.

Soames wanted to shake hands with the man, as you might with a prisoner-of-war, to show that war's the same for all. But it wasn't and isn't. This man could be one of the worst people on earth, not a captured chaplain like he looked. That was how it was. As you get older you get less savage. 'Hand over that bottle of wine then.' It would ease things along, the time of waiting. A relief seeing them go without him . . . down that . . .

*

He watched them, knowing himself in the wrong. The prisoner had no helmet but his hands were freed to hold on by, a rope round his neck. Luis took the gun, loading one shot under the prisoner's eye. 'Just in case,' he'd said. That was reasonable enough. 'It'll still be in there when I get back, you'll see.'

You could hear the falling scree and stones inside the hill, a low voice every now and then at first, then dead silence from underground. The sea was getting lighter now – darkness draining out. The morning star still sharp, fading unwillingly. An old actress. Silent, far up and out, gulls patrolled their flight-paths, each one half an arc. Here's hoping the discipline underground's as good as those birds. The sky, now – that's the thing you could hardly believe, how it is, here in the south on a bare coast. Why should the Greeks go any further than here? And they hadn't. Why yearn for an after-life paradise when you had one in front of you? Soames lit one of his black cigars and had another swig of wine – white, from Cassis by the label. Crisp as the dawn air. There was a combination of things here that in normal circumstances would make him happy. Splendour all around and good tastes within. But pleasure these days only reminded him how soon he'd be alone to enjoy it. The familiar thought returns. Wasn't love enough, that she goes to die on me? A wrong question, irrational, unscientific, indecent. But returning every time.

Sitting on stony ground brings those last days before the Liberation to mind, out on the garrigue with the enemy heading for home. Few got there. The heat then! Marvellous. Dead bodies along the roads, burnt-out trucks, bloody vengeance in towns and villages. Too bad for anyone with a mark against his name and not enough time to take cover. Cover was what this man Michel had found and kept, he must be one who knew a lot and put what he knew to good use for thirty years. Till this morning. He'd reckoned without Luis, the Gitan who'd seen the inside of their special camps. And now those old Resistants and their kangaroo justice ready for him down there below sea level. How many of them? Two, three, maybe. So by tonight Luis is away in the Camargue where the tight-arse from the Préfecture won't know how to find him if there's trouble. Not with all the Gitans there are in the Camargue, brown and hirsute and wild as boars in the undergrowth. The gendarmes never penetrate far inside private land there due to bulls all over the place. We'll have bulls, right away, essential precaution. Tomorrow. And the market for Egyptian Arab horses rises, rises. There's no horse snobs like the French horse snobs. But just loving those thoroughbreds the way he did, that could be a brand of snobbery of its own. Racial. One of the worst come to think of it – what led so straight, so easy, to the camps. Better drink deeper from the Cassis bottle, spread a bit more haze around the dilemma.

Wine can blur the outline of one problem, bring another into a prominent place. It was happening now. Something about the logistics didn't click. If Alain was the guide, why had Luis gone down first? He wasn't the one who knew the way but he'd passed the gun to Alain and gone ahead with the rope-ladder rolled over his shoulder. Well, it could just be that he had to fix the irons. Probably not much room down there, a tight squeeze in the dark. Crushed – Soames moved his shoulders and arms, shaking the idea off. That was plausible. Alain from just behind could tell Luis the way ahead, they both had a light in their hats. Fair enough. But the ladder. If the men already there had used one to get down, why take another? That didn't click either, not in a million years. Something must explain it. Well – maybe the others had just used a rope but Luis knew they'd need more, being inexperienced. He had to get that man Michel into a deep cave and deliver him in one piece. Yes, maybe that was right, and a ladder was the only way. The problems seemed to retreat into the blur again.

But there was something else, lurking in there. Only an impression. A thing he didn't want out in the light. Without the wine, maybe he wouldn't have let it out, but now there it was, pretty distinct. Didn't Alain and Michel know each other already – from before? And quite well? Almost intimately, as if Michel – if what Luis said about him was true – had . . . worked on Alain, the way they did in those days? It was like sensing the knowledge between two animals with reason to hate or fear each other. Even if the two of them hadn't spoken, the impression was in the air around them, of a shared foul experience.

Soames stood up, knocking over the near-empty wine bottle that had helped these things into the front of his mind. Michel had spoken, muttered something, he was sure of it. Just a word under his breath, while Luis was crouching to enter the hole in the ground. The word, what was it? – "Iscariot." That was all. Not much. But not a thing you'd say to a mere guide you didn't know. He, Soames, had heard it, registered it and dismissed it. Why? Because he didn't want to know? Why not? The same reason a guard can refuse to hear a sound out there in the dark – fear before duty. The war veteran and ally of the Resistance had gone wrong. Was it age? Or death in the house . . . next him in the bed?

No. It was terror of being trapped in some tunnel, arms pinned, paralysed. Like in the tank, watching his foot burn off. A fear he couldn't master, branded on him, and the fear of showing it even greater. And there was his father before him – trapped in a coal seam off the Cumbrian coast, never come up again. He should have gone with them, leg or no leg, to see after Luis. It was his duty. His right. Soames advanced on the hole and slowly began to enter it. Sweating, holding down the fear, his mind only on the return climb. An old soldier, even a *mutilé de guerre*, he can't choose the soft way out.

He might see lights, or shout down to Luis, or find the ladder fixed to the rock. There was still light above him – still time to cry off. The sun soon to come over that hill and the sea turn blue.

Soames, insecure because of his disability, slipped on the dark scree a couple of metres inside the opening shaft and fell as if down a chute. Inelastic, the artificial leg jammed against the stone with his weight behind it, pain all concentrated in the stump. It wasn't the first time, he'd had a fall or two. He tried to move. The fall had carried him beyond the light. He managed to free the leg by retracting his hip in a way he'd learned. The exercise of a skill can be its own reward. He wasn't impotent in the bowel of the earth. The flame of his lighter showed a space cramped as a tomb. A rope knotted to an iron in the stone dropped into an almost vertical shaft. Without a torch, that would be like jumping down a well. The lighter went out. A draught of air from below – perhaps this cave opened out on the sea. Those Resistants could have another exit, that would be just like them. It was a good thought – Luis could have been telling the truth after all. Soames put a flame to a bit of paper from his pocket. What he saw came as a shock, in the flickering light.

There were bones – a human skull. Yet, by degrees – after that first shock – it began to feel like a sort of company, in a way. There'd been none in the tank, just him, the others got out before the fuel went up, and left him. Soames laughed. That skull there in the rock, it raised morale. By the size of it, it was a woman. So, in a way, he was bedded here with a woman. It could be worse. He put his face to the opening of the shaft where the rope vanished into darkness, and shouted as loud as he could, 'Luis! Luis! Don't fuck about, Luis. Come up here!'

His voice, like a loose stone, rattled and boomed down in the dark. No answer came. Soames shouted again. Nothing. There was the rope, there was the hole below. He must go on. The skull smiling in the light of the flame seemed to tell him so. Down there, it seemed to say, is the action. Duty. Four metres or so, Luis had said, then a passage with an elbow, before the drop. Here's where you could do with a drink. See how far down the flame shows. He lit the remaining corner of his paper and passed his arm as far as it would go into the shaft. The stone was like layers of frozen pastry, you'd think this shaft was built by some crazy mason. The flame was near the end of the paper. 'Luis! . . .'

The blast and the rush of air came in almost the same moment. The pressure on ear-drums was like having both sides of your head knocked in with a stone. Through the blackness came the familiar after-smell of explosive. And a new silence with it, deeper because of that noise. It wasn't the fear that tore Soames now – he'd as good as won against fear. It was conflicting claims. Luis was down there where the explosion came from and God knew what he was up to. God alone knew if the explosion had left him whole. To say nothing of the carbon monoxide an underground explosion can generate. And in the Camargue was Ida. Which way did duty lie? If he turned back, would he always think he'd been too afraid to go on? You're not meant to put a woman's claims first – you attend to survival of the species with the woman, of the unit with the comrade. That was how it was meant to be. But Soames was old and he'd paid his dues in the man's world. Now he turned away from that shaft and the region of heroism. Above him was a disc of grey light. On hands and one knee, with the useless leg trailing behind him, he began the re-ascent of the scree. A handicapped man could do nothing here. He would get help . . . later. Till you're sure there's no other way, you don't call in help on a clandestine operation.

The strong light washed down and over him. He was almost there, the top of his head level with the opening – his heart going hard . . . when he heard the shot from below. A single shot – it could be from any revolver, not necessarily his. First the explosion, now the shot, though Luis was meant to be out of the way before any execution. Still, if there'd been a shot it mean the explosion hadn't blown them all to kingdom come. They could have been opening a second exit – enlarging the hole where the draught came from. On reflection, the shot and the explosion were good signs, they meant Luis's part in the proceedings was over. Soames was out in the air now, exhausted but free. He lit a cigar and gave a thought to the woman down in the terrors of the shaft. She hadn't got out, poor darling. Or maybe she'd been thrown in when her day was done. It didn't bear thinking about. There was a bit left in the bottom of the bottle.

Remember Luis was athletic and full of fire and his love waiting for him not far away. He would climb out of that hole any moment now, Soames was sure of it. Tomorrow they would look at the new land he'd bought, the thatched *cabane*, gates and fences, water supply, septic tank. There'd be a sort of happiness for a few months . . . there could be no new emergency now. He swallowed the last drop.

There were sounds rising from the shaft – falling stone, a scrabbling on scree – 'Luis!' A huge relief got to Soames, in spite of the scrabbling. Luis was in a hurry to get away and so was he. 'You hear me there?' No answer. Now he could hear another noise, a sobbing, it seemed – a sob on each breath like a man in battle order at the end of a run beyond his strength. Soames knew the limits in himself, but what were Luis's limits, and what could drive him past them? Instinct – that was his mark. 'You hear me, Luis?' he shouted again, louder. 'You've got the gun?'

But it wasn't Luis's head that finally showed, after what felt a long time, down there at the end of the shaft. It was Alain the guide, his face grey under the helmet too big for him. He must have been sent up on his own with a message. Bad sign. He was within reach of the surface, still making that noise now with a distress awful to hear. Soames's heart froze at the sound. He put an arm into the shaft to pull the little fellow out. 'Take hold of that,' he said, and felt his hand gripped by a hand cold as the stone down there.

*

He was holding his other fist clenched tight in front of his chest, near the heart, like a child with one treasure in the world. That's how he looked, an old child a bit wrinkled in the early sun. All his body was shaking, his head and mouth, it was like a fit he was having.

'Where's Luis? What's going on? For Christ's sake sit down.' But the little fellow didn't sit. He clutched the hand in front of him and stood there breathing noisily, mouth open, face all wet. Till this moment Soames had forgotten his flask, stuck in a back pocket. He passed it to Alain. 'Try a shot. It helps. Take a breath.'

Alain stood there, not drinking, whisky splashing about on the stone from his trembling. 'We must go away quickly,' he said, voice loud because his breathing wasn't under control.

'Go?'

Alain lifted the fist so it was in front of his face. 'It's something I've to give Maître Vipont.' The shaking had turned sporadic but more violent. Soames took hold of his arm and tried to steady him.

'Drink some of this. Go on. Or I'll pour it down your throat.' He waited. 'Where's Luis?' he already knew the answer couldn't be good. It would be a very bad thing, to be faced whatever it was. 'Is he hurt? What about the others?'

'There are no others,' Alain said, as if that was the only part of the question he'd heard. Soames tightened his hold on the arm. What was this little bugger saying? He seemed the enemy now. No others. Luis had lied after all.

'Luis – he's . . .' Soames shrank from saying it. But this Alain, the enemy bringing bad news, he wasn't delivering, he probably couldn't.

291

'He's done for, down in that cave, that's right isn't it?' Luis's race was run, Soames knew it the same way you know that night must come. The turning world.

'Yes.'

'Why?' The shaking seemed a bit less. Some sort of strength had passed from one to the other, and Soames didn't let go of the arm because he needed the contact.

'He showed me how to use the gun.'

'On the captive? Was that the shot?' If there were no others, who was this Alain who Luis had said was a guide? Vipont must be somewhere behind the lies.

'No. Not Michel. But the water's rising fast.' Alain drank some more whisky. His voice sounded quieter. 'He's walled in. When the rock fell on Luis it walled Michel up. In the confessional of Lazarus.'

'Luis set an explosive to wall the man into a hole in the rock? Was that it?'

'Yes.'

'And caught it himself?'

'The explosion cracked the wall. There was a lot of dust and the sea started in.'

Now at last Soames saw what had happened, because he knew Luis. Luis hadn't wanted a quick, decent exit for Michel – a bullet in the head, neat work by old Resistants. He wanted Michel to learn from the inside what horror was. And Bernard Vipont had understood that. Luis was going to take his girl from him – the Gitan from nowhere would carry off the sole apple of the rich man's eye. So a trap had been set, to bring the law down on him. That's how simple it was, Soames believed. The trap was Michel, the man of Birkenau. And it had gone wrong, the sea was flooding in. 'Luis gave you the gun?'

'Yes.' He would have to be taken through it, word by word.

'The water was rising and he showed you how to pull the trigger. That's how it was?'

There was no need of an answer. Luis would point to the place at the side of his head and he'd say, 'Do it now' – something simple. With the Karolys, death was only just under the skin. Soames must find out who this fellow was who'd done the work he'd have done himself, if he'd been there. 'Do you work for Vipont? Is that it?'

'No.'

'Then what are you?'

'I'm from the convent where Michel was hiding . . . I brought him to Luis. I did it for him.'

'You're some sort of a religious?'

'Until Luis came.'

'Did you leave my revolver with the other man – Michel?'

'I couldn't help him. There was only one bullet. I left the gun in Luis's hand. I closed his fingers on it.'

It had taken guts to do all that. Appearances meant nothing. Soames took the whisky flask and drank what was left – not much. Not enough. Ida would know what had happened without him even telling her. What ran from her to Luis and back was a lifeline and she'd have felt it snap. 'What is it you've got there?' Why would Luis want to send something to Vipont at the end? Maybe it was really for Marion, to remember him, besides what she was carrying. Alain opened his fist, still looking at it. In his palm lay a rusty steel medal with engraving on both sides. You couldn't make it out for the rust. Names, it seemed, and a design. 'Luis gave you that and said it was for Vipont?'

'He told me where to find it. He wanted to send a piece of painted stone but it was too heavy. He said Maître Vipont will know where this came from?'

'Where does it come from?'

'There are some bones in there. A woman. It was with them.'

When Soames put out a hand to take the medal Alain closed his own again, shutting it up tight. 'Give it here and I'll hand it to Vipont when I've had a look.'

'No. Luis told me to give it to him. It was me he told.' He was shaking again, as if he'd shake to pieces.

'Do what you have to do.' Soames felt there was nothing left inside him now – he was a shell, an empty man. 'Then where will you go?' he asked, all the same. He understood what he was about. When Luis was a lad out of the camp, he'd felt sorry for him. But he'd lost Luis, his comrade of the next generation was gone. Now he felt sorry for this poor specimen of an Alain. 'So where will you go?'

'Nowhere. On the street. The docks. Some of the sailors off big ships use people like me, I know. Luis said he'd put me to work with horses.' He was looking at Soames as he said it. Then he put his hand up in front of his face. 'That's too late.'

Soames didn't answer. It wasn't a question. The sun was hot on the back of his neck as he stared out at the sea. From up the hill behind them, from over beyond the crest maybe, there were voices. Still a good way off. 'We'd better get out of here. We can't do anything if the water's rising. Just block the hole and say a prayer.'

'Prayer helps no one,' Alain said, and Soames felt he understood him better.

'Then we'll take that medal to Vipont, you and me, and tell him what he's done. And I'll show him another thing, before long . . . in store for the loving father Vipont.'

Soames turned to limp off this battle ground where the day'd been lost. Sooner or later someone would find the hole and explore the burial place – find his revolver too. It could be a long time off or it could be soon. You don't look out for certainties, when you've been around. If you can extract half a tooth, rip out half an eye . . . it's something, a bit clawed back from fate, *baxt*, the enemy. It's a score.

# Chapter Fourteen

ANYONE WOULD BE afraid, not just a man unhappy with his motives.
Marion was beside the swimming pool, lying on her stomach with one
leg raised behind her from the knee, swinging it slowly back and forth.
Her hair was wet and some of it had escaped the loop holding it
behind her head. The series of terraces and their tended trees, the
balustrades and urns and steps, drew the eye downward to the big
cypresses at the bottom of the garden. Bernard could see the motor-
bicycle from the window at the side of his study, just inside the gate,
leaning against the wall. He'd found Michel's revolver where it had
fallen on the steps, and now it was in his safe. That motor-bicycle
must be disposed of, and the sooner the better, though no easy way of
doing this came to mind. It was the sort of detail Luis would . . . have
taken care of.

However, there were more urgent things and they were what
frightened Bernard. An over-indulgent father builds up no credit
balance to fall back on when times go hard for his children in the
domain of the emotions. In a family you can only be safe by the rule of
fear; Bernard had heard that, and read it and disbelieved it. Now he
knew it was right, and the dread rose from his stomach. Maybe he'd
tried to buy a permanence of love, not win it. You can't buy that in a
family, only in a brothel. Marion was going to need a woman with her
now. Bernard lifted the house telephone and called Juanita.

She stood listening to what he had to say, without expression. This
made it difficult to know how much to tell and what to conceal. Fear
tempted him to say more than might be wise, but as he spoke he

sensed an understanding behind her guarded eyes.

'The sapeurs-pompiers will retrieve the body,' she said at last, after he'd stopped and they'd stood a minute silently looking down at the swimming pool two terraces below.

'No. They can't. The whole cave's below sea level. Only divers could get in.'

'They have divers.'

'The entrance is blocked.'

'But you know where it is.'

'I won't send any sapeurs-pompiers. A burial place can be a secret for the few. Sometimes it's better. You don't fish a body from the bottom of the sea.'

'Now I know what you want,' Juanita said, turning from the window. She stood still in the middle of the room with her back to him, then she went to the door. 'You want me to protect you. You gave your authority to a crime and Marion's lost her lover, and you're afraid of her.'

'Yes.'

'I know you've told me lies by leaving out most of the truth. But I'll help you because I'm sorry for you. Love in this house is under a bad sign. I'll have to tell Marion that too.'

'When she wants me, I'm here.'

'I don't think she'll want you.'

When Juanita had gone, Bernard drew his curtains closed and sat in the dusk of his study. He wept with his hands in front of his face, his chest heaving. Not to be wanted by Marion wasn't what he'd expected. He needed her to want him – it would have comforted him, calmed the dread. It was impossible to believe she wouldn't want him, even to think it was unnatural. Juanita exaggerated. Yet she'd been steady and reticent, for her. White-faced, even cold. Women had reserves of unexpectedness which it was wrong to try and gauge, and he'd never done that. The unexpected was part of what they had to give.

He must see Albertas. Those researches through the clerks' mafia must be halted before they went too far and dangerous curiosity was aroused. And Bernard needed support from someone who knew him maybe better than he knew himself. He rang the office.

'Albertas. Can you come out to the Villa Vipont?'

'The dossiers form a mountain before me on my work-table, Monsieur Bernard.'

'I need you at once. '

'You're in some trouble?'

'Yes.'

'I have no car.'

'Take a taxi.'

Marion was no longer by the swimming pool. Bernard let the curtain fall back, opened the window onto the courtyard and stepped out. From here there was a covered passage to reach the gates of the Villa without meeting anyone. He walked along it and passed out into the quiet street, lined with oleanders the size of trees, to wait for Albertas in his taxi. He felt again how he'd always relied on Luis, not just as an accessory on the windy side of the law. Luis had been the closest thing he had to a friend; now he was just a solitary attorney with a stricken daughter. Thank God – there was Albertas.

'This way.'

'Is no one supposed to see us?'

'This is the quickest.'

Like Juanita, Albertas accepted the story with reticence. To both of them, Luis had been an intrusive element and the decencies required that relief at his disappearance be masked. But where Juanita thought of Marion, Albertas had his mind on the Public Prosecutor. That was one of the reasons Bernard had sent for him.

'I commiserate with you on the loss of your associate, Monsieur Bernard. How will we deal with the disappearance of the man Weiss? You told me the Prior of that convent is the Prosecutor's brother.'

'You know his chief clerk quite well, I think?' Bernard said.

'We've had dealings over the years, naturally.'

'You count him a friend?'

'We share a certain *fréquentation*. He's the brother-in-law of my cousin.'

As Bernard thought, they were fellow-clansmen. 'You must talk to him, Albertas. Weiss was sheltered and protected for years. The authority for protection like that comes from much higher up than a Public Prosecutor, as we know. It's political, it's State lies and secrecy. That's dangerous for anyone in the way . . . anyone not covered.'

'If only you hadn't spent all these years . . .'

'Not heeding your advice, running down enemies – but it was worth it. Now we must take measures. Tell Caraman's chief clerk that everything we know about Weiss is on record in our files. Haven't we bought a computer? Say it's all in that. Don't try and tell me how the thing works. If ever a rash step is taken against us, just say the material will be made widely available.'

'How?'

'Never mind details. Say that researchers in Anglo-Saxon universities would be fascinated. Their press too. Tell him over a bottle of your best burgundy. I'll send you a case tomorrow.'

For the first time in Bernard's memory, Albertas looked at him with a sort of admiration. 'It's the stratagem of a real professional,' he said.

'You mean a clerk, Albertas?'

'I mean a blackmailer, Monsieur Bernard.'

They left it at that. These were just words and to use more would devalue tacit understanding. 'There's no time to lose,' Bernard said.

'I'll call him from here,' said Albertas. 'That reminds me. Madame Ghazakian telephoned three times today.'

'I haven't time for Madame Ghazakian now. And I'm not in the mood.'

'She has a visitor from England who knows you. A Madame Molyneux who, it seems, would be enchanted to see you again.'

There, at least, was someone who would still be enchanted. Mrs Molyneux inhabited a world where Bernard's record was quite clean. To her, he was a gentleman, a man who drank whisky. And if Caroline was inviting him it meant that the Inspector hadn't reached her yet. Probably he wouldn't. Enquiries into the violent death of a prostitute don't get much diligence. Also, a visit to Caroline's would postpone . . . for a few hours . . . 'Madame Molyneux? Now there's a distinguished woman, Albertas.'

Albertas did what he'd never done before, he put a hand on Bernard's shoulder. 'Let me advise you, Monsieur Bernard. You're tired and hurt and frightened, I can see it. Go to Madame Ghazakian's and relax in the company of the distinguished Madame Molyneux. Tomorrow will be time enough to face what you have to face here.'

'Yes, I will. Thank you, Albertas. You've supported me in a crisis, as I hoped you would.' There was something he'd forgotten, something important. Ah yes. 'Can you stop the investigations? Cause them to dry up? I mean about Weiss in Lorraine and Lyon. I'm afraid we might be traced. If anything reached the ears of those people in Anglo-Saxon universities . . .'

Albertas put on the look of any man in control of mysteries. Bernard had last seen it on the face of the Prior up at the convent. 'We must consult about that tomorrow,' he said.

*

Umberto looked reduced in self-importance. Caroline must have disciplined him. But he'd kept his job so he had nothing to reproach Bernard with.

'You look tired tonight, Monsieur Bernard,' he said.

'I am. It's been a full day Umberto. So, let's see – no news of the little Sonia?'

'She hasn't come back. They often disappear, the very young ones.'

'They're safer here.'

'It's why Madame Ghazakian is strict.'

'I know. I was sorry to get Sonia into trouble.'

'I was afraid you'd never be allowed here again, Monsieur Bernard. But the English lady is in the boudoir.' Umberto's eyes expressed wonder. 'Are all English ladies so lively? I thought they were a quiet people, without much exterior. Madame Molyneux has the exterior of a *prima donna assoluta*.'

'The Roman legionaries left descendants all over England, especially the north. I expect she's one of them.'

'That would explain everything,' said Umberto. 'Madame Ghazakian isn't at all well. If the house closes, perhaps I'll go to Liverpool like those early Romans and work for Madame Molyneux.'

Caroline didn't sound unwell to Bernard who could hear her laughing with Mrs Molyneux all the way down the corridor leading to the little boudoir. Seeing them contrasted side by side, he thought Caroline seemed modest, almost bourgeois, very French, however Armenian she might be. She stood up as he came in. 'I must leave you to talk together a moment,' she said.

Mrs Molyneux's eyes and teeth flashed, and the golden streak in her hair made the gilding of the boudoir look pale and faint. 'My dear,' she cried as soon as Bernard was in the room, 'how delightful to meet again! I was heart-broken when you didn't return to Liverpool from your quest in the country. I had all our resources ready and waiting for you. I was looking forward to it. You had only to indicate your tastes in your own way. I'm sure we could have pleased you, through and through.' She embraced him enthusiastically, jewellery pressing into his shirt front.

'What a joy to see you,' Bernard mumbled, not so sure he was up to her vitality this evening after all. Then an idea came to him, lightening one of the dark aspects of his problems. 'Are you here on a recruiting drive, dear lady?' he asked.

'I'm here for a little holiday and because Caroline told me she's not well. I was worried. I wanted to see her.'

'Umberto mentioned it. What's the matter?'

Mrs Molyneux took his arm and led him into the illuminated court where she made even the marble deities look bourgeois. 'Caroline has always suffered from occasional petit mal as you know. Well, now it's turned into the real thing.' She sounded almost triumphant about this change for the worse, yet her eyes had an expression of true sorrow – a histrionic temperament at large.

'She has seizures?'

'Dangerous ones. You know there are degrees of grand mal. Hers is drastic. She has the Sacred Disease in full force.'

'How terrible.'

She laughed. 'Nothing's for ever. Not even love. We all have some little problem or other. The thing to do is pay the least possible attention to them. I heard from Madeleine for the first time for many years, about your visit,' she continued.

'She helped me and I showed my appreciation. It was a legal question.'

'I know about it. She asked me to contact you when I said I was coming here. She's worried about her daughter.'

'I'm glad to hear that. I've got the girl safely and I think she should go to her mother. It occurred to me already, dear Mrs Molyneux, that you might take her back to England with you. I'm going to give her an independence – like a dowry – so she can choose what to do when she gets away from where she is now.'

'And where is she now, Monsieur Vipont? In your house? In rooms you've taken?'

'Certainly not. She's far younger than my daughter.' At this, Mrs Molyneux laughed again, but wholeheartedly. 'She's with some nuns who are my tenants in a historic building in the old town.'

'Some of my best recruits have come to me straight from the nuns.'

'If I send her to you, will you promise to put no pressure on her? I mean when she sees your house she may prefer it to going to the mother she doesn't know. It's my duty to deliver her to her mother, whatever happens afterwards. I'll cover the expenses, naturally.'

'For such an open-handed man, nothing is too much trouble,' said Mrs Molyneux. 'I've always specialised in lawyers – you'll send me your colleagues next year when there's an international forensic congress in Liverpool. It's expected to bring a lot of money into our businesses. I always say it's the drama of the court that gives lawyers such imagination.' She looked about her. 'How vulgar these statues are. I wonder Caroline can abide them, year after year.' Her spirits seemed to be sinking, dramatically. 'Our work can get so repetitive,' she said.

'Meeting you was part of a great happiness I had in seeing the land of my forefathers,' Bernard said, taking her hand and squeezing it. Mrs Molyneux's mood mustn't be allowed to slip downhill, it might drag his with it. The lights of pleasure returned. 'I'll have the girl brought here tomorrow.'

'And I'll look after her. You have my word.' Mado would probably end up with her anyway. He drew closer to Mrs Molyneux, to show due regard.

By the time Caroline reappeared, Bernard was feeling extremely tired and would have liked Umberto to carry him to his car and drive him home, but she was an old friend and the Sacred Disease inspires pity as well as terror. He took her hand affectionately and kept it in his. He was too tired to think of anything to say so he just gazed in sympathy. She looked pale but relaxed, more so than when he arrived. Perhaps she'd just had a fit. He hoped to God she wouldn't throw another while he was still here. But the thought of home, now he remembered what was waiting for him, was almost worse.

'There's no more time for quarrels about nothing,' she said. 'You know now my end is near. I must wind up my affairs.' It was easy to see she'd been at school with Mrs Molyneux. In the dull life of their convent they'd created a world of dramatic fantasy, and kept it going. Their successful, expensive houses of business were the natural outcome. 'You must come tomorrow and advise me about the succession laws.'

'You exaggerate, Caroline,' said Bernard.

'Not at all. I've been warned. Any big effort at the time of an attack can finish everything – it's why no sufferer from *grand mal* can have a life insurance.'

Bernard was staring at the wrist of the hand he held. She wore a fine chain with a small gold medal on it which he hadn't seen before. It was engraved with some symbol . . . He took the object between his fingers. Chased on one side was a design like a palm-tree with two branches – a Greek Y, an upsilon. He turned it over. Caspar, Melchior, Balthazar. Three kings.

'Tell me what this signifies, Caroline.' He put his free hand in the coat pocket where he now carried the steel medal Alain had brought him, engraved with the same symbol. The Huguenot cross, that other relic of the cave, was round his neck in the traditional way. Twin tokens of mortality. He'd rubbed the rust on the medal away in the secrecy of his study, with wire wool.

'It's a trinket worn by people struck by the Sacred Disease, Bernard. A talisman. An ancient thing. Superstition says you can't come to harm while you wear it but it's only a charm, alas.'

Knowledge – the light of knowledge poured into Bernard's mind where the dark ages had been. He let go of her hand and stood up. As her hand fell, the weight he'd always carried seemed to disperse like a smoke ring spent on the air. He felt young and light as in that early afternoon of 1944. That poor girl, Julie – it was her condition, it was ecstasy and effort, not some brutality of his that took her from her goats and from Raimond. An accident, just an accident, had set its seal on the hot wax of his days. He remembered the letter to Raimond from his father – 'she had the sickness still.' Bernard turned his back on the floodlit statues and walked to the door. He didn't answer the voices, disappointed and querulous as they sounded now behind him. He no longer needed this kind of house, those charades, any impresario. Cure, never to be forced, had come in its own chance way and he was going home. Now he could face Marion and give her strength, he had so much to spare.

The whole world was fresh, even in the stifling heat of the August night. He took the lightning that struck far out on the sea where the first Greek ships had sailed in – bringing alpha and omega and upsilon – for the flash of understanding that heals.

*

'I warned you.'

'You must speak to her again, Juanita. I'm her father. She needs me. I need her. I can help her. I feel full of strength, it's flowing over me. Pouring out of me.'

'Save it up for the house of ill-fame when you go there tonight,' said Juanita bitterly.

'I shall never go there again. I don't need to.'

'Then I haven't prayed for you in vain.'

He must let Marion come to him, he mustn't try to go to her. Tact and goodwill and love would prevail. He telephoned Albertas.

'Please tell those nuns to deliver the girl Mado to Madame

Ghazakian's house. Whatever I owe there, settle it. I won't be going back. And what was it you wanted to tell me – about the researches?'

'Something a little worrying, Monsieur Bernard. We should meet.'

'I'll come at once.'

When he saw the paintings in his office, Bernard realised with huge relief that he no longer needed the secret collection in his attic, any more than the charade at Caroline's house. The Courbet windmill had ground the grain of his vengeance. The trust could be wound up, all he needed was a deserving beneficiary. It was too late in the day to pin anything on the Caraman brothers, even though he felt sure they somehow belonged with the names on his list.

'Please sit down, Albertas.'

Albertas sat stiffly opposite him. 'A rather curious development has overtaken us,' he said.

'From the clerks . . .?'

'Someone has talked too much,' Albertas admitted. 'It seems there's been a follow-up in the Anglo-Saxon world. A group of researchers there, very potent and highly funded people, I think.'

'Americans?'

'Of course. A Jewish research group.'

'Researching what?'

'War criminals in hiding and art works stolen from deported families.'

'They know Weiss? Or knew him, rather?'

'They seem to think so. They telephoned again this morning from New York.'

'Speaking French?'

'Speaking it more classically than you or me, Monsieur Bernard.'

'What do they want?'

'They want revenge, for one thing. I explained that according to my information, the man Weiss or Singer has already paid his debt. They want to recover a painting they say he stole. A work of great value by one, Georges La Forest, showing a gitan fortune-teller, a simpleton, and a pickpocket. It was taken from the house of the most powerful Jewish family in Lorraine.'

'And there are surviving relatives?'

'Very redoubtable ones I believe, Monsieur Bernard.'

'I must see the Prosecutor immediately.'

'I had a long talk with his clerk last night.'

'Satisfactory?'

'Most satisfactory.'

There wasn't a day to lose, not a morning. Bernard had heard about these groups of vengeance. They were like Luis, doing the neglected work of society, but doing it with the help of huge subsidies and worldwide chains of influence. He walked across to the Prosecutor's office in the Palais de Justice leaving Albertas to warn of his coming. Caraman, paler than ever, received him in a darkened room where no sound penetrated from the outside world.

'We're in deep waters, Monsieur le Procureur,' Bernard said at once.

'And it's you who put us there, Vipont.'

'Not altogether. I don't ask to know State secrets or be told about relations with the Vatican, but it's clear that Weiss has been very well looked after. It wouldn't do for that information to spread.'

'Our clerks have already thrashed the matter out, I believe.'

'A detail remains to be cleared up. A substantial one.'

The Prosecutor put his head in his hands and groaned. 'I have a severe migraine headache coming on,' he said.

'You must postpone giving in to it,' said Bernard. 'Weiss had a stolen painting in his possession at the convent. I took it as a dowry for his daughter, but I've a liking for the girl and I'm providing for her myself and sending her to her mother to be educated. The painting will go back to the convent.'

'They won't want it.'

'Your brother must have known something about its provenance. It hung in the library. I don't give him any choice.'

The Prosecutor nodded and made a gesture of surrender with his hands. 'Very well. I'll go up there when my migraine passes and warn him.' He was being reasonable. He was reduced.

'I'm glad you say so. And I'll arrange delivery tomorrow night under cover of darkness. The Prior should expect to see a van at eleven o'clock. There'll be some other items also.'

'Weiss had a collection? Surely not?'

'No. I have some collector's trove. A kind of memorial to my father.' Did the Prosecutor flinch? Or was it the migraine shadow passing over his eyes? 'I'm bestowing it on the convent as an ecumenical offering.'

'Why would you choose the Couvent de la Génératrice Immaculée to do that?'

'I failed to resolve the problem of Brother Raimond's inheritance and they'll lose the land that means so much to them. We upset their way of life, Karoly and I. Brother Alain left them and your brother accused us of being an alien influence. I feel there's a debt but once these things are inside the convent I'll consider it settled. And you and I need never mention the Weiss episode again. For as long as you remain discreet, Monsieur le Procureur, the gift guarantees my discretion and yours. Especially yours. I'll cease to collect. The memorial will be complete.'

Bernard had never imagined himself leaning on Caraman in such a confident, blatant, triumphant way. It seemed now that everything must go right. He was on a winning streak. As soon as he got home he rang Albertas.

'The people in New York telephoned again. They're sending a delegation. A commando, I think you'd call it,' Albertas said.

'Excellent. Inform them at once that you've traced the La Forest and a number of other works with doubtful histories to the convent at Luminy. After that, it's their affair. They must adapt their methods to local conditions. You can take all the credit for yourself, and the reward if there is one. I'll arrange delivery tomorrow night.'

'I believe your father would have approved your sagacity, Monsieur Bernard.' It was the only real compliment Albertas had ever paid him, and like any unique thing it was priceless.

*

Among the orange trees on the terrace overlooking the sea there was a stone bench, the ends carved in the form of horses heads. Bernard sat on it in the dusk, waiting. He'd heard a car stop beyond the cypresses and the high wall, out on the Corniche road, then the engine turned off. It was a public road . . . one had no right to object to the presence of an unseen car outside the garden gate. But he wished it would start up and go on.

Juanita had said half past eight and he'd arrived at eight. It was the first day of September and the sun was already below the sea when he came down the steps. The young fruit on the trees was still green but if you looked you could find one or two with a stain of colour – or was it just reflection from the western sky? He heard a soft footfall on the steps above. Should he stand? No, he must seem passive, receptive, strong. It was easier to be all that in a sitting position.

Marion came no nearer than the foot of the steps, where she stood facing him, frozen and contained. Bernard smiled at her because her presence always made him smile, there was no purpose in it, it was automatic. Marion didn't answer the smile in any way. If he hadn't felt so strong he'd have been more afraid.

'Won't you sit here on the bench?' She shook her head. He looked at her more closely. Her face was so young, there was no mould for the cast of despair. But he could see it just the same, it was in her eyes. Now they turned down and seemed to measure the cypresses and the wall, then came back to him. Bernard felt his own love fly out from him to enclose her and bring her to him among the orange trees. '*Kennst du das Land, wo die Zitronen blühn*?' – he had a record of the Wolf setting of the poem and it always moved him excessively, for a song. The longing and the loss. And here and now, loss was reaching out to him like the cypress shadow.

This silence must be broken. 'Come,' said Bernard and patted the stone beside him. 'Give me your hand to hold. My heart's breaking for you, Marion.' He believed it, he wanted the current of his new strength to flow through the contact of hands, then all would be well. Everything would be all right – difficult, but all right. 'Come.'

'I have come.' Her voice was small and hard, her mouth unsteady. 'I'm going to leave you. I'm leaving the Villa Vipont and I'll never come back here. Never.'

React before there was time for belief – 'But it'll be all yours, Marion, one day soon.'

'Oh, you'll live for ever,' she said with bitterness in her voice. Even so, the movement of her mouth suggested to him the smile that would usually have gone with these words.

He tried to follow up the advantage. 'Not without you. Come here and sit next to me and see how we need each other.'

Marion shook her head again. 'I'm going away,' she repeated. 'To the Camargue, there's no secret about it. To have my baby where Luis wanted it.'

'You're pregnant, Marion? You let yourself . . .?'

'I didn't let myself. I chose.'

'Did he know?'

'I told him the day before.'

'Who else?'

'Juanita. And Monsieur Soames.'

'You've told Soames?'

'Oh, he already thought it . . . it was he who . . .'

'First put the idea?' A general always has a master plan, Albertas had warned him of that.

'And Luis told him he was right.' Marion's face was still as ever, cold as a garden statue under rain.

'And you've spoken to him on the telephone?'

'Yes.'

'Did he tell you exactly what happened?'

She raised her hands and held them in front of her as if to fend something off. 'I don't think so. I think that should stay down there with Luis under the sea. It's what you told Juanita and it's what I said to Monsieur Soames, to stop him.' Bernard stood and took a step towards her. He could see that if he came any nearer she'd turn away and go back up the stair. He couldn't bear for her to turn from him. But he had no more means, his powers were spent. He wondered about other mammals – did any of them do this to the being that gave them life? He doubted it. It was a human prerogative.

'When will I see the child?' he asked.

'When it wants – if it wants to.'

'And where will you go?'

'I'm going to Monsieur Soames. I'll learn how to help with the horses. I can do veterinary work.'

'Ida – Madame Soames, she's dying. Did you know that?'

'Of course. But she'll wait. And then he'll need me to look after the house.'

'You don't know anything about looking after a house.'

'I'd have done it for Luis.'

'You mustn't be dependent, Marion. You must have money of your own.'

'I don't want any money. There's land there in the Camargue. Money's the worst thing . . .'

'Will you leave me with nothing . . . nothing at all to do for you?'

She shook her head as if to clear a thought away, then turned and started down the terrace steps. Now he knew what that car was, out there on the Corniche. He watched her go – life setting under the hill – a last flicker, a breath, the dark. At the gate in the wall Marion half turned, looked upwards at the house and the orange trees, then she was outside, the gate was shut behind her – darkness fell on the terraces of the Villa Vipont. Bernard heard the engine of Soames's waiting car start up.

\*

If there were sounds out there in the world now, they didn't reach him. For all he knew, the universe could have stopped. Probably death was a bit like this. Timeless, separation for ever, from yourself. If he'd just had the firmness of character a father should have and known how to keep his distance . . . to protect them both . . . but that presupposed a normal life, feelings shallower though safer than his had ever been. He'd been a parasite, he knew that; a man without friends, a paternal deviant.

The light was going now; at the meeting of sea and sky visible from his study window the gilt and purple were joining the dark. So the world was still turning after all. Bernard stood up and drew the curtains, then turned on his lamps. Sitting at his desk he tried to weigh himself up, judge himself less. He'd propped his head on his hands, eyes closed, elbows supported on the desk top, but after a minute or two of that he straightened up. The posture of despair didn't fit him. Or he it. He surveyed his centre. To his surprise, it seemed to be holding. If Marion was no longer there to fill it, what was? You don't think much about strength when you have it, it's more a preoccupation of the weak. Yesterday, Bernard would have been destroyed; today it seemed he was getting through, still on the surface, head above the black waves. Borne up, probably, by a nature of cork and a new buoyancy of mind. He looked in the mirror and there he was. He felt ashamed of this hardiness, as if he'd caught himself not grieving when grief was indicated; not hanging himself from the nearest tree when that was what any man who'd loved his daughter too well should do. An image of loss struck back at him – the passenger in the Jaguar, her empty place in the Bentley . . .

Still . . . reflecting on it . . . all might not be lost for ever. The day you can no longer keep ahead, do all you can to keep up. Never drop out. Juanita and Marion would stay in touch. Discuss the course of pregnancy and such vital matters. The genetic inheritance of the child. Even its grandfather, perhaps. Likenesses . . . features . . . the female underground, like the clerks' mafia, must be put to contribution. Now – already – was the time to do something. Doing something was always the right way, always had been. He rang Juanita on the house telephone.

'Please come to the study.'

'Why don't you come to the kitchen if you've something to say?'

'I thought – I hoped – we could sit here and talk more peacefully.'

'That means you want sympathy. You needn't look to me for any.'

'Are you coming, Juanita?'

'Are you ordering me to come, Monsieur Bernard?'

'No. I'm inviting you. You'll give me pleasure if you do.'

'Better not count on that,' Juanita said, softening.

What was it Luis had said? That he didn't feel so bad, because of Juanita – something like that. Bernard rearranged the furniture so a pleasant warm lamplight would fall on her in the chair where he proposed to put her, and a dimmer light on himself.

'Well,' said Juanita in the doorway. Neither the word nor her voice was encouraging.

'Please sit down,' Bernard said. 'I mean . . . won't you take that chair, it's the most comfortable.' Juanita sat and looked hard and long at him without speaking. 'So. My Marion doesn't live with us any more,' he said.

'I think it's better for both of you.'

'And my attic's empty and unlocked.'

'I heard you go up there and down several times in the night. And outside.'

'Now we can deal with the rats.'

'Have you really asked me into your study to talk about the rats, Monsieur Bernard? We could have done that on the telephone.'

'No. No. Would you like a glass of champagne? I have some here.'

'Yes, I would like that.' She seemed to settle deeper into the armchair, and took the champagne glass in a more robust hold than Caroline ever did, using all her fingers like a peasant woman.

'The house is going to seem empty,' Bernard said.

'It's too big.'

'Just for two people, yes.'

'What two people do you mean, Monsieur?'

'Will you call me by my first name, Juanita?'

'I don't think so. I may return to Spain at the end of the week.'

'But I don't believe you will.'

'My confessor will advise me.'

'Surely you don't think staying here with me is a sin you have to take to the confessor?'

'I think it a sin to breathe the same air as a man whose conscience isn't clear.'

Bernard could understand that. It corresponded to a subjective problem he'd long had. He extended a hand to touch hers, glancingly. 'I think you've guessed that my conscience is as clear now as those snows on the Sierra Nevada you often mention,' he said.

'Then you can be calmer, at last. All the same, you're a heretic,' Juanita said, and he could tell by her voice that this was no disadvantage in her eyes. She must be one of those women who really prefer outsiders. He'd always thought so, actually, ever since she came to work for him. He leaned forward a little into the light.

'Should we get into my Bentley and drive out somewhere for dinner, Juanita?' he asked.

'No,' said Juanita sharply. 'While I work for you, I'm your housekeeper and a man with a clean conscience doesn't take his housekeeper out to restaurants. That much I do know without help from the confessors.'

'If I dismiss you here and now from my service, then will you come?'

A smile broke slowly over Juanita's face, transforming it into a face of triumph – singular as a Goya. 'If you dismiss me without a month's notice, I'll sue you.'

'But you'll come out to dinner?'

'Where?'

'On the Vieux Port.'

'Will we see the yachts from the table?'

'Certainly.'

'You must wait while I change.'

Usually, Juanita used a service stair from her room on the first floor. This time she came down the main one. Bernard stood at the bottom and watched her. Marriage had taught him that you can't hurry a Spanish woman and so the delay was no surprise. She wore an outfit in black and gold – a confection like Mrs Molyneux's polychrome hair – which looked quite expensive, the emphasis falling, as with Spanish furniture, on decoration rather than structure. You could never mistake it for French. He didn't mind that – on the contrary, he preferred it – it seemed all the less bourgeois. She looked like a housekeeper on an outing and he didn't mind that either. Within the dress was a woman as good as any other – better – didn't Luis say she was a jewel? Bernard knew you must take what chance you get, with the female mafia. And hadn't he done enough harm already, chasing in the forest of imagination?

She was watching him, as he watched her coming down. 'You know no one could ever look like her, to you,' she said when she reached the bottom step. He put out a hand because in her eyes was the same expression – bruised, belligerent – he knew from Marion's.

'We'll think about something else,' he said.

'Tomorrow, we'll decide what we can think about.'

It was a Catholic solution, to be going along with.

\*

'I won't be coming to the office today, Albertas. And perhaps not for some time.'

'I wish you a rapid recovery, Monsieur Bernard.'

'You know Marion has left me?'

'Your succession will bring her back one day. It's the advantage of our inheritance laws. You can't disinherit her and natural affection will resurface in time, before you die.'

'Thank you, Albertas.'

'And there's the cash-flow question.'

'I'd thought of it.'

'Patience is all you need.'

'And outside interests.'

'There'll be plenty of work waiting for you,' said Albertas.

He would take the ferry over to the islands, do what he'd wanted to long ago. Get in the sea, hope it might scour down to the last stain by its lashing of salt – put his head under as Luis's head was under, stayed under, in the drowned cave. But he felt so buoyant now he knew he would live to breathe again. And meantime at the Villa Vipont – meantime – Juanita could be in the middle of a call from some telephone cabin down in the Camargue. It wasn't too soon for that to happen. He couldn't believe it was too soon.